**Keith Stuart** is an author and journalist. His heartwarming debut novel, A *Boy Made of Blocks*, was a Richard & Judy Book Club pick and a major bestseller. His third novel, *The Frequency of Us*, was a BBC2 *Between the Covers* pick and Radio 4 *Book at Bedtime*. Keith has written for publications including *Empire*, *Red* and *Esquire*, and is the video games correspondent for the *Guardian*. He lives with his wife and two sons in Frome, Somerset.

 @keefstuart

 keef.stuart

 @Keefstuart

*Also by Keith Stuart*

A Boy Made of Blocks
Days of Wonder
The Frequency of Us

# LOVE
## IS A
# CURSE

## KEITH STUART

SPHERE

SPHERE

First published in Great Britain in 2024 by Sphere

1 3 5 7 9 10 8 6 4 2

A CIP catalogue record for this book
is available from the British Library.

Hardback ISBN 978-0-7515-7299-5
Trade Paperback ISBN 978-0-7515-7298-8

Typeset in Electra by M Rules
Printed and bound in Great Britain by
Clays Ltd, Elcograf S.p.A.

Papers used by Sphere are from well-managed forests
and other responsible sources.

MIX
Supporting
responsible forestry
FSC® C104740

Sphere
An imprint of
Little, Brown Book Group
Carmelite House
50 Victoria Embankment
London EC4Y 0DZ

An Hachette UK Company
www.hachette.co.uk

www.littlebrown.co.uk

For Michael and Eileen Vockins

One need not be a chamber to be haunted,
One need not be a house;
The brain has corridors surpassing
Material place.

Far safer, of a midnight meeting
External ghost,
Than an interior confronting
That whiter host.

Far safer through an Abbey gallop,
The stones achase,
Than, moonless, one's own self encounter
In lonesome place.

EMILY DICKINSON,
From 'One Need Not be a Chamber to be Haunted'

# Prologue

# **Batheaston, 1892**

She kissed her daughter and squeezed the tiny girl for as long as she dared, because this would be the last time. Once the precious cargo was lowered back into the cot, Camille turned away and left the room immediately. Her whole body shook in protest as she walked down the hall, but she fought to control it. This was necessary. It was the only way to ensure the safety of her child. The only way.

She put on the red dress she'd had made. It was an exact likeness, as far as she could remember, of the one she had seen that night.

Downstairs, the maid was in the kitchen peeling potatoes, humming to herself.

'I am just stepping out for a walk,' said Camille, her voice thick and wavering. 'I may take a stroll up to the manor. Please can you check on Daphne if I am not back within the hour?'

'Yes, ma'am.'

'She'll be hungry when she wakes up.'

'Yes, ma'am.'

'Good,' said Camille, absently. 'Good girl.'

She left the house, taking only a small bag, a lamp and a flask with her. It was early evening and the high street was quiet, the stores already closing in the dimming light. The track to St Cyprian's Court would be muddy, but she was wearing her stout boots and it didn't matter if the hem of her red dress got ruined – she wouldn't wear it again. Crossing the street, she waved to a woman she vaguely recognised from church and started up the hill, the hedges bristling in the wind either side of the narrow road. The breeze stilled for a moment and, in the deadening quiet, Camille whispered to herself, 'Be strong, be strong.' This was, after all, the course of action she had planned for weeks. It would be the end of it all – the constant fear, the dread, that some harm would come to Daphne if she did not act to protect them both. The track turned sharply to the left, and when she rounded the corner, she saw a large black dog in the lane fifty yards ahead, its eyes almost luminous in the low light. It watched her for a few seconds then padded into the trees. Above her, branches groaned and rustled. Starlings whirled in the brooding sky.

After another turn in the track, the old church hove into view, its tower already black against the clouds. She would not go in there, she could not even bring herself to get close. And although that is where it all happened, it was not the source of the evil. Instead, she followed the track up to the mansion itself. It had been home to the Seymour family for hundreds of years, but now they were gone, and a beastly presence occupied that vast gothic building and all its grounds. Camille was here to exorcise it at last. She lit her lamp and stood watching for a moment. Then she retreated and waited ...

Once the house was dark, it was not hard to find a quiet way in.

A servants' door at the side was often left unlocked, allowing the staff to leave and enter the building at all hours. There would be perhaps four or five staff in the main building; most resided in an annexe at the rear, but their accommodation was distant enough from her plans to allow their escape.

Inside now, Camille made her way quietly through the scullery and kitchen, into the servants' corridor running behind the main ground-floor rooms to the library, situated directly under the master bedroom. She took the flask out of her bag and opened it, the sharp smell of paraffin filling her nostrils. She splashed the contents onto the drapes and across the bookcases, she splashed it on the furniture and the Persian rug.

For a moment she paused, thinking of her blessed daughter who she would not see grow up, of her husband, who would struggle to understand her disappearance. But their safety was what motivated her. They would never be entirely free until this place was razed to the ground and, pray to God, taking the curse with it. She had tried to leave no record of the terrible event that tormented her, and surely her husband would never disclose it to their beloved girl. He would protect her.

Then she threw her lamp to the floor. The fire caught, a blue-ish flame following the paraffin trail up to the books where pages browned then ignited. The curtains were quickly ablaze, multi-coloured flames burst from a large painting hanging above the fireplace. The heat rose at a frightening pace. Calmly, she walked to an armchair and sat down amid the fiery ruin she had brought forth, satisfied that she would finally have her peace from the demon that had brought itself upon her.

They say the flames reached up to the clouds that night. The hellish orange glow was even visible from Bath. Black smoke billowed out like spilled ink across the sky. Many local men ran up the track when the fire was spotted, but there was nothing to be done and no chance of getting a water pump up there. All the witnesses could do was watch open-mouthed as the inferno swallowed the building.

# Chapter One

# How It Began

I was fifteen when I found out that my family is cursed.

We were gathered at my aunt's ramshackle home, a converted medieval church hidden away in the woods outside Batheaston. It had once stood on the estate of a country house named St Cyprian's Court, but that burned down many years ago and the church was left semi-derelict until my aunt bought it. The stone walls were crumbling, and the ancient windows were so thick with muck, the few meagre shafts of light that made it through were weak and jaundiced. I sat on a threadbare sofa with my sister, Nikki, both of us silent and clenched. Several of my aunt's old London friends were gathered in a conspiratorial scrum in another corner, murmuring to each other amid the cloying smoke pouring from an incense burner precariously placed on a pile of glossy magazines. Along the north wall was a row of metal shelving units stuffed with books, records and weird prototype sculptures shaped from doll parts and broken computers. At intermittent points there were large industrial radiators. And in the centre of the nave was my aunt herself, lying barely visible in a huge antique four-poster bed, its curtains drawn on three sides, with only the side facing us left open and lit by a single spot from above, like a ghoulish stage set. She was dying, and this gaudy, monstrous flourish was the way she wanted to say goodbye. My mother was at her bedside, inside the curtain, leaning in towards her sister, their voices indiscernible across the echoing chamber. The whole tableau had the look of some dark gothic painting – if only Auntie had been well enough to paint it.

Lorna had been famous once. She was one half of an artistic duo, alongside her 'creative partner' Reggie Macclesfield whom she had met at the Slade School of Art in the 1970s while sharing a studio with a bunch of other students making cutting-edge computer and video art. Lorna and Reggie specialised in weird animatronic sculptures of demons and witches made out of shop-window dummies and TV screens and wires and metal. They were fascinating and horrible. The art world adored them. Then something big happened and the duo broke up. Auntie never told me anything about it, but afterwards she fell into drugs and alcohol and disappeared for two years. When she resurfaced, the art world had moved on. The church was her home, but it was also supposed to be her studio. Her plan had been to make new art alone, but it never transpired, not even when the cancer brought her a ton of attention. A few months after their break-up, Reggie won the Turner Prize alone.

I was bored and didn't know how to behave. Was I supposed to be crying? No one else was. So I sat picking my black nail varnish off, sighing to myself. I took my phone out of my pocket so that I could text my friend Jess and ask her to grab a book from the library. Nikki tutted at me loudly. 'It's for school,' I mouthed, but she shook her head. 'Go outside if you have to,' she rasped. 'I'll get you when it's your turn to see her.' I rolled my eyes, got up and flounced outside.

It was a relief to be in the open air, breathing in the heavy scent of the earth and trees. This had always been a spooky place. Two sides of the building were surrounded by an overgrown graveyard, the weathered headstones half sinking into the weeds and slime. And then there were the woods, thick and dark, encroaching on the church's boundary wall as though determined to engulf it. I used to play out here, climbing the withered branches, making dens. It scared me a little, but I was also fascinated. I would circumnavigate the building over and over again, running my fingers along the cold stone, imagining who had touched it before. I felt that I knew every inch, every scar.

While I waited, I did another circle, following the greenish paving slabs around the exterior, avoiding the nettles. After I'd almost completed a circuit of the entire building, I batted some brambles out of my way and spotted something I didn't recognise. Low down on one of the slightly newer sections of the porch wall, which had clearly been part of repairs some time ago, there was a heart shape carved gracefully and deeply into the surface, and in its centre were the letters, 'R. W. & D. R. In love. 1915. For ever.' I was still examining the beautiful serif letters when I heard Nikki calling my name from the church entrance. The time had come for me to sit at Aunt Lorna's side and I wished it to be over already.

The thing is, I loved my aunt. I adored her. I was obsessed with her. She was so different from the rest of the family. Strange, scattered, angry and impetuous. You never quite knew what she was thinking. She was a punk and then a goth, she was obsessed with witchcraft and horror, but also robots, computers and sci-fi . . .

I definitely took after her – the books I read were ghost stories, the first make-up I ever wore was her thick sludgy mascara and blood red lipstick; the bands I loved were Bauhaus, Joy Division and Siouxsie and the Banshees, drawn from her huge record collection. Lorna saw in me a kindred spirit, a fellow weirdo. Like her, I'd always had a dark imagination, my sketchbook filled with monstrous imaginings. I would stay with her for most of my school holidays, something my mum actively encouraged. I was not exactly an easy kid. I was volatile and obnoxious and I carried within me this subtle sense of dread that I couldn't explain. It lingered at the back of my mind, whispering of sadness to come. Mum couldn't handle it. As an architect specialising in very sensible austere office design, she struggled with my unpredictable behaviour and wild mood swings. I was never surprised when it was time to pack me off to the church in the woods. Lorna would often take me to London. We'd buy vintage dresses and army boots in Camden Market, we'd go to exhibitions, gigs and gallery openings. Sometimes Reggie was there. In the taxi afterwards, she'd cry and say she'd screwed everything up, and then we'd laugh about it, her heartache. I didn't understand, I just thrived on the drama. There was never any drama at home, not even when Mum divorced my dad. He just disappeared from our lives when I was seven, leaving almost no sense of himself behind, like a brief haunting.

A few years ago, Lorna started to get tired and breathless, and she lost so much weight. She looked ten years too old. Then she admitted she had lung cancer. Three months ago, she became too ill to move, but was enjoying the attention – so she had her huge industrial workbench taken from the nave and replaced with this lavish antique bed so that she could rest in grand comfort while receiving journalists and acolytes. Moths to a dying flame.

Yesterday, the call came in from her manager: she wanted to say goodbye to her friends and family. But I didn't want to say goodbye. I wasn't ready.

I followed my sister back inside, allowing my eyes to readjust to the darkness. As the heavy oak door closed behind us, I stood stupidly staring for a few seconds, watching my mum and her sister finishing their final chat. Just before they parted, my aunt reached for something – a small red satchel – and handed it to Mum; they gave each other a meaningful look. Then Mum walked away towards the rabble of artists, and my sister nudged me in the ribs.

'Go on,' she whispered.

I shuffled forward, slowly and self-consciously, across the stone floors with their etched memorials to long-dead people, towards the wraith-like figure at the heart of the room.

What greeted me was a scene of human ruin. Auntie Lorna, emaciated and pale, was almost lost beneath myriad blankets and quilts. She was half sat up, her greying hair matted, her old Cure T-shirt stained and baggy. The small chamber, enclosed within the thick curtains, had a horrible musty-sweet smell that I instinctively hated and feared. All around her lay books and newspapers; her bedside table was a bombed-out pharmacy of scattered pill bottles, used tissues and little plastic cups. There was an IV drip hanging beside her, the tube leading under the bedclothes.

'Auntie,' I said, and my voice broke into a squeak.

'Come in,' she said. 'Sit down next to me.'

I edged towards her, making my way through piles of clothes and photos and junk, then pulled myself up onto the bed, unable to look my aunt in the eyes, afraid of her and what was coming.

'Cammy,' she said. 'I see you are grieving me already.'

I looked down at my black T-shirt, black cardigan, black Docs. 'I like to be organised,' I said.

9

She tried to laugh, but it came out as a scary hissing, choking sound. 'You get me,' she said. 'That's why I saved you until last.'

I smiled and finally looked at her properly. Her eyes were liquidy, her mouth all drooping. I hated myself, but I overwhelmingly wanted to run out of there, run far away. This person wasn't my aunt. This wasn't my hero.

'I know,' she said softly. 'I've let myself go.'

She smiled again and I did too. She took a cigarette out of the packet by her bed and lit it. 'How are you? How's school?'

I shrugged. 'I've got some exams next week.'

'Have you revised?'

'Not really.'

'Good. Exams are a tool of the patriarchy.'

We were silent for a second.

'Are you happy?' she said.

'I don't know. I guess?'

'At your age, not knowing is good enough. It's something to build on.'

I knew I should say something to her, tell her that I loved her, but I didn't want to get it wrong. Nobody prepares you for moments like this.

'Auntie, I . . .'

She lifted her skeletal hand and placed it on my arm. There was no weight to it at all.

'Shh,' she said. 'I know. I know.'

For the first time I felt the sting of tears in my eyes.

'Do you have good friends?' she said.

I thought of Sarah, Jess and me messing about this morning, listening to music, laughing.

'Yeah, they're good.'

'You need three types of friends to make it through life: the fun ones, the ones you can talk to, and the ones who can get you out of a mess. Ditch the rest. Ditch the ones who use you and give nothing back. Learn to spot them.'

'I will.'

'Be nice to your mum. She loves you. In her own way. Things haven't been easy for her.'

Her hand slipped away and her eyes closed. I leaned in.

'Auntie?'

She suddenly started, as though shaken awake, and looked back at me, her eyes focused and alert at last. 'One last thing,' she said. Her voice was so faint I had to get even closer. 'Did your mother tell you about the curse?'

I looked at her, confused. 'The ... the curse? You mean, like, periods?'

She smiled. 'No, an actual curse. A real curse.'

'I ... I don't think so.'

'I thought she wouldn't. Deborah has always shied away from the dark side of the street.'

She looked over at her library.

'Do you remember the books we used to read together when you were a child?'

'Yes. Those old ghost-story collections. I loved them.'

'Your mother hated that I read them to you. She said that they put scary thoughts into your head. Do you remember what you said to her when she told you that?'

'No.'

A shadow passed across the bed, and Auntie wheezed, watching it go. She flicked ash onto her blanket, then her eyes were back on me.

'You said, "But, Mummy, those thoughts were already there."'

I looked back towards my mother, who was now sitting on the sofa with Nikki. She was watching us.

11

'Cammy, listen,' said Lorna. 'There is a curse on the women in this family, there has been for hundreds of years.' She said it matter-of-factly, as though it was the most normal thing in the world, then she took a long drag on her cigarette. 'You ought to know.'

This would have been a lot for most fifteen-year-olds to take in. They might have assumed she was delirious or joking. But not me. It wasn't just the stories we'd read together. She'd always believed that the supernatural is just science we don't yet understand; her mantra was that Arthur C. Clarke quote: *any sufficiently advanced technology is indistinguishable from magic.* 'Listen,' she'd tell me. 'If we are prepared to accept that subatomic particles can exist in two places at once, we should also accept that the dead are among us. And the dead *hate* us. We take from them everything they once had and we don't look after it well enough.' I believed in curses, I had read so much about witchcraft. But could *we* really be cursed? My thoughts swirled in the thick air. I looked out towards my mother, as though hoping for guidance from someone outside this weird little haunted grotto. My aunt chuckled again.

'It's all right, I don't expect you to believe me,' she said, her pathetic attempt at a laugh dissolving into another coughing fit. And she suddenly shifted to utter seriousness. 'But you will.'

I swallowed deeply.

'What . . . I mean, what sort of curse?'

She took a deep, laboured breath, then pointed at me.

'Us Piper girls, we can't . . . ' She stopped for a second, as though to compose herself. Her breath crackled in her chest like kindling on a fire. 'We can't have the things other people have. It always ends badly.'

'What? What always ends badly?'

'Relationships. Romance. Everyone gets hurt. Obliterated. When we fall in love, something terrible comes for us.'

She looked away, falling back into the pillow.

'Auntie, I don't know what you're trying to tell me.'

She coughed again, lightly at first, but then horribly loud, over and over, her pale face reddening with the effort and pain.

'You are capable of great things, Cammy. But you must be independent. Do you understand?'

I nodded.

'The rest of the family, they all tried to pretend it wasn't real. It got them nowhere. I succumbed to it too. But you, you must face it.'

'I'll try . . .'

'There is a secret for you to uncover. There is proof. It all ties together.'

'I don't understand. What . . .'

Another coughing fit, a horrible wet, hacking sound. 'Just go now, my darling. Go.'

I stood up, the combined weight and weightlessness of the moment bewildering me. All I knew for certain was that I wanted to do what she told me. I did very much want to get out and get away. But as I slid down from the bed, I heard her breathe in again.

'Cammy, turn around, look at me for a second. Be what you want. Do what you want. But . . . just . . .'

She stopped and there was a silence so deep I dared not breathe through it.

'Just don't fall in love.'

# Part One

# A CURSE

# Chapter Two

## Ten Years Later

As soon as I heard the voice, I knew something terrible had happened. Even on a crackly mobile phone connection, with the background noise of my hi-fi blaring out the Jesus and Mary Chain, there was something in the tone, some hint of highly practised professional empathy.

'Hello. Is that Camilla Piper?'

'Yes?'

I reached over and switched off the music. There was a bustling in the background on her end. Urgent voices but also a shriek of laughter somewhere distant. I was already running through the possible scenarios. Had my mum fallen ill? Had my sister's house burned down? A gruesome montage of family disasters swam into view.

'Miss Piper, I'm phoning from Southview hospital in Bristol. Do you know a Benjamin Jones?'

For some reason, it was the last name I expected to hear.

'Um, yes I do?' I said it as a question because, in that critical moment, there was a small part of me thinking, *Do I? Really, do I?*

'He's my boyfriend.' I said the last part as though reassuring myself as much as informing the woman on the other end of the line. It still felt weird to say that word. I'd never really done relationships before.

There was a crackle on the line.

'Miss Piper,' the voice replied. 'There's been an accident.'

Wait, let's go back a little bit. My name is Camilla Piper, I'm a jewellery designer and I live in Bath. After my aunt died, I stumbled through the rest of my teenage years, failing all my GSCEs first time round, then doing them again. A-levels and a gap year followed, then I studied art at Birmingham University. When I graduated, I did not know what to do with my life, so I began to unravel. I relied heavily on my sister, Nikki. She was always the sensible one, the clever one. When she was six she told her teachers she was going to design spaceships for a living, which made them laugh; then she graduated from Bristol University with a double first in computer science and was immediately snatched up by an aerospace firm based in a converted warehouse on the Bath waterfront. She is now coding rocket guidance systems. When I left uni, she offered me the garden flat beneath her house on Widcombe Hill, until I got on my feet. I insisted on paying rent, but she knew I couldn't afford to, so she charged an insultingly small amount just so that I could feel better about myself.

On the positive side, I always knew I had an escape route thanks to my aunt's will. While she left Nikki enough money for a mortgage deposit, she left me the church. I wasn't old enough to drink or drive, but I owned a listed building and two acres of land including a decommissioned burial ground. That was weird.

For a decade, I couldn't face going in there; the memories of my aunt were too raw, and, to be honest, without her there to protect me, I was scared of it. So, after uni, I lived at my sister's for eight months. It was a difficult time. To say the least. I'd gone from being part of this vibrant, edgy art scene with lots of friends and events and exhibitions, to a hermit-like existence in the suburbs. While Nikki's career was booming, I was in a total creative slump. While she was building a life upstairs with her brilliant job and her new boyfriend Justin, a marketing executive at her firm, I was bingeing on takeaways and Korean horror movies, sinking into despair. I have always had this horrible feeling of impending doom. Even as a toddler, I felt it skulking about at the back of my mind. But in those post-university weeks it started to eat me alive. Nikki tried to pull me out. She knew I'd done well on my jewellery design course at uni, so she converted her garage into a workshop and had a beautiful jeweller's bench installed. She loaned me the money for second-hand tools, and never expected to be paid back. But I had no ideas, no inspiration, nothing was coming in. I don't want to get into it, but I became utterly miserable. Then my sister went away on a dream work trip to NASA in Washington, DC and my nosedive culminated in one idiotic, destructive weekend that I have blanked completely out of my mind. I stuck it out in the flat for a month after that, but it became unbearable to be in that space. I couldn't go to Mum's because she'd moved from Bath to London while I was at uni and her chic new apartment was too small. We'd end up killing each other. I also knew she would interrogate me about why I'd left Nikki's. Then one night I came up from the garden flat to borrow some milk. Nikki's back door was open, so I knocked and went in and heard Justin and Nikki talking in the kitchen. 'Come on,' he said. 'It's time she moved out. Think of the rent we could get on that flat.' I knew eventually he would do this.

The next day, I packed up my things, arranged for my tools and workbench to be collected by a moving firm, and told my sister I was going to live in the church. It was time.

I remember the day of the move so well. It was a frosty December morning – the solstice – the darkness only just lifting as Nikki drove us up the narrow lane from Batheaston. I hadn't made this short journey for a decade, but it was imprinted on my memory. I knew I would see the tower first, solid and dark, rising above the gnarled old oak and ash trees. We turned a corner and there it was in the near distance, like a warning. I shivered at the sight of it.

'Are you definitely sure about this?' Nikki asked for the tenth time that morning.

'I'm sure,' I said, and tried a weak smile. 'In for a penny, and all that.'

'You can work here for a few days, see how you get on. You don't have to move straight in. We've no idea what it's like inside.'

'I'm sure it's fine. Roland has been looking after it.'

We reached the boundary wall that circles the graveyard and followed its jagged curve to the small dirt layby on the north side of the building. There was a shiny red Jaguar XJS parked there already – Lorna's manager Roland Jeffs was here. We pulled up next to it and got out of the car. The sky was a grubby white, a great silence hung in the cold air. Nikki opened the rusted iron gate, beckoning me in. 'Your mansion awaits,' she said.

Looking up at the building that morning was like seeing a ghost from my past. Beyond the stretch of overgrown lawn was St Cyprian's Church, its Bath stone walls seeming grey and cold in the shadow, its dark arched windows revealing nothing of the interior. There it was again, that tremor through my bones. The last time I had been here was to say goodbye to my aunt. Now I was here to stay. To somehow make it my own. Nikki opened the boot of her car and dragged out my backpack, then handed it to me.

'Do you want me to come in?' she asked.

'I'll be fine.'

'You can always change your mind. Text me if you want to come home.'

I looked back at the building, and then saw Roland coming out of the small doorway.

'This *is* home,' I said.

Roland waved and I waved back. He pointed towards the building and then disappeared inside again.

'Just . . .' Nikki paused for a second. 'Just be careful. It's an old building, the electricity and heating might be dodgy. And what if there's a thunderstorm?'

It was a family joke, how terrified I was of storms. I always have been. When I was a child, I'd climb into Mum's bed and cry and shake all the way through. At university, I got friends to stay up with me all night playing music – anything to avoid the sound. I even had recurring nightmares about it. I'd see images of lightning, burning trees, women screaming. If I was left alone, I'd have panic attacks so bad I thought I was dying.

'I'll be fine,' I said. I hugged her, took up my bags and walked through the gate towards the entrance. I could smell the mud and rot from the woods beyond.

Inside, the first thing that hit me was that it seemed smaller than I remembered. The arched windows were not as grandiose, the wooden beams that supported the roof looked lower. But otherwise, this was the St Cyprian's of my childhood. The chilly nave with its flagstone floors darkened by dirt and wear, the line of memorial stones down the central aisle. The whitewashed walls, the plaster scarred and pockmarked, covered with ancient brass plaques. My aunt's metal shelving units were still standing, filled with her books and records. There was a smattering of Lorna's furniture – her old sofa, two battered armchairs. I threw my bags onto them. The four-poster bed was gone. She had asked for it to be smashed to pieces and burned in a sort of pagan death ceremony on the lawn. Her sculptures and sketches were all gone: some she sold, but the rest? Maybe she burned those too.

'You're early,' said Roland, emerging from the chamber below the tower, which had been Lorna's bedroom and would now be mine. 'I was just making the old place feel a bit more homely. Had a new bed put in there, fresh duvet, the works – a little welcoming present.'

He was a stocky man in his early seventies, weathered, but still imposing, his face like a block of granite. He'd been a boxer as a young man, then a nightclub bouncer, then he was employed as a minder for a 1970s rock star. The whole time, he studied arts management at a local college – when he was too old to protect people with his fists, he did it through shrewd business acumen. There were always whispers of gangland connections, which Lorna loved. She trusted him implicitly. 'We had a survey done last week,' he continued. 'Building structure, electrics, damp. The works. The place is in decent nick for its age. The heating can be a bit temperamental, but it should keep you from dying of hypothermia. You'll need to keep on top of garden maintenance: you'll find tools and a petrol mower in the big outbuilding just down the path among the trees. Oh, and the surveyor said you should look into getting some sort of lightning conductor on that tower.' I felt a wave of nausea at the thought of being here during a storm. 'Your aunt left a small fund to cover the bills and minor repairs, so call me if you have any problems.'

We stood for a few seconds looking about, not sure what to say.

'Oh, I almost forgot,' he said, reaching into his coat pocket. 'She insisted I give this to you in person.' He handed me an envelope.

I opened the envelope carefully. There was a single sheet of paper and a short handwritten note.

*My darling Cammy. Welcome home. Be careful – this building has a history. But then don't we all? I hope you are productive here. If you are lost, look for the truth, it's deep inside.*

It was typical of my aunt to be thoughtful, strange and terrifying all at the same time.

'All good?' asked Roland.

'Yeah.'

'You're brave,' he said. 'I'm not sure I'd sleep here. Place gives me the creeps. Always did.' He held out a bunch of keys, most of them old and rusted. 'Good luck, love.'

With that he sauntered off towards the door, before turning again.

'You remind me of her,' he said.

'That figures, I stole her whole look.'

'No,' he replied. 'It's not that.'

After I heard the faint sound of his car pulling away, I stood for a minute, allowing my ears to adjust to the silence. Noises started to filter through – a tapping coming from somewhere in the walls, rooks cawing outside in the trees. Then one of my bags fell off the chair and crashed loudly to the ground.

I took my phone out of my pocket and called Nikki.

'Do you want me to come back after work?' she asked.

'Yes.'

'Do you want me to stay over tonight?'

'Yes.'

'I'll bring some wine.'

While waiting for her, I took my stuff through to the tower chamber and filled the wardrobe with my clothes – black jeans, black shirts, a few dresses. There was a large antique mirror on the wall and when I looked into it, I saw *her*. *Her* hair, the smoky eye make-up she taught me to apply, the multiple ear piercings she convinced Mum it was okay for me to get, the septum piercing she paid for the day she told me about the cancer. I was her niece, but sometimes, looking back, I was one of her sculptures too.

When Nikki arrived, she stood in the entrance for a while looking around.

'Jesus,' she said. 'Are you sure about this?'

'Just give me the wine,' I replied.

Our glasses filled, Nikki wanted a tour, so we walked through to the cloister, which Lorna had converted into a kitchen, with the altar as a worktop – a feature that she thought was amusingly sacrilegious considering how awful her cooking was. She had also had an AGA fitted at great expense, just beneath the stained glass window, which depicted a woman in a red shawl holding the decapitated head of John the Baptist. We walked through the narrow door to the little private chapel that Lorna had used as an office. Her desk was still there, as was her computer and two filing cabinets. I checked all the drawers hoping to find some stack of her undiscovered art, but it was all letters, bills and other boring paperwork. Back in the nave, as we walked along the shelves, Nikki ran her finger across the spines of Lorna's books on the occult, demonology and robotics, her sci-fi and horror novels, her art monographs. We browsed through her records and found the Cure's *Staring at the Sea* album, so we put that on and sat together on the old sofa, looking around, taking in our surroundings.

'Do you think you'll be able to work here?' she asked.

'I'll let you know. I might need a few more bottles of this.'

'It's a shame all her art is gone – that might have helped.'

'Oh God, no. That would have been completely intimidating.' I took a deep sip of wine. 'What's happening in the space travel business?' I asked.

'I'm doing a lot of very complicated maths at the moment.'

'Can I help?'

'That depends. How are you on computational fluid dynamics?'

'I like to think I can hold my own.'

She laughed. We sat in silence for a while as 'Charlotte Sometimes' played.

'I'm sorry I was such a terrible lodger,' I said. And I suddenly felt like crying.

She put her hand on my shoulder.

'I don't think that person was you,' she said. 'I think it was . . . just a sad lonely ghost.'

I kicked her in the shin. She kicked me back.

I gritted my teeth, and asked, 'How are things with Justin?'

'Yeah, all fine. He was on TV last week, being interviewed by the BBC about the aerospace industry in the southwest. He looked pretty good on camera.'

'I thought the camera never lied?'

She kicked me again. 'I'm tired,' she said.

We shared the big bed in the tower chamber. When I switched all the lights off we were plunged into the blackest darkness I have ever known.

'Jesus,' I said. 'I might need to leave a lamp on.'

'How will you cope when you're sleeping here alone?'

'I'm just going to have to lure someone here.'

'Oh yeah? Have you got a victim lined up?'

'You know I haven't.'

'It's not Auntie's whole curse thing, is it?' She grabbed me by the shoulder and made a spooky noise. 'Wooooooh! You must never fall in love! Never!'

'Get off me!' Nikki let me go and turned over. The sound of an owl in the trees somewhere. 'You don't believe in it at all, do you?' I said.

'No. The universe is weird enough as it is.'

'But that's exactly it. The universe *is* weird.'

'Good night, Cammy.'


For the next few weeks I was busy settling in. I bought a knackered old Land Rover, so I could bring all the rest of my tools, and an old oak dining table and some chairs from a house clearance auction, so I could eat meals like an adult. I cleared some space in the centre of the nave and had the removal men put my workbench where Lorna's had been. I unpacked my charcoal block, my motor polisher, my soldering kit, a new rolling mill for shaping rings and bracelets, a whole box full of pliers, burrs and hammers. It began to feel like my place.

At first, I found it hard to sleep – the total darkness, the thought of its history, the people who had passed through; the graves outside just metres away. On the second night, I was awoken by a creaking sound coming from the tower above me. I tried to open the little trapdoor that led up there, but it was nailed shut. There was a flutter of wings and a loud cawing. The next night, the pipes gurgled and the sound was like demonic laughter. I started to realise the church had . . . an atmosphere. It wasn't really something I could explain, just an odd feeling, like when you know somehow that you are being watched. I told myself it was Lorna. Often, I caught the scent of her favourite perfume on the air, the old notes of ylang ylang and patchouli. It seemed to follow me around the church. I found that weirdly comforting.

The uncanny feel of the place was inspiring too. I spent hours flicking through Lorna's books on the occult and folklore, looking for jewellery design ideas. Goth was in again, so it made sense. I learned about the witch marks carved on to the door of the church. I sketched symbols, skulls, totems, and figured out how they might be crafted into rings and necklaces. Within a month I'd made up some rough prototypes, launched a website and an Instagram account. I messaged Lorna's old agent and she got me some press coverage. As soon as people knew I was Lorna Piper's niece, the orders started coming in.

Over the coming months a routine developed. Every day I worked into the evening listening to records, then I read or watched movies. I started to clean the windows and scrub the floors. When the graveyard and lawns got overgrown, I ventured into the outbuilding. There was a short ladder, a range of gardening tools, metal buckets. Against one wall was propped a large dangerous-looking sledgehammer. I found the petrol lawnmower among piles of empty wooden storage boxes. A few YouTube videos later, I'd taught myself how to use it. Occasionally on a Friday afternoon, Nikki would drive over from the city centre and we'd have a drink at the Black Dog Inn down the lane. The locals called us the odd couple: she wore her smart work clothes, I was always in black. But they accepted us; it was nice in there.

That was where I met Ben.

# Chapter Three

# Boyfriend in a Coma

The afternoon the hospital called, I had this weird thought that it might be the police. Ben and I had been seeing each other for several weeks, but I had this sudden idea that maybe he was some sort of conman. What if he'd just cleared out my bank account and flown to Brazil? (Although on my bank account he'd be lucky to make it to Brighton.) But then I pictured him with his floppy fringe and baggy jumper and his work boots not done up properly, the laces trailing behind, and felt a twinge of guilt and compassion. No, that wouldn't be it. I'd experienced selfish psychopaths – Ben did not fit the mould. And we had been texting each other, barely an hour before, flirting, joking, messing about. I tried to remember the last text I'd sent him. It was something soppy, I knew that.

'Miss Piper,' the voice said. 'Did you hear me? There's been an accident.'

I snapped back into the room.

'What's going on?' I asked.

'I'm afraid Benjamin has been involved in a car crash. We're trying to contact his family, but we've been unable to reach anyone. Yours is the number he's called most.'

For a microsecond, I was kind of pleased by this confirmation of our relationship, but that was quickly replaced by a flood of shock and fear.

'Is he all right?' My voice had gone weirdly high pitched. I became hyper aware of my surroundings, the bare stone walls, the tools spread out across my work desk, everything within reach and ready. Everything normal.

'I'm afraid he has sustained a serious head injury. He had to be airlifted to Southview.'

My brain began to sizzle and splutter like a cheap firework. The words were not making sense.

'Ms Piper?'

'Yes, I'm here.'

She said a few things that just didn't go in, and then, '... so if you report to A&E someone will help you.'

'Yes,' I said again and ended the call.

For a few minutes, I sat staring at the phone screen, wondering how, in a matter of moments, my life had just completely capsized. Then I grabbed my car keys.

The Accident and Emergency room was eerily quiet. I expected chaos and carnage everywhere, but instead there were rows and rows of empty seats. A mum was sitting with two small children, one with a hand wrapped up in makeshift bandages, the ghost of a bloodstain showing through. Two middle-aged men were sitting three seats apart both huffing and sighing, telegraphing their impatience to each other. I walked slowly towards the reception desk, feeling dreamlike and distant.

'Can I help you?' a woman behind the counter said. She was wearing over-sized glasses, which cruelly magnified her poorly applied eye make-up.

'I got a phone call. My boyfriend has been brought in. His name is Ben . . . Ben Jones. He was in an accident?'

The woman jabbed at her computer keyboard.

'We're trying to track down his family. Do you have any contact details for them?'

'No, I'm sorry. I mean, I know they live in Abu Dhabi. Is he okay?'

'Someone will come through and help you. Just take a seat.'

I sat a few seats down from the mum with the two kids and I gave her a pained smile. She turned away. The waiting area was cold and white and smelled of chemicals.

'Camilla Piper?' a voice called. It was a woman in a navy-blue uniform, hugging a clipboard to her chest. Her short dark hair was flecked with grey, and her smile was kind and indulgent in a way that made me feel scared for what might be coming. I stood up too fast and my head swirled for a second.

'Follow me,' she said.

She took me through a set of double doors, along a bright corridor then into a small warm room with a window, three plastic chairs and a framed photograph of some sunflowers – I wondered to myself how many lives had been quietly ruined in here. 'Sit down,' she said. And I did. She glanced at her clipboard, flicking through some pages and what looked like an X-ray. I watched, feeling a horrible sense of impending doom, the clock ticking ever louder on the wall behind me. Through the window, I could see a stretch of lawn, shady beneath dotted trees, and people going about their lives. A young couple hugging, a man in jeans and a dressing gown smoking on a bench, a woman in a long red dress standing amid the trees, seemingly looking up at me.

'Now, I don't know how much you've been told,' the nurse said, drawing my attention back into the room. 'But it seems Ben's car veered off the road and hit a tree. He sustained significant head injuries in the impact. He was stabilised in A&E then had some tests, including an MRI. Thankfully, it looks like there is no significant bleeding so we're not looking to operate at this time, but he has swelling and contusions on his brain.'

She looked up at me, and I knew I was supposed to ask a question, or just react in some way, but I had nothing. My mind was blank, my foot tapped fast against the leg of the chair.

'Okay, but . . .' I was trying to form the words into a question, but they wouldn't go. How did I get here so quickly? Why was time moving so fast all of a sudden? I felt tears on my face before I understood that I was crying. 'Will he get better?'

The woman took a packet of tissues out of her pocket and handed me one.

'We have to see how he does in the next twenty-four hours. We've put him in a medically induced coma to give his brain a bit of time to recover. I have to warn you that there is a chance of lasting damage. We won't really know the extent until he wakes up. There may be quite a long, difficult road ahead. You need to be prepared for that. He seems strong though.'

'He is.'

'Now, Camilla.' She paused. 'Can you tell us anything about where he was today? Where was he driving back from?'

'Um, some sort of festival.'

'Had he been drinking? Had he taken anything at all? Any drugs?'

'No, it wasn't that sort of festival. It was a horticultural show in Cheltenham.'

'What about medication? Anything that could make him sleepy?'

'No. I don't think so. No.'

'Does he have any health issues? Is he epileptic?'

'I don't know. He hasn't told me.'

'We're just trying to establish what happened, you see. Because he was travelling at speed when he came off the road and, according to the police, there's no evidence that he applied the brakes. So either he was incapacitated somehow or . . . he got distracted.'

And in that moment, my stomach felt like it was dropping through my body.

Because I'd sent him a string of texts. I wanted him to know I was looking forward to seeing him. Because it was so nice to have found someone like him. Because even though we'd only been going out for a few months, I thought I might be falling for him. In fact, I was sure of it. I texted him that much. Did I send it?

Was it right before the crash?

'Can I see him?' I whimpered.

'Not right now, there are more tests to do. Go home, get some rest – you've had a shock. Come back tomorrow. We'll let you know if anything changes.'

I left the hospital in a daze, the shock submerging me like quicksand. As I stood near the main entrance, I had a flashback to the memory I had managed to turn into a silly story, a myth, a joke. That day my aunt died. Her final warning to me as she faded.

And, with a horrible certainty, I took out my phone and looked at my outgoing messages. The last one I sent to Ben.

*I think I might be accidentally in love with you just a little bit.*

They came to me in a flash, the words Lorna had whispered to me on her deathbed. '*Us Piper girls, we can't have the things other people have . . .*' The phone dropped from my hand, the screen shattering on the cold dead concrete.

*

All the years I'd spent trying to take the sting out of that moment, that weird revelation. I'd got through university hardly worrying about it. Or so I thought. Wasn't it odd how I'd never had a proper relationship while I was there? Was it just a coincidence I'd never wanted to?

'When we fall in love, something terrible comes for us.'

Now, finally, was it here for me?

## Chapter Four

# **Emotion**

Usually, the Black Dog pub was deathly quiet on a Friday afternoon – just a couple of old locals nursing half-pints of bitter over a game of chess or a crossword puzzle. But on that particular Friday, a few months after I moved to the church, Nikki and I walked in to find a rowdy table of twenty-somethings all wearing green polo shirts emblazoned with the logo of a landscape gardening firm, clearly very excited that work was over for the week. We had to squeeze into a small nook beside them and it was difficult to hear each other amid their jostling and laughter. For a while we sat in comfortable silence, sipping our drinks, checking our phones until Nikki got a message notification.

'Oh, Justin's home,' she said.

I pretended not to be listening. Recently, during a surprise weekend in Paris, he'd got down on one knee and proposed to her at the top of the Eiffel Tower. I felt sick when she told me the details.

'I gotta go.' She finished her drink and stood up. 'Hey, you should come, too. I'll make supper, open a bottle of wine, you can stay over.'

'Three's a crowd,' I said.

'Come on, Justin would love to see you.'

A memory played in my head. And then some words. *It's time she moved out.*

'Oh, we both know that's not true,' I said.

I stayed, reading a book of Vernon Lee's ghost stories, which I'd found in my aunt's library and had become obsessed with. Eventually, the guy next to me, who I'd barely noticed, turned around and said, 'I'm sorry for all the noise. Did we scare your friend off?'

He was quite tall, with a broad face and a long fringe that flopped over his eyes, like a public schoolboy in a Merchant Ivory film. However, there were also streaks of mud on his face, shirt and hands, which offset the look quite effectively. He seemed self-assured and engaged with life. Not my usual type at all.

'No, it's fine, she had to go anyway.'

'Do you guys live nearby?'

'My sister lives in Bath but I'm at the old church down the road.'

'You live there? I thought it was derelict.'

'Nope, it's mine. I inherited it from my aunt. She was an artist.'

He nodded, knowledgeably. 'We're working just behind there, at the Coach House.'

There was another peal of laughter from his table and he turned towards them again. I figured that was the end of our conversation, but as I looked down at the page I was reading, he said, 'I'm Ben, by the way,' and he was back.

'I'm Camilla.'

It looked like he was about to try and shake my hand, but then had second thoughts.

35

'What's the church like? It looks kind of rundown from the outside.'

'Yeah, it's like that inside too.'

'So what do you do?'

'I'm a jewellery designer.'

'Oh, what sort do you make?'

Now he had turned almost completely around, his back to his friends.

'Mostly silver stuff – rings, bangles, quite chunky and sort of gothic, I guess.'

He noticed the ring I was wearing, a thick silver band with a winged skull at its head.

'Is that one of yours?' he asked.

'Yeah. The skull is inspired by a carving on one of the headstones in the graveyard. The wings are meant to suggest that a person's journey does not end with death.'

I held my hand closer to him so he could see it better, and for a second he held it so that he could examine the ring more closely. His fingers were rough on my skin.

'It looks kind of weathered and ancient. How did you do that?'

'I make the mould of the skull in wax and then sand cast it. Basically, you pour molten metal into the imprint and it solidifies into the shape of the design. But the process leaves lots of tiny pockmarks, which makes it look old.'

'Do you have stuff like this for sale?'

I found myself wondering if he was asking for himself or as a gift for a partner.

'A small collection,' I said. 'I do some bespoke work too.'

'It's really good.'

'Thank you. What are you doing at the Coach House?'

'We're reworking the grounds. The place was completely

overgrown. The owner has given us free rein. It's the first space I've had design input on so … it's a big deal for me.'

'That's really exciting.'

He gave me a self-deprecating shrug. One of his friends let out a loud laugh, leaning backwards and bumping him hard, splashing his pint across the table. I had to jump up to avoid the river of beer as it cascaded over the edge and on to my seat.

'Shit,' he said, leaping up too. 'I'm so sorry.' He started trying to stem the flow with a beer mat and then noticed that my jeans were soaked. He took off the checked shirt he had tied round his waist, leaning forward to try to mop me up with it.

'No, don't worry!' I said, and found myself grabbing his arms to stop him. 'I'll get a cloth from the bar.'

'It's okay, it's an old shirt,' he said. And we stood like that struggling with each other awkwardly for a few seconds until we realised the whole place was silent and his workmates were staring at us, smirking.

'Get a room,' one of them whispered, and the rest laughed.

I stared at them, pissed off at their childish insinuation, and I noticed that Ben's face was reddened with embarrassment and anger.

'Fuck off, Jonah,' he spat.

There was a long awkward silence, and I didn't like the dynamic that was emerging: that I was somehow already becoming a possession of Ben's for him to feel defensive about.

'Well,' I sighed. 'I have to go.'

I backed away from them all, this weird staring tableau that had, a few seconds ago, been a group of mates laughing. I'd ruined their evening without even trying. Outside, I looked at my phone; it was barely 7 p.m. For some reason, I didn't want to go back to the church. I considered driving to Nikki's but then she would definitely rope me into her Friday night with Justin, and we'd end up eating pizza, awkwardly watching some shitty reality TV series while I prayed he wouldn't try to talk to me. The thought of it made my heart sink.

Just then, I heard the door of the pub open and shut again. When I turned, it was Ben, holding my book. I'd left it on the seat and it was clearly drenched in beer. He wiped the cover off with his hands.

'I'm sorry about that,' he said.

'It's fine. It's just an old book.' I didn't want to tell him it was my aunt's, and that she'd written lots of notes inside that I loved reading as much as the stories.

'No, I mean my workmates. Jonah is such a dickhead sometimes.'

'Really, it's fine. Don't worry.'

He looked at the writing on the cover of the book. 'Ghost stories by Vernon Lee?'

'Yeah.'

'I've not heard of him.' He handed it to me.

'Her,' I said. 'Vernon Lee is a pen name. Her name was Violet Paget.'

'Is it good?'

'It's really good. Maybe when it dries off, I'll lend it to you.'

There was another big peal of laughter from inside the pub, and Ben threw back an agitated glare. 'Listen,' he said, turning to me. 'I don't suppose you want to get out of here, do you? I really fancy seeing a film. Do you want to go and see a film?' Immediately, I heard the voice of Lorna in my head, urging caution. She had taught me to see predators everywhere. But I also saw pizza night with my sister. With Justin.

'Right now?' I said. I toyed with the book in my hands, feeling the stickiness of the beer on the cover.

'Yeah, there'll be one starting at the Little Theatre at eight, right? We'll just make it.'

'Do you know what's playing?'

'No. Do you?'

'No. It might be terrible.'

Slowly, almost imperceptibly, the idea was moving from a spontaneous and unlikely gesture to an actual plan.

'It might be,' he said. 'But it may also be the best film we've ever seen.'

There was something about him, his kind of quiet nonchalant confidence, that made the possibility not completely unenticing. In that moment, the easiest thing for me to say turned out to be, 'Okay, why not?'

That was how it began – although it didn't feel like a beginning at the time. I wasn't looking for anything or anyone. It just felt like a convenient way to stay out longer. But that's the way these things often come at you, isn't it? Everything begins as a distraction from something else.

There were two movies showing that night but the one I insisted we see, despite some reservations from him, was a Polish horror film. It was about a woman living alone in an old house in the middle of a forest. At night, she begins to hear these awful screams, but each time she goes into the woods to investigate, all she sees are shadows flitting between the trees. During the day, we see her silently going about her life, cooking, reading and cleaning, but there is one room she never enters, and the camera always lingers on the closed door. As the film goes on, the screams get closer and closer until, at the climax of the movie, she looks out of the window and she sees them at last – hundreds of awful skeletal figures in tattered clothes, clawing their way through the undergrowth towards her house. She tries to barricade the doors, but they get in anyway, and when she runs up the stairs they slowly follow. Finally, she bursts into the one room we have never seen: it is the bedroom her deceased mother slept in and, on the bedside table, and along the mantlepiece, there are framed black and white photos of her mother in the uniform of a Nazi concentration camp guard. The camera cuts to the ghosts, clawing their way into the room, and they are wearing the rags of blue and grey striped prisoner uniforms.

I loved it. Aunt Lorna introduced me to horror movies, way before I was really old enough to watch them. *Blood on Satan's Claw, The Wicker Man, The Exorcist.* It wasn't just that she was extremely irresponsible. I always got the feeling she was testing me, seeing what I could cope with. That was the basis of our relationship.

'Jesus,' Ben said as we walked out into the darkening night. 'That was intense.'

He sat down on the kerb opposite the Cross Bath. I sat too. We stretched our legs out into the cobbled road.

'Do you regret inviting me now?' I said.

'No. It was amazing, just . . . really dark.'

'It was kind of a European version of Japanese *onryō* films.'

He looked at me baffled.

'*Onryō* – it means vengeful spirit. In Japanese folklore, they come back and kill their enemies, and the children of their enemies and so on.'

'That's . . . fine,' he said.

'My sister won't watch Netflix with me any more because I always choose Asian horror films about haunted apartment buildings.'

'Shall we get a drink?'

I looked at him. His eyes were big and brown behind that glossy fringe. But I was still only really seeing him as an escape route from home.

'Yeah, sure. But I have a strict three-pint limit.' What I didn't add was, I need to stay in control. Anyway, this is always a good test of a man's character. How does he react to self-care around alcohol?

'Very sensible,' he said. Then he smiled and it was a smile I was already getting to know and, despite myself, like. And as we walked back towards Union Street, passing the shops and cafés, I noticed he had a kind of loping stride, long and sure, like nothing bothered him. It was nice to be with someone confident. After a quick drink in the West Gate, we moved on, past the Victoria Art Gallery, which had an exhibition about the Bath Blitz, to a pub near Pulteney Bridge. We sat in the beer garden, revealing nuggets of our life stories to each other. He lived in a shared house with two friends (both women) and still had £15,000 in student debt to pay, despite the fact he dropped out of a law degree at UCL after barely a year. He'd only gone to appease his dad. I told him about how my aunt had left me the church, how my sensible sister, with her nice home and long-term boyfriend, had let me live in her basement flat until I could summon the courage to move. There were things I left out.

'Was that weird?' he asked. 'Living beneath your sister and her boyfriend?' I felt a gnawing in the pit of my stomach, but wanted to keep the conversation light.

'You have no idea,' I said.

The night went on and I switched to Coke, he stayed on beer. Nineteen eighties soul was playing on the sound system and the tables around us were getting packed with students in their best going-out clothes. His words were beginning to slur, but I stuck it out.

He quizzed me on my favourite music, I tried to find out more about his family, the usual things you do when trying to establish common ground and parameters with a stranger you might be falling into a friendship with. I soon realised he wasn't one for analysing his decisions. He didn't want to talk about quitting university, for example.

'It was an impulse.' He shrugged. 'I didn't think it through. Do you know what I mean?'

I shook my head.

'I've made some big mistakes,' I said. 'So now I *always* think things through.'

It was easy, that's the thing. From the very first moment, he was comfortable to be with. You know how sometimes, you meet someone and it just feels like you've known them for years, that you don't have to put on a front or awkwardly scramble about for common ground? That's how it was with Ben. I didn't have to market myself as someone more vibrant and interesting than I was. But that easiness also made me feel edgy and uncomfortable. I didn't *want* to like anybody. At the end of that first night in Bath, after we sat out under the evening sun, talking and laughing, we stood for a while silently watching the boats bobbing on the Avon. Then we said goodnight and he leaned in towards me. Instinctively, I jerked backwards, turning my face away.

'Shit,' he said. 'I'm sorry. I just . . . God, I'm so sorry.'

'No, it's fine.'

'I was just going to kiss you goodnight. On the cheek. Nothing . . . serious.'

'Honestly. It's fine. I'm just . . . Look, let's swap phone numbers. If you still want to?'

'Yeah, definitely.'

After that we said goodbye again and I watched him walk off

towards the bus station, then disappear around a corner. I was embarrassed by my reaction to him. Here was an interesting guy, and we'd had a good time, but I'd already scared him off. Sometimes I could see my whole future rolling out ahead of me like an empty motorway. Is that what I deserved? I checked my phone and there was a message from Nikki.

'Did you stay at the pub long?'

'I ended up going to the cinema with one of the guys who sat next to us.'

'Give me details!'

'I'll tell you about it when I next see you. Don't think I'll hear from him again.'

He called me on Sunday morning.

'Do you fancy going for brunch?' he said, like nothing awkward had happened.

I looked at my phone screen. It was almost midday.

'I think we're a little late for brunch.'

'Lunch then? Oh wait, are you a lie-in person? Have I woken you up?'

'No, it's fine.'

I was wandering aimlessly around Bath town centre, drinking takeaway coffee, window shopping with imaginary money.

We met up ten minutes later at a pub near the Assembly Rooms, with a row of tables outside providing a view of the city. He was wearing jeans and a baggy cardigan over a T-shirt and his hair was a little windswept. He looked as good as he did on Friday night. We started browsing the food menu, and just dropped back into the groove. He chatted about Friday and how, when he got home and finally checked his phone, there were dozens of messages from his workmates asking where he was. I told him that Nikki

43

couldn't believe I'd just gone off to the cinema with him. 'I'm not very spontaneous,' I told him. We both ordered steak frites and Diet Cokes and laughed about wanting the same things. I asked what he did yesterday.

'I worked all day, then crashed out at home, watched Netflix, went to bed. You?'

'I went into Bristol. Had a nice lunch in Clifton Village. Bought a dress. Went to the Watershed and saw *another* weird film.'

'Were there dead people crawling out of a forest?'

'Not this time, sadly.'

The food arrived and while eating we gently unpacked more of our lives. I told him about growing up in Bath, spending most of my holidays with my aunt, how Mum had moved to London as soon as I left for university, how my family seemed to be threadbare and scattered.

'I never knew any of Dad's relatives and I never will because he just sort of disappeared after the divorce. I only met my mother's mother Elizabeth a few times. She split up from my grandfather and apparently no one ever saw him again.'

'The men are often disappearing in your family.'

'It sounds sort of suspicious when you put it like that.'

I'm not sure if I even thought about the curse in that moment. I was just enjoying talking to him. Maybe I should have been more careful. But then we moved on to his life, and the shadow passed. He said that after he dropped out of uni, he ended up studying horticulture part-time at Wiltshire College, living with friends, doing bar work to keep his head above water.

'Why horticulture?' I asked.

'When I was seven my dad got a job in Abu Dhabi,' he said. 'I didn't want to go, so they left me behind with my grandparents.'

'Wow, that's harsh.'

'No, it was good. I loved Nanna and Grandad. They had an allotment and they let me help them grow sweet peas and loads of different vegetables. They took me for walks and taught me how to identify trees and wildflowers.'

'So we were both basically raised by relatives other than our parents.'

'Is that how you got into making jewellery? Spending time with your aunt?'

'She always wanted me to work in art somehow. She took me to loads of museums and galleries and explained everything to me. It could be embarrassing though. She'd quite happily stand there in the Tate and loudly slag off some new exhibition if she didn't think it was good work. We were asked to leave a couple of times. She'd always promised that one day we would collaborate on a sculpture. But after she died, I didn't really feel that I could be an artist like her. I just like quietly making things.'

'Is it creepy in that church at night? I've heard stories about it.'

'What sort of stories?'

'I don't know. That it's haunted?'

'I think it possibly is.'

'God, it must have been *really* bad living with your sister and her boyfriend . . . '

A memory bubbled up into my brain and I had to swallow quickly to keep my food down. A strong breeze blew across the tables as though someone had rushed past us, sending several menus fluttering to the floor.

'Are you okay?' said Ben. He put down his knife and reached for my arm. 'You've gone really pale.'

'No, I'm fine,' I said, trying to be comfortable with his concern. 'Are we getting dessert?'

'Oh,' he said. 'Let's just lay down a ground rule right now. We will *always* get dessert.' It was the first acknowledgement of any sort of ongoing commitment, any sort of future that contained us both.

And still, it would have been so easy for me to walk away, to just not answer my phone when his number came up. I knew I could ghost him, I could ignore his messages for however long it took. Starve the thing of oxygen. While we talked, I was picturing how I would tell him that I didn't want to see him again, that I just didn't need anyone right now. A dark corner of me whispered that I deserved to be alone again.

But somehow I didn't end it. I met up with him again on the following Wednesday evening. We went for a stroll through Sydney Gardens, stopping to watch a Pullman train pass on its way into Bath station. I was testing Ben's horticultural knowledge, pointing to plants and flowers in the decorative borders and asking him to identify them, which he did, using both the English and Latin names.

'I have no way of knowing if you're making it all up or not,' I said.

'You'll just have to trust me,' he replied, holding out his hand for me to hold. I took it. He was most interested in the wildflowers hiding along the walls and among the trees. He spotted a little blue one and immediately dug a dog-eared notebook out of his bag and started scrawling something on the page with a pencil.

'What are you doing?' I asked.

'Oh, I record unexpected sightings,' he said. 'And I do a little sketch.' He knelt there for several minutes, scribbling feverishly as I sat on a bench nearby and checked my phone. 'Sorry,' he muttered. 'I won't be a minute.'

But I didn't care. It was cute.

The next afternoon, we met in the Black Dog. This time I was wearing the dress I bought in Bristol and I wanted it to make an impact, but Ben was grubby and tired from digging out soil to make a new lawn, and he seemed a little distant. By the time we'd finished a pint he was yawning and stretching.

'Are you okay?' I asked.

'Yeah, just a long boring day.'

'Maybe we should call it a night. I need to pop back to the studio anyway. I've got some emails to check before I start work tomorrow.'

'You don't have email on your phone?'

'No. I like to compartmentalise. Work email stays at work.'

He looked disappointed that our evening was coming to a premature end.

'Do you want to come with me?' I asked.

We wandered down the lane in the evening warmth, wafting midges away, breathing in the sweet smell of cow parsley. There was something luminous about it, the golden hue of the light, the bees buzzing in the hedgerows. I had this pleasant feeling of déjà vu. When we reached the crumbling brick wall surrounding the church grounds, I swung open the rusty gate, then we ducked through the trees, and emerged into the overgrown graveyard, cast into sudden darkness by the shadow of the old building. 'Cemeteries are amazing for wildflowers,' Ben said. 'Lots of very rich soil.' Then something caught his eye amid the foliage and he wandered off.

'Be careful of the gravestones,' I said. 'Some of them are a bit hidden. I'm always tripping over the dead.'

He stopped beside a tuft of weeds and put his hand amid them, before gently pulling away a bloom made up of dozens of tiny purple flowers.

'That's pretty,' I said. 'What is it?'

'Vervain,' he said. He was already taking out his notebook. 'It's quite rare in this area. According to folklore, it was supposed to provide protection.'

'Protection against what?'

47

'Evil spirits,' he said. 'Black magic, that sort of thing.'

'Oh,' I replied.

'There might be germander speedwell here, cuckooflower, yarrow . . .'

While he was talking, I just happened to look up at the tower. Three of the four belfry arches were enclosed with slotted covers, but from where I was standing, you could see inside. The old bell had been taken down in the early nineteenth century, so now it was empty. But when I opened my mouth, I saw something up there that silenced me. There was a figure in the shadows. Dark and still. Barely a silhouette. The outline of a pale face. A hint of red cloth.

Then it was gone.

'What is it?' asked Ben, following the direction of my gaze.

I tried to point but my arm wouldn't move.

'I thought I saw someone up there,' I said. 'Staring down at me.'

A wind picked up and blew through the branches of the trees, sending the leaves into a rustling chorus. *Shhhhh. Shhhhh.*

'I can't see anyone. Is there a way up?'

'There used to be a ladder inside, but it collapsed a long time ago and the trapdoor was nailed shut.' I remembered the second night I stayed in the church, hearing the rook cawing inside the tower above me and realised I was shaking a little. I knew it was just a shadow, I knew it. But still . . .

'I'm heading inside,' I said as calmly as possible. 'Are you coming? I have beer in the fridge.'

In the nave, I handed him a can and he asked to see all my equipment. The polishing motor and ultrasonic cleaner, the blowtorch, the rotating vice. He picked up and studied the tools with interest. Explaining it all helped me to regain my composure.

'I'd better sort these emails,' I said eventually. 'Will you be all right for ten minutes?'

'Yeah,' he said looking around. He started going through the records, then looked at a couple of the old memorials on the wall. I could tell he was getting restless. 'I might have a quick wander outside.'

'Okay. See if you can find any more spooky flowers.'

I watched him walk out into the graveyard supping his beer and I had a moment of weird clarity: I like this boy. It felt odd to even say it to myself, to allow him to pass through the invisible barrier I maintained between convenient distractions and actual people, actual friends. I booted up my laptop with a stupid smile on my face, and spent a few minutes going through my inbox, deleting spam, reading a couple of thank-you messages from satisfied customers, clicking through three new orders. There was a pleasant lightness to everything. I took a sip from my beer and luxuriated in it. Then, through the buzz of cheap alcohol, I heard a weird sound. A slight scratch from somewhere above me, then a stomp, stomp, and the sound of roof plates shifting.

'What the fuck is that?' I whispered to myself. I shot up from my chair and sprinted for the door, skidding on to the cobbled stones beyond the entrance, almost afraid to look up there again. But it was Ben, stepping gingerly across the roof tiles towards the tower.

'Um, Ben, what are you doing?'

'I just want to have a look,' he said, as he shuffled closer to the tower.

'I'm not sure how safe it is.'

'The roof is really solid. I'm being careful.'

'I'd rather you got down.'

'I will, I just want to . . . '

'Ben,' I shouted. 'I'm serious, get down! NOW!'

He stopped and turned towards me, shocked by my tone. 'Shit, I'm sorry,' he said. He walked towards the edge of the roof, his head bowed in solemn regret. Then he bent his knees and jumped to

49

the ground with a resounding thud.

'I'm sorry. I should go,' he said. He looked genuinely crestfallen. It was the first time I'd seen any sort of vulnerability in him.

'You don't have to go! Just ... don't climb on my ancient church, okay?'

'I know. Look, I'll go. I'm tired. I should get home and sleep.'

'Sure, okay. Text me tomorrow, if you want.'

'I will.'

He gave me the smallest glimpse of that smile of his.

'Why *did* you go up there?' I said.

He shrugged. 'I wanted to make sure there was no one hiding. I once saw this movie about a psychopath secretly living in a family's attic, and they didn't know until he started killing them. I was thinking about you, out here alone ...'

'You were worried I had an axe murderer in my belfry?'

'It sounds stupid when you say it out loud.'

'I think maybe that's because it *is* stupid.'

'Okay, well, I'll go.'

I watched him lope off through the graveyard and out onto the woodland path. Then I went straight back into the church without looking up. Without looking towards the tower.

Later on, I drove over to have coffee with Nikki and told her about the little disagreement. She looked at me with mock horror.

'You sent him home?'

'No, *he* decided to go home,' I said.

'You sent him home for being naughty!'

'That's not what happened!'

'No, it's good to stand up for yourself. So when are we going to meet this renegade?' she asked.

'I don't know.'

'Are you ashamed of your boring older sister?'

'Don't be daft.'

'So it's *Ben* you're ashamed of?' she said, prodding me in the side. 'Is he hideous? Is he?'

I laughed despite myself. 'No, that's *definitely* not it.'

'Ah, so you're worried I'll try and seduce him? Maybe, I'll tempt him into a threesome with me and Justin.'

And then somehow it wasn't funny any more.

Once again, I wondered if I'd scared Ben off, but once again he waited a day then called me to ask me out – this time to an exhibition of historic botanical illustrations (what else?) at the Holburne Museum.

We met every night that week. He'd walk over to the studio when he finished work. Sometimes we'd go for a drink; sometimes we'd wander up the hill into Cowleaze Wood, or along the brook towards Bath, holding hands, watching our shadows stretch out over the path in front of us. It was June and there were oxeye daisies, forget-me-nots and yarrow along the hedgerows. I knew how to identify them now. Thrushes and nuthatches sung in the low branches. He took me to his place in Larkhall to introduce me to his housemates. I knew it was a big deal. Meg was tall, beautiful and stupidly thin, with tumbling auburn hair and an obvious crush on Ben, to which he was pretending to be oblivious. Rose was a trans girl, an anime fanatic with pink hair, extremely funny and geeky, and also in utter thrall to Meg. It was quite the dynamic. We had an awkward night in the Salamander pub, all four of us, Ben and Rose jabbering on about some video game they'd played while Meg and I tried to suss each other out.

'You're not his usual type,' she said, nursing a vodka, lime and soda. Classic power play.

'Oh?' I said. 'What's his usual type?'

'He tends to go for conventionally pretty girls.' She took a sip of her drink.

I smiled sweetly at her. 'I suppose the problem with conventionally pretty girls is that they can be quite bitchy.'

Later as we walked out of the pub, I took Ben by the arm.

'I'm sorry about all the tension between me and Meg,' I said.

'What tension?' he replied. Then he darted off after Rose to steal the woolly hat she was wearing.

The next weekend, on a spur of the moment decision, we bought a tent and drove to Dorset. We camped at a site overlooking the sea; the owners sold goats milk and homemade pasties from a little shack. We sat on the hill drinking beer and watching cruise ships pass slowly by in the distance, their lights reflecting across the water.

And because we were a little drunk and sharing a tent, it was bound to happen and it did – on top of the polyester sleeping bags, among empty crisp packets and crushed lager cans. Not exactly the royal suite at Claridge's, but it was nice.

Things developed through the long, languid summer. Picnics on little Solsbury Hill, a music festival in Bristol. He took me to meet his work friends and to see the garden he was helping to redesign. He showed me plans of what they would plant and explained to me how they were laying the scalping and foundations for a level bedding area. 'Afterwards we'll put down some compost to reinvigorate the soil,' he explained enthusiastically. I offered to help and ended up ferrying a wheelbarrow filled with weeds and brambles back and forth to a skip. Then I sat and watched him sketching and planning, his face furrowed in concentration. There is something so beguiling about a man who unabashedly shows care and competence.

As autumn approached I took him for a long weekend in London. We stayed at the Standard near King's Cross, and the next day, we went across to the British Library and looked at the original manuscript for *Jane Eyre*, which was on display. We walked into Soho, then up to Fitzrovia. I wanted him to see the Grafton Arms pub. It felt like an important moment.

'This is where my aunt Lorna met Reggie Macclesfield,' I told him as we took a seat away from the throng of the bar. Our table was sticky with spilt beer and there was a jam jar of wilted flowers in the centre. We both looked around the place, tired by our long walk but exhilarated as well.

'So this is like hallowed ground for you,' he replied.

'Definitely,' I said. 'I wouldn't bring just anyone.' He stretched his arm along the top of the seat behind me. 'They met here one night in the 1970s, and then they were barely apart for twenty years.'

The Cure came on the sound system, the opening chords of 'Friday I'm in Love'. I felt dizzy with it all. He took out his notebook and for a while he sketched the flowers in the centre of the table, while I idly checked my phone. When he finished he put down the book, leaned across the table and kissed me.

'Shall we go back to the hotel?' he asked.

'But it's your round,' I said.

'I promise you, one day we'll meet here again. What's the time?'

'Nine-thirty.'

'Okay, in exactly one year's time, we'll meet here again at nine-thirty, and I will buy you a drink. We'll have Old Fashioneds because we'll be sophisticated adults by then.'

'Okay,' I said, kissing him back.

'Promise me,' he said. 'Whatever has happened by then, promise me we'll do it.'

'I promise.'

I felt happy in a way that I knew I was not entitled to be. In a way that felt unsafe.

A week ago, he told me there was a big garden design event he had to go to in Cheltenham, a work thing, and that he'd be away for three days. That's when I realised this was something serious – because I knew I'd miss him. In his company, the doomy thoughts that often clouded my mind faded into the background. The voices that warned me of some lurking disaster became a whisper. But the thing is, when I watched him drive away from the church at seven-thirty that morning, I had an unpleasant feeling that I couldn't place in my groggy, half-asleep state.

It was only later, with a cup of coffee and a slice of toast inside me, that I realised what it was.

Fear. The old fear. The one that felt ancient inside me.

That something malevolent was there, waiting in the darkness at the edge of the fields.

# Chapter Five

# **The Ward**

When I left the hospital I called Nikki at work. I wasn't expecting any help, I just wanted to hear her voice. But the first thing she said was, 'I'll be with you in twenty minutes.' She didn't think twice about it. When she arrived, she gathered me up and took me to her house, then she made me tea and listened while I told her everything about the accident: the injury, the prognosis, the text message. She stroked my arm like she did when I was little.

'It's my fault,' I said to her. 'It's my fault this has happened.'

A dozen thoughts were flashing through my brain at once; little memories from the past few weeks, the guilt of the text messages, and behind it all the dark spectre of something else, something I hardly wanted to acknowledge. This was all too much to take on, all too early, too soon. I'd been getting along fine alone, and now this. And now *this*.

'It isn't your fault,' said Nikki. 'You don't know what happened, it could be anything that distracted him. He could have fainted or had a seizure. And even if he did read your message, it was his choice to look, not yours.'

She was always good at this, my sister; rationalising everything, breaking it down so that anything dark or troubling was efficiently discounted. It must have been weird growing up with me, always insular and morbid and prone to silent drama.

'You don't think ...' I paused for a second, watching for Nikki's reaction. 'You really don't think it has anything to do with the curse?'

She gave me a look of solemn pity. 'Oh, not this.'

'It's just that feeling I have – it's always been there, this fear, this dread. But it isn't just mine. Do you understand? Do you really not feel it?'

She gave me a strained smile.

'No, I don't feel it.'

'Auntie did. Auntie believed in it.'

'Auntie had issues. We all know that.'

'But the fact that this happened to Ben right after I sent him a message to say—'

'Cammy, stop it! He's had a terrible accident, you're still in shock, but this isn't the way to deal with it. Just listen to yourself! Auntie was not ... she just found what she wanted to find.'

'I don't know,' I said.

'That's because she practically brainwashed you. It's her fault you got obsessed with all that stuff.'

'That's not true,' I said. 'She listened to me, she believed me.'

'She put it all there!'

'No! It was always there.'

'Anyway,' she said, moving in close to me and lifting her arm over my shoulder, 'you're forgetting that we have incontrovertible proof that there's no curse on the family, preventing us all from being in love.'

'What's that?' I asked.

She gave me a playful slap on the arm. 'Me and Justin! We're in love! We're getting married! He is a good man and nothing terrible has happened to us. So that's it, case closed, right? Right?'

I smiled but I didn't answer.

Later that day, when I got back to the church, there was a rook standing on the branches of a yew tree just outside the graveyard. A flashback hit me. I was six or seven, and I was visiting my aunt. We were outside the church, and there were rooks perched along the wall, cawing and fighting.

'They give me the creeps,' she said. 'They always have.'

'Why are there so many?'

She took a long drag on her cigarette.

'In some mythologies, crows, rooks and ravens are said to be harbingers of death,' she said with a disinterested flick of ash. 'It is also thought that they can convene with the spirit world.'

'What does that mean?'

She took my hand as we trudged along the muddy path. 'It means they see dead people, walking around like regular people.'

'Be serious!'

'I am serious. They bring messages from those who have passed over.'

'What sort of messages?'

A wind took up and rustled the browning leaves.

'Nothing good,' she said.

Two days later, I was allowed to see Ben. He had been moved to the critical care unit, which had a nicer waiting room with its own vending machine and tea-making facilities. The atmosphere was very different to the casual impatience of A&E. It was sincere and respectful, like a library or cathedral. The people who came here were under no illusions – they knew how serious it was.

While I was waiting to be shown on to the ward, I thought about what I would say to him, even though I knew he would not be conscious. They say that people in comas can hear you talk, but is that the same for induced comas? Are the rules different? I wanted to tell him I was sorry, and that I would come as often as I could. I thought about bringing music he might like, or a field recording of countryside sounds to remind him of his job, but I didn't know the etiquette of this place, or how you are meant to act around people who are seriously ill. Was it okay to mention the outside world, or their lives as they used to be? That thought sent my stomach plunging like a dull weight. Would the Ben I knew ever wake up, or would it be someone else? How would he ever forgive me?

The nurse who had shown me to the waiting room appeared.

'You can come through now,' she said. And as we walked to the double doors she smiled at me – a rehearsed, reassuring smile. 'We've managed to track down his parents,' she said. 'They're going to try and come later in the week. Will you be coming too? It might be good for them to have a familiar face around when they arrive.'

'Oh, we haven't met yet,' I said. Her smile faltered for a second but she quickly recovered.

'Come this way,' she said. The ward was white, all white – the walls, the beds, the strange plasticky floors – like a weird vision of the afterlife. Around each patient were gathered clusters of futuristic machines, beeping and whining and breathing. She was leading me towards a partitioned area, behind which I could hear the sound of rhythmic wheezing. She pulled back a curtain, and there he was.

There are moments in life that nothing can prepare you for. No matter how many times you may have seen similar scenes enacted in TV dramas or movies, the cold reality is shockingly different. When I first glimpsed Ben in that bed, surrounded by screens and digital readouts, a Spaghetti Junction of tubes sprouting from his body, I gasped out loud. My head swam. The nurse took hold of my elbow.

'It looks scary, but it's okay,' she said. 'Sit here.'

She guided me to a chair next to the bed and lowered me onto it. And it hit me like a sledgehammer how unprepared I was for this, how I had carefully structured my life to avoid personal catastrophe. I liked to be alone, I liked to work, to drift and think – how did I get here when I had taken such care? And then I looked at Ben, his face bruised, blackened and misshapen, his hair stuck to his forehead, his eyes swollen shut. The grief of it made me lightheaded.

'Stay for as long as you like,' said the nurse, as though this was normal. 'Call if there's anything you need or want to ask.'

She was about to leave, but I turned to her urgently.

'Can I hold his hand?' I asked.

'Yes,' she said. 'Just be gentle.'

When she left, I slowly reached out, afraid to make contact in case his fingers were icy cold. This fear took my mind racing right back like a horror movie jump cut, to my aunt's deathbed, her skeletal hands dyed yellow with nicotine and sickness. But when I touched Ben's fingers they were warm and his hand felt strong, and I could feel the callouses on his skin from where, just a few days ago, he had been digging up soil.

'Ben . . . it's me, it's Cammy.' My throat started to hurt, like I was swallowing something big and sharp. 'I'm so sorry, Ben.' I felt tears pooling in my eyes, but I didn't want them, so I took a lot of deep, silent breaths in time with his ventilator and started jabbering.

'You've been here almost a week, but you haven't really missed much. I'm really bored without you. When you're better, there will be a lot for us to catch up on. I recorded a TV documentary for you. It was about Kew Gardens. I thought you would be interested. When you're better, we can watch it together. We should go and visit, there's a Premier Inn really close by. If you still like me. If you forgive me. I'm so sorry. I shouldn't have messaged you. None of this should have happened. I can go. If that means you're safe, I can leave you alone. Just, wherever you are, please come back soon, okay? Ben? Ben, I think about you all the time.'

There was no answer, no movement. The machines were more in touch with him than I was.

As I walked back along the muddy path to the church, the shadow of the spire jutted out across the grass, like an arrow pointing towards me. The air was still and sullen. I unlocked the door and pulled it open, and on entering the nave, I saw, for a brief moment, the bed in the centre of the room, the wraith-like figure within it, and the question on her lips, 'You know about the curse?' I didn't then but I do now. Is it real? Aunt Lorna believed in it, and out of everyone in our little family, she was the one I listened to and trusted the most. She was so smart, a genius. She saw the world in a different way. For her it was filled with omens and spirits. She would take me on her lap and say, 'You see them too, don't you?'

And I said yes.

The next day, I sat by his bed for three hours, listening to the beeping rhythms, watching him not wake up or even stir. I went home, I slept, I woke up crying, balled beneath the covers. The same thing the next day, and the next.

On the fifth day of Ben's coma, I decided I had to do something. I had to know what Lorna was trying to warn me about that

day – even though everyone else thought it was bizarre and ridiculous, I didn't. I needed to know how *she* discovered the curse. I
spent a frustrating afternoon rifling through her bookshelves and
filing cabinets trying to find a diary or notebook or a folder marked
'Family Curse'. But I'd looked through those bookshelves hundreds
of times, and the cabinets were crammed with bank statements,
contracts and bills.

It wasn't until later on, sitting down with a mug of tea, that I
realised something. There was only one place I'd ever known her to
write anything personal . . . her website. Lorna had been one of the
first artists to go online. She'd set up a webpage in the early 1990s,
which she'd kept online ever since. Could there be something
hidden on there about the curse? I sat at my desk, flipped open my
laptop and typed in the URL. The screen came up and there it was:
looking exactly as it did when she first launched it, complete with
crudely animated images and ugly stock fonts. Although she could
have easily updated the look of the site to make it more modern,
she never did. She said she preferred the anti-corporate, hacker
aesthetic of the 1990s internet. Across the top of the screen ran
its title, Anathema, alongside a pixelated black and white photo of
Lorna standing beside one of her sculptures. Below the photo was a
set of icons linking to different sections. One went to her blog, but
I'd read those entries so often I knew them by heart; it was mostly
her theories on art interspersed with darkly funny musings on the
effects of cancer treatment. Another icon opened a page of images
from various exhibitions, another listed links to sites that Lorna
had been interested in at one time or another. There was even a
guestbook, which I clicked on, skim-reading through the hundreds
of messages from admirers of her work, most of them from the
1990s, a handful expressing grief after her death. The icon I had
the highest hopes for was labelled 'Press' and contained links to

dozens of articles written about her art – perhaps there would be profiles of her, with quotes and personal details, that I'd not read? A few took me to old versions of the BBC, *Frieze* and *Guardian* sites, but these were just reviews of specific exhibitions and didn't tell me anything new about her. As I clicked through the rest, the links were almost all dead, a useless string of 404 error screens left abandoned by long-lost publications.

I was about to give up when a final link caught my eye – it was set apart from the others on the screen and written in a colour that made it hard to spot against the background. Lorna had referenced it as 'My final interview', and it was with a magazine I'd never heard of called *Vitrine*. It was the title of the article that really made me catch my breath: 'A cursed vision: whatever happened to Lorna Piper?' A cursed vision?

I clicked the title.

There was no hyperlink.

A little more online research revealed that *Vitrine* closed in 1998 and never had its own website. There were several other references to the interview around the web, but no transcriptions or scans. I discovered that the founder and editor of the magazine was an entrepreneur and art collector named Margot Erwitt who died in ... 1998. According to a short obituary I found, she had a son named Christopher. Another Google search. There was a Christopher Erwitt working as a curator at Bristol Museum, his email address was there on the page. Could it be the same person? I opened Gmail and wrote a quick message explaining who I was and asking if he was Margot's son. If so, did he have any copies of the magazine? The cursor hovered over the Send icon, my finger poised to click. Was this stupid? Was this a weird thing to do? I realised if I sent this message then it was suddenly real – someone else would be involved. My fears would be out there in the world beyond me and my sister. I got up and walked away. I lay on my sofa and, despite myself, I fell asleep. I dreamed that Ben was on the roof of the church. I was screaming for him to get down but no sound was coming out. A tree fell and smashed into the building. I looked for Ben and, amid the rubble, I saw a broken body. Then I woke up.

I went over to my laptop and before I could think it through again, I clicked Send.

## Chapter Six

# Ben Wakes

Arriving at the hospital the next day, I was a mess. There was worry for Ben, worry for myself, there was the undertow of being put into this fraught situation where I wasn't in control. It was coaxing out the worst in me.

'Some good news,' said the nurse who buzzed me in. 'We're bringing him out of the coma. The doctors are gradually reducing his sedation, so he could wake up at any time now. He's a popular lad – you're the second young woman to visit this morning.'

'Oh,' I said, and then I couldn't help myself but add, 'who else has been in?'

'One of his flatmates,' the nurse replied. 'Tall girl, very pretty. Meg, was it?'

I sat by Ben's bed, trying to fend off a lot of ridiculous, unfamiliar feelings. Why had she come alone? Why hadn't Rose been there too? *Tall girl, very pretty.* God, how pathetic, what did it matter?

Ben was lying unconscious next to me, surrounded by life support machines and all I could focus on was how weird I felt about Meg.

So I sat and I waited. I stared out of the window at the clouds passing silently across the sky. I listened to the beeps and the nurses chatting about last night's *Love Island*. For them, this was just a regular day, just a normal place to be. I watched other visitors coming in wearing fraught, hopeful expressions. Mostly, though, I watched Ben, analysing his face for any signs of wakefulness, holding his hand, imagining the feeling of his fingers twitching against mine. But nothing was happening. After two hours, I went down to the hospital shop. I wanted to get him something just in case, but I realised I didn't know what he needed when he was ill. I didn't know that part of him yet. I opted for a bottle of Lucozade and a copy of *National Geographic*. Walking back to the ward, I stopped in the waiting room and got a coffee from the machine. It tasted like hot mud. I took it back to his bed and sat down. I took another sip, grimaced, checked my phone, casually glanced up at Ben, not expecting any change, expecting to just sigh and look back down at my phone.

His eyes were open.

It felt like my brain was being hit by every possible emotion at once. Elation, shock, relief, fear – all firing, all colliding and exploding. For a second, I was struck completely dumb by the panic of it. Then I looked around wildly.

'Nurse!' I shouted. 'Nurse!'

I turned back to him. His eyes were glassy and fixed ahead.

'Ben,' I said. I took his hand in mine. 'Ben, it's me, Cammy.'

Finally he turned his head.

'What . . . ?' His voice was a thick, groggy slur.

I just sat there with my mouth open, unable to speak, completely unsure of what I should be telling him.

65

'I'm just seeing if there's anyone who . . .'

He was looking around, trying to take in his surroundings. 'Where . . . ?'

'You had an accident in your car,' I said. 'You're in hospital. It's going to be okay now.'

He made an effort to sit up but slumped back into the bed. 'Can't move my leg,' he said, fear in his eyes. 'Can't move arm.'

Finally, the nurse was there, ushering me away. For a few seconds, I stood in the middle of the ward, utterly adrift, getting bumped by people passing by, still holding the plastic cup of horrible coffee. Then I wandered, as though in a daze, to the waiting room once again.

Two hours later, it was a consultant who called me back into the ward. She was in her fifties, her greying hair cut into a severe bob.

'We have been giving Ben some tests,' she said. 'Cognitively, he is doing well. He is confused and is having some trouble with words, but his comprehension and awareness seem to be good. However, he has some bruising to his brain. This is very common in car accidents because the head gets rattled about quite a bit. The problem is, the swelling can prevent some of the messages getting from his brain to his muscles, and that's what is happening to Ben. He is experiencing paralysis down the right side of his body. It could be that he'll be able to regain movement when the swelling inside his skull goes down; the messages need time to rebuild fresh pathways. He will certainly need physical therapy, but we don't know how much, and we can't say to what extent he will recover. It's very early days. Do you understand?'

I nodded, but I didn't really. It was far too much to take in.

'You can sit with him now,' she said.

I walked back to the bed and sat down. He turned and looked at me with a slightly drunken expression.

'Don't know what's happening,' he drawled.

'I don't either,' I said. 'But I'm here. I'm with you.' I took his hand again. 'We'll find out together.'

He lay there just staring at me blankly, not blinking, no emotion. It was unnerving, as though he was trying to remember who I was.

When I got back to the studio later that afternoon, I felt utterly exhausted. I sat at my workbench, dazed and numb, hemmed in by the heavy silence. On my phone there were a dozen WhatsApp messages from Nikki demanding an update, but I couldn't face her interrogating me for medical facts. Instead, I went to lie on the sofa, drifting into a weird half-sleep in which I could hear the beeps and whirrs of the machines surrounding Ben.

I was awoken by a light tap on the door, followed by the sound of it being slowly pushed open. I sat bolt upright, still not properly awake and vaguely terrified. It's not that I never had visitors – I got supplies delivered regularly and once in a while passing ramblers would pop their heads in to ask directions. There were even times when art students turned up hoping to glimpse Lorna Piper's studio. But people didn't usually push open the door. An elderly woman peeked cautiously into the room and, on seeing me, she took a few steps into the nave. She was wearing an elegant scarlet coat and her face was hidden beneath a vintage felt hat. When she looked up, it was immediately clear she had once been very beautiful, her eyes still a glimmering oceanic blue, her cheekbones high and defined, giving her face a feline quality. I wondered perhaps if she was looking for the fancy new housing development on the other side of the meadows.

'Can I help you?' I asked.

'I do hope so. I'm looking for Camilla Piper?'

Her voice was friendly, but there was also a husky, almost

flirtatious quality to it that was weirdly alluring. I found myself feeling a little tongue-tied.

'That's me.'

'And you design jewellery, is that right?'

'Yes.'

She walked towards my work desk and put out her hand for me to shake – she was wearing exquisite silk gloves. 'My name is Joan Pendle. I'd like you to make something for me.'

I shook her hand and stared at her, not quite able to get to grips with the unfolding scene.

'You do take commissions?' she asked.

'Oh yes,' I said. 'Yes, I'm sorry, it's just that most enquiries come via the internet . . . '

'I don't use the internet.'

'That's fine, I . . . ' I looked around at the mess: Coke cans everywhere, unwashed plates, dirty clothes. 'I'm sorry about the state of the place. I don't really get many visitors.'

'I'm not surprised. You are rather hard to find. We drove past several times before I saw the little parking area by the road. Do you have something I could sit on, or shall I stand while we conduct our business?'

I jumped up and brought over the chair from beside the polisher. 'I'm sorry,' I said, feeling childish and subordinate. She pushed the chair closer to me and sat down, placing a beautiful Chanel handbag on her lap.

'I would like to you to make this ring for me,' she said. From her handbag she took a piece of folded cartridge paper and passed it to me. It was an elegant watercolour sketch, like a fashion illustration, showing a woman's hand wearing a beautiful twist ring. There were blue stones set where the ends of the band crossed.

'It's gorgeous,' I said.

'I owned it for many years, but lost it recently. Is this something you could recreate?'

I studied it again, trying to focus.

'It's not my usual style, but I could do it. It might take a while for me to source similar stones. Are they sapphires?'

'I don't know,' she replied. 'But let's say they are.'

'And the band – is it silver or platinum?'

'Platinum. It should be platinum.'

'It will be quite expensive.'

She waved the subject away dismissively.

'That's not important.'

'I wouldn't be able to start immediately. I'm afraid I have a few other commissions to finish first.'

'I understand. There is no particular rush, although I am not getting any younger.' She gave me a wry smile and then took a card out of her bag, which she placed on my workbench.

'All my contact details are here.'

And then she got up to leave, our strange little meeting over already. I looked at the ring again and felt a sudden sense that I had seen it before. Some faint memory, locked away at the back of my brain.

'Can I ask how you found me?'

She smiled. 'People are easy to find these days. There is no such thing as a stranger.'

She looked at me for a few moments, her expression changing to something unreadable.

'You do look so much like her,' she said. 'It is almost uncanny.'

And then she left.

## Chapter Seven

# What Meg Wants

The next time I went in to see Ben, I was walking up the ward feeling hesitant about how he would be when I stopped short: Meg was in the seat next to him. Her back was towards me, but I could see that she was leaning in very close to the bed. I approached quietly, wanting to study her, to hear what she was saying before she knew I was there. But she was silent.

'Hi,' I said.

She turned round, a little startled and seemed to blush a little – or was I imagining that?

'Oh, hi.'

'How is he?'

'He's asleep now. He woke up a while ago and was really confused and angry. They said that's normal.'

For a few moments we remained there together, looking at Ben, until it became too awkward.

'I'm going to get a disgusting coffee from the machine,' I announced. 'Do you want one?'

'No, I'm going to head off. I'll walk down with you.'

She gathered up her coat and bag, and we left the ward in silence. I stopped at the vending machine in the waiting area and, as I made my selection, she stood close by, giving me this strange, synthetic look of sympathy and understanding.

'You know, you don't *have* to do this,' she said.

'Have to do what?'

'Keep visiting him. Keep seeing him.'

I knew it. I knew this was coming.

'Why wouldn't I?'

'It's just, look, you two have only been a thing for a few weeks. This is a lot to take on. He might need many weeks of treatment. I'm just saying that no one will judge you if you walk away.'

The machine gurgled as the cup dropped into the little delivery slot. I could hear the BBC news channel playing on a TV in the corner of the room.

'I'm fine,' I said quietly, focusing my attention on the cup filling with vile industrial sludge. 'Thank you.'

'You may be fine now,' she said. 'But what about a month from now? Or two months?' There was a short pause. I could tell she was looking at me. 'And honestly, I don't mean to be rude but I'm not sure you're what he needs right now.'

Finally, I did look back at her.

'What do you mean by that?'

'You do have quite a dark vibe.'

'Dark vibe?' I repeated.

'Look, sorry, I didn't mean anything by it. Just . . . I don't think he needs anything complicated or upsetting at the moment. So maybe it would be better if you just . . . let him go.'

'Better for who?' I asked.

'For Ben obviously.'

I took the steaming cup from the dispenser, maintaining eye contact with her, trying to work out what to say. My hand was shaking so much, the coffee swilled out scalding my skin. Eventually, she held her hands up in mock surrender.

'Look, whatever,' she said, but her voice lacked some of her previous confidence. 'Do what you want, just remember he's fragile.' And then she walked away. As I watched her go, the adrenaline faded, replaced with something much more insidious and gnawing. What if she was right? What if I was no good for him? Maybe I had nothing to offer. Maybe it would be best if I slunk away – from the hospital, from Ben.

Behind it all were the lingering thoughts that made my stomach swoop. The curse. Lorna's words – that I had to be alone. And beyond that, the thing that was much more primal and innate: the sense of dread, skulking about at the back of my mind. The insistent thought: you're bad for him. You're bad.

But I did go back to him. I walked slowly to his bed and sat down, placing the coffee cup on his bedside table next to the copy of *National Geographic*. I picked it up and started flicking through, trying to escape from myself in the glossy photos of faraway places.

'Read,' said a hoarse, quiet voice.

I looked up and Ben was staring back at me, a strained, lopsided grimace on his face.

'You're awake?' I said. 'How are you feeling?'

He shook his head slowly. 'Bad.'

'Is there anything you need? Can I get you anything? Do you want the nurse?'

He shook his head again. Then with great effort he lifted his arm and pointed to the magazine.

'Read,' he said. 'Please.'

So that is what I did. For two hours, I read to him. I read articles on shipwrecks of the African slave trade and melting icebergs on the Antarctic peninsula. I read a piece about an amateur horticulturist who set up a website in the late 1990s to collect and swap information about rare roses and went on to build one of the largest collections in the world. I drew the curtains around us, and climbed onto the bed beside Ben, shuffling as close as I could, and I kept reading. I was halfway through an extremely long article on the use of street security cameras to track wildlife when I realised he was asleep. Looking down, I saw that his hand was on my lap. I picked it up and held it. I could feel his fingers faintly tremoring like the heartbeat of some tiny creature. Like butterfly wings.

That night in bed, I lay for hours, going through everything from the past few days, my thoughts spiralling down strange rabbit holes of guilt and possibility. I kept returning to Lorna's final words. *Just don't fall in love*, and the inevitable follow-on: had I placed Ben in danger? Would he be safer without me? But then I remembered his hand on my lap, and I thought about how crazy it was to think that some ancient curse had followed my family through the generations. How could I possibly believe that?

I couldn't visit the next day – I had three commissions to finish. While working, I kept being drawn back to the mysterious Joan Pendle. I examined the sketch again and knew I'd need to use a different, more precise technique. It would take some thought.

The following morning, I was back with Ben. This time his face seemed a little less swollen, but his skin was a weird yellowy colour. He barely registered me as I sat down beside him. He was staring out of the window.

'How are you?' I said. 'You look better.' I noticed that his eyes were teary. 'Ben?'

73

Slowly he lifted his arm to point out of the window.

'The tree,' he said. 'Can't remember what it's called. The flowers over there ... I ... '

'Don't worry, it'll come back to you.'

He had sunk back down into the bed, his face furrowed in confusion.

'Can't feel anything,' he said. 'So tired.'

'It's okay,' I said. 'Just get some sleep. I'll stay.'

'Don't want to sleep,' he drawled. 'I keep seeing it. Whenever I close my eyes, I see it.'

'The accident?' I asked. 'You're seeing your accident again?'

'No,' he said. 'The bell tower.'

'Oh you don't have to worry about that! I'm not cross any more. It's all forgotten.'

He shook his head. 'There's someone up there.'

A wave of prickling tension went through me.

'What do you mean?'

He turned with agonising effort, his eyes wide and unfocused. 'She's watching.'

'Ben, there is nothing there. That day, I just saw a shadow or something. I think you've had a nightmare, that's all.' The ward had become suddenly quiet, as though everything beyond us was fading far away. 'Besides, why would there be someone up there watching you?'

He shook his head once more.

'Not me. You. She's watching you.'

On the drive home, I rationalised it to myself. It was the pain, the confusion – just some drug-induced dream. Ben didn't really know what he was saying. I'd looked up at the tower a couple of times since that afternoon and I'd never seen anything again. But there was a part of me that couldn't help thinking about the curse. What it was and how it worked. I tried to block it out, but I couldn't. Lorna had told me there was a line of tragedy tracing all the way back through the family for many years. She'd told me there was proof. Perhaps the answers were out there if I wanted them. And I did. I wanted to know who else had been through this.

More importantly, I wanted to know if I could escape.

# Chapter Eight

# The Museum

The next morning, I spent the first few minutes of the day trying to avoid thinking about Ben, or the fear gnawing at me about my aunt's parting message. But then I made the mistake of dragging my laptop out and checking my emails and, among a few boring work messages, I spotted a name I didn't immediately recognise. Christopher Erwitt. It took my groggy brain a few moments to recall that I'd contacted him about his mother's interview with Lorna. He wanted to meet for a coffee and a chat.

*Here we go,* I thought.

I hadn't been to the Bristol Museum in years. There was a school trip once, I must have been nine or ten – we had a guided tour of the Ancient Egypt section and we all stood around for what felt like hours gawping at mummified corpses before spending our allotted pocket money in the gift shop. I bought a postcard of an open sarcophagus and Mum wouldn't let me put it up on my bedroom wall. I was obsessed with cursed tombs and Egyptian mythology for several weeks afterwards, much to the concern of everyone (apart from Lorna, naturally – she was delighted). It was weird to be coming back here, with a curse of my own.

The afternoon was grey and featureless, a fine haze of rain hanging in the cool air. I parked in a decrepit old multi-storey, and walked the short distance to Queens Road, past the parade of cafés and takeaways. The museum looked quite grand in the low light, its famed Venetian gothic frontage seeming to almost glow, despite the gloom. Inside and up the marble steps, the vast entrance hall was as cavernous as I'd remembered, the Ancient Egypt section beckoning to the right.

We'd agreed to meet at the museum café at two and I was already five minutes late. As I was walking through to the café, my footsteps echoing on the tiled floors, I realised I had no idea what Christopher looked like. I should have searched for his biog on the website or done a Google image search. In the end, it didn't matter: the café was almost empty. There was a little group of mothers huddled near the play area, watching their kids rummaging through the dressing-up box, and a couple of old grannies who seemed to have brought their own tea in a thermos flask. And then, across the other side of the seating area, was a lone man perched at a small table reading *History Today*. He was wearing a blazer, jeans and a pair of chunky black-rimmed glasses. He looked younger than I was expecting, late thirties maybe, with an almost handsome, bookish face. There was a scuffed leather satchel hanging on the back of his chair. He looked up, saw me staring and gestured for me to go over.

'You look a little like your aunt,' he said, standing up then reaching out to shake my hand. 'Sit down. Can I get you a drink?'

I asked for a coffee and he shouted 'Two coffees please, Jane' to a bored-looking teenage girl behind the counter. She tutted audibly.

'So,' he said, turning back to the table. 'You're here about the article my mother wrote?'

'Yeah. It was a profile of my aunt, but I can't find it anywhere online.'

'I'm not really surprised about that. The magazine only ran for a few issues and never had a huge circulation. No website, no online presence at all. It's a collector's item now.'

'Was she a journalist?'

'Oh God no,' he said, laughing. 'She was a collector and patron. My father worked for a pretty big petrochemical firm and she redirected his assets into art on a pretty industrial scale. She supported a few well-known artists – including Lorna and Reggie. She treated the magazine like her own personal journal, really. She only covered people she was interested in. She couldn't abide the Young British Artists, which made her a bit unfashionable in the 1990s. She was quite a character. And she absolutely adored your aunt. She was a little obsessed with her, I think. She seemed very drawn to the supernatural element. And she loved the fact your aunt ended up buying this rundown old church in the middle of nowhere. She actually visited while she was writing the article. Did you know that? The two of them became quite close.'

The girl from the café counter brought over two large cups of coffee and a little jug of milk, squinting at us both and then trudging away. Christopher poured milk very slowly into his coffee, stirring it with deliberate care. It seemed as though he was thinking about something very deeply.

'And you work there now,' he said, 'as a jewellery designer?'

'Yeah, I've been there almost two years.'

He nodded, still stirring his drink.

'What's it like? The church, I mean.'

It felt so odd to be here, having a normal conversation with a stranger while Ben lay in hospital, barely functioning.

'It's an amazing space, but it's always cold. Really quiet, too . . . Kind of spooky, I suppose.'

He looked up at me quickly.

'Spooky how?' he asked, his tone a little more urgent.

'Oh, you know, it's an old church. There's a graveyard outside. There is a kind of darkness and loneliness about it.'

'I see,' he said, leaning forward. 'I have to admit, this is why I wanted to meet you.'

'Oh?'

'Has anything happened to you there? Anything strange?'

*She's watching you.* 'Um, no,' I said. 'Not really. It's a bit eerie at night, there are a lot of scary noises, but it's an old building. Why?'

'A couple of years ago, we had a local historian, Bob Hunt, come and give a talk entitled "Somerset and the Supernatural". You probably know that witchcraft was rife throughout the county, well into the nineteenth century, and there are thousands of ghost stories. We got chatting in a pub after the talk, and somehow the church came up in conversation.' He paused, stirring his coffee and then taking a sip. I felt a growing tension in the air. 'He said it is supposed to be haunted. It's mentioned in one of his own books about local folklore.'

'Haunted?' I repeated, trying to sound as casual and unaffected as possible. 'What by?'

'The stories are all quite vague. Just . . . a presence. Whatever it is, old Bob told me in no uncertain terms to stay away. It's supposed to be bad luck to see it.'

A sudden chill. Goosebumps on my arms.

The flash of red in the bell tower.

I think the look of shock on my face was obvious.

'Oh, don't worry,' he said. 'Bob was a bit of a crackpot, to be honest.' He shifted slightly uncomfortably on his chair. 'It got me thinking for a while, though, and when I received your email it brought everything back.'

'Does your mother mention something about it in the article?'

'Oh, the article,' he said. He opened up his *History Today* magazine and inside were three sheets of paper stapled together. 'I hope you don't mind. I only have one copy of the original, so I don't really lend it out. I have photocopied the piece for you.' He handed it to me. 'She doesn't mention ghosts. Not directly. But there's some pretty odd stuff in there. To be honest, I was hoping you might know a bit more. Did your aunt tell you anything about the history of the church?'

'Nothing I remember.'

'The visit made quite an impression on my mother. She took dozens of photos. Here . . . '

He reached into his satchel, pulled out a small folder and handed it to me. It was filled with black and white photographs of the building: the nave, the tower, the graveyard.

'These are incredible,' I said.

'You can keep them. I've had reprints done.'

It was strange and somewhat reassuring to find someone else as interested in Lorna as me, even if it was more about his mother. But there was something in his tone, something going on under the surface I couldn't quite place. I was desperate to get away and read the article, though, so I drained my coffee and put the photocopied sheets and the folder in my bag.

'I'd better be off,' I said. 'It was cool meeting you. Thank you.'

'My pleasure. If you need anything else, you know where I am.'

He sat and watched silently as I put on my jacket and slung my bag over my shoulder.

'After the article was published, Reggie Macclesfield got in touch with my mother. He'd read it and wanted to respond. She ended up interviewing him. I'm thinking of giving the recording a listen, maybe writing the piece myself. Would you like me to send it to you if I think there's anything relevant?'

'Yes,' I said. 'Please do. She didn't write a piece about him then?'

'No, the Lorna article was the last she ever wrote,' he said, looking down and wrapping his hands around his cup as though for warmth and comfort. 'She died two months later.'

Outside in the hazy rain, I felt almost guilty that I had dragged someone else into this little psychodrama I had created. He seemed like a serious, intelligent person: how could I tell him I was being driven by the fear of a curse on my family? But then, *he* had asked me about the church, about whether I'd seen anything weird or spooky there – it was him who brought that up. And was it just a coincidence that his mother had died so soon after visiting Lorna?

I had a bracelet I was supposed to be finishing off, but as soon as I got in and heaved the heavy oak door closed behind me, the lure of the article proved too tempting. I made a cup of tea and sat down on the sofa, then looked at the first page. The main image was a photo of my aunt, standing outside the church, wearing her black motorcycle jacket and Bauhaus T-shirt, cigarette in the corner of her mouth. Classic Lorna. The photo was taken from below so she seemed to be looming over the viewer. Above her you could see the church, all dark and foreboding, and my eye was drawn to a series of dark blobs along the ridge halfway up the tower. When I looked closer I could see that they were rooks, perhaps a dozen of them, perched in a neat line, seemingly looking down towards my aunt or possibly, alarmingly, towards the camera itself.

I didn't realise that this image would so precisely set the tone for the article, and everything that would follow afterwards.

### 'A cursed vision: whatever happened to Lorna Piper' by Margot Erwitt, *Vitrine Magazine*, Autumn 1997

There are strange symbols etched into the door to Lorna Piper's studio, a decrepit church hidden away amid gnarled trees on the outer edge of a sleepy Somerset hamlet. One is a hexafoil, a six-petal flower enclosed in a circle, another shows two interlocking Vs. 'They are witch marks,' she explains as she beckons me inside. 'The parishioners used to carve them as a protection against evil spirits.' She runs her bony fingers along the indented curves. 'Obviously they don't work, because *I* live here now.'

A fortnight ago, during the last warm days of early autumn, *Vitrine Magazine* was astonished to receive an email from Piper. No one had heard from her in three years. The spring of 1994 saw the abrupt end of her creative partnership with Reggie Macclesfield, after making some of the most extraordinary art of the 1980s. Neither would say what happened, just that they separated 'by mutual consent' according to a terse joint state-ment. She immediately announced that she was cutting herself off from the London art scene, bored with its endless parties, celebrity gallery openings and leech-like hangers-on. She put her work into storage and disappeared. Eight months later, Macclesfield won the Turner Prize with his first solo piece. Piper only made one comment at the time, to a reporter from *The Times*: 'I wish him all the best. Perhaps the £25,000 prize will bring him the happiness he was unable to find while working with me.' Like many other art publications, I'd sent her dozens of interview requests since then, but heard nothing back. Until that email.

The content was characteristically terse and opaque. 'Margot, you have always supported my work. I want to introduce you to my new studio. I have a tale to tell. The church isn't just the setting of the story; I think the church *is* the story.'

I readily agreed, though if I'd have known what was in store over the days that followed, I would perhaps have taken more time to think it through.


## Day one

She meets me at the church lychgate wearing tatty black dungarees, her dark hair in two long plaits. Beyond the graveyard, her new studio looks like any small parish church, the weathered Bath stone walls dotted with yellow lichen. Yet, there is an odd disquiet to the place, a strange kind of unrest that I can't quite explain. The tower casts a long shadow like a dagger across the grass.

'Wine?' she asks, as she shows me inside.

While she opens a bottle in the cloister, I look around. The interior has apparently been left as she found it, the windows blackened with dirt, the flagstone floors uneven, the walls scarred and bare, apart from several stone memorial plaques. Most of the old wooden pews are gone, although a few rotting benches remain, as does the raised oak pulpit, which is riddled with woodworm and on the point of collapsing. There is a musty odour of damp earth about the place, mixed with something sickly sweet like decaying vegetation.

But Lorna has brought something of herself into this ancient place. There are rows of industrial-looking shelves, some packed with books, others with records, and several with odd natural objects: old birds' nests, an animal skull. There is a large workbench in the centre of the nave, a ratty sofa and two original Charles Eames lounge chairs placed opposite each other nearby. But there is no sign of any new art in progress.

When we sit down together, I ask straight out: what happened after her sudden exit from the art world? 'I had a bad couple of years,' she says. 'Depression, drugs. I hit rock bottom, then just kept tunnelling. I ended up in a rehab centre in the Cotswolds, got clean, started depressurising, trying to figure out where to go next.' What she decided about her art was that her obsession with the occult and the supernatural contained within it a multitude of mysteries and revelations about her own past. 'I had a rather sad childhood,' she says. 'I grew up in St Albans in the 1960s, and it was just this quiet little commuter town. Mum was a housewife and my father was an accountant. They were fond of each other, but their relationship was very formal and distant in a way that I couldn't understand. It was as though they were living separate lives in the same house. Often, my mother seemed unhappy and frustrated and trapped. I blamed dad for that.'

At the age of two or three, Lorna had a frightening experience. 'We were driving somewhere, and a bird, I think a crow or a rook, flew into the windscreen with a sickening thud and died instantly. There was blood all over the glass. It doesn't sound like much, but I was terrified. It felt like the beginning of a nightmare I'd always known was coming. I started to have awful dreams. I'd see birds clawing at my bedroom window, trying to get in. This progressed to frightening visions of people I'd never met, but felt I knew somehow.' Her father tried to reassure her that these were just bad dreams, but Lorna knew they were manifestations of something she felt deep inside: a lingering sense of fear and loneliness. For reasons she couldn't understand or articulate, she was certain that someone or something was watching her, and that they meant her harm.

The way she coped was art: she would draw what she had seen in her dreams, or craft it out of modelling clay. 'There was one occasion, I drew something I had seen in my sleep the night

84

before – it was a group of women sitting around a table holding hands, and in the background there was this dark figure looking over them, something very threatening. Father took the picture off me. He said that it was strange for a little girl to even imagine such things, but when he showed it to my mother her reaction was very different – she seemed to recognise it somehow.' Lorna recalls the conversation they had.

'What are the people doing at the table?' her mother had asked.

'I don't know,' replied Lorna. 'Talking.'

'What about?'

'Something sad.'

Her mother nodded and leaned right down so that she was at eye level with her daughter. Then she pointed at the dark figure.

'And who is this?'

'I don't know,' said Lorna, looking away. 'I didn't draw that person.'

A few years later, Lorna got into her parents' room and found a box hidden at the back of a bedside cabinet. Inside, she discovered a journal her mother had written. The book opened to a particular section: Elizabeth wrote about discovering the name of her 'birth mother', her 'real mother', Daphne Ricard. Lorna did not understand. Was her mother adopted? No one had ever told her. 'I can recall reading a little further,' says Lorna. 'There was something about an awful secret. A tragedy. A curse. But before I could find out more, my father walked in. He was furious, ripping the journal from my hands and sending me bawling to my room. Later, I heard raised voice downstairs, then my mother came to see me. She looked ashen-faced. I asked her about Daphne and I remember that she grimaced as though in pain. Then she said, "You don't want to know. It's best not to know." I forgot about that night for many years. It wasn't until I got here that I remembered. Isn't that odd?'

As she got older, Lorna sought solace from the tension and boredom of home in books. Her mother had a small collection of Penguin classics, which Lorna precociously raced through. Her favourites were the gothic novelists: the Brontës, Walpole, Radcliffe. Her tastes grew darker. She joined the local library and ordered books on witchcraft and the supernatural, hiding them from her parents like a guilty secret.

At eighteen, she fled to London, ending up in a squat in Hackney, where she started to make sculptures out of whatever weird stuff she could find. She would spend days scouring the old East End scrapyards, bringing back shop-window dummies, pushchairs and burned-out televisions, turning them into eerie statues of demons and monsters. In 1975, she applied to study Fine Art and Sculpture at the Slade and was accepted on to a diploma course. She began to make large installations based on Victorian gothic paintings – devils constructed out of wire and metal and circuit boards, kneeling on the chests of sleeping mannequins. Then Reggie came along.

They met in the Grafton Arms pub, down the road from the Slade. He was in a little corner with several other young men, most of them wearing polyester shirts and kipper ties like mathematics lecturers; she was with a girl named Patty Egan from her course, both of them in ripped drainpipe jeans, Docs and mohair jump-ers, nails painted jet black. 'When we sat down with our drinks, I remember Patty looking over at the group and explaining they were from the Slade's electronics lab,' says Lorna. 'She found it hilarious that they were trying to make art on computers. But I was intrigued.'

One of the group was different to the others, tall and weirdly refined with a messy mop of curly hair. He was wearing a burgundy leather jacket and tight, striped trousers like a tall Marc Bolan. It was Reggie. Later, Lorna went up to the bar, and he stood beside her, eyeing her cautiously as they waited to order. She recalls the conversation perfectly.

'You at the Slade too?' he had asked.

'Yeah,' she said, with a disinterested tone.

'Fine art?'

Lorna says she lit a cigarette and nodded, blowing smoke in his direction.

'I'm in the computer lab,' he said, wafting the smoke away. 'I design robots.'

She twisted round to face him. 'Robots?'

'Well, computers that talk. I'm experimenting with speech synthesis and artificial intelligence.'

'You came to art school to make HAL 9000?'

He laughed. 'Something like that.'

'Why?'

'Computers are the future of art.'

'Bullshit.'

'Okay,' he said, unperturbed. 'What do *you* make?'

'I make sculptures of supernatural beings, monsters – stuff from paganism, ritual, myth. I'm very interested in the gothic and uncanny, but with a modern edge. I call it techno-folkloric art.'

'You want to scare people?'

'Always.'

'Right,' he said, leaning in against the bar. 'So these monsters you make – imagine if they could turn to the viewer and speak.'

And that was that. For the next four hours, until they had to be physically thrown out of the pub, they talked about art, horror, computers and machines. She told him things she'd never told anyone – about how scared she always felt, about how she was certain a tragedy existed somewhere in her past; she told him about finding her mother's journal. He didn't dismiss it. At a house party two nights later, the two of them sat on the stairs and discussed their theories on technology and superstition. As drunk couples pushed by, he said he was fascinated by the idea of shared recollection – he believed memories and experiences could be passed down through generations as psychic engrams, like units of information, like computer programs. They knew, as the music pounded and thick cannabis smoke turned the air to fog, that they had to work together. But there was something else she knew. 'I really fancied him,' she says. 'I'd never met such a kindred spirit.'

When the party ended, she invited him back to her student hovel. They lay next to each other in her bed, and began to draw up a manifesto for their art. Their work would consist of terrifying, revelatory installations fusing traditional sculpture and new technologies.

'We need to make ourselves part of the art,' Reggie had told her. 'Like Gilbert and George, but . . . '

'Totally impassive and unreadable.'

He moved closer.

'Like Kraftwerk. Like we're technicians producing these incredible visions as though they were just . . . '

'Computer printouts.'

Lorna remembers leaning against Reggie's shoulder, then she turned to him. 'There was something beautifully feminine about his face,' she says. 'The way his hair fell about his eyes in curled ribbons. I began to feel almost woozy with excitement and anticipation. It seemed inevitable that we would kiss, and I wanted to. I wanted whatever was going to happen next. But nothing happened. He kind of jerked away with this horrified expression on his face. It was clear to me in that moment that all he wanted from me was art. It was . . . oh well.' She pauses, and looks away,

88

and her eyes look suddenly moist. 'One of us apologised. I can't remember who.'

As dawn came up and the sun began to filter through the tattered curtains, it was decided that their relationship should be as inscrutable and sterile as machinery. Every time she thought of that moment over the years to come, Lorna said she would feel a distinct throbbing pain in her chest.

They started their working relationship together. They built animatronic demons from scrap metal, the limbs controlled by computer programs. Their work, *Zoltan II* (1982), was a pastiche of an arcade fortune-telling machine featuring a robotic figure who would dispense horrifying predictions to spectators, using a speech synthesiser and language processor. *Séance* (1983) featured a group of mannequins around a table, holding hands, as spotlights strobed and a robotic medium listed the spirits of dead people. The British art scene was snobbish about their work, but they were picking up interest elsewhere; a famous hip-hop artist used their sculptures in one of his videos, which brought them interest from cool galleries in New York and Tokyo. They dropped out of the Slade and set up a workshop in an abandoned slaughterhouse in Barking. By the mid-1980s they were being exhibited all over the world as well as working on special effects for a string of horror and sci-fi films. When reporters asked about their relationship, Reggie spoke for them – he said it was purely artistic, purely mechanical. It was their image. They appeared together at openings, unsmiling and slightly apart in identical black and silver outfits, behind metallic sunglasses. There was a famous *South Bank Show* interview with Melvyn Bragg where Reggie said he was asexual – he didn't want a partner, a family, none of that stuff interested him. 'I agreed,' Lorna says. 'I said I felt the same, even though it made me so sad.' She tells me that by the mid-1980s, her and Reggie were spending so much time in their workshop, they dragged a mattress in and slept there, next to each other but apart. 'Sometimes, I'd have a nightmare and wake us both up,' she recalls. 'Reggie would calm me and fetch me water, and then he'd go and sit at his computer to do some programming. I'd watch him from the bed, feeling reassured by the glow of his screen.' Then he'd crawl back into bed as the sun was coming up and she would lie there watching him. She would say to herself, 'If I reached out, I could touch you, Reggie.' But she never did.

There were times Lorna couldn't work, when a dark cloud would sit above her and zap all her energy. Reggie always made her feel safe, but she was beginning to realise she needed more from him. 'One weekend, I decided I needed to get away so I went to see my mother,' she says. 'She left my father when I was eight years old, and my sister was two. We lived in a little flat in Brighton, and when sis and I left home, she stayed. That weekend, I just wanted to see her. I needed to ask her something.' When Lorna arrived, she saw that her mother had aged quite gracefully. There was a strange restless air about her, like a train passenger in a waiting room. Although she made Lorna feel welcome, she spent a lot of the time in her armchair looking out of the window, out towards the sea, as though she were waiting for someone.

The two of them took long walks along the beach each morning. They drank tea on the pier. Elizabeth cooked delicious French meals. On the final day, during a stroll across the cliffs towards Hove, Lorna told her mother about her feelings for Reggie.

'That time I read your journal when I was a child,' Lorna said. 'You wrote that we were cursed never to love.'

'You shouldn't have seen that.'

'Is it true?'

Her mother gave her a sort of wan smile. 'Love is hard for us.'

'Reggie is not like Dad.'

'Oh, darling, I was never in love with your father.'

Lorna stopped in her tracks, the waves crashing in a few feet away. She wasn't surprised. She'd always known, but it was hard having it confirmed so casually. And there was something Elizabeth wasn't saying. She was keeping something back, a secret.

'So I shouldn't tell Reggie how I feel? I should just forget about it?'

'I can't make that decision for you. But you must understand, you can't have what other people have.'

'What do you mean?!'

Elizabeth started walking again, wrapping her scarf around her neck.

'Mum,' Lorna yelled into the wind. 'Is it coming for me?!'

Her mother turned, and called through the wind, 'If you are feeling like this, it is already here.'

That night, Lorna packed her things, and ran from the house. She caught the train back to London, her mother's words sounding in her ears. She was desperate to see Reggie, to tell him how she felt, but she couldn't face losing what they had. She would have to keep it buried. She could see no future in art, in life, without him.

At the studio, he was sitting alone in the dark, chair pulled up to the large, barred window, the headlights from passing cars illuminating the room with shards of orange light. His hair was unkempt and wild, like a romantic poet. He stood when he saw her.

'Where did you go?! I've been so worried!'

'I went to see my mother.'

'Are you okay?'

'I will be.'

He approached her in an almost uncertain way, as though frightened. He looked beautiful.

'I really missed you,' he said.

Her arms felt weak. He put his hands on her face. 'I really missed you,' he whispered.

They kissed. Her bag dropped from her hand. All her resolutions shattered.

Back in the church, in the present day, she gets up and lights a cigarette. 'That's enough talking for today,' she says. There are tears in her eyes. Later, I lay awake in the bed she made up for me on the sofa in the nave. I hear her pacing the floor for hours.

## Day two

I get up to the smell of bacon cooking. Lorna is in the kitchen making doorstep-size butties and fresh coffee. I tell her that yesterday we talked a lot about the past, so I suggest we move on to the present. She nods, relieved.

A year ago, Lorna discovered that the abandoned St Cyprian's Church near Batheaston was up for sale, and she was immediately interested. Her family had lived in this area of Somerset for many generations and she saw it as a sign. It would be a symbolic homecoming. When she called the estate agent they told her the church had been built as a place of worship for the owners of St Cyprian's Court, a lavish manor house that burned down in mysterious circumstances in the late nineteenth century. 'The church had been on the market for several months with little interest,' she explains. 'Lots of people had been to see it, but none returned for a second viewing, so the price had been significantly reduced. Apparently, there's some dark legend attached to both the house and the church. Anyway, the estate agent hinted that if I were to make any sort of offer it would almost certainly be accepted.'

The building turned out to be semi-derelict, hidden among gnarled ancient trees like a scene from a horror movie. It even has an ancient crypt – only accessible from the outside, via a narrow staircase and a low door. Lorna says it is empty. No stone coffins, no skeletal remains. Just dirt floors and arched ceilings and rats shuffling in the dark corners. 'Perhaps I will demand to be interred here when I die,' she laughs.

She fell in love with the place immediately. 'I felt like the girl in some gothic fairy tale,' she says. 'Lost in the woods, all alone, stumbling upon an enchanted building and then falling asleep inside. I knew that something would come – something vital and terrifying would wake me up at last. It was strange because the church seemed so imposing and unwelcoming, but it was also familiar. I felt like I was supposed to be there.' She discovered that before his conversion to Christianity, St Cyprian had been an occultist and sorcerer. That sealed the deal. She put in what she thought was an insultingly low offer, and twenty minutes later, the estate agent called back to tell her it had been accepted.

It cost a small fortune to repair and update the building, renovate the ancient heating system, and organise electricity and phone connections. But it still felt wild and disjointed from the modern world. The only sounds were the wind, the creak of swaying branches, the rooks squawking. 'I noticed them on the first morning,' she says. 'They were gathering in the trees at the edges of the graveyard.' It is clear they bothered her.

In the evening, we have a whisky together, our faces illuminated by a dozen candles. As we talk, shadows creep along the ancient walls. 'Do you hear it?' she asks. 'A shuffling sound, like small feet, like wings spreading and closing.' But all I can hear are the tree branches scraping against the windows. I say to her in a joking way that perhaps we're not entirely alone here and not entirely safe.

93

'That's good,' she says. 'That is where creativity comes from. At night, while I lie in bed, there are whispers in the air, but I cannot hear the words.'

## Day three

We spend the morning constructing several extra shelving units that will hold all her art materials, prototypes and several abandoned projects, which are due to arrive from the storage facility in Wapping. A delivery truck turns up crammed with wooden crates. She has hired a couple of art students from Bath University to help unpack them. There are concept paintings, 'imperfect' pieces that she never showed, preliminary models of sculptures you can now see in Tate Modern or MoMA. There is a series of life drawings created on a computer and printed on dot-matrix printer paper, which she hangs on the south wall between the plaques dedicated to long-dead people. She enjoys the irony of this placement. One of the student helpers, a rather serious girl named Pandora, dressed in bootcut jeans and a vest top, expresses concerns that the damp atmosphere is likely do lasting damage to some of Piper's works. 'Degradation is an essential element of art,' she tells her. 'The modern lust for preservation is ghoulish and neurotic. Things want to rot. They desire death.' The student scuttles away, chastised. Piper lights her seventh cigarette of the morning.

The girls stop for lunch, perching on a box crypt in the churchyard, eating their sandwiches. We overhear them talking.

'Are you going to Tom's party tonight?'

'Maybe. I'm seeing Mansun at Moles. I could swing by after that. You?'

'I'm pretty knackered. Some of those sculptures weigh a fucking ton. That robot head, Jesus.'

'What's she doing out here anyway? I guess she's upset about that whole Turner Prize thing.'

'Shit, that's got to hurt. The moment Reggie Macclesfield ditches her, he wins it for his own work. Then everyone starts saying he was the real talent and she was holding him back? Fucking Yoko Ono–John Lennon bullshit. She *is* pretty mental though. Why does she still dress like a goth? Christ, it's the nineties.' They spot a crow watching them eat and one of them shoos it away.

'This place gives me the creeps,' the other one says. 'I can't believe she sleeps here.'

'Probably in a coffin.'

'While smoking a fag.'

With that, they collapse into laughter.

When the girls leave, the church is quiet again and Lorna is surrounded by the detritus of her life's work. 'When I first bought the church, I did think a lot about occasionally opening the space up, using it as a combined studio and gallery,' she says. 'Not for preening critics and snobbish art wankers – I don't want them wandering about in here, mentally assessing the value of the works in the wake of my artistic break-up. No, I want to make the space available for young artists, people like Reggie and me with weird visions and ideas. I'd like to support the next generation of outsiders. For now, I'll keep this place just for me. Perhaps I *will* sleep in a bloody coffin.'


## Day four

Lorna tells me that last night she dreamed she was working alone on a sculpture, seated in her armchair next to a solitary candle. Gradually, she became aware that someone – or something – was very close to her. When she looked around, she thought she saw, in the thick darkness, a pair of small black eyes, watching, waiting. She was so terrified she couldn't move or make a sound. 'When I woke this morning I found this on the bed.' She hands me solitary black feather.

I wonder if this really happened. I wonder if she's playing with me.

We spend a couple of hours staring at her unfinished sculptures, her sketches. 'They meant nothing to me any more,' she says. 'What were Reggie and I even trying to say with those wretched machines? I came here to make something about *me*.'

But who is she? Who is she without Reggie, who had never loved her at all? She suggests a walk to the local inn. We leave the churchyard and wander along a narrow path through a meadow dotted with wildflowers. We pass a large building site, which Lorna says will be an exclusive modern housing development named St Cyprian's Court, where the manor once stood, and a little further on, a large, much older building named the Coach House. Its garden is chaotically overgrown, and from it sprouts a large For Sale sign. 'This will all be gentrified soon,' she says with a sigh.

When we get onto the road again, a hazy fog falls and it takes us a while to find the pub, the Black Dog, a ramshackle cottage with a rusty sign hanging at an angle from the wall. Inside, it is like a scene from some Sunday-evening costume drama. Pockmarked stone tablet floors, ancient wooden tables, a charred inglenook fireplace, yellowing walls lined with sepia photographs of huntsmen on horseback. Two old men in flat caps droop over half-pints of Guinness, their slavering dogs sleeping at their feet. We fetch drinks at the bar and sit near the window, where she looks out on the empty fields and the grey clouds above. What exactly is it she is looking for out here?

'Inspiration,' she sighs. 'Something new, or maybe something very old. I don't know.'

We sit in silence for a few moments.

'Bad weather coming in,' says a voice from the other side of the room. It's one of the old men, his cragged face now turned in Lorna's direction. Why is it that men feel completely unable to leave women alone in a bar? She nods, not wishing to encourage him, but he is not to be rebuffed.

'You at the church then?' he says.

How could he possibly know? I wonder.

'Yes,' Lorna replies. 'Have you seen me there?'

'Word gets around.' He takes a sip of his drink. 'You all right in there, are you?'

'Yes, it's a very interesting building.'

The other man looks up and contorts his face into an unreadable expression. The two of them exchange a glance.

'Do you know about the church?' she asks them.

The woman behind the bar looks up, suddenly interested.

One of the men shakes his head. 'Nobody goes near it,' he says. 'Nobody with sense, mind.' He looks back down at his drink, swirling the glass in his hand.

'What do you mean?' Lorna asks. Silence. 'I said, what do you mean by that?'

'It's just an old, ugly place,' the other man says. 'He meant nothing by it.'

Lorna looks at them, clearly expecting some follow-up, but none comes. Tutting, she turns back to the window. She must feel a long way from the sophistication and fun of the Colony Room Club. That was part of a different life. So where is she now? The afterlife? She turns away from the window.

'What if I can't work?' she says. 'What if it really *was* all Reggie?'

Back at the church, with evening drawing in, she lights dozens of candles and we settle down into moth-eaten old armchairs with a bottle of claret, and then another, and another. We talk about art and her fascination with the occult. Just before midnight, the wine finished, we go outside for a cigarette and look up at the night sky. Beyond the branches of the ancient trees, beyond the black clouds, there are distant stars twinkling. 'You are dead!' she suddenly yells up at them. 'You died thousands of years ago! You just don't realise it!'

As we turn to walk back into the church, I stop in the doorway in mild surprise. Despite it being a calm night, with not even the slightest wisp of a breeze, all the candles have gone out.


## Day five

Lorna wakes in a mood of pensive darkness that I am now becoming familiar with. When I emerge from my makeshift bedroom at eight in the morning, I find her sitting in the kitchen staring at the stone altar.

'Did you hear it last night?' she asks. 'Did you hear the noise?'

She has started to hear a tapping sound in the church at night. A quiet, patient rap at the small door in the north transept. (In church architecture, it's known as the devil's door. They were meant to lead demons out of the church.) Tap. Tap. Tap. Like someone knocking. She says she crawled out of bed and stalked quietly to the door, her feet slapping on the cold stone. But when she lifted the latch and opened it, there was nothing outside.

'Something is coming,' she says.

I heard nothing at all.

Today, no work is done. Instead Lorna sits smoking cigarette after cigarette, watching the sun come up then fade away. She said this building saved her from despair, but has it? One thing is becoming increasingly clear. There is a horrible sadness here. It oozes from the flagstones, it is in the walls. Dread, rising like damp. You can feel it weighing you down as though your clothes are sodden. It hums in the air. Had it always been here, or did Lorna bring it? I think it is both. Lorna tells me she's had the same feeling inside her since she was a little girl – that she was somehow doomed. The church amplifies it and reflects it back at her. Sometimes she wanders along reading the epitaphs on the walls – these solemn expressions of grief and respect to lords and generals and clergymen and their wives. She asks out loud, 'Which of you haunts this building?' Because something does.

## Day six

For hours she drinks and she studies her inventory of broken circuit boards, mannequin parts, mutilated toys. But she can't see how they will fit together in new ways – all she sees are the cursed robotic beasts she had constructed in her old life. Her mind bereft of ideas or inspiration – the frustration is maddening.

'I think this place was a trap,' she announces as night falls. 'I felt certain there was a story for me here. I felt it in my bones – some strange connection to my past. When I walked into the church I thought I could hear my ancestors whispering to me. But no, something tempted me in and then it started draining my life away.' She stands up and walks to the altar, sloshing wine from her glass. 'You summoned me, but there is nothing here!' she yells, as though addressing the building itself. 'Well, I'm not scared of you! Whatever you want from me, come and get it!' Then she sinks down onto her knees, spilling red wine on the stone. I rush over to her, worried that she's about to pass out.

'Lorna, come on, let's get you to the chair,' I say. She looks at me. 'I've lost everything.'

Suddenly there is a thick atmosphere in the room. It feels like a terrible pressure around us, like tension mounting, a vice gripping shut. For the first time I feel what she has been feeling: that we are not alone.

At that precise moment, there is a thud at the door.

It is not a tapping this time, but a loud insistent bang. The noise makes Lorna sit up with a start. For a few seconds we stare at each other, unable to say or do anything. Then come two more bangs on the ancient wood, the noise resounding around the building. Someone is out there.

'Who is it?' she calls, her voice shaky.

I've been in some strange situations with artists in my time: I was shouted at by Tracey Emin, thrown out of Francis Bacon's studio, but I've never been actually frightened before.

There is a long silence, long enough to make me wonder if this is really happening. But we can both feel it. The presence of someone. Lorna drags herself off the floor and towards the porch, moving as silently as she can through the gloom. Beneath the door, I can see a shadow moving.

'Who is there?' she calls, louder this time, with an edge of anger. 'This isn't funny.'

She steps closer to the door, then leans forward slowly, meaning to place her ear against the oak.

'Lorna, it's me.'

The sound of the voice makes her leap backwards in shock and surprise. I am cowering behind the armchair, wondering why we are not calling the police, but when I peek out again, to my astonishment, she is opening the door.

'Do you know who it is?' I whisper.

100

'Yes,' she says. 'It is the past. The past has come back for me.' She puts her hand to the key and turns it, before dragging the door open.

'I'm sorry,' the figure at the door says. 'I'm sorry to turn up so late.'

Lorna is silent for a second, as though calculating the risk of inviting our visitor in.

'You'd better come in.'

Lorna walks back into the nave unsteady on her feet, and following close behind is the Turner Prize-winning artist Reggie Macclesfield.

They sit together, Reggie in one armchair, Lorna in the other. I hover nearby. She introduces us to each other. He shakes my hand. 'I read *Vitrine*,' he says. 'The only art magazine that isn't complete shite.'

'Do you want me to go?' I ask them.

'No,' says Lorna. 'Stay. Please.'

Reggie nods his approval.

I go to the kitchen to make them both coffee. Lorna offers Reggie a cigarette, which he snatches greedily. Then she says, 'Why are you here?'

'Oh, I'm speaking at an arts festival in Bath.'

'No, why are you *here*? Why now?'

'I don't know.'

I bring over the coffee, then retreat to the kitchen, pretending to wash up, but watching them. She stares at him, her face blank.

'You're here to gloat.'

He smiles. 'This is an amazing space,' he says. 'Are you working?'

'I'm trying.'

101

Reggie reaches into his coat pocket and drags out a large pewter hip flask, twisting off the lid in one practised motion. He offers it to her, but she shakes her head. He pours a generous glug into his coffee.

'I tried to go teetotal,' he says. 'But I failed. I've been failing since you left London.'

Lorna snorts. 'The Turner Prize was a failure?'

His face takes on a sort of desperate grimace. 'It meant nothing.'

'Yes,' she says, 'I've heard those words before.'

He sunk into the chair as though an agonising pain had passed through him. It was clear they were reliving some half-buried trauma. Now he is back, sitting in her church, her studio, looking desperate and contrite.

'Why are you here?' Lorna repeats to him.

He looks her in the eyes for the first time tonight. 'I want to work with you again.'

This is too much for Lorna – she lets out a howl of something like laughter, but much darker and more pitiful. Like a wounded animal.

They sit in silence for a while and the tension tingles. Underneath everything, I realise, there is still a crackle of possibility in this relationship. The electrical charge they generated has never gone away. The church suddenly feels full. A congregation of two. Reggie draws a small notebook from the same pocket as he had taken the flask.

'I have ideas,' he says. 'Just snippets really, new technologies, ugly unformed things. But with you ... they could be something. They could fucking sing.'

He tries to hand the book to Lorna but she knocks it away.

'Imagine it, if we started making art together again as a team. We'd have galleries queuing up to exhibit us.'

'Don't,' she hisses.

'Just look. I'm not asking for you to agree to anything tonight. Just take the book and read my notes. Look at the sketches.' His eyes blaze.

'Reggie, please,' she says. 'Don't do this.'

'But Lorna . . .'

'Don't do this.'

He walks towards her, the book still held out like a gift or a peace offering. There is something crazed about him now. 'Just take the book and look at it. Just give me a chance. You owe it to us!' With that, he grabs her by the wrist and forces the book into her hand. I know I should stand up and intervene, I should protect her. But I'm frozen in my seat. It feels as though I am watching theatre – it is shocking and intimate but it is also something I cannot intrude upon. Lorna is so shocked by his gesture that she takes the book. But it is just an instant. With all her might, with everything she can muster, she pushes him away and throws the book across the room. It hits the stone wall with an explosion of pages and photos and inserted notes and sketches.

'Fuck you, Reggie!' she screams as he scurries over to gather the wreckage of the book together. 'I can't do this again! I don't need you.'

Suddenly he is furious too. 'Really?' he says, his voice snide and cruel. 'You're doing fine out here? You're making art without me?! Look at you, look at this place! All this old shit you've kept. It's a fucking mausoleum, it's a graveyard! You are buried here.' There is something crazed about him now. 'Just take the book and look at it. Come back to London, give me a chance. I know things will never be like they were between us, but maybe they can be something new.'

I am sure it would have been so easy for her to submit. All three of us know that if she went back to the city, back to her partnership with Reggie, they would be able to create something together, and that people would take notice. But she doesn't submit.

'I came here to find something of my own,' she says quietly. 'My past, my history. A story, any story. Maybe you're right. Maybe there is nothing here. But I have to try.' Her eyes glisten in the candlelight. 'Why did you do it?' she says, almost in a whisper. 'Why did you leave?'

He looks down, unable to meet her eye again. A shabby caricature of himself.

'If you don't know, if you really never knew, there is no point in answering.'

He gathers the book together and puts it down on Lorna's workbench.

'This is an incredible building,' he says. 'There is something very weird about it. But you won't be happy here. This is not where you will make your grand statement. It is going to swallow you whole.'

With that, he walks away, pulling open the door and disappearing into the empty night.

We sit up and talk into the early hours. It feels more like a therapy session than an interview.

'The day you got back from your mother's. That kiss. It led to something, didn't it?'

'Yes,' she replies.

After the act, the atmosphere was immediately wrong. Lorna says she knew it was already doomed. She sensed from him a silent regret. She can't remember who said it first, that it had been a mistake. Reassurances flowed between them. 'We'll forget about it, put it behind us, it will be fine.' But it wouldn't be. A spectre lived in the room with them now. As they lay naked, entwined in each other's arms on that mattress in the studio, surrounded by unfinished work, Lorna's world began to collapse in on itself.

In the following weeks, they didn't speak of it; the awkwardness and regret seeped in like a poison mist. They argued over work, they cancelled commissions and exhibitions. Lorna was pushing him away, for his own good she believed. Then one day Reggie packed his bags. 'This is too painful,' he said. 'I can't do it any more.' And he was gone.

I tell her there is still such a chemistry between them, it lit the building up. She nods reluctantly. 'Those times we would work together in the studio for days without sleeping or bathing. The same energy as young lovers. Almost exactly the same. I hate the fact that I can still feel it.' She lights another cigarette. 'Five minutes with him and I can actually feel dormant parts of my brain firing up again.'

We sit and drink and smoke and talk. There is incense burning on a small side table and the thick, spicy odour of patchouli permeates the air.

'When Reggie asked me to go back to London, I felt a presence. I had a sense of other women being close – it hummed in the air. And at last, I heard my ancestors speaking softly to me.'

'What did they say?'

'They said, don't go.'

'But can you live here, in this haunted house?'

She breathes out a fog of cigarette smoke.

'All houses are haunted,' she says. 'One way or another.'

'But will you be *happy* here?'

She scoffs at the question. 'Happiness? Do you think that is what I am looking for? Artists don't want happiness, we want immortality.' With a struggle, she extricates herself from the chair and shuffles off towards her bathroom. It seems the interview is over, but then she turns back.

'I'm sorry, I couldn't give you any new work to write about,' she says. 'I hope your time here wasn't wasted.' I assure her it wasn't. 'Something happened here in this place and I am part of it. It is close. It is very close indeed.' She looks out through the windows. 'Do you see them out there? In the trees, on the gravestones – dark shapes shuffling, watching.'

But all I see is a half moon and the silhouettes of branches reaching out towards each other in the night. There are no birds at all.

## Day seven

This morning the sky is grey and low. Inside the building the air feels charged, as though a storm is brewing. While I pack my things, Lorna sits in her armchair with a cigarette, watching me. It feels as though she is stewing, like some mystery is hanging here waiting to be resolved. I take my bag to the car and place it in the boot. Walking back to the church, I can't help but feel disappointed. I haven't witnessed some great resurgence. I haven't seen new art.

When I get in the church, Lorna is standing stock still looking towards the devil's door, her eyes wide. I'm about to ask what is going on, but she shushes me.

And then I hear it, the tapping. Tapping at the door. The sound of tiny feet on the roof, on the stone pavement outside. She walks over and, in one movement, flings the door wide open. Dead leaves blow in across the cold stone floors. She is standing there, her arms open, ready to embrace whatever is lurking outside, whatever it will bring. Creativity or madness or death. In a moment of calm she turns to me and smiles.

'It's here,' she says.

There is a whoosh of air and movement as something flies in. It passes very close to her face then out towards me, then away again. Shocked, we both look around for the source.

And there it is on the lectern of the old wooden pulpit – a large black crow. It shuffles a little and then settles, staring directly at Lorna with its tiny black eyes. Slowly, she starts to edge towards it, not wishing to scare it away. But, in fact, the bird shows no sign of fear. It stays, and it stares.

'Hello,' she says. It pecks at its feathers briefly but does not look as though it will fly away. She steps closer, edging past her workbench, which she knocks with her hip causing a loud scraping noise. The bird does not move. Closer, she steps, closer still. It looks away and shuffles along its ancient wooden perch. When she reaches the foot of the narrow stairs leading up to the pulpit, the crow momentarily opens its wings and Lorna stops dead, thinking she had finally frightened it, but it seems to be merely stretching. Stretching and waiting. The steps look rotten and weak, and I can only watch as she tentatively places a foot on the first one and tests it. It creaks but it holds. The bird turns towards her. Another step. She grasps the handrail, and I edge forward, expecting at any moment that a stair will crumble and Lorna will plummet straight through. Another step, and I wonder to myself, what on earth will happen next? Will she reach out? Will it hop on to her hand?

Slowly, with the soft wood groaning beneath her, she leans forward to make the final step on to the pulpit landing – it is then, finally, that the bird takes one last look at her and launches itself away in a flurry of feathers. The shock of the movement unbalances Lorna and in a panic she grasps for the lectern. Now, the step beneath her foot finally gives way. Her leg falls straight through, the stair exploding into rotten splinters beneath her, and in desperation she grabs at the handrail, which somehow stays firm, preventing her from crashing entirely through the staircase and on to the ground below. For a few seconds, she hangs there, shocked. I run towards her, and reach up, trying to support her as she slowly pulls herself up, dragging her body on to the raised floor of the pulpit where she lies, trying to catch her breath.

I ask her if she's all right.

'I think so,' she replies.

Eventually, she looks around and sees a small cupboard beneath the lectern, hidden in the shadow.

'I've never noticed that before,' she says.

Then she reaches out and opens the cupboard door. I move round so I can see inside as well. There in the little dark space are the mottled sepia edges of what look like pages.

Is it an old bible?

She reaches and takes it.

It is a bundle of old papers, tied up with twine, and as she draws them out, we realise together that they are letters. Several are still in their opened envelopes, the stamps crossed with blurred print, the addresses handwritten on the ancient paper in faded ink. I catch site of a date on the corner of one. June 1915.

I hold on to her as she clambers slowly down the remaining steps, clutching the letters to her chest like priceless artefacts. She goes to her workbench, sits, and slowly unties the twine from around the pile. The paper looks as dry and delicate as ancient papyrus. The sheets are stained a reddish brown and many are torn. Lorna holds them to her face and breathes them in. I ask her what she smells. 'There's the faintest hint of perfume,' she replies. 'Something very soft and floral. But there is something else, lingering just beneath. I don't know. It's like dirt and blood and terror . . .'

She studies the signature at the bottom of one page and suddenly looks bewildered. She hands the letters to me, almost as though she wants me to confirm that they are real. I look at the sloping signature at the bottom.

Daphne Ricard.

'My grandmother,' she says. 'Daphne Ricard was my grandmother.'

Lorna begs me to stay with her while she reads the letters. I make us strong cups of coffee. Apparently, half of them are written by Daphne, the other half by a young soldier named Robert Woodbridge.

When she finishes reading, she puts the letters down, her face pale and drawn. 'My God,' she says. 'Daphne fell in love with him and then . . . something came for her. Something terrible. It had come for her mother too, and God knows how many women in the family before that. It was a curse. An awful curse. The one my mother talked of. Now, I know. Now I understand.'

Outside, in the trees and along the roof of the church, in the belfry and atop the gravestones, dozens of shiny black birds have gathered and their cawing fills the air. The sound is almost deafening.

Lorna Piper came to a tiny village in Somerset to find out more about her past, in the hope that it would inspire her art. Now she has uncovered a tragic family secret. She wants to know how this church links to her ancestors and where the curse originated. She is terrified but also inspired. She is determined that when she discovers the horror at the centre of it all, she will capture it in her art.

'It will be my greatest work,' she says as we hug goodbye. 'And my bitterest warning.'

# Chapter Nine

# **Realisation**

Lorna didn't make the curse up – she had it in writing, from my great grandmother. Or at least that's what the article claimed. As soon as I finished reading, I turned the pages over and started again, took a highlighter from my desk and underlined words and phrases. I paced around on the old stone floor, reading and thinking, reading and thinking, my mind whirling. The things that happened to Lorna in this place, the letters just being there all that time – what did it all mean? I knew my aunt was an eccentric, I knew she liked to play with expectations, to create controversy, so the article couldn't be entirely relied upon. But I didn't believe she was a liar. The local historian who Christopher mentioned said that there were legends attached to this place, confirming what the men in the pub had apparently hinted to Lorna and Margot. But if it was true, how did it connect to a curse on my family?

When I finally snapped out of it for a few seconds, I realised it was getting dark. Shadows were crawling down the walls, the tower chamber was already in blackness. I felt, very suddenly and clearly, that I didn't want to be in the church that night. I really, really didn't want to be alone. So I did what I always did. I called Nikki. I called my sis.

'Can I stay over tonight?' I asked, while hurriedly gathering up my car keys, bag and jacket from the work desk. I knew that Justin was away at some space expo.

'Yes, of course. Are you okay? You sound stressed.'

'Yeah. Just a weird day. I'll tell you all about it.'

I was just about to bolt for the door when I had that irrational fear you get as a child, the one where you're running up a dark staircase to bed and you're sure something is following you. I was absolutely certain someone else was in the building. A thick sludgy silence engulfed me. It was as though the air itself was waiting for a sound, a movement. I kept thinking of Lorna's words in that article. *Something is coming.*

Slowly, I walked towards the main door, still listening, still waiting. When I was close, I took a deep breath as though I was about to swim through some kind of dangerous underwater cavern, then I grabbed the handle and pushed. Nothing. It wouldn't budge. I pushed again. Nothing. I thought maybe I'd locked it, so I pulled the key out of my bag and tried it. No, it was unlocked. I took a step back and shoulder barged the door. This time it gave a couple of millimetres as though ... as though someone were holding it closed. A sickening fear shuddered through me.

I ran instead to the devil's door at the north transept, and it opened with a reluctant groan. A rush of cool air hit me, along with the smell of wet earth. Branches were rustling in the wind, a crescent moon was visible just above the treeline. I slid out, slowly closing the door behind me. Then I switched my phone torch on and looked both ways, out towards the gravestones, and afterwards, reluctantly, at the main entrance.

There was no one there.

Another breath, then I bolted fast, sprinting down the muddy path towards the car, navigating by the weak light from my phone. Halfway, I got the sense again of something behind me and turned. I was sure I saw a figure standing dead still amid the headstones. Looked again with the torch. Nothing. Waves of terror turned my insides to ice water as I ran towards the car, dragging my feet through the mud.

I was so preoccupied, I didn't see the exposed tree root knotted across the path.

My foot hit it and I stumbled, falling awkwardly into a thick clump of weeds and bushes. My hand hit something hard and cold. A stone. A single gravestone, lying in the earth, hidden amid the undergrowth. The name was obscured and half worn away, but I could see the first letters: C-A-M-I. Horrified, I scrambled to my feet and ran, smashing the gate open and hurling myself at the car.

When I got to Nikki's, I banged on the door, and virtually collapsed into the hallway when she opened it.

'God, what has happened?' she said, helping me in. But I was too breathless to speak. She set me down on her sofa with a cup of tea and sat with me for several minutes while I waited for my heart to calm down. The events tumbled through my mind as pictures and moments, irrational and confused.

'I was reading an article about Lorna and the church and I just got spooked,' I told her.

'Spooked by what?'

But I couldn't say. It was like a nightmare – terrifying at the time, but when you try to explain, it falls apart in your hands and the parts aren't scary any more. She had work to do, some programming task no one else could figure out, so she sat next to me with her laptop, debugging rocket timers, while I watched *The Exorcist 3* on Netflix.

'Don't you want to watch something relaxing?' she asked.

'This is relaxing,' I said.

Later I pulled out the now-crumpled pages of the article and looked at them again. It was as though, just by reading about Lorna's experiences, I had awoken something in the building. Or in myself. I'd always felt slightly unsettled there but never threatened. Not until tonight.

I knew that I would have to find those letters; they might be a vital link in the chain that could lead me backwards to the source. Surely Lorna hadn't thrown them away? How could Margot not have enquired further about their contents? The sceptical part of my brain was still thinking that Auntie had invented the whole thing. All that business with the rooks. I'd seen and heard them in the trees, and sometimes on the tower, but they never tapped at the windows. I still wondered if she'd faked finding family artefacts hidden in the church – a way to get the art world interested in her work again. But she had told me about the curse just before she died, and that the answers were there if I looked. Why would she do that if she didn't think the curse was true? Why would she mislead *me*?

The next day, I had the morning free before going to see Ben again, so I decided to return to the studio and begin a more forensic search. As I pulled into the parking space just behind the church wall, I felt a heavy sense of trepidation, recalling the way I had left the place the previous night – the figure amid the graves. But now, in the morning sunlight, through the frame of the tree branches, the church looked as it always did: ancient and quiet, the honeyed stone walls dappled with lichen. I was just being silly.

I'd obviously just completely freaked out because of the article. There was a light breeze and the sounds of song birds. There were no rooks lurking in the withered branches or along the roof, watching. I avoided the headstone I'd stumbled into, the one that appeared to have my name on it. Surely, it was just a figment of my imagination, I didn't need to examine it again to know that. Instead I walked quickly to the church door and slowly pulled it open, trying to ignore the witch marks as it creaked stiffly on its hinges. I'd found those odd circles inspiring. Now they had taken on a slightly different light. What were the people here afraid of?

Inside, everything was as I'd left it. My workbench ready, my tools neatly stored. It was time to put last night out of my mind and be pragmatic. I was here to look for something, so that's what I would do. I'd already been through the office and the filing cabinets – definitely no ancient letters in there. The pulpit was long gone, rotted away to nothing, so I checked in all the kitchen cupboards, behind the shelving units, searched for hidden cubbyholes in the walls. I was sure I wouldn't find anything, but it was filling the hours before my visit to Ben. I moved with precision through the chancel, the nave, the tower chamber, looking under furniture, along sills and the heads of columns. Nothing. Just dust and stone and long-dead insects.

There was one place that I didn't go, that I had never been. The crypt. I almost felt it beneath me, the dark, silent expanse. But Aunt Lorna had said she'd only been down there once and never again. It was empty and cold. She'd since bricked it up and brambles and ivy had grown over the entrance, sealing it behind intestinal labyrinths of branches and vines.

By midday, I'd still found nothing, but I was covered in grime and my joints ached. I took a shower and changed, trying to make myself look vaguely normal for the hospital visit. I would have to switch modes, putting all this craziness to one side so that I could be there for Ben, whatever that meant.

As soon as I got to the ward, I was taken aside by one of the doctors. She guided me to a little consultation room and sat me down on an uncomfortable plastic chair. I was too dazed to really get worried.

'So, I think you know about Ben's memory loss,' she said. I recalled him desperately fumbling for the names of trees and flowers. 'He seems to be suffering from a form of agnosia, which means he's having trouble identifying certain objects. In Ben's case it's nature: trees, flowers, animals. It is rare, but it can happen as the result of brain trauma.'

'Will he get it all back?' I asked.

'It's possible,' she said. 'But he'll need help. He's lucky he has you.'

I felt that horrible sunken feeling of doubt and guilt in my stomach. I wasn't a carer. I wasn't up to this. He deserved better.

'Don't look so worried!' she said. 'When he moves to the Cotswold rehabilitation centre in Painswick, the amazing psychologists there will work very intensely with him. Your job will just be to keep him talking.'

'He's moving?' I asked.

'Yes, I'm sorry, I assumed you knew? His parents have arranged the transfer. He's leaving on Friday. He'll have his own room, access to a state-of-the-art gym, therapy sessions – sort of like a luxury spa, but for brain injuries.'

I paused for a millisecond longer than I meant to, thinking how much time that would add to my journey. 'That's great! That's really great.'

When our little meeting was over, I went to the bathroom and stared at myself in the mirror. Baggy mohair cardigan, black jeans, hair a mess, pale and haunted. Who could I possibly help? A patient came in and I had to pretend to be washing my hands. I swallowed hard, then walked back to the ward.

Ben was sitting up in his bed in a dressing gown, a rubber ball in his right hand.

'Had physio,' he said. 'Got to keep trying to squeeze this.'

'How are you doing?'

'Still foggy. Confused about stuff. Can't really move my arm or leg. They said it'll take time.'

'And your parents have got you a place in a rehab centre? Will they be coming over to help you move?'

He looked away.

'They can't come now,' he said.

'What? Why?!'

'Some big business thing Dad's working on. They sent me that.' He pointed to a new iPad on the cabinet next to his bed. 'So we can FaceTime.'

'Are you all right with this? It seems like they should drop everything if their son is in hospital after a car accident?'

'It's fine.'

'I mean, they're moving you all the way to Painswick and they're not even going to be there to help you settle in?'

Somehow, even in his groggy state, Ben picked up on what I was thinking.

'You don't have to visit if you don't want to,' he said.

'I do! I do, Ben, I just have to plan my week a bit better, that's all. Do you need help with moving? Do you need me to bring anything?'

'No, Meg is helping. She's packing up a bunch of stuff from home.'

'Oh . . . okay.'

116

'It just made sense, you know, her sorting it. Because she lives there.'

'I get it.'

He took my hand in his.

'Are you sure?'

'Yeah. It does make sense.'

Awkward silence. I looked momentarily at the time on my phone, and became extremely aware that Ben had noticed.

'So what are you up to?' he said.

'I spent all morning searching for something in the church and I've had absolutely no luck finding it.'

'What are you looking for?'

'The past, I suppose.'

'Well, where did you last put it?'

'Ha ha,' I replied. It was the tiniest glimpse of the Ben I knew. 'I just found out that my aunt once discovered a bunch of letters hidden in the church. They were written by my great grandmother. I've looked everywhere for them. She must have stored them somewhere else.'

'Why do you need them?'

'They just have some information about my family. Something I need to know.'

'What about the . . .' he seemed to be struggling for words. 'The filing things? The metal things.'

'The cabinets? They're just crammed with bank statements and bills – the letters definitely aren't there.'

'There might be a clue though?'

'I don't really have the time to play Miss Marple. I've got a lot to do, I'm getting behind on orders and . . .'

'And you've got to waste time with me.'

'That's not what I meant. I just don't want to spend hours

117

rummaging through my aunt's papers when I know the letters aren't there.'

I felt myself getting irritated and I didn't know why.

'Bring them.'

'Huh?'

'When you come to rehab, bring the papers. We can go through them. I need something to do.'

'Okay. If you're sure.'

I leaned down and kissed him on the lips. After a moment, he drew away, his expression clouded with concern.

'You'll get bored of me, won't you? Eventually.'

'Don't be silly!' I replied.

'I think about you all the time.'

'I think about you too.'

'No,' he said. 'That's what you said to me. When I was . . . asleep. I heard you.'

'You did?'

'Yes. I held on to it. It felt safe.'

I kissed him again.

'Thank you,' I said.

'What for?'

'I don't know. For saying that, for feeling that.'

He smiled and looked at me.

'What have you done with your hair?' he asked.

'Absolutely nothing. Do you like it?'

'It's wild.'

We both started laughing. Then he stopped and was serious again.

'Thank you for coming,' he said. Now his eyes were glistening. 'I'm so sorry for putting you through this. I wish I could remember the accident. I don't know what happened.'

'It doesn't matter. You've just got to focus on the future.'

'I'm scared.'

'I know.'

'What if I don't get better?'

He put his arm up over his face, and I knew it was because he didn't want me to see him upset. It was a child's gesture and I felt it in my heart.

'Oh, Ben,' I said. 'Just give it time. We'll get there. We'll deal with it.'

A physio came in to take Ben to another appointment. I kissed Ben goodbye and walked into the corridor. I made it a few steps before I had to stop and put a hand on the wall to steady myself. I was crying before I even knew it. The shock of it, the weirdness of Ben being so vulnerable. It made the horrible guilty feeling at the back of my mind edge its way forward out of the gloom. Because what if it *was* my fault? What if the thing that came for my aunt was now coming for me? For us?

And another hidden part of me knew, with dark, horrible certainty, that I deserved it.

# Chapter Ten

# The Letters

It took an hour to drive to the Cotswold brain-injury rehabilitation centre, a collection of modern buildings with clean white walls and vibrant orange roof tiles surrounded by acres of neat lawns and sculptured flowerbeds, with some woodland at the border of the grounds. This would be Ben's new home for however long he needed treatment. Approaching the car park, I drove past several people in wheelchairs navigating the wide concrete pathways with speed and finesse. A few others were being gently pushed by smiling staff. It looked like there was a large canteen on the ground floor of the main building, which opened up onto a veranda with a view over the fields. Effort had clearly been made to conjure the effect of a country hotel, but there was something unavoidably institutional about it. I could not quite imagine Ben here – young chaotic Ben, bounding about outside with a shovel or a wheelbarrow. How could he be confined in this way? The thought made me feel momentarily sick. I parked up and grabbed my bag and a dumb little present I'd bought for him, wrapped in Superman wrapping paper as a joke, which was seeming more tasteless with every passing minute.

Inside, the reception area was bright and glassy, with lots of jazzy modern paintings on the walls – paint swishes in rainbow colours – like the stuff you find in budget chain hotels. I approached a young woman behind the long white desk and she looked up at me from her Apple computer.

'Hey, how can I help you?'

She had the bright smile of a spa receptionist.

'I'm here to see Ben Jones.'

After checking a few details, she gave me a visitor pass, and guided me down a sunny corridor, lined with wide wooden doors. We stopped at one with Ben's name on a little LED panel beside it. She pressed a buzzer and I heard a woman's voice shout, 'Come in.' At first, my heart slumped because I thought it was Meg, and I really didn't want to have to share him again. But as we walked in, I saw that it was a smartly dressed middle-aged woman sitting beside Ben, who was upright in his bed.

'Hi, I'm Valerie,' she said. 'I'm Ben's occupational therapist.'

'Oh, should I come back in a bit?'

'No, it's fine. I'm just finishing an assessment. It's nice to meet you.' She turned to Ben. 'I'll see you tomorrow morning for our appointment. It's in your app,' she said, pointing to his iPad. She slipped past me, leaving a trail of expensive perfume in her wake. We were not in an NHS hospital any more.

'Hi,' he said. His smile was coming back. He looked a tiny bit more like himself. The bruising had gone down a lot and his face was alert rather than weirdly vacant. I could recognise him as my boyfriend and not some stricken, haunted figure covered in wires.

'Hey.'

I took the chance to examine the room. It looked like nice university accommodation – a bed, a desk, bookshelves, a big window overlooking the gardens, a flatscreen TV mounted on the wall. But there was also an alarm button and a bedside table on wheels.

'Well, here you are in rehab,' I said, sitting in the armchair next to his bed.

'My parents always told me this would happen,' he replied. It was definitely him. The old Ben.

'How are you? Is it okay here?'

'It's better than hospital. I have a big TV. Meg brought my Xbox. There's a swimming pool and a gym. And a multidenominational prayer room.'

'That's going to be useful for you.'

I tried not to focus on the detail about Meg.

'What's that?' he asked, pointing to the present.

'Oh, this is just something silly for you.' I handed it to him.

'Um, you might have to help me open it,' he said.

'Shit, sorry, of course.' I sat down on the bed next to him and loosened the paper, then passed it to him. He pulled out the contents – it was a guidebook to trees and flowers, with lots of colour photos. When I went up to buy it, the woman in the bookshop said it was perfect for children.

'I thought maybe it might help you remember,' I said. 'We could go out and find some together. When you're ready.'

He put it on his lap and flicked through the pages silently, with a furrowed expression. I thought perhaps I'd messed up, reminding him of all the knowledge he had lost or at least mislaid. But then he turned to me, and said simply, 'I love it.' He held my hand, and we just sat in that moment for a little while, looking at each other, our fingers interlocked, the room bathed in soft sunlight, birdsong from the gardens outside the window. It felt like there were good emotions inside me. They just needed switching back on.

Someone brought dinner in for Ben, a chicken pie, peas and potatoes that actually looked edible. I helped pull the table around so he could eat in bed. He switched the TV on and we watched the news as he ate. Halfway through a story about the economy, I noticed he was having trouble spearing the potatoes, so I silently took the knife and started cutting them in half for him. We didn't speak, he just let me. Looking back, I realise now it was one of the most intimate things I had ever done for another human being. I experienced such a rush of love in that moment, it almost took my breath away. When I finished he smiled at me.

'This is what it'll be like when we're old,' he said. I seductively licked the gravy from my fingers.

Once he'd finished, he put the plate aside and said, 'Now, where are your aunt's documents?'

'You still want to do that?'

'Yes. I've cleared my schedule.'

So I went back to the car, opened the boot and dragged out two huge folders filled with papers.

'Shit,' he said when I walked into his room, struggling not to drop them.

'Well, you asked for this. And there are four more files in my boot.'

'Put them on my desk,' he said. I took the plate away and dumped one of the folders on his table, then pulled out a wedge of papers for myself.

'What am I looking for?' he asked.

'I don't know. Anything weird?'

'That's really helpful.'

I settled into the armchair by the bed and began to scan through the printed letters, bank statements and invoices.

That's what we did together for the next two hours, slowly working through the pile. There was a little kitchen area in his room, so I made us tea and opened some ginger biscuits. It felt strange to be spending so much time together, just quietly doing something, as though we were a normal couple relaxing at home. For a few minutes, I almost forgot about the dread I was feeling, the creeping fear of some malevolent supernatural force trying to encroach on my life. Here we were in this sunny room, just the two of us, and Ben getting better, looking better every day. And it was something of a relief, as we approached the end of the task, piles of papers neatly sorted into categories, that nothing had shown up that was relevant. My most exciting find had been a letter from Tracey Emin, which Ben wanted to put on eBay to pay for a new games console. A dead-end would be good for me. A dead-end could be a sign that there was nothing to look into. But then, while I was skimming through a letter from the curator of a gallery in Hälsingland, I noticed that Ben was staring intently at one piece of paper.

'What is it?' I asked.

'I thought you said you'd all lost touch with your granddad?'

'Yes, when he and my grandmother divorced, he moved away. No one saw him again. How the hell did you remember that?'

'I don't know. I think I remember everything you've told me. It's like it's stored differently in my brain.'

'Oh,' I said.

'So, who told you that he'd disappeared?'

'Mum. Why?'

He handed me the piece of paper. It was a photocopy of a letter from Blackwood House care home in Hertfordshire, confirming the details of a trust set up by my aunt to support a resident in perpetuity.

The resident's name was Donald Piper.

My grandfather.

'Oh shit,' I said.

'Do you think he's still alive?' asked Ben.

'I don't know. I doubt it. He'd have to be a hundred at least.'

Ben pointed to the phone number at the top of the page.

'There's only one way to find out.'

Before I could overthink it, I took out my phone and dialled the number.

# Chapter Eleven

# **Donald**

The rain came in just a few miles before the M25. It started lightly, but all of a sudden my windscreen was being pummelled by raindrops the size of tennis balls, and the traffic slowed to a crawl amid the downpour. I turned on the radio and gazed outwards at the headlights reflecting in the saturated road surface.

For most of the tedious three-hour drive to St Albans, I was rationalising my actions to myself. This is normal, this is a normal thing to do. Travelling halfway across the country to ask a long-lost relative about a family curse. It must happen every day, surely? Whoever answered the phone at Blackwood House that day was extremely nonplussed by my enquiry. It was as though they spent a large part of their working day fielding calls from the families of misplaced elderly residents. She confirmed that he was indeed still alive and that I could visit him, but that he was very frail. I chose not to confront Mum about all this just yet – I wanted to see him first.

Driving through the gates to Blackwood House, it became immediately clear this wasn't some modern purpose-built care home. It was a huge Victorian gothic mansion, its dark brick frontage forbidding and austere, a multitude of peaks and spires black against the sky. On either side of the main entrance, there were two turrets with decorative battlements and rows of winged gargoyles perched menacingly at the corners, giving it the look of some wretched horror-movie castle. I parked in one of the guest spaces, sat in the car for a second, then got out and headed to the doorway.

Inside, the entrance area was similarly imposing, its charcoal tiles and blackened oak-panelled walls creating a gloomy atmosphere untroubled by the light coming in through the stained glass windows. Above a long reception desk, a row of large paintings portrayed dour Victorian men and women, staring gloomily out at unwary visitors. A lone woman in a starched white blouse sat behind a desk, ignoring me.

'Hi, I'm here to visit Donald Piper,' I said in an assertive voice. 'I have an appointment.'

I'd tried to dress as conservatively as possible, in a black wool sweater and a tan skirt I'd somehow stolen from Nikki. But when the receptionist lifted her thin pointed face to me, she seemed deeply unimpressed.

'I'll call someone to help you. Take a seat.' She pointed to an antique Chesterfield sofa on the opposite side of the hall.

Five minutes later, a young man in a red polo shirt appeared and introduced himself as Kevin.

'I'm a carer here, I look after your grandfather. Let me take you up. The lift is this way.' I followed him, past a grand sweeping staircase, to a small elevator that looked a hundred years old, with an iron trellis instead of doors. 'He's on the top floor, the attic level,' Kevin continued. 'It's where the servants would have once lived. It's

127

mostly staff accommodation now but there are a couple of residents up there. Apparently, your aunt picked the room.'

'She came here?'

'She must have. It was before my time.'

Could Lorna have brought Daphne's letters back for him? They were written by his mother-in-law after all.

The lift juddered to a halt. He wrenched open the trellis.

'Now, I must warn you,' he said as he showed me out. 'Your grandfather has fairly advanced dementia. He's not likely to recognise you. Also, he can become quite irritable and angry. I'll give you some privacy, but there are alarm buttons around his apartment so just press one of those if you need me.' I felt like Clarice Starling being taken to the dungeon where Hannibal Lecter was imprisoned.

Donald's apartment was at the bottom of a long, low corridor with a polished wooden floor that squeaked beneath my footsteps. I knocked and waited, then pushed the door open. The hinges groaned loudly.

It was a large bare room with a slanted ceiling and a window at the far end looking out over trees. There was a small dining table and a sideboard, and a doorway leading through to the bedroom. A few framed black and white photographs lined the walls and a large carriage clock stood on an ornate mantlepiece, the ticking echoing around the room. Donald was seated in an armchair, a blanket over his legs. He looked impossibly old, his body hunched and desiccated, his hangdog face drawn into a rictus frown. He was staring at an LCD television. It was switched on to an old black and white movie, but the sound was muted. He did not seem to be aware of my presence.

'Hello?' I said. 'Donald?'

He turned to me slowly and scanned me with red, watery eyes.

'I don't want my lunch yet,' he said in a high, strangled voice. 'I have my lunch at one p.m. and dinner at six-thirty p.m.'

'I haven't brought you lunch. I'm here to visit you. My name is Camilla. I'm your granddaughter.'

He turned back to the TV, his head nodding silently.

'It's lovely to meet you,' I said. 'We didn't know where you were. I'm sorry we've not met before. How are you doing?'

No reply.

I wandered up to the photos on the wall. One was of a young man in a military uniform standing in front of a bomber plane. The next was a wedding portrait, the same man standing beside a pretty woman in a simple silk wedding gown. There was something in her eyes that looked immediately familiar. It had to be Elizabeth, my grandmother.

'Is this your wedding day?' I asked, louder this time, clearly enunciating every word as though speaking to a child. I stood for a while, waiting for him to respond to me, to do anything, but instead he just sat nodding, watching the TV, his tremoring hands clasping and unclasping the arms of the chair. I glanced through to the bedroom. Perhaps that was where he kept all his personal things.

'That's your bedroom through there is it, Donald?' I asked.

'I have my lunch at one p.m. and dinner at six-thirty p.m.,' he replied.

I looked around furtively, wondering if they had any sort of security cameras in here, but nothing was obvious, so I started subtly side-stepping towards the bedroom, my eyes on Donald all the time.

Inside, the room was dominated by a large bed with some sort of motorised frame. Around it stood a wardrobe, a chest of drawers and a bedside cabinet, all in the same dark wood as the furniture in the living room. There was an odd atmosphere – the dust seemed to hang in the air as though frozen in aspic. Quietly, I walked over to the wardrobe and opened the doors. Nothing but a row of musty trousers and blazers. The chest contained socks and underwear, folded shirts and sweaters. I lifted them all, but there was no hidden stash of nostalgic keepsakes. Everything had the same smell of wood polish, moth balls and some sort of medical detergent. I knelt down and looked under the bed, hoping to find a box or an old suitcase filled with personal trinkets, but there was just a pair of tartan slippers. God, I thought, a six-hour round journey for a slightly creepy visit with a relative who doesn't even know me. I was just getting to my feet again, when I looked up and gasped in shock.

He was standing right there in the doorway.

'I know what you are looking for,' he said.

For a second I was struck dumb. He'd caught me going through his things. My mind was racing, trying to come up with an adequate explanation.

'I'm sorry, I was just . . . '

'I knew you would come back for it one day.'

His eyes were completely impassive.

'I think you're confused,' I spluttered. 'I've never been here before.'

He didn't answer. Instead he shuffled towards the bedside cabinet.

'I kept it for you, Elizabeth. They took almost everything but I kept this.'

I knew I had to tell him I wasn't his wife – it would have been the ethical thing to do. But instead I watched him as he opened a drawer. I watched as he reached inside. And I held out my hand when he offered something to me, wrapped in a plastic bag.

'Thank you,' I said. I looked inside.

To my disappointment, it wasn't the letters. Instead it was a battered old hardback book.

'I let Lorna out of my sight for a few minutes,' he said in a cracked voice. 'When I found her, she was in our room, looking through your bedside cupboard. This was on the floor beside her. I didn't mean to read it. I couldn't help myself.'

'It doesn't matter,' I told him.

'You're still so beautiful,' he said softly. 'You look just like you did that day.'

'Thank you,' I said again, slowly pushing the book into my satchel, hoping he had more to give me. He slid the drawer shut.

'Is there anything else?' I asked. 'I was hoping you'd kept some old letters?'

He looked at me and, gradually, the smile he'd been wearing faded into a look of utter despair and dejection.

'I didn't understand at the time, why you did what you did. I suppose I do now. All I ever wanted was to keep you safe. I loved you.' He moved to put a hand on my arm, but I stepped away.

'I think I'd better go,' I said, circling round him and then edging backwards towards the door. 'It was nice to meet you.'

'You're leaving me again?' His voice was taking on a strange urgent tone.

'Yes,' I said. 'I'm sorry.'

Something darkened in his face, the vacant affection replaced in a second by despair and fury.

'You are a whore,' he rasped. 'You wrote it all in that book and you knew I would find it. You knew I'd find what you had been up to!'

I got the door open and walked down the corridor, trying to maintain a cool detachment.

Then he was in his doorway. 'Come back! Oh please, Lizzy, don't leave me again.'

But I was pressing the lift button, and as the doors opened, I looked back one last time to see him in the corridor, his hands to his face, weeping hopelessly.

When I got to the car, I opened the plastic bag expecting the book to be some old novel with sentimental value. But when the pages fell open, I realised they were all handwritten. Inside the front cover was a name.

Elizabeth Piper.

Donald's parting words came back to me. *You wrote it all in that book and you knew I would find it. You knew I'd find what you had been up to.*

I hadn't found the letters, but I had stumbled across something that might prove equally useful. If I wanted to discover what it was that haunted Lorna, that still haunted me, who better to go to than Lorna's mother?

Instead of heading home, I decided to drive to Mum's. When she moved to London, everything happened quickly for her. She immediately got a job with a cutting-edge architecture firm based in Bethnal Green. She sold the family home, left Bath behind, and bought an apartment in a brutalist 1960s tower block, which had recently been refurbished. There was now a concierge in reception and the lift smelled of lavender and eucalyptus rather than urine. I stood for a few minutes outside her door to gather my thoughts, then pressed the buzzer. As soon as she answered, before she could even greet me, I held up the letter from the retirement home.

'Do you recognise this?' I asked.

'Hello to you, too,' she replied. 'What on Earth are you doing here?'

She took the letter from me and studied it for a few seconds. 'I see,' she said.

'Did you know about him? Did you know all this time?'

'You'd better come in.'

I followed her into the vast living room; there was quiet classical music playing, and the lights were on very low. Her desk in the corner of the room was glowing from the light of two huge monitors.

'I'm just finishing some work,' she said, padding through to the kitchen area. 'Do you want a drink?'

'I'm fine.'

'You look like you need a drink.'

'I said I'm fine.'

I sat down on her expensive and uncomfortable sofa.

'Well, I'm having a drink,' she said, opening the fridge and pulling out a bottle of white wine. While she filled her glass, she watched me, trying to gauge my mood.

'Did you know about this?'

'No,' she said. 'Not exactly. I suspected Lorna might have got in touch with him towards the end but, to be honest, I was never interested. Mum left him when I was two. He was never my father in any meaningful sense. But Lorna remembered him. She'd always blamed him for how miserable our mother was, and how tense the house felt when she was a child. But maybe she tracked him down and felt sorry for him.'

'This family is so weird,' I said.

'I can't argue with that,' she replied. 'Where did you find this letter?'

'It was in her filing cabinet. I think she wanted me to find it.'

'Why?'

'She wants me to know the truth.'

'What truth? Oh God, not this stuff about the curse again? When are you going to realise she made things like that up all the time?'

133

'But she didn't make it up. She had proof.'

'Proof?'

'She found a bunch of letters in the church; they were written by your grandmother during the First World War. The curse is mentioned in there. I've looked everywhere for them, but they're not in the church. Do you know where they might be?'

She did a big theatrical sigh.

'Cammy, this obsession of yours – it's not healthy.'

'Mum, I just want you to tell me if you know where they are.'

'I don't,' she said, getting up and walking back to the kitchen. 'Lorna probably lost them or threw them away. Now, do you want some dinner? Are you staying over?'

There was something a little odd in her manner, something evasive, but then, I suppose I had turned up unannounced at her home and started an interrogation.

'I can't stay,' I said. 'I've got things to do.'

'Fine.'

I got up.

'Sorry to barge in on you,' I said.

'You can barge in anytime you like.'

At the door, we hugged in our habitual, slightly awkward way. Then I asked, 'Did your mother ever mention it? Did she ever talk about a curse?'

'My mother hardly talked about anything,' she said. 'She was very detached and ethereal. I always got the feeling she was frustrated by her life, like she was waiting for something else. I learned how to exist as an invisible girl.' She gave an awkward laugh.

I didn't tell her about the journal. I don't know why. I just wanted to read it first, to experience it without the cloud of Mum's scepticism.

*

134

It was almost midnight when I made it back to the church, but I didn't feel tired. I poured a glass of wine and curled up on the sofa with Elizabeth's notebook. There was a moment of apprehension about what I would find and what it would mean. But I opened the book and began to read anyway.


## The journal of Elizabeth Hopkins, 1958

I was thirty-six years old when I discovered the truth about my mother – and, by extension, myself. It is almost inconceivable to me now, a few short weeks later, that I am on a train to Bath, and from there I will take a taxi to the village where she lived. I will have answers at last. But on the way, while I have time, I need to write it all down so that I can make some sense of what is happening. I must work out where to go next. I need to be methodical. I don't think I have written anything longer than a shopping list in twenty years. How does one start?

I suppose, from the beginning.


Growing up, I didn't have the slightest clue where I came from. I was adopted as a baby and my new parents were very conservative, insular people. They always claimed not to have been given any details about the tiny child they took away from the mother and baby hospital. There was no official adoption process back then, it was all done privately and surreptitiously, like a kind of hostage exchange. My real mother was young and unmarried, that's all my parents would ever tell me. But from the way they looked at each other whenever I asked awkward questions, I knew there was more to it. They held a secret about me and they had never intended for it to get out.

When did things start to feel wrong? It seems there has always been something inside me – an unnamed fear I couldn't quite express. As a child, I had terrible nightmares. I would wake in the dark screaming and screaming until my throat swelled and my voice was lost. My parents would ask what I had seen and I would always say the same thing, 'There is someone in the dark, watching me.' One night, after they had calmed me down and put me back to bed, I got up again and wandered groggily into their room, desperate to be with them. And as I tiptoed to their door, I heard my mother say, 'You don't think it's true, do you – what she wrote in that letter? About the curse on their family?'

I can still remember what I felt. An icy sense of recognition that sunk into my insides, freezing the blood in my veins. At last, I had a word for what was wrong with me. A curse. Something I had learned about from fairy tales. After that, there were mumblings and disagreements coming from their room. I could not make them out – until I heard my father say, 'Our daughter is not cursed!'

Now, looking back from today, so many years later, I know that he was wrong.

My expedition towards the truth began when Lea and Arthur moved in next door. They arrived in a beautiful glossy black car, which Donald later identified as a Jaguar Mark VII. Arthur, who was rather thin and stooped, got out first and walked slowly round to open the door for his wife. I expected a middle-aged lady to step out, but I was utterly transfixed by what emerged instead: a woman clearly much younger than him, her hair cropped short like a boy's. She was wearing a beautiful pale blue pinafore dress. There was something graceful and almost artistic about the way she moved, like a motion-picture starlet. Arthur reached back into the car and pulled out a Moses basket and I heard the cries of a

136

very small baby. I thought about popping out and asking over the low hedge that separated our driveways if there was anything the family needed, but then their removal van arrived and there was a lot of hubbub, so I thought it better to wait. Instead, I watched from my living-room window as the movers brought in boxes, and the young woman wandered up and down, rocking her baby in her arms with a sort of lazy disinterest. I remember that Lorna eventually dragged me away to help her with some colouring, and then I started on my usual Tuesday afternoon chores, dusting and tidying the bedrooms, washing down the bathroom. When Donald got home from the office he was annoyed to find that dinner would be slightly late. He likes to eat at 6.30 p.m. every evening, on the dot. Later, I bathed Lorna and put her to bed, then came down to read the *Picture Post* and listen to a concert on the wireless. These were the rituals around which I shaped my life. They made sense once, I suppose. They helped ward off the other feelings.

The next day, I was dusting the living room when I saw my new neighbour walking along her path pushing a pram. She was wearing an exquisite woollen coat in pillbox red and seemed almost luminous in the drab grey of the afternoon. She turned momentarily and caught me watching – I was going to duck away but she smiled very brightly and waved. I thought about asking Donald if we should invite them over for drinks at the weekend but I knew he would demure and say he was too tired for guests. I tried to remember the last time we had entertained. Sometimes, I just wanted something to happen.

It was choir practice that night and when I got home quite late in the evening Donald was up in Lorna's room. I found him sitting up on her bed reading the *Telegraph* while she slept across his lap.

'She had a nightmare,' he whispered.

I felt the colour drain from my face as I recalled my own night-time traumas as a child. I felt guilty that she had inherited them. 'What was it about?'

'Nothing, don't worry,' he replied. I let myself believe him.

He was a good father, a good man.

I met Lea properly the next morning. Lorna and I took a small walnut cake around and when she opened the door, I was surprised to see she was still in her bedclothes. 'Oh goodness,' I said. 'Have I woken you up?' She just laughed. My plan had been to drop off the cake and leave, I didn't want to be a pest, but she beckoned us inside, and needing no extra encouragement, Lorna bolted straight past her, winding between the tea chests piled in the hall. Lea put the baby out in his pram in the back garden, found some paper and pencils for Lorna, and then we sat in the front room drinking tea, surrounded by unpacked boxes.

She introduced herself and told me she was twenty-four years old and that Arthur worked for the War Office in some top-secret capacity. Her father had been a journalist but he was killed when their home was destroyed during the Blitz so the rest of the family moved to Edinburgh. 'My mother told me that the worst thing in the world had already happened to us so now we were free to do what we wanted in life.' It was a philosophy I somewhat envied.

Lea studied French and philosophy at King's, and when she graduated, she spent two years in Paris working as a model and an au pair for a high-ranking member of the Admiralty. She told me she had met Arthur at the famous Aux Folies bar. 'By then I was rather tired of Paris,' she said. 'And he was very clever and interesting. He used to design wireless sets but then the War Office took him because he had intercepted some vital German communication about a new sort of bomb. I'm not supposed to know, but

I pick things up. Anyway, we went out a couple of times and had long conversations about art and science and then he said, "Why don't you marry me and we'll get a nice flat near Whitehall and be very happy?" That seemed like a good offer. Then Noah arrived and we moved here.'

She made my life seem positively dull but still insisted on hearing all about me. I told her how I'd been adopted, then grew up in St Albans. I told her how I moved to London and spent five years working as a typist for an advertising company.

'I loved it,' I said. 'I was lodging with another girl, Heather . . .' I stopped there for a moment to gather my thoughts. 'We had a lovely time, a wild time. But my parents were desperate for me to be married, so I came back and courted Donald, who was younger than me, but very mature. He worked for a big firm and made good money. It seemed like the right thing to do for everyone. A year after our wedding, both my parents died within a month of each other. Tuberculosis.'

Lea looked shocked and I was desperate not to bring the mood down. 'Anyway, you think you had all the excitement in Paris,' I said. 'But we holiday regularly in Margate.' She laughed out loud at that and I rather blushed at the idea that I had entertained this cosmopolitan girl. I was so conscious of the gulf between us – she was beautiful, stylish and well-travelled and I had done very little. But she was so pleasant and vibrant that I started to feel at ease. And when Lorna brought over a picture she had drawn, Lea showed genuine interest and my daughter was thrilled with the attention. When she had toddled back to the table, Lea lit a cigarette, leaned forward and said to me, 'So what do you know about your real mother and father?' Her forwardness caught me by surprise. No one had ever asked about it before. 'Oh God, was that too personal?'

139

'No ... no, it's fine, it's just ... no, I don't know anything. My parents told me they didn't keep any records.'

She nodded, a look of thoughtful consternation on her face.

'And you never looked into it?'

'No.'

'Why not? Do you mind me prying?'

'No ... I wanted to, but it upset my parents when I talked about it, and I ... I wouldn't know where to start.'

'Arthur would,' she said. 'He has loads of contacts. He could have a snoop for you – at least get you started. It would be exciting!' Her eyes seem to light up at the prospect.

'I don't know,' I said. 'Donald thinks it's best left in the past.'

'But it's not about Donald,' she said, putting her hand on mine. 'It's about you.'

Just then, we heard Noah start bawling from the garden.

'Dammit,' she said. 'The little bugger is supposed to sleep for another hour. I'll just see to him, stay here.'

And as she moved, her hand slid along mine and a little way up my arm.

The next day we met in the park. She pushed Noah in a lovely pram with shiny silver wheels, and Lorna lolloped behind us in her new wellington boots. I asked Lea something like, 'How are you finding motherhood?'

'Boring and exhausting,' she replied. She lit a cigarette and blew out smoke. 'I do love Noah with all my heart, it's just, we have very different interests.'

I'd never heard anyone talk about motherhood like that, as though it were an inconvenience rather than the point of life.

'What do you like to do?' I asked. 'When you're not being a mother.'

'I like to dance and drink cocktails,' she said. 'But I think it'll be a while before I try those again. I used to go to the pictures a lot. When I lived in Paris, it helped me with my French.'

At last, something I could contribute!

'Do you know the Academy cinema on Oxford Street? They show European films. Heather and I used to go quite regularly.'

She looked impressed. 'You watched French films in London? How sophisticated!'

I blushed again. 'But I don't go any more.'

'Why not?'

'Donald doesn't like to go into London at night. He says it's dangerous. He says if I want to see a picture I can go to the Odeon here in St Albans, but I'm not as interested in the American films.'

'What are you interested in?'

'I liked thrillers the best. And horror films. There was a Danish film I saw, *Häxan*, about a witch. I find them very therapeutic. Does that seem odd?'

Lea stopped and looked at me. And I still can't believe what she said next.

'There is something dark in you, Elizabeth. I could see it there, right from the start. You have secrets.'

I felt oddly affronted.

'What on Earth do you mean?' I replied.

'Gosh, I've done it again. I just say things how I see them, and sometimes it comes out very badly. Please, forgive me.'

But I was very upset and irritable, and we hardly talked on the way back home. When we got to our houses, she said. 'It was lovely to see you. I'm so relieved to have interesting neighbours.' I don't think I had ever been called interesting before. With that, she took me by the shoulders and kissed me on the cheek. I jerked back a little, somewhat startled. 'I'm sorry,' she said, laughing. 'I sometimes forget I am not in France any more!'

When I got home, I ran the vacuum cleaner through the hall, and cleaned the dining room. I planned the meals for the weekend. And somehow, those boring tasks felt more bearable in her afterglow. That evening, I stood at the bedroom window watching the sun drop below the houses opposite, thinking about Lea and how we had parted. I realised that I could still feel the brief contact of her lips on my cheek.

There were a few days we didn't see much of each other. They had decorators around, and I was busy organising Lorna's fifth birthday party. But she lingered in my head. Then one morning I popped over next door, meaning to see if Lea needed anything from the shops, and the front door was open. I could hear Noah crying somewhere in the house. I ducked my head in and called out, but there was no answer. Very gingerly, I stepped into the hall and called again. Nothing apart from the baby's distressed cries, which I could now tell were coming from upstairs. Thinking perhaps Lea had fallen asleep, I started up the stairs, hoping not to startle her or the baby. When I got to the nursery, Noah was lying in his cot alone, bawling, his little face beetroot red. I picked him up and said, 'Shh, shh, where's Mummy?' I walked towards the master bedroom and tapped at the door. No answer. From inside, I could hear jazz music playing, but nothing else. I pushed it open and looked in.

She was on the floor, sprawled half upright against the wall in just her pyjama top and stockings, surrounded by gramophone records. There was an empty bottle of schnapps at her side and several stubbed out cigarette butts in a bowl.

'Lea,' I said. 'Lea?'

Her eyes opened and she focused on me with a groggy stare. 'I rather fancied a drink,' she slurred loudly over the music. I put Noah back in his cot, then returned to Lea.

'Let's get you into bed.' I tried to pull her on to her feet but she was a dead weight. 'Come on,' I said. 'You have to help me.'

With superhuman effort, I dragged her up until she was sitting on the edge of the bed, then she rolled herself on to her back. Then she stared at me as though trying to work out who I was. Somehow, she still looked beautiful. A damaged ingénue.

'This was Daddy's favourite song,' she said. 'Noah has only slept for twenty minutes.' She struggled to raise a finger to her lips. 'Shh,' she whispered. 'I think he's trying to kill me.'

With that, she passed out.

I took Noah down to the living room, which was a mess of nappies and soiled muslin squares, the settee dusted with talcum powder. I found a tin of Cow & Gate, and mixed up a solution. He drank it greedily. When he had finished, I took him out to the garden, winded him, and laid him gently in the pram, before pushing it forwards and backwards for a little. When I went back inside, I began to pick up and fold the unused nappies, gathered the muslin cloths and put them in the basket in the kitchen, and washed up all the dirty crockery I could find. When I went back to her, she was still sleeping. For some reason, I knelt beside her and took her hand in mine, as though I were caring for a sick child. I recall looking out of the window, at the street, the town, this place that had contained almost my whole life. It seemed so small and pale now. When I finally looked down at Lea again, I was shocked to see that she was awake and staring at me. Slowly, we both looked down to where I was holding her hand. Instead of pulling away, she tightened her fingers around mine and closed her eyes again. Then I called

Arthur and asked him to come home. He took the family away for the weekend.

The following Wednesday, she came over to my house, looking apologetic. I put the kettle on to boil and she sat with me in the kitchen. Lorna was at the table, making a mess with some clay and a bundle of sticks from the garden.

'I'm sorry for what happened,' she said. 'I'm a horrible person, a horrible mother.'

'Nonsense. My God, you have a lot to deal with: a baby, a house move . . . it's a wonder you're functioning at all!'

'I don't really feel as though I *am* functioning.'

'That is completely normal, I assure you. I was exactly the same. I was a wreck with Lorna. You just get through it, and things get easier, day by day. I promise.'

'I hope so.'

'Here,' I said. 'There is nothing tea cannot solve.'

'Maybe I should try Noah on it.'

'With a drop of brandy, perhaps.'

'Oh, please do not mention liquor to me. I'm so ashamed.'

We went through to the living room and sat together on the sofa, sipping our tea for a few moments. I liked having her here in my house. She brought something with her. A freshness.

'Were you really a wreck with Lorna?' she asked.

'Just after she was born, I developed what our doctor called "a nervous condition". I felt very low, I could barely care for my baby. For a long time, I was lost. It was as though some poisonous fog had descended upon me. I don't know what I would have done if it hadn't been for Donald. There had never been what you might call a great passion between us, but the way he cared for me then, so delicately, I became quite hysterical over him. I thought, if he supports me, if he helps me through this, I will love him for ever. And then I started to have these terrible nightmares; I'd be with Donald and the baby in our home, and I knew something awful was coming to take them from me, some monstrous figure edging towards the house. It got to the point I was afraid to sleep.'

'I expect that happens to a lot to new mothers,' she said. 'It's the exhaustion and the upheaval, and . . .'

I stopped her. 'I've had dreams like that before.' Then I told her about the recurring nightmares when I was a child, and the hushed conversation I'd overheard in the dead of night. *Our daughter is not cursed!*

'So you think you are cursed?' she said, turning to me.

'I know it,' I replied.

I found the letter when I was fifteen, I told her. It was in my mother's keepsake box. They were out and I was being nosy. The envelope was tattered and smudged. It was addressed to 'the new mother of my baby girl'. I memorised every word, every heartbreaking apology and explanation. She begged them to take good care of me. But the lines that haunted me were not about love. 'There is something my baby girl should know for her own safety. There is a curse on our family, something ancient and vengeful. My daughter, your daughter, cannot fall in love, it will only end in tragedy. I know this sounds like madness, but it is true. Please believe me. Something is watching. Protect her for I cannot do it, though I wish I could. I write this from a place of darkness. Help her stay in the light.'

Lea was looking at me with unguarded astonishment. The room buzzed with tension.

'An ancient curse,' she said. 'How frightful.'

It was such an understatement, I burst out laughing. The ludicrous tragedy of it all, raw and open, but somehow rendered unreal by her. With Lea close to me, I felt safe.

145

'You think I'm mad, don't you?' I said, burying my face in my hands, suddenly embarrassed. 'You think I'm a maniac!'

'No,' she said, shuffling closer. 'I think you're fascinating.'

'Oh don't!'

'You are!'

She pulled my hands away from my face. 'You are,' she said again. Then she lifted her hand and gently pushed my hair away from my eyes. I found myself unable to react; the softness of her touch made me woozy. Lea's face was close, her eyes locked on mine. I could feel her breath on my cheek. And then Lorna ran in and I hauled myself up to greet her.

Something was beginning to unlock inside me. Every day, I'd get my household tasks finished as quickly as possible, then I'd take Lorna next door and while she drew or entertained Noah, Lea and I worked on the house together. Having followed a guide in *Homemaker* magazine, we stripped all the walls in the bedrooms and hung the beautiful new wallpaper that Lea bought from Peter Jones in Sloane Square. We unpacked all the tea chests, overhauled the nursery and ordered new fixtures and fittings for the kitchen. Donald didn't seem to mind, as long as dinner was always ready when he wanted it. 'She's a bright young thing,' he said once. 'It is good to see you happy.'

At 3.30 p.m. every afternoon, we had a break from decorating. We'd drink fresh coffee, which Lea made in a French cafetière and then listened to popular music on Radio Luxembourg. The world had long been a closed room to me – now it felt as though a shaft of light had entered. Often when I looked into her eyes, she would nod, as though I had spoken my thoughts aloud. They hung in the air between us, silent but real.

*

I allowed myself to remember that I'd had one friendship like this before – the one I tried to blot out of my mind. But that was years ago. The other neighbours in St Albans, the ladies at choir, they were all perfectly pleasant in a brittle way – there was always an edge to everything, a sense of competition. Who had the cleanest house, who cooked the right meals, whose husbands had the most important jobs, whose children were the brightest. Everyone smiled at everyone else, but they were jockeying for position. With Lea, it was not like that. It felt more like a childhood friendship: intense and unguarded. At the time it felt lopsided: I was sure she didn't need me the way I needed her, and I found myself wishing that she did. But the uncertainty was part of it. In every other part of my life, I understood the routines, I knew what to expect, I knew what the limits were. But with Lea, I didn't.

I didn't know what her limits were at all.

She started to feed me further little snatches of her life. One day, Lorna and I were at her house and she showed me a photo album, filled with pictures of herself modelling clothes for Dior and Balmain. 'That is Barbara Goalen,' she explained, pointing to another woman in one of the glossy images. 'She taught me so much. We were very close friends – as close as two people could be.' Her eyes flicked to me, as though watching for a response.

'Do you miss it?' I asked. 'It must be so dull here in comparison.'

'Sometimes,' she said. 'But it wasn't all glamour. It was hectic and confusing, and not always safe. The men see you as an object. They wanted to use me up.' I thought she was adding those provisos for my benefit so that I didn't feel jealous or self-conscious about my tedious life story.

I paused and then found myself asking, 'Do you miss your friend Barbara?'

'No,' she said. 'Not now I have you.' She smiled and lit a cigarette. She looked thoughtful for a few seconds, and then, 'I have something for you.' She reached into her handbag and pulled out a manilla folder, which she passed to me.

'What is it?' I asked.

'Open it, darling,' she replied, putting her hand out and stroking my arm. Her touch was so easy, so natural.

Inside, there was a single piece of folded paper. I looked at her and she urged me on, so I took it out and unfolded it. Then I stared at it, unable to register what it was I was seeing. An official crest, some typed words, a signature. Again, I looked at her, bewildered.

'Oh, Lizzie,' she said. 'It's your birth certificate. Well, a copy of it anyway.' Then she pointed at a name. 'And that is your mother.'

I think, perhaps, I went into shock for a few seconds. My brain fizzled and blanked, like a television set being switched off.

'Arthur pulled a few strings,' she continued. 'Do you know what else he has found? The address your mother lived in when you were born. It's in Batheaston, near Bath. And I was thinking, we could take a trip there, me, you and the children. It will be an adventure, Lizzie, a real adventure!'

Her words echoed around the small tidy room. The sound of it seemed to mock me.

'How could you?' I asked in a trembling whisper. 'How could you simply delve into my life like that?'

Her face fell into a look of sheer horror. 'But I thought . . .'

'I told you! I told you I didn't want to know.'

'No, you said that *Donald* didn't want you to look.'

'What difference does it make?! You went ahead and did it anyway.'

'I did it for you! I thought you'd be pleased.'

'Why? Why did you ever think that?! I dread it, I dread knowing!'

'But if you know, then you can . . .'

I stood up from the sofa. 'I need to go,' I said. She stood up too.

'Lizzie, please.' She put her hand on me again, but this time I brushed it away with more force than I intended and she sunk back on to the sofa.

I paced over to the dining table and dragged Lorna up into my arms. 'We're going,' I said. She tried to grab at the paper she'd been drawing on, but I was too fast. She still had a crayon in her hand as we left the house. Once inside our home, I fell to my knees in the hall, my eyes blind with tears, still clutching Lorna, my little girl.

'What is it, Mummy?'

'Go to your room.' I could barely speak the words.

'Mummy, I'm scared.'

'Go!'

She ran up the stairs and I lay there alone, sobbing. It was as though someone had died. It was an uncontrollable grief. But I didn't know who it was for.

When I woke the next morning, I decided to clean the house from top to bottom. A proper spring clean. I had a strong compulsion to keep busy, to empty my mind and not pause for a second. I tidied the bedrooms, dusted and polished, I tore the bedsheets from the beds. I scoured the bathroom tiles and scrubbed the floor until my hands were red and raw. I cleaned the carpets in the hallway and down the stairs. I moved out the sideboard in the living room so that I could dust and clean the carpet behind it; the same with the dresser in the kitchen. How could she think that was acceptable? I washed all the bedsheets, then hung everything out in the garden, my back to *their* house. I heard the doorbell twice during the morning, but I ignored it. The phone rang but I let it ring in

149

case it was her. If Donald needed me he was going to have to come home. I felt that I never wanted to see her again.

But oh, she haunted me. One image kept flashing into my mind: her face an inch from mine, the scent of her and the way I suddenly felt almost drunk on it. It would have been so easy to close my eyes and slip towards her. But what would that have meant? Did she even know what she was doing? Was she just a silly girl looking for silly thrills? And then she'd handed me that damn folder, and the thought of it made me more furious.

I washed, I scrubbed, I cleaned, I hated her.

By 3 p.m. I was exhausted. My hands were chapped, my eyes sore from the fumes. Lorna had fallen asleep and so I found myself lying on my bed, attempting to construct a plan for the future. Certainly, Lea and I could no longer be friends, she had destroyed that. But while I simmered, another quieter voice was wondering how I could possibly live without her. She had opened the door to a different life in which I knew who I was, and I had slammed it shut. I was frightened. I had to protect Lorna from whatever it was that dwelt in me.

For a month, I tried to move on. I settled back into familiar routines. Housework in the mornings, afternoons out with Lorna in the park, evenings in with Donald. He noticed that I was more attentive, more interested in his tales of workplace politics. I was taking greater care over meals, trying out new recipes from *Woman's Weekly* and *Good Housekeeping*.

'You have not been seeing Lea so much,' he said one evening from behind his newspaper.

'No, we've fallen out,' I said. 'I think she is rather immature.'

'A lovers' tiff?' he said.

'Don't be ridiculous. What do you mean by that?'

He pulled down the corner of the newspaper and gave me a sad smile. 'I was just joking, my dear.'

And then one night I was putting Lorna to bed when we heard a ripple of thunder in the far, far distance.

'Is it a storm?' she asked.

I tucked her blankets in tighter around her.

'Yes. But you don't need to be afraid. It is a long way away and by the time it gets to us, you'll be asleep and it will pass over.'

I kissed her forehead. She looked up at me. 'When the storm came, the man died.'

I opened my mouth to speak, but my throat wouldn't open. I had to force the words out. 'What man?'

'The man outside the church. He wanted to help me.'

A rumble of thunder. It sounded closer now. It seemed as though I could feel the tremors within me.

'I think you have just been dreaming.'

'No, it happened. A long time ago. Something was there. It wanted to get us.'

'What wanted to get us?'

'You know, Mummy.'

'I don't, darling. I don't know. You can tell me.'

But it was a lie. I did know, I'd always known. She looked back, she stared into my eyes.

'The curse, Mummy. The curse on us.'

I thought she must have heard me telling Lea about it. I'd always been so careful to protect her. But I realised, in that moment, hiding from it wasn't the answer. The past always comes out, the only question is how we face it.


The very next morning, Lea opened her front door to find me standing there, eyes sore from lack of sleep, hair dishevelled.

'I have to go to the house in Batheaston,' I said.

'I know,' she replied.

'And there is something else I have to tell you about my past.'

'I know.'

She put her arms around me and I let her.

'I'm scared,' I said. 'I'm scared to go back.'

'It's all right,' she whispered. 'I'm coming too.'

That is how we came to be on this train, Lorna, Lea, Noah and I, speeding through the Wiltshire countryside towards the west of England. It was an easy lie to tell Donald – a weekend away, visiting a relative of Lea's. It would after all leave him free to play golf with his colleagues. But it felt like a transgression. I had barely been out of St Albans since we married. He kissed me at the front gate and held his daughter close. There was, in the moment, an odd sense of finality.

We have adjacent rooms at the Grand Pump Room Hotel in Bath, paid for by Arthur. I do not know what Lea told him. After unpacking, we spent what remained of the afternoon wandering the town, the four of us like a little family. We saw the Circus and the Royal Crescent and browsed the shops on Milsom Street. I had a giddy sense of freedom. For a moment it felt like a holiday. Tomorrow, we will head out to Batheaston and we will discover the truth about my life, or at least try.

The following morning we ordered a taxi and the doorman helped us to bundle Noah's pram into the boot. The drive out to Batheaston was short and the jolly driver wanted to know what plans we had in the village. I told him I was visiting long-lost family and he seemed excited about that and began to ask questions that I didn't have answers to. Then he pulled up at the side of the road, just a few hundred yards along the high street and said, 'There it is.' He pointed towards a rather beautiful Georgian townhouse, with large sash windows and a portico entrance supported by lavish Ionic columns. In front was a neat garden bordered by a low hedge entangled with rose bushes. This was my mother's home. This is where I came from.

While the driver helped Lea take out and unfold the pram, I took Lorna by the hand and just stood staring at the building, feeling a rush of confused emotions. What is one to feel when confronted with a past they never knew? I was aware that, although it looked like a beautiful home, what I felt most was sadness.

With Noah safely in the pram, we walked together, the four of us, along the low hedgerow to the gate.

'What shall I do?'

'Knock at the door,' said Lea. 'Or I can, if you want?'

'No,' I said. 'Thank you, but no. Lorna, stay with Lea for a moment. Mummy won't be long.'

I opened the wooden gate slowly and quietly. Through the windows, as I walked forward, I could see ornate furniture, bookcases, an antique lamp, a teak writing desk. Had my mother used any of these? Before I was ready, I was at the large front door, painted a glossy red. There was an electric bell and I rang it. The shrill sound screamed inside the house. My heart was thumping now, I felt my breath in short gasps.

Nobody came. Not for several seconds. I was just about to turn back, when I heard footsteps inside, and then the sound of a latch being lifted. The door opened inwards to reveal a woman in perhaps her late forties, in a stiff tweed skirt and a cashmere pullover. Her greying hair was expertly styled, her face intelligent and severe.

'Can I help you?' she asked.

But what was I to say? That my mother had once lived here? That I was given away as a baby and now I was back? For what? Oh yes, to trace the source of some awful curse that I had heard my parents speak of in the black of night and then discovered for myself in a letter. She would think me insane. I opened my mouth and it hung there, wordless, for what seemed like hours.

'If you are selling make-up,' she said, 'I'm afraid I am not interested.'

'I'm not,' I managed. 'I'm here because . . . I think my mother lived in this house. I'm sorry, this is going to sound very odd. You see, I was given up for adoption and I just discovered who my real mother was. And I was wondering . . . I was just . . . '

'Your mother lived here?'

'Yes.'

'She was one of the Ricards?'

A spark of excitement.

'Yes! Yes, she was Daphne Ricard. Did you know them? I mean are you . . . '

She gave the faintest shake of her head, and when she looked back to me, the emotion I saw in her eyes was pity. She sighed deeply.

'I'm afraid you've had a wasted trip,' she said. 'They moved just after the Great War. There was some family tragedy, I believe. I don't know much. We bought the house from an agent. We had no contact with the family at all.'

I stood in silence, bereft, tears pricking at my eyes, an impossible mix of feelings swirling in my head.

'And you have no forwarding address?' It was Lea, standing beside me now, Lorna in her arms. 'No way to contact them?'

The woman shook her head again. 'I'm sorry.'

'How about your neighbours?' asked Lea. 'Might any of them remember the Ricards?'

The woman stole a look at her watch.

'I'm afraid I don't really know many of them. I'm hardly here. I'm

154

a theatre producer and spend most of my time in London. I have a telephone meeting in just a moment, actually. I am very sorry I couldn't be more helpful.' Both of them turned to look at me. I felt like a lost child. The woman at the door put her hand on my arm. 'Would you like to come inside and have a look around at least?'

But I didn't. I had no feeling for the place; I had not come to see unfamiliar rooms and objects. I had come for her.

We said goodbye and trundled away. I was shellshocked, I think, and not sure really where to go or what to do. We walked further up the high street past a couple of little shops; a delivery boy passed us on a bike, the basket on the front handlebar loaded with parcels. Noah grumbled occasionally but Lorna was quiet and thoughtful. After a few minutes we reached a sign pointing up a narrow steep lane.

St Cyprian's Church, 1 mile.

Something awoke in my brain; I can't explain the feeling. It was almost an electric shock of recollection.

'Can we walk up there?' I said. 'Just to look?'

'Why? Do you recognise it?'

'I don't know.'

Lea looked doubtfully at the lane and then at the pram. 'I don't think we'll be able to get this damned contraption up there,' she said. She looked around. 'How about I take Lorna and Noah to that teashop over there. We could get a cream bun and wait for you. What do you think, Lorna?'

Lorna nodded but looked at me with a pensive and uncertain expression, fiddling with the hem of her skirt.

'If you don't mind?' I said to them both.

'Not at all, it will be fun!' said Lea.

She took Lorna by the hand and guided her towards the teashop without looking back. I turned to cross the road when I heard

Lorna call, 'Mummy!' She was tugging at Lea's hand trying to free herself from Lea's grasp. 'Mummy,' she shouted. 'Don't go to that church.'

The lane was hard going in places, the cobbled surface giving way to a rough muddy old track and, as it rose up above the town, it got steeper still until my legs ached with the effort. On each side of me were dense woods, dark and pungent with the smell of rotting timber. There were no sounds at all apart from the cawing of distant rooks. At last, I rounded a sharp corner and there, rising above the treeline, was the grey tower of the church, tall and somehow foreboding. Walking closer, I could then see the old stone wall bordering the churchyard, the trees at certain points crowding on to it as though trying to burst through. There was around the whole place a strange humming sound, like an electrical substation. It got louder as I drew closer to the church, like a warning. The old copse gate was rotten and loose and, as I pushed it, it swung awkwardly at an odd angle. The building was becoming more visible now, dark amid ancient yew trees, the gravestones densely lined but poorly kept, sprouting from the earth like jagged teeth. A wind came up, rustling its way towards me through the leaves. I pulled my coat tighter and ventured forward towards the porch, where I ran my hand along the old wooden door, tracing several odd shapes carved into the surface. I kept asking myself, why am I here?

Then the door began to open all by itself, creaking loudly. Beyond it I was certain I could hear voices whispering in the blackness.

What I felt was a sudden unfathomable terror. At first, I walked away slowly, but then, out onto the lane again, I began to run, losing my footing once or twice on the treacherous surface. My heart and lungs were hammering and, about halfway down, I retched into the hedge by the road and started to cry. I was filled with fear, almost frenzied with it. But I knew I had to get myself together before I saw Lorna. I took a compact mirror out of my handbag, straightened my hair and tried to rub away the blotched mascara. But as soon as I walked into the teashop and Lea looked up at me, I saw in her face that I had been unsuccessful in my efforts. Together we gathered up the children and took a bus back to Bath. On the journey, Lea did not ask what had happened. Instead, she silently took my hand as I gazed out of the window, Lorna asleep on my lap. I wished I was brave, I wished I had the strength to face what was waiting in the past for me.

Back at the hotel and ensconced in our rooms, I thought the day was over but then Lea knocked quietly on the door between our rooms. When I opened it, I almost gasped. She was wearing a beautiful belted dress in black and white check, with a tight bodice and a pencil skirt.

'Noah is fast asleep,' she whispered. 'Is Lorna?'

'Yes, unbelievably.'

'I think we could use a drink, don't you?'

We took dinner at the French restaurant in the hotel. Lea had to help with the menu. We ordered entrecôte minute steaks with dauphinoise potatoes. When we finished, we sat up at the bar for Martinis. We were getting tipsy and, for a few precious moments, I felt liberated, as though I was suddenly someone else, some other woman. Perhaps the woman who stayed at the advertising agency, who didn't crawl back home. Who didn't keep things hidden. I told Lea what had happened at the church, how I'd felt something odd in the air, and how the door had started to open.

'You must think I'm an absolute idiot,' I said.

'Not at all. It sounds creepy.'

'But still, I'm furious with myself. I am desperate to find the truth.'

Lea twirled the cocktail stick in her drink. Something changed in her expression. 'Are you?' she said.

'I'm sorry?'

'Are you desperate for the truth? Really?'

'What do you mean?'

'It's just that I'm not sure you'll be ready to confront your past until you face the truth about your life now, at this moment.'

'What truth?'

She gave me a patient smile as though what she was about to tell me was the most banal observation she could make.

'You don't love Donald and you never have. Not in that way. You can't.'

I looked at her in stunned silence. Once again, she had overstepped the mark, barging into my life like a prizefighter. In the background, I noticed a piano had begun to play. We were surrounded by couples swooning over each other.

'How dare you?' I said. 'How dare you make presumptions about me? Who on Earth do you think you are?' I stood up, knocking over my glass, spilling the contents all across the table. A few other guests looked round.

'Elizabeth, please sit down.'

'I thought we were friends. But you ... you're a bully. A cruel, deceitful bully.'

I stormed away, pushing past a group of men in black tie who were laughing loudly, up the beautiful mahogany staircase to the first floor. Once inside my room, I wanted to slam the door shut, but Lorna was asleep so instead I paced up and down, up and down, across the thick carpet, my hands clenched into fists, muttering and mumbling, eyes filled with tears that I didn't want, that I rubbed angrily away. And then, I heard Lea unlocking her door and going into her room. I waited for her to try to knock on the interconnecting door, relishing the thought of ignoring it, of making her sleep on her accusations and the damage they had done to our so-called friendship. When there was no knock, I was even more angry and agitated. How could she just slope off to bed as though nothing had happened? But, as I finally sat down on the edge of the bed and put my head in my hands, I took some very deep breaths and allowed my mind to clear. I would have to confront her, that was it. As soon as it was light, I would tell her how beastly she had been.

At first light, I knocked on her door. She opened it almost immediately, as though she had been waiting, and stood before me, silent and sorry. And all I could say, the only words that would come out in that moment, were not the ones I had expected to say.

'How did you know?'

Because she was right. She was absolutely right about me. At last, I let myself remember.

And then I confessed. It all just came away, like melting ice.

Heather and I were flatmates, then friends, then we were something else. We didn't even know what it was called. All I was certain of was that I had to keep it from my parents – they would have been horrified. Those were the truest days of my life. We had a year enjoying the London we discovered together. Nights out, cocktails, then a show or a picture, sometimes a concert. The Gateways club, down the unlit staircase, other women watching us from dim corners. Looking back, it was the only time in my life I didn't feel scared, that I forgot there was something right on my heels. But always in the back of my mind was the letter. The warning it contained. I let myself be seduced by it.

'Not long after, everything fell apart,' I said. 'It was a lazy Saturday morning, we were in bed. Somehow, I'd forgotten my mother was coming to visit – I always marked it in red on the calendar, but not this time. It was as though I brought it on myself. She let herself into the flat and found us together. The look on her face, I will never forget it. It wasn't anger, it was grief – as though she had found my dead body. She walked straight out of the flat and I was too shocked to follow. Later, my father phoned. He was crying with rage. Lea, it was horrible. He said they weren't sure how they could go on being my parents. I begged them not to disown me, but he said I had to come home, they would stop sending me money for rent. So that's what I did. And goodness, how keen my parents were to snatch me out of that life. How they pressured me to settle into the plan they mapped out for me. Husband, house, children. The avenues all closing in until only one remained. And look where that led me. Housework, dinner ready at six-thirty p.m., eaten in silence, then the radio, a book at bedtime, a peck on the cheek. I buried myself in those daily rituals. Donald is a good man, but it's just ... the woman who tidies his house and makes his dinner and sleeps in his bed, it's not me. The person who is here with you, *that* is me. I feel like, when I'm with you, I could be brave.'

'You *are* brave,' she said. 'But you must face your past and what it means.'

It was so odd to look at her in that moment. She knew all my secrets now.

'The church,' I said. 'I have to go back to the church.'

We made the same arrangements as the day before. Lea took the children to the teashop, and I walked up the steep lane alone. Once again, there was the tight corner and, once again, just behind, I

160

saw the church tower looming above the trees. I ducked through the gate and walked along the stony path to the porch. I had to remember what Lea had said. *You are brave.*

Tentatively, I tried the church door.

It was unlocked.

I pushed it, and the ancient hinges groaned as it gave. A smell hit me, of old stone, dust and mould, and as I stepped inside I had an overwhelming feeling of déjà vu. The dark stone floors, the scarred walls, the windows almost black with dirt, they all felt utterly familiar ... but not to me. How could I explain it? I felt as though I was viewing this solitary place through another's eyes. With every footstep further into the nave, I felt not so much watched as ... accompanied. I had to keep looking around, sure that Lea had come to find me and was standing at my shoulder. No one was there, and yet, I was certain I was not alone.

'Hello?' I called. My voice echoed around the nave, upsetting the weird stillness. 'Hello?' I said again.

I read every inscription on the walls and the stone tablets on the floors; there was no sign of anyone with the surname Ricard. The chamber beneath the tower and the small private chapel beyond it might have hidden secrets, but there was no sign of any parish records, or anything at all that suggested people had ever worshipped here. Back in the nave, I wondered what I ever expected to find. But that odd feeling of being *seen* was still there. There was a presence all around me. The sound of whispering again. I walked over to the pulpit and wondered if there was anything up there on the little platform. My foot was hovering over the first step when a voice from behind stopped me dead.

'I wouldn't if I were you.'

I spun around in shock to see a middle-aged man standing in the doorway, bulky and serious, a toolbox in one hand and a thermos flask in the other. He was wearing dark blue moleskin trousers and a grubby white shirt, the sleeves rolled up his arms.

'The wood is rotten,' he said. 'Your foot will likely go straight through.'

'Gosh, you gave me a fright.'

'I'm sorry,' he said. 'I was surprised to find anyone in here. Not many people make it up to this church. It's a lonely old place.'

He walked further in, towards me, setting his flask and toolbox down on one of the pews. I found myself taking a nervous step back until I felt the bump of the cold wall behind me. After all, what men had I spoken to in the last five years apart from Donald? The butcher, the doctor, the vicar – all ancient whiskery old duffers, red-faced, jovial, harmless. I had no idea who this was.

'Are you looking for something?' he said. 'A student of church architecture perhaps? Sorry, my name is William. I'm a carpenter. I own the furniture shop down in town.'

'I'm Elizabeth Piper,' I said.

'The parish has a small grant to maintain this church, so I come in my spare time and try to keep it from falling down. My father was the local stonemason and he repaired the porch many years ago, so I feel duty bound to protect his legacy. I know a fair bit about it if it's the building you're interested in.'

'I'm trying to find out about my mother – I was given up for adoption as a baby. I found out recently that she lived in Batheaston, so a friend and I decided to come and see if we could find any of her family.'

'And you came here looking for her grave?'

'No,' I said. That was the first time it struck me that she was very probably still alive somewhere. It was a thought I'd need to deal with at another time. 'I saw a sign for the church and, for some reason, I just felt I had to come and see it.'

162

We stood in silence for a few seconds, looking around.

'There are no parish records here?'

'Oh no,' he said. 'All that stuff is long gone.'

I nodded.

'Well,' he said, picking up his toolbox again. 'I'd best get to work. Some of the guttering has come loose on the north wall. Give me a shout if you need anything.'

'I ought to get back into town,' I said, sighing.

We walked out through the porch together and into the churchyard.

'It was good to meet you, Mrs Piper.'

'And you.'

I started off along the path again, feeling oddly bright considering my failed venture.

'I hope you find what you are looking for,' he called after me.

I turned back to him. 'I'll just have to walk through town shouting, "Does anyone remember Daphne Ricard?"'

I laughed, but he didn't. He stood and stared at me.

'I knew her,' he said.

'*You* knew her?'

'Yes, I was very young, five or six perhaps; my father often used to bring me out on jobs with him. He was working on this church with an apprentice of his, a young man – Robert Woodbridge. I got to know him a little. Your mother and he were friends. Very close friends, I think. She used to visit him here while he worked.'

'My God,' I gasped. I started walking back towards him, and now it was he who was edging away. 'Do you . . . do you know what happened to her? Do you know where she is now?'

'I don't,' he said quickly. 'The family moved away, I believe, a few years after the war. I don't know much.'

I kept walking towards him. I wanted to sit him down and drain

163

every scrap of information I could from him. 'What was she like? What do you remember?'

'I was very young,' he said. He had a ladder laid out by the path and he picked it up and placed it against the wall. 'She was pretty. Seemed kind. She liked to read, I remember that. Always had lots of books in her satchel, always rode a bicycle. She disappeared after the war. There were lots of rumours, but no one outside of her family really knows the truth of it. I am very sorry, I really do need to get on.'

'I just . . .' He was climbing the ladder now, toolbox in hand. 'I just have one last question. This is going to sound odd, but did she ever talk to you about a curse? A curse on her family?'

He stopped climbing. He had his back to me so I couldn't see his expression, but he rubbed the back of his neck, as though he was dealing with some difficult quandary. I thought he was about to tell me I was mad.

'She didn't have to tell me,' he said. 'Everybody knew. People talked about it in the village.'

'What did they say?'

Behind us, amid the dark branches of the yew trees, I could see black shapes gathering, black feathers glinting in the half-light.

'Just that a curse had befallen the family,' he said. 'And that it had something to do with Daphne's mother. Camille Redferne, I think her maiden name was. She'd had some sort of supernatural experience – an encounter. There was a death involved. The horror and grief drove her mad. She ended up in an asylum, and later, I'm afraid to say, she died in the fire at St Cyprian's Court. Daphne was a very intelligent young woman, she deserved a bright future. But the disaster that befell her mother, people around here think it was transferred on to her. A generational curse.'

He must have seen the look of horror in my eyes. 'Oh don't

164

worry, I'm sure it's a lot of superstitious nonsense.' He eyed me with pity then, and I think a kind of grim fascination. 'Although I have to say, it's odd, it's very odd that you should find yourself drawn to this church,' he said.

'Why?'

'Because whatever it was that happened to Camille, it happened here.'

I left that church in a daze. Finally, it was confirmed beyond my mother's strange letter. Something really had been haunting my family for many years. Could it be that as soon as we commit to love, something strikes, laying waste to our hopes, our lives? I felt I would have no choice, but to abandon whatever was happening between Lea and myself. The weight of that thought crushed my heart.

I barely talked to Lea on our way back to the hotel. Lorna, picking up on my emotional state, buried her head in my chest during the taxi ride and wouldn't let go of me. Back at the hotel, Lea said, 'Something happened at the church, didn't it?' I could only nod. We stood for a while in the grand foyer, slightly lost.

'If you'd prefer, we could take supper in our own rooms tonight?' she asked.

But as sure as I was that we had no future, that was the last thing I wanted.

'Let's feed the children and get them settled,' I said. 'And then let's have dinner again. Just you and I. It's our last night after all.'

We decided to change for the evening, and once I had put on my dress and make-up, I gathered the courage to knock at the adjoining door. 'Come in,' called Lea. Cautiously, I went through and Lea was at the vanity table applying lipstick. She was wearing an exquisite gold halter-neck cocktail dress, which seemed to have glittery thread woven into it so that it caught the light and sparkled with her every movement. She looked just as she did in the photos of her modelling days – almost too beautiful to be real. She turned to me.

I had chosen a dress I'd made for a dinner party last year, black with small silver buttons down the front of the bodice. Before leaving for Bath, I'd added some lace to the cap sleeves, an attempt to make it a little more chic and Parisian.

'Do you know, I have just the thing that will go with that dress.' She scrabbled around in her suitcase and brought out a small black velvet-covered box, which she opened to me. Inside was a necklace lined with tiny sparkling diamonds.

'It's from Cartier in Paris,' Lea said. 'Will you wear it tonight?'

I didn't have time to answer. She took the necklace from the box and slowly, gently, opened it around my neck and moved behind me. 'The clasp is small,' she said. 'I have to get close.' Her voice was quiet and breathy and the sound of it, together with the feel of her fingertips brushing my skin, sent ticklish sensations all through me. It was so unfamiliar, to be touched like this, to be treated so tenderly, with such attention. I almost wept.

'There,' she said. 'Perfect.'

We ate in the French restaurant again. The pianist played Cole Porter songs and the candles flickered on every table. For a little while we didn't speak. It seemed we were both wrestling with thoughts we couldn't express. But eventually, I told Lea about what had happened in the church and how it made me feel. As ever, she listened without comment or interjection. Once shared, the burden seemed lighter.

There was a dance happening in the hotel ballroom; a good jazz band from New Orleans was playing. Having checked that the children were still asleep, we decided to go. Walking through the foyer tacitly hand in hand, people bustled past us, smoking and shouting and kissing. When the door to the ballroom opened, there was a rush of sound and heat, a peal of drums, a trumpet wailing, an explosion of chatter and excitement. Young couples, groups of men in smart black suits and hats, a small stage almost entirely obscured by swirling cigarette smoke, and somewhere in there, the jazz band playing. We found a little booth at the edge and ordered drinks, tapping our feet to the music, taking in the sights. It was a blur of low light and bodies, and the glint of brass instruments; we cupped our hands over each other's ears to talk, and then more drinks, and the swirl of dancing, the joy of it, the sheer joy, the rhapsody of being free and noisy and alive.

In that moment, I felt an odd rush of euphoria. Perhaps it was the drink, I don't know. But I felt light and unburdened. Being with Lea in that beautiful hotel, talking in a way I couldn't with Donald – and being listened to. It seemed as though anything was possible.

And suddenly we were back out of the ballroom, seemingly in one swift, giddy movement. We stood facing one another outside the door to Lea's room. Her skin was damp and still flushed with sweat from the dancing and music. I could feel that my hair had come loose from its careful styling.

'I don't want to be alone tonight,' I said.

She opened her door and stepped slightly to the side, giving me space to walk in if I wanted.

'I could put Noah in with Lorna,' she said.

'Yes.'

'We'll have to share the bed.'

'I know.'

She reached up and took my face in her hands.

'Something is going to happen,' she said.

'I know,' I replied.

Afterwards, we lay on our sides, Lea behind me and very close, her arm resting on my shoulder. I felt alive, my heart pumping. It was like seeing in colour for the first time in years. I took her hand and held it to my chest. Part of me wanted to stay here for ever, in this room, in this moment. I was conscious of the fact that this was a fantasy, but perhaps this time it could hold? Perhaps we could hide from it, claim some ground?

Lea kissed me on the shoulder and she asked, 'What are you thinking?' I turned to face her, to look at her in this way for the last time.

'Later today, I will have to go back to Donald.'

She shook her head.

'Listen to me. Whatever destroyed my mother and her mother before her, is in me too. This is for the best. But if we're careful . . .'

'We could still be . . . good friends?'

'A secret,' I whispered. 'From the whole world.'

'I wish it didn't have to be.'

She stared out beyond me towards the window, a quizzical expression across her face. The sun was shining in. Her skin glistened like honey.

Three hours later, we stood at our garden gates, summoning the courage to say goodbye, Noah in his pram, Lorna in my arms. I wondered how much my daughter would remember of all this. Would I have to explain it one day? Would she know anyway?

Lea leaned forward and kissed me on the cheek.

'So this is it. Back to our old lives?'

'Not quite,' I said. 'Just be strong. You were always stronger than me.'

She turned away.

Donald greeted me with a kiss. He didn't ask about the weekend. I went upstairs to unpack my things.

Some people say they know the moment they fell in love. I don't think that can be true. It's not a light switch that goes on and off, it is a sequence of tiny shifts in mood and meaning; the touch of a hand, a kind word, a night out, a weekend away, a kiss, a sacrifice. Each adds delicate new layers, like a tailored suit. The exact process is hidden from us, perhaps for good reason. I am in love with Lea, though given the chance, I would have chosen not to be. We can never have what other people have. But in that moment, I hoped we could have something.

I will stay with Donald. I have to try. It is not fair on him to live this lie and to think it true. But the illusion must be maintained. Perhaps he will never know that our marriage was over the day the new couple drove up in their smart car, and the woman with the boy's haircut climbed out. As good and kind as he is, Donald never made me feel how I felt with Lea the night she took my face in her hands and said, 'Something is going to happen.'

Two days have passed. I keep the journal in my bedside cabinet. Donald respects my privacy and would never pry inside. I want to maintain this record of Lea and me. I mean to add to it as much as possible.

But already part of me knows that disaster looms. Last night, I dreamt that I came home and he was there waiting for me, looking deathly pale and dishevelled.

And on the armrest of the chair, beside his shaking hand, was this very journal.

# Chapter Twelve

# **Finding Camille**

It was way past 1 a.m. when I finished reading. A blueish moonlight was coming in through the windows, occasionally broken by bats fluttering past like spectres. At first, I'd breathlessly skimmed the text, my focus darting about looking for clues and keywords amid the jumble of revelations, but on the second and third read-throughs, I began to calm down enough to fully digest the story. This was my grandmother, these were her words, her experiences, captured in her own journal. The truth as she saw it. This was the journal Lorna found and read as a child. It's how knowledge of the curse was passed. Lorna had always talked about her parents' loveless marriage, how it was part of what inspired her to rebel and become an artist. But she'd also inherited a sense of frustration, dread and fear, as did Elizabeth. The nightmares, the heartbreak, the doom. Did it slip down to all daughters in the family tree, spreading outwards like a disease? To Lorna, my mother with her failed marriage, to my sister? To me?

The key revelation was Camille. My God, that name. Camille/Camilla. The symbiosis of it. I walked through to my little kitchen to make a coffee, switching on lights as I went. It was now clear that belief in this curse went back at least three generations. I also knew that something had taken place at St Cyprian's, something terrifying, which seemed to bring the curse to light. Camille suffered a complete mental collapse as a result, and even after she seemed to have recovered, she died in mysterious circumstances. It was so much to take in. So many questions remained.

She died in mysterious circumstances . . .

The gravestone. The one I fell over the night I thought I saw someone lurking in the church grounds. The one with my name on.

I grabbed a torch and ran from the church, into the grounds. A thin fog drifted across the wet earth, the sounds of rustling among the trees. Across the lawn, to the lone grave on the north side of the building. I knelt beside the flat weathered stone still buried in weeds, took three long deep breaths and started to rip them away. The same letters were revealed at first, C-A-M-I, then L-L, the carving worn down to the faintest scratch. Finally, with one broad sweep, I cleared the rest of the undergrowth away, and gasped.

CAMILLE RICARD

1862–1892

CHERISHED WIFE AND MOTHER

LOST AND NE'ER RECOVERED

OUR LOVE TRAVELS WITH HER.

The next morning, I thought about phoning Mum and interrogating her about Elizabeth and Lorna, and what I'd learned. But I knew there was no point. She'd be evasive and dismissive, she'd mock me. Instead, I settled back in front of my laptop and googled Camille, hoping there might be a reference to her or to some sort of disaster at St Cyprian's, but none of the results was relevant. There was nothing at all for Lea either. I realised I needed to start being methodical about this. I decided to sign up to one of those family-tree sites to access birth certificates and census records – it wouldn't provide much information about my ancestors' lives, but it would give me the basics. I also wondered if there were any old newspaper articles about Camille or St Cyprian's, and another half an hour on Google led me to the British Newspaper Archive, which required another paid subscription, but that gave me access to hundreds of years' worth of local newspapers. It was already late morning, but I was becoming obsessed now. I typed 'Camille Redferne' into the archive's search window and watched dozily as the display blanked and the computer whirred. Then eight results came up. I sat forward, instantly awake, and started scrolling through. Disappointingly, five were clearly about a different Camille as the dates were way out, but four came from the Bath paper during her lifetime. The first was about her appointment as a curator at the Bath Royal Literary and Scientific Institution after several years as an active member. It was deemed a remarkable achievement for a woman. The second was a report about an event she had organised entitled 'The Science of the Spiritual', with speakers from the Ghost Club and the Psychological Society of Great Britain. According to the article, it was an enquiry into the scientific basis of ghosts, premonitions and other supernatural phenomena, but there were few details. It was odd, though, that she was clearly interested in these things, just like Lorna. Just like me. Then there was a story concerning a meeting of the Institution in which Camille stepped down as a curator for health reasons – it was dated 1883, so was surely a reference to her breakdown? Finally, a report on her suspected demise in the fire at St Cyprian's Court. Although her body had not been found, several witnesses saw her walking up to the house that night and she had been missing ever since.

I printed all the news stories out, cleared my dining table, which I never used anyway, and laid them all across the surface with the letters, the journal and the copy of the article about Lorna. I needed to visualise everything together. Then I set down my laptop amid the papers and searched for St Cyprian's on the newspaper archive. There were dozens of results from the 1700s onwards; it was going to take hours to trawl through them all, but by this time I was falling asleep at the keyboard. I needed to go to bed. The past would have to wait.

A fortnight went by. There was just too much going on in my life. I had to reorganise all of my work to fit in with driving to the rehab centre every day, which eventually became every other day because I was exhausted and the petrol costs were killing me. I'd neglected the ring I was making for Joan Pendle, so I went back to that. It was intricate and laborious work, melting down casting grains of platinum in a crucible, pouring the molten liquid into the skillet, cooling it into an ingot I could work with, crafting two collets for the stones. There was a relief in having total control of something. For a few moments I could just concentrate on this one object, this slither of precious metal.

During that time, Ben was tested and analysed and questioned by a whole range of kind, smiling experts. He had a team of them: a physio, an occupational therapist, a psychologist; they had a timetable of therapy for him that took up a lot of his days – he slept for the rest. He was still frustrated by the lack of communication between his brain and the limbs on his right side. Even as he started feeling more awake and alert, his physical progress was negligible.

On the last Saturday of November, I turned up late as I had two necklaces and a complicated ring to finish. Ben had ordered pizza and lined up something for us to watch on Blu-ray. Part of me felt too exhausted for it.

'What have you chosen?' I asked.

'A surprise,' he said. 'It's very romantic.'

The food arrived and I climbed on to the bed next to him. As I helped myself to a huge slice, he hit play. It was the director's cut of the film we watched in Bath. 'There's a lot more gore,' he said. 'They've added in a whole torture scene.'

I put my arms around his neck and kissed him. 'You know me so well,' I said.

And he did. I'd fallen into the habit of seeing him as another chore, something passive I had to provide for. But he wasn't. He was thinking about me too. I allowed myself to forget about the curse – or, at least, I momentarily convinced myself that it couldn't affect us here. Even if it *was* real, hadn't it already done enough to me? I really needed to live in this moment. I needed to be normal – and what could be more normal than lying in bed with your boyfriend, eating pizza and watching a Polish horror film? When we finished eating, he put his head against mine.

'Thank you for coming,' he said. 'Even though you're really busy.'

'I'm glad to be here,' I said. 'I *need* to be here.'

Just as we were getting to the climactic sequence where the decomposing bodies start crawling towards the house, I looked down and realised something.

'Um, Ben,' I said.

'Yeah?' he replied distractedly, not turning away from the screen.

'Ben . . . you're holding my hand.'

'I know.'

'Ben, it's your *right* hand.'

And together we stared at the unexpected yet instantly familiar sight of our hands interlocked, his fingers curled around mine.

From that moment, it seemed like a switch had flicked back on inside him. The internal communications system was rebooting. As soon as he started getting some motion back in his arm, his leg decided it was time to work too. His lead physio Greg, a ridiculously muscular bundle of positive energy, wanted to push it with exercise. 'We have to get his muscles really working again,' he explained. 'The sooner we start, the better.' At first, they were using a winch over his bed to get him up and about, but then, as he got stronger, they moved on to a sort of body board so he could slide into a wheelchair. Even then, the progress was too slow and painful for Ben and he got angry sometimes. One morning I got a text from him saying that he'd be in the gym when I arrived and that I could join him there, if I liked. To play along and get in the mood, I wore an old pair of grey jogging bottoms and a Nike T-shirt that I once bought because I thought I might get into running, but then never did. I put my hair into a stupid ponytail to complete the athletic look, and drove out.

The gym looked like it belonged in a really expensive hotel, with floor-to-ceiling windows looking out on the gardens, long rows of running and cycling machines lined up, and a general air of physical productivity. When I got in, Greg was helping Ben over to the parallel bars and I saw that Ben's face was bright red with sweat and effort. He barely acknowledged me as he slowly manoeuvred into position. I sat cross-legged on the floor a few feet away, next to a rack of free weights, and watched as Greg leaned in and provided quiet, thorough instructions on what to do, and how Ben should shift his legs without losing grip or balance. For a while, I felt like I was in one of those movies where an injured sports star fights his way back to fitness before winning some crucial tournament. I felt a guilty tinge of relief at being able to lose myself in someone else's drama, even if it was my boyfriend's. With Greg's hands on his waist, Ben slowly pulled his leg forward, his face fixed in a rictus mask of determination, his arms shaking with the strain. Slowly, his foot slid and shivered forwards while Greg said, 'Yes, that's it, that's it,' and I joined in. 'Well done, Ben. Oh my God, well done!' A smile began to break through on Ben's face, as he wrenched an arm forward on the pole. But then, his confidence growing, he leaned in and put too much weight on the leg. In a horrible lurching movement the limb crumpled under him and he collapsed on to the soft mat, almost taking Greg with him.

He smashed his fist down into the floor and yelled, 'FUCK!', his voice dense with rage.

I wanted to lighten things up again, so I told him, 'Ben, that was amazing!' But he turned to me, his eyes flashing with anger.

'Don't!' he shouted. 'Just fucking don't!' I looked at him, too stunned to respond. 'Can you just wait in the canteen? Or come back later or whatever? I can't do this with you sitting there.'

'Sure,' I said, trying to hide how upset I felt, but hearing the quiver in my voice. I got up slowly and walked to the door, feeling embarrassed and stupid in my gym kit.

I was a long way down the corridor when Greg ran out after me, calling my name.

'Listen, Cammy,' he said when he got to me. 'Don't take it personally. I see this all the time. It's why we never insist that visitors get involved with rehabilitation. Residents get idiots like me poking and pushing and testing them all day. Sometimes, the last thing they need is for visits to become part of that. Most patients just prefer to keep things separate. Does that make sense?'

'Yeah,' I said.

'Okay, I'd better get back before he seriously injures himself.'

He jogged away and I briefly thought about waiting for Ben, but I didn't want it to be awkward. Instead, I texted, saying I had to get back for work and that I was sorry, and then I drove off.

I kept feeling guilty about just disappearing on him, and the next day I had to go and see a supplier in Bristol, so I decided to take a detour on my way home and turn up at the rehab centre as a surprise. As it was quite a bright, warm afternoon, I figured we could buy coffees in takeaway cups and sit outside together. I fantasised about how pleased he would be at this unexpected treat.

Walking up towards the main entrance, I glanced towards the gym and then stopped in my tracks. Through the huge windows I could see Ben on the parallel bars again, edging his way along with that look of grim determination on his face. Behind him I could see a woman standing close by, watching, and I assumed it was another physio – until she shifted out of the shadows and I saw that it was Meg. She was in her fitness gear – a leotard, Lycra leggings and expensive-looking trainers, and she had her arms lifted ready to catch him if needed. And indeed, within a few seconds, his arms gave and he started to fall forward. She immediately ran in and took hold of him and the two of them crumpled on to the crash mat together. When she lifted him to his knees he was laughing.

I stood in silence for a few seconds unable to rationalise what I was seeing.

I backed away, almost colliding with a woman passing behind me in a wheelchair. Then I was walking very quickly to my car,

177

desperate to be gone before anyone saw me. *What does it matter?* That's what I kept asking myself as I thundered along quiet, criss-crossing B-roads. *It's better this way, surely? Surely, this is the best possible outcome. Ben would have someone, I'd be alone and no danger to anyone.*

*I'd be alone.*

I had to stop in a layby because my eyes were watery. I put my head on the steering wheel for a really long time.

## Chapter Thirteen

# Fear and Loathing in the Garden

The next morning, I stepped outside with a cup of coffee. The sky was grey and the church grounds looked wild and sullen. The grass needed mowing and several of the gravestones that hadn't already sunk into the mud were slowly disappearing amid weeds. There was a stillness in the air. The only sounds were the endless rustle of leaves and, I noticed with slight apprehension, the cawing of rooks somewhere amid the branches. Once again, I felt absolutely certain I was being watched. Shadows lurked and flitted in the spaces between the trees. Someone could be there, a few feet away, and there would be no way of knowing. When I went back into the nave, there was such an odd feeling in the room, as though the air had only just settled after recent activity. I felt sure I could hear, or at least sense, the echo of someone else having just been there. I caught the smell of patchouli on the air again. 'Lorna?' I called.

I decided I had to get on with work. I powered up the hi-fi and switched from the record player to the radio so I'd hear some human voices. Then I sat at the bench and started working on a pendant I was making for a client in Whitby, carving the delicate wax mould. I went back to Joan's ring, placing the sapphires, delicately soldering the claws then teasing them over the sparkling surfaces of the precious stones. But as I worked, I found myself wondering about what had happened to Camille in this building; then I strayed into thinking about the older tales attached to the area, the superstitions, the ghost stories. Something was driving me and it wasn't idle curiosity – it went much deeper than that.

I managed another hour's work before setting off to see Ben again. After the murky morning, it was a bright afternoon, the low sun casting a burnt-orange haze over the countryside. I had Meg's words in my head from that time on the hospital ward – *I'm not sure you're what he needs right now* – and as I drove I tried to interrogate myself about my feelings. Did I need him? I certainly didn't need the two-hour round journey practically every day. The thought of his recovery stretching out for months made me queasy. What would happen when he left the rehab centre? Would he be able to work, or even live independently? What would my role be in that? Was I expected to be his carer? But the question that simmered beneath it all was Meg's. Did he need *me*? Was I a good enough person to get him through? In my head while parking was the image of Meg helping him up. The two of them laughing.

Walking towards the main building, I spotted Ben by the entrance. He was sitting in a wheelchair, with a book on his lap, wearing a light blue sweatshirt, his hair ruffled in the soft breeze. He looked good. Thin and slightly drained, but good.

'What are you doing out here?' I asked.

'Waiting for you,' he said. 'I'm learning how to use this thing.

You can steer it with one arm, look.' He put his hand on the wheel, pushed and it moved forward. 'I've got the book you bought for me. They reckon if we go out and actually look up some flowers it might jumpstart something in my head. Do you want to go for a walk?'

The shock of this unexpected development stunned me into silence for a few seconds, but eventually I managed to blurt out, 'Sure!'

And then he was off along the path, not bothering to wait for me. It reminded me of how he was before – the confident stride that seemed to say, if you want to come with me, fine, if you don't, that's cool. But I did follow him. We took a path along the lawn to the first of the elaborate flowerbeds, where he stopped and handed me the book. Then he sat there staring at a row of dainty little flowers, like a chess grandmaster contemplating a tricky move.

'Okay, it's autumn, that narrows it down,' he said.

I had no idea, so I started flicking through the book, but even though it was supposed to be for children, it was clearly structured for people who knew vaguely what they were doing.

'Have you found it?' he asked.

'Not yet.'

'Okay, we'll come back to that.'

He pointed to some bright magenta flowers behind us, and this time I found them in the book.

'I know what these are,' I said.

'Give me a moment,' he replied.

But as he sat in silence it looked like nothing was coming. It was painful to watch. It was horrible.

'Okay,' he said quietly. 'What are they?'

'They're hesperantha, I think. Look.' I tried to show him the book but he pushed himself away.

181

The same thing happened at the next display and the next. We'd stop and I looked them up in the book. I started reading little bits of information to him to see if that jogged his memory, but it didn't.

'Maybe it'll be easier with wildflowers,' he said. So we left the asphalt path and followed a rough track into a little wood, but it was hard for him to push himself on the woodchip surface.

There were lots of white flowers with pretty petals and even I knew they were sneezewort because he had shown them to me before, but he stared at them blankly. He stared and stared.

'Do you want a clue?' I said brightly.

But the hope had gone.

'This isn't working,' he said. 'Let's go back.'

'Wait, I think I have it here, maybe it's . . .'

'I said let's go, Cammy!'

He tried to turn the wheelchair but the wheels weren't getting any purchase, and it looked difficult to manoeuvre. I hated seeing it. I felt sad for him but also angry. I was angry that he couldn't do what he used to do.

'Let me help,' I said.

'NO! Leave me alone!'

As soon as I got his wheelchair free and on to the path again, he pushed himself away. He didn't wait for me and, this time, I didn't follow.

Chapter Fourteen

# The Red Satchel

It was Mum's birthday and she invited Nikki and me to her apartment for the weekend. I was not looking forward to it. When the three of us got together, there was always a modicum of tension, like we were hiding something from ourselves and each other.

I arrived early Saturday afternoon and Nikki was there already, sitting at the breakfast bar with a glass of sparkling wine. Mum was assembling some sort of salad. Fleetwood Mac was playing in the background. 'Here's our poor girl,' said Nikki, dropping from the stool and sprinting over to hug me. Mum waved and blew me a perfunctory kiss. Then she sauntered to the fridge and pulled out a bottle of Prosecco.

'How are you? How is poor Ben?' said Nikki. Her voice had a tone of performative sympathy that made me feel a sharp pang of anger. Mum handed me a flute almost overflowing with bubbles.

'He's fine. He's getting stronger every day,' I replied. I didn't want Nikki to think of him as some kind of invalid, some sob story to coo over and patronise. That wasn't him. Even stuck in a rehabilitation centre, semi-paralysed and depressed, he was twice the man Justin would ever be. God, how I wished I could say that out loud. Instead, I smiled and took a swig of the wine.

'And how about you?' asked Mum, putting a bowl of Kettle Chips on the counter. 'How are you feeling about it?'

I sighed and thought about how to reply. This visit got heavy really quickly. 'I just feel . . . guilty. Confused. Scared.'

'I bet that's normal.'

'It doesn't feel like there's anything normal about my life right now.'

Nikki nodded. 'Mum told me about your little excursion to see Granddad. Tell me what happened!'

'Nothing much. I was looking for something.'

My sister pushed and prodded, and eventually I gave in and told them about the journal. Its revelations about Elizabeth and Heather, Elizabeth and Lea. The curse. Camille.

'Oh my God, Granny was gay?' Nikki exclaimed. 'Mum, did you know this?'

'No. I mean, your granny was always very guarded, but . . . Cammy, why didn't you tell me you'd found this?'

'You have to show us!' Nikki said. 'This is fascinating!'

Then I had to go through the whole story again, in minute detail. And while they obsessed over Elizabeth's love life, I kept trying to bring it back to the revelations concerning Camille and the curse.

'You're *still* obsessed with that whole thing?' said Nikki.

'Doesn't it seem odd to you?'

'It's confirmation bias,' she replied, taking a sip of her wine. 'You're expecting to find some kind of uncanny family history so all

184

the evidence points in that direction. And really, this whole curse thing is just a symptom of your worries about Ben.'

I stared at her for a second. 'Thank you, Dr Freud. How much is this consultation going to cost me?'

'I'm serious,' she said.

'But I've always felt like this – I've always felt like there was this kind of weird darkness at the edge of things, just waiting to close in on me.'

'I think you need to stop listening to Lorna's goth records.'

'Nikki!'

She put her hand on my arm and shot me her sympathetic smile. 'Look, let's put the journal to the side for a second and deal with the issue at hand. Which is Ben. You've got to decide what to do about him.'

'He needs me.'

'We already know that,' she said, jamming another crisp into her mouth. 'But the big question is, do *you* need *him*? I know that sounds selfish, but you can't be with him out of sympathy alone. That's not fair on him. Sometimes you need to be cruel to be kind.'

Over dinner, the talk passed from our grandparents on to Nikki's job and Mum's latest client while I silently tried to get the image of Ben and Meg out of my head. When I tuned back into the conversation, they were reminiscing about some camping holiday that I barely remembered.

'Do you have the old family photo albums?' slurred Nikki.

Mum sighed. 'Yes, they're in my storage cupboard somewhere.'

'We have to see them!'

With much protestation Mum got up, and Nikki followed her as she walked down the hallway. I could hear them talking and laughing, and not wanting to be entirely left out, I picked up my glass of wine and wandered out to join them. I'd never seen inside the storage cupboard before – it wasn't actually a cupboard at all, but a whole room next to her office and the door was always closed. I was almost expecting precarious piles of overflowing cardboard boxes, but no, this was Mum, so the space was incredibly tidy and ordered, with bespoke shelving units lining the room, each carefully filled with lever-arch files and labelled storage containers, like some sort of bank vault. There were a few anomalies among the pristine plastic boxes – an ancient Canon word processor, an architectural model of an office building, a weathered satchel, a couple of moth-eaten teddy bears – but otherwise Mum had managed to completely compartmentalise her memories. I grudgingly admired her for it.

As I stood in that room, watching my sister and mother pull files from the shelves and search inside for our childhoods, I had a strange feeling I couldn't quite place. It prodded at my mind, like a distant bell chiming. A memory of something. Then Nikki shouted, 'Found them!' while waving several red, embossed photo albums around. And so we traipsed back to the living room and gathered together on the sofa, turning the pages of the albums, to images of Nikki and me as toddlers, all dinky summer dresses and fat little legs, and hands covered in cake and ice cream. As the pages turned, it was interesting to see our characters diverge as we hit our teens; Nikki in her designer labels and pastel colours, me in black, in army jackets and knackered Docs.

'My goodness, what a miserable goth bitch you were,' said Nikki.

'Hasn't she changed?' replied Mum, putting her arm around my shoulder. They cackled together like witches.

Around 11 p.m., Nikki started to yawn and stretch and talk about needing rest after a long week, so the party was over. She got the guestroom, I got the sofa. Lying between the Egyptian cotton bedsheets, it was easy to think rationally. I *was* being paranoid. I *was*

186

freaking out over what to do about Ben. In the space of a few weeks my life had transformed from quiet, predictable routine to chaotic drama. The sensible option would be to drop my investigation into the past. What could I possibly find there? But I kept coming back to that odd sensation I'd had in Mum's store cupboard, the ghost of a memory brushing past me.

Eventually falling asleep, I dreamed I was walking towards the church on a cold afternoon. Covering the roof, and along each window ledge, and in and around the tower, were hundreds upon hundreds of rooks. They cawed and clamoured and ruffled and pecked, and I knew they were bringing a message.

I woke suddenly at 3 a.m., bathed in sweat, breathing hard, my head thudding. Once I'd calmed down, I still had that odd feeling again of something half-remembered. I got up and went through to the kitchen for a glass of water and, as I stood there drinking, it came to me.

That satchel.

The one in the store cupboard.

It was the one my aunt gave to Mum on the day she died.

# Chapter Fifteen

# **A Discovery**

By the time I woke up on Sunday morning, the other two were already out. Mum left a note in the kitchen: 'Good afternoon. We've gone shopping, back later. Phone if you need anything.'

I didn't feel guilty when I flicked the light on in her storage room. She had, after all, technically lied to me. The satchel was in the place I had seen it the previous evening, wedged between shoeboxes and photo albums. It was almost definitely Lorna's – I had seen it a few times at the church when I'd stayed with her. Carefully, I reached up and pulled it free. The clasp was shut, and I was momentarily disappointed to see that it had a lock on it. Was I going to have to find the key, force it open, or just give up? To my relief, when I pushed gently at the lock, it opened easily. I looked inside and gasped.

It was a bundle of old letters tied together with a length of twine. The handwriting was beautiful and ornate, though the ink was fading and the paper was dyed sepia with age.

Daphne's letters. They were here all along.

I was just about to untie them when there was the slightest noise behind me, followed by a shadow moving against the wall. I held my breath.

'You're awake then,' Mum said. I jumped, then swirled around in shock, almost falling backwards into the shelves.

'Jesus, Mum, you scared the shit out of me!'

I stood there like some dumb creature caught in the headlights of a speeding car on a quiet country road.

'I saw you looking at the satchel when we were in here with Nikki,' she said. 'I saw the little cogs whirling.' She made a rotating finger gesture next to her head. 'Those letters were written between your great grandmother and her boyfriend, while he was fighting in France in the First World War. But I suspect you already know that.'

'Why didn't you tell me you had them?'

'Because I knew this would happen. You are becoming obsessed.'

'There's something in here about the curse?'

She gave me a concerned expression. 'They're very fragile,' she said. 'You need to be extremely careful with them. You need to be extremely careful with *all* of this.'

'You think I'm crazy, don't you?'

Her phone buzzed and she looked down at it momentarily.

'I think you've had a terrible shock,' she said. 'I think you blame yourself somehow for what happened to Ben. And just like your aunt, you think there is something dark and terrible at the heart of it all, something that has been passed through the family, and you're going to spend all your energy trying to track it down.'

'And you think I'm wasting my time?'

'I think you have the capacity, as she did, to make things darker than they are. And I think that impulse is destructive.'

189

'Then why?' I said. 'Why did you let me stay with her so much? Was I that much of a nightmare to care for?'

'Let's not do this.'

'No, I want to know. Was I so awful as a daughter, so fucking unmanageable, that you were prepared to dump me on your mad sister?'

'That's not how it was, Cammy. You wanted to go, and you told me every chance you could how much you hated it at home.'

'I was a teenager! Of course I hated it at home!'

The small, closed silence of the storage room was becoming oppressive. It felt like the walls were closing in on us.

'She needed you around,' Mum said in a quiet voice. 'You adored her and she needed that. You both had art in common, and that was something I didn't really ever get. She gave that to you. If I made you feel like I was pushing you away, I . . . I feel very sorry for that. I am very, very sorry for that. There was never a moment I didn't want you at home. I missed you every day you weren't there.'

I had never heard her be like this before. Apologetic and hurt. It was almost unbearable. I felt a compulsion to lighten things.

'Are you sure that there was never a *single* moment you didn't want me there?' I asked, smiling. She welcomed the change in mood.

'There may have been *some* moments. Just one or two.'

We giggled. She put her hand out to my face and turned it.

'You got another ear piercing?' she said.

'Yeah, a few weeks ago. You've only just noticed?'

'There are so many, it's hard to keep up.' She stroked my chin then let me go. 'I love you,' she said. 'You know that, don't you?'

I put the box onto the shelf and hugged her. She was stiff in my awkward arms.

*

Mum let me take the letters home. She put them in a Tupperware container for me like a packed lunch. It made sense to read them where they were found, like some sort of ritual. Had Mum read them? Or had she just stored them away? Was there something in here she was afraid of me seeing? When I got in, I took the box to the big table where I'd laid out the other documents, the journal, the magazine feature, then carefully removed the letters. There was a dozen of them, Daphne's written on thick paper that I expect was once creamy-coloured and luxurious. The others on military stationery. All the pages had scuffs and tears, and as Lorna had observed, there were splatters of what looked like mud across them. As I ran my fingers over the surface of one page, it occurred to me that I was the third generation of my family to touch these brittle artefacts.

I sat down at my office chair, switched on my big industrial lamp and angled it over the letters. Laying out the first one in front of me, I saw that it was dated January 1915. It was more than one hundred years old – a faint voice from our distant history.

What was it going to tell me?


## The letters of Daphne Ricard and Robert Woodbridge


### Daphne to Robert

I am writing this letter straight after seeing you off at the station. I feel wretched about how I left things. I am haunted by how it must have felt to propose to marriage, only for me to turn away, unable to respond. But, darling, I am afraid. I am afraid of how I feel about you, and what it means. We both know what my father expects. I am to marry a man of whom he approves, a lawyer, an accountant, a doctor, anything else is unthinkable. He sees this as my purpose, even in this age of utter turmoil. If he ever finds out I spent the weekend with you in Bridport and not with Eliza's family in Weymouth, I have no doubt I'll be disowned. I can trust Eliza, she is my closest friend, but this is a small village, things get out.

And now to sit here, picturing you going back to the hutments in Salisbury, packing all your things, boarding a ship, your heart full of hurt and disappointment, knowing what it is you are heading into. It is unthinkable. And yet it is all I can think about. I keep recalling the day you enlisted. The sky was cloudless, and the air was so dense and hot. While you signed yourself away, I was with Eliza, sketching the view over Bathampton Down. There were children playing in the river, seeking shelter under the weeping willows. The war seemed like some distant fantasy. And then those weeks you spent yomping around Ashton Park with a spade for a rifle, like it was all a lark. The oddness of it. I couldn't believe your barracks were in the empty buildings of the Bristol International Festival where I'd once explored a Malaysian rubber plantation and bought tea from an Indian bazaar. Now it is a place where men learn to fight our foreign enemies. When we first met, you were repairing the wall of a church, now you are learning how to gut a man with a bayonet. When I see the young soldiers in Bath, parading the streets in their spotless new uniforms, laughing and joking about the battles to come, I can't help but think that isn't you. You are a craftsman, you make things with those hands. I can still feel them on me.

My only consolation is that you are not going to Africa or some other distant place. France is just a step across the Channel. You are not far from home, Robert, you are not very far at all.

## Daphne to Robert

Before we parted, you begged that I keep you up to date with news from home. Well, I have news, Robbie. I have discovered something about my mother, something that has been kept from me my entire life. It feels wrong to trouble you with this, considering where you are and what you are there to do. But the act of sharing is a selfish comfort to me and, therefore, I must continue.

Yesterday afternoon, I returned home after a long bicycle ride down to Bradford-on-Avon, and instead of going straight into the house, I decided to sit on the little wooden bench on the lawn beneath the kitchen window. It was such a lovely sunny afternoon, and I knew as soon as I stepped foot inside, my stepmother would find some chore for me to be getting on with. I'd been sitting there lost in my book for perhaps an hour, when I heard our housekeeper Mrs Lewis in the kitchen, talking to the new maid, Ethel, who has come fresh to us from the cottage orphanage at Avon House. The girl was enquiring about our family, and the subject turned to my father and stepmother.

'But what became of the first Mrs Ricard?' the girl asked.

There was a long silence and I thought perhaps they had moved away to another room, but then I heard Mrs Lewis say in a quiet voice, 'We are not to speak of her, and certainly never in the presence of young Miss Ricard.'

I froze, almost not daring to breathe in case I gave away my presence. All my father has ever told me about my mother is that she was a fine, intelligent woman and that she sadly died soon after I was born of a long illness. I never asked anything more because it upset him so. But I had always sensed there was something I was not being told. A secret that everyone else in the village was privy to except me. Whenever I walk into a shop or get on the tram, I have a sense of conversations suddenly ending, of people looking away, biding their time until I have left. It has made me feel like a kind of pariah.

However, I knew Mrs Lewis could not keep hold of her discretion. She has always delighted in vexing me. It was her who told Father that I was visiting Eagle House, where Emily Blathwayt was providing a refuge for the suffragettes who had been arrested and beaten. All I did was serve them tea as they sat in the garden covered in bruises, half-mad with shock and trauma. Father was livid. He said I had been conniving with anarchists.

So I closed my book and listened, and sure enough Mrs Lewis continued.

'Miss has been told a story about her mother and how she died, but it's not the truth. She was a difficult woman, you see, she had terrible trouble with her nerves. Before she married Mr Ricard, she was in an asylum. He met her afterwards and nursed her back to life. She was happy with him for a while, but she started to fall apart again after Miss Ricard was born. And then one day, she just disappeared from home. People said they'd seen her walking up towards St Cyprian's Court and that very night the house burned down. She was never seen again . . .'

I sat there, paralysed by shock for several minutes. A whole lifetime of deceit unravelled in an instant. But what frightened me most was that, somehow, I already knew. I knew there was something wrong with my mother. And I've always had this awful feeling deep inside myself, like a slither of shrapnel in my heart, that whatever it was that had happened to her would one day happen to me.

How I wish you were here with me now. I still do not understand why you felt you had no choice but to enlist. I know there was pressure from your father, the tyrant, who was disgusted that you didn't follow him and your brothers into the military. After they fought with the British Expeditionary Force at Marne, I realise the pressure must have grown. But you despised him, didn't you? He's bullied and belittled you all your life. What does it matter what he thinks of you now? What does it matter in the end?

## Daphne to Robert

It's been almost a month, I am desperate to hear from you. I am spending much of my time at the church. We are providing support for women in the village whose husbands are fighting. We hand out food packages and help where we can with matters at home. The children look bereft and confused.

Eliza and I played tennis this afternoon. She is always asking about our night at the guesthouse. She is barely a week younger than me but now sees me as impossibly mature and sophisticated. We are in a ghost-story phase, devouring the tales of Vernon Lee and Mary Elizabeth Braddon. I suppose it is our way of coping with all that is going on. I'm not sure these stories are good for me – the tales stir those old feelings I have, the dread at the very back of my mind. Worse still, Eliza has a new housekeeper, Gwen, who is of ancient Somerset stock and knows many hoary old folk tales about the local area. She told Eliza that a vengeful ghost haunts St Cyprian's Church! But when Eliza took me to the kitchen to meet her, she went very quiet and refused to share any stories with me. She avoided us for the rest of the afternoon. It was as though I frightened her somehow. Why?

My sleep has been very troubled. I keep having the same dream over and over again. I go to the church to see you, but you are not working outside and the building looks different, the trees much closer and wilder. And when I open the big oak door and look in, it is so dark and there is mould everywhere, and you are not there either. But there is a woman, a young woman in a red dress, standing in the aisle with her back to me, looking down at something. I walk towards her, but for some reason I am very, very scared, and when I am close, she slowly turns towards me and points – and I am so terrified I cannot scream. That's when I wake up.

How I miss you, Robbie. You helped banish these thoughts while you were here.

This afternoon, Mrs Lewis was out shopping and my stepmother was visiting friends, so I took advantage of an almost empty house to search for evidence of my mother. I scoured shelves, cupboards and closets, I flicked through books, I even lifted carpets and looked for loose floorboards, but I found nothing. My father's erasure of her is so complete, so deafening. I have nothing to hold. It is so odd, how a life can just be removed. I will keep looking. I have to.

You will be careful, won't you? I am begging you to stay safe and not to take risks. You must remember at all times that you are important and needed.


### Daphne to Robert

Where are you? Can you tell me? Every day, I check to see if a letter has arrived from you, and every day Mrs Lewis asks who it is I am so desperate to hear from. She knows, I'm certain she knows about us.

A new battle of sorts has begun in our home. Father has decided that I am to become governess to my young stepbrothers until such time as they attend school or that I marry, whichever comes first. As you know, I had set my heart on applying to study English Literature at Girton College. However, Father insists that education is harmful to young women; he says that exams make us neurotic and that conspicuous intelligence is unattractive to prospective partners. I protested loudly, and he got up to go to his study, but I followed and told him the world is changing and that it needs clever women more than ever. He turned on me with such a fury and shouted, 'For God's sake, Daphne, it was such ideas that destroyed your mother!' then he slammed the study door and locked it. What did he mean? He hasn't spoken to me for two days. I know he loves me, and he was such a caring father to me as a child, but my God, he does not know what to do with me now. I wish he would tell me what really happened, perhaps it would help me understand. It may even help him to unburden himself. But I daren't push.

I'm sorry to go on, you are facing much greater concerns. But it is horrible to feel powerless. There are always eyes on me – my stepmother, my aunt, our housekeeper, neighbours, family acquaintances. A man can have no idea what it is like to be monitored in this way. My hope is that, if I can't change the way my father thinks, perhaps the war will do it for me. Several of the younger clerks at his firm have enlisted, and there is a lot to do, so he is talking about the prospect of having to employ women. I'm sure the idea fills him with unbridled horror.

Have you met any new pals in your battalion? Are there any other keen readers? Ethel is trying to teach me to knit. She tells me the soldiers need warm woollen socks and that it is our responsibility as women to provide them. I have started a pair for you, but surely the war will be over by the time they are finished.

I am so afraid. The silence is terrifying. Sometimes I steal a glimpse at Father's newspaper before he takes it away from me, and I have seen some of the reports, the casualty lists. In the village I hear women talking, crying, swapping stories of the men and then boys they have lost already. You would tell me, wouldn't you, if you were injured or afraid? I can't face the thought of you being alone out there.

P.S. This morning, I walked past the locked door of my father's study and it struck me: if there is anything about my mother somewhere in this house, it will be in there. The problem is, there are only two keys – the one Father keeps with him at all times and the one Mrs Lewis uses to clean the room once every week. She is under strict instructions to let no one else in. But that is my new mission, I have to see inside.


### Robert to Daphne

My darling, I cannot tell you how wonderful it has been to receive your letters. I am sorry I haven't replied sooner. It is difficult to find the time to sit down with a scrap of paper and a sound mind. You have asked what it is really like here, and I shall try to tell you. You'll notice this letter comes in a green envelope. These are handed out on a monthly basis and pass through the system uncensored. They are meant for men to write to their sweethearts, but we have to sign a waiver to verify they contain only personal matters. I am going to break the rules somewhat.

If man's aim with this war was to create a Hell on Earth, then he has surely succeeded. We have spent the last five days in the frontline trenches – I have slept for perhaps two or three hours in all that time. I am with a small unit responsible for trench repairs, so we are kept close to the action. I've known most of the other fellows since we enlisted, they are decent men. Teddy and Bert are labourers on the railways, working on the Great Western line down in Cornwall. George Johnson is a civil engineer, he is twenty-two but looks much younger. He has a two-year-old daughter who he is absolutely potty over. His wife sends long elaborate letters about the little girl's escapades and they amuse us all. He keeps a photo of them both in the breast pocket of his uniform. This is his first time out of London – the lad can't believe how far the fields stretch, how there can be nothing on the horizon but hills and sky. I've been reading Emily Dickinson to him and he's asking interesting questions. I feel rather paternal towards him.

The rain has been ceaseless for over a week. Our dugouts are flooded and the duckboards along the floor of the trench have rotted so anywhere we rest we're up to our knees in mud. The men who have been here longer wear uniforms mangy with lice – they have to burn the buggers out of the seams with candles! The German artillery bombardment has been continuous for the past two days, huge explosions that make the whole planet shake. We call the shells 'coal boxes' because they throw tons of pitch black dust and smoke into the air, and it gets into your nose and mouth and lungs, it's all you can taste.

Daphne, death is everywhere. When the fighting is fierce, bodies are left to rot in the wasteland beyond the trench – these were once men with families and parents and wives, now they are corpses, bloating in the rain.

There has been one bright spot at least. Last night, there was a gap in the shelling. We managed to drain the dugout and get a brazier going, so we had a little light and warmth. I took out my copy of *Jane Eyre*, almost giddy at the prospect of a few moments to read. A new officer was trudging through the mud, checking on the men, and he stopped by me.

'Charlotte Brontë?' he asked. I looked up and saw a kind, rather handsome face smiling down at me in the most pleasant and indulgent way.

'Yes, sir,' I said. 'Rather soggy, I'm afraid.'

'It's a miracle you've kept it at all. Is it your only book here?'

'It is, sir. I did have a copy of Matthew Arnold's poetry, but Johnson over there used it as toilet tissue.'

The officer laughed. 'Please do keep this one away from him. That is no fate for a Miss Eyre.'

'No, sir.'

'You're a scholar, are you?'

'No, sir, not really. I'm a stonemason. But I do like to read.'

'Me too,' he said. 'Me too.'

The others sat about, frozen by this unexpected intrusion into our routine. The captain seemed to sense their discomfort.

'Good,' he said. 'Good work.' He stood for a few seconds, as though unsure what to say, or where to go next – it felt for a bizarre moment like a chance meeting at a pleasant garden party. Finally he said, 'I'd best get on, check the rest of the line.' And then he wandered away with a sort of relaxed insouciance, like a groundsman inspecting the pitch at Lord's. Later, one of the other men told us his name is Captain Guy Seabright. His father is said to be a close friend of General Haig, no less. The word is, he led his men with great distinction during the opening months of the war, but those battles took a toll.

I am being self-indulgent by not responding to your own news. What a terrible shock for you to find out about your mother in that way. Is there no one else in the village you can talk to? Did she have no other relatives nearby?

Please do not give my ill-timed proposal another thought, it was rash and manipulative. The thought of you is keeping me alive, but everything beyond this mud and slaughter feels somehow unreal. I close my eyes and try to recall how we met, how we became friends, but the details are blurring. Do you think, when you write back, you could tell me the story from your point of view? I need to know it happened. I need evidence that our world still exists.

## Daphne to Robert

My goodness, what a relief to hear from you. I almost wept when Ethel brought your letter to me! But how quickly my elation turned to horror and concern when I read of your plight. What madness that men must live, fight and die like this. It is a sort of Armageddon. All I can do from here is pray for your safety, which I do incessantly.

You asked for a story about how we met, so let me try to recount it. On that day, my intention had been to cycle along the valley path to Ashwicke, and if I had done so, I would never have chanced upon you. However, due to a flood, I was forced to take a detour and, much to my disquiet, I found myself heading towards the ruin of St Cyprian's Court. I was always wary of that house, due to the role it seemingly played in my mother's demise. There are all sorts of legends and stories attached to the place. When I heard there were plans to build a lot of new houses there, I felt somewhat relieved that the estate was to be erased from the Earth for ever. That afternoon, as I cycled alongside the boundary wall, I looked in through the trees at the edge of the grounds, towards the old church. It had fallen into such a terrible state, I'd always assumed it too would be pulled down, but there were three men there clearly conducting repairs: you, your boss and his young son.

I told you afterwards that I had stopped to catch my breath. That isn't true. I stopped to watch you. You looked very dashing in your heavy white shirt, the sleeves rolled up, and your tweed trousers tucked into those stout boots, like some explorer from a boy's comic book. Then you came over to me. And as you walked through the trees, the dappled sunlight gave your skin a sort of golden sheen. You were beautiful, Robbie. I felt such a tremor of excitement as you approached. Did you know?

'Are you lost?' you asked, wiping the sweat from your brow.

'No, I live nearby,' I said. 'I am riding my bicycle.'

'So I can see.' You smiled, looking down at the machine. And I blushed at the idiocy of my reply.

We were quiet for a second, and the world swam back into focus. There were thrushes singing in the trees behind you, the rustle of leaves, the clang, clang, as your colleague chipped at a stone block.

'I like your trousers,' you said. It was only at this point that I remembered I was wearing my cycling bloomers.

'I had them made especially. They allow more freedom than a long skirt. Nobody knows I wear them. It's a secret. Father would be angry.'

'I won't tell,' you said.

'What are you doing here?' I asked.

'I'm a stonemason. Well, an apprentice stonemason. We're carrying out some repairs on the old church. It was struck by a falling tree during the big storm of 1888. After that, it was donated to the local parish, along with funds for its restoration. I suppose nobody got round to it until now. It's rather an odd place. I hear there are ghost stories attached to it.' You fixed me with that smile again. 'Are you heading anywhere particular?'

'No,' I said. 'I just like to ride. I'll find somewhere with a bit of shade and perhaps sit and read for a bit. I can never be out for long.'

'What are you reading?'

I took my book out of my satchel and handed it to you.

*The Tenant of Wildfell Hall?*' you said. I must admit, I didn't think you'd know it, but you surprised me. 'What do you make of Gilbert? He's a little impertinent expecting Helen's affection after all she's suffered.'

'He's in love,' I said. 'We have to expect men to be silly and selfish under those circumstances.'

You burst out laughing.

'You read the Brontës?' I asked.

But before you could reply, there was a distant bellow from behind you.

'Mr Woodbridge,' the voice shouted. 'Do you think you might delight us with your company at some point this afternoon?'

'That would be my employer, Sid,' you said. 'He's brought his lad along today, so he's keen to show who's boss. I'd better go. It was nice to meet you, Miss . . . ?'

'Miss Ricard. Daphne Ricard.'

'Pleased to meet you, Miss Ricard. My name is Robert Woodbridge. But my friends call me Robbie.'

'Robbie!' the voice called again. 'Get back here, you lazy bastard!'

'And what charming friends they are,' I said.

'Goodbye, Miss Ricard, I hope we have the chance to speak again.' With that you doffed your cap.

'I hope so too,' I said, forgetting that if my father or stepmother had heard me speaking so informally to a strange man they would have confined me to the cellar.

As I watched you, all I could think about was how exciting it was to strike up a conversation with a young gentleman outside of my rather small circle of acquaintances. I had not thought that this was the beginning of something. But then, just as I sat astride the saddle and pushed down on the pedal, you called out again.

'I'll be working here for several weeks,' you said. 'I get a little time for lunch at midday, if you were to ride this way again.' I didn't reply, but as I cycled along the narrow path, I found that I was already constructing reasons to come back that way. I did not realise at the time it would be almost every day.

Indeed, I became adept at finding excuses to be out on my bicycle. I took on chores for my church group, I made deliveries for my stepmother and picked up shopping for elderly neighbours. I was a most helpful young lady. At the same time, the intensifying drama of world events helped to divert attention away from me. It was easier to be furtive when all over Europe, countries were moving against each other.

You and I went for walks along the valley, we had picnics in quiet corners of lonely fields. We swapped novels and poems, and talked about Keats and Dickens and George Eliot. You asked questions about me – real questions, about the things I liked and thought. No one had ever done that before. My father had me brought up to be quiet and respectful; the last thing he wanted from me were opinions. He expected me to give myself to the family, to help my stepmother and my brothers, like a sort of glorified house servant and governess, until I was old enough to be handed over to some suitable man who would treat me in more or less the same fashion. But that's not the person you saw.

The person you saw was me.


### Robert to Daphne

A cold, dark week. The word is, a major offensive is being planned, so everyone is jittery. The anticipation is horrible. We watch the wasteland for movement and sleep in the trenches like rats. Your mind drifts, your grip on the world starts to loosen. Sometimes I hold your letters, just to remind me that you are there. Can I smell your perfume on them, or am I imagining that? I don't know how long I can hold on. I just don't know what matters any more. I must sleep now. I'll write more tomorrow.

The shelling started again last night. My unit received word that a guard post two hundred yards down the line had been hit, collapsing a section of the trench and burying two men and a sentry dog. Our orders were to repair the wall and rebuild the post as quickly as possible, using whatever materials we could salvage. I thought of old Sid Moss teaching me how to carefully chip away at some ancient piece of stone. How to prepare a lime mortar. My work on St Cyprian's Church now seems like a strange dream. The world outside is fading.

I loved reading the story of our meeting. The memories took me out of this place for a few moments. Please send more.


### Daphne to Robert

As you wanted, here is another memory from home. This happened, Robbie, this was real. Please keep this letter safe, please do not share it with the other men.

June 21st, 1914, a hot, bright afternoon, the sky an endless sea of blue. It was your last day working on the church and you wanted to show me the finished article. Together we walked the exterior, and you pointed out the smooth new blocks of stone you had laid, the stylistic touches to make them match the originals.

'Gosh, it is rather hot, even in the shade,' I said, removing my hat and fanning myself with it under the freckled light of the trees.

'We can go inside for a second,' you said. 'It's cool there.'

I followed you around to the wide oak door and you held it open for me as I passed. Sure enough, the air was deliciously cold, and it was so quiet, the only sound coming from our footsteps on the stone flags, the echo of it through the building. We stood at the rear and looked at the stained glass window, so close to one another, I felt sure we were touching. The close smell of you made me feel languorous and dizzy. Your breath quickened. We stayed like this for a long time, understanding, I think, that something was going to happen, but not sure what or how we could bring it about. The silent pews faced away from us in their solid, determined lines. I felt momentarily awkward, so I began to walk down the aisle, trailing my fingers across the back of each seat, aware that you were following close behind.

'I used to feel rather scared in here,' I said as we walked. 'It was as though I was never quite alone. There is a feeling about the place, don't you think?'

'Yes,' you said. 'I do. I really do.'

I looked up at the old arched ceiling all hung with cobwebs. Patches of light from the windows formed glittering shafts across the timbers. We came to the wooden steps of the pulpit and stopped, not quite side by side.

'The silence is strange in here,' you said. 'I think there is something in it.'

Closer now. The slightest sheen of sweat on your forehead.

'What?' I asked. 'What is it?'

You looked up and around the interior, then back to me.

'A sort of longing, perhaps?'

We stared at each other, but somehow couldn't move, couldn't touch – it was too much, too big and brave a step. Instead, you shuffled away, seemingly fascinated by the old walls. For my part, I backed into the handrail leading up to the pulpit, the wood still smooth and glossy under my hand. And I began to walk up the steps, thinking that I had never done this, that the pulpit was, of course, out of bounds to me and always would be. And when I reached the lectern, I leaned forward and looked out towards you, as though preparing to preach. But I didn't want to say anything, and I didn't want you to either, I wanted you to understand, just by looking at me, what I needed from you.

And you did.

Without taking your eyes from me, you began walking towards

the pulpit. Slowly, almost too slowly, you put a single foot on the bottom stair, then step by step, the wood creaking beneath your feet, you climbed up to me.

'Is it safe?' you asked.

'No,' I said and I held out my hand to you. 'It's not safe. Come on.'

You took my hand and climbed the last few steps. Nearer, higher, until we both stood on the wooden stage. Slowly, we pressed together. I lifted my hands to your face and you stopped me, but only to remove my gloves. I traced my fingers along your jaw, I swept your hair out of your eyes, your cologne was spiced and heady, like incense. You leaned forward. I leaned too and our lips touched, closed at first, then parted. Everything else I knew in the world dissolved in a giddying swirl. It felt like such a miraculous contrast, our first kiss, against the cold, dry austerity of the church.

## Robert to Daphne

It is now Wednesday. Or perhaps Thursday, I'm not sure. We're moving forward, a major attack on a key German position is now all but certain. After a ten-mile march through mud and wind, we're billeting at a small village at the foot of a rather picturesque hill range. On the first night I slept for several hours in a barn and it felt like the royal suite at Claridge's. I've done what I can to wash my uniform and clean out my service rifle, and there is a good canteen here, so we have eaten well. Most of the local population has left, but a few pedlars still linger about selling postcards of nearby attractions, mostly battle-scarred buildings and ruined countryside views; they also offer to take photographs of us which can be sent back home. I'm not sure I'd be happy for you to see me in this state.

It has been a pleasant day. Earlier, the rest of my unit joined a raucous soccer match with some men from another company.

They played on a stretch of pasture pocked with craters, so it was not exactly the FA Cup final. I was sitting on a low stretch of wall, watching them run about and writing this letter, when the officer from the other night, Captain Seabright, came over.

'Hello again,' he said, sitting beside me. He took out a silver case and offered me a cigarette, which I took and then we sat there silently smoking for a little while. What I didn't notice amid the squalor of the trench was that he has extremely bright blue eyes and his hair is yellowish blond, which gives him a very Scandinavian sort of look. We got idly chatting, and he told me that he went to school at Rugby, then studied Classics at Oxford before attending Sandhurst for officer training. He is not at all like the other officers, who are snooty and distant with us, he seems to be one of those men who can get on with just about anybody. He has a wonderful air of affable detachment, as though the war is a sort of amusing entertainment. After sitting for a while, he invited me back to his billet for tea. He had a room in a lovely old house by a nearby stream. He took me up and, do you know, next to his bed, he had a metal chest containing bookshelves, which were crammed with novels by Dickens, Eliot, the Brontës, all in excellent condition.

'It's my portable library,' he said, while putting a kettle on his little stove. 'It gets transported to wherever I'm billeted.'

'How on Earth did you fix that?' I asked. It seemed incredible to me that this man had managed to bring such an extravagant thing to the front, and that the army was ensuring its safe transport around France! But he simply shrugged and smiled, and then he said, 'Actually, blow this, let's have a proper drink.' And from a small wooden cabinet he produced a bottle of red wine and two glasses.

'So,' he said. 'What do you make of Jane Eyre's Mr Rochester?'

And do you know what? We sat and drank wine and talked about literature for over two hours! It was like a sort of mental bathe – I could feel the grime of fear and horror washing off me. Outside, we could hear through the open window that the lads had swapped from soccer to cricket. On that wonderful afternoon, with Captain Seabright lying on his bed, and me lounging in a comfortable armchair beside him, we sat and read and chatted as the sounds of birdsong and the thwack of leather on willow drifted in from outside. Just before I left for the evening he handed me a book. 'I thought you might like to borrow this,' he said. 'But please don't let Private Johnson get his hands on it.'

It was a rather battered collection of Matthew Arnold's poetry.

'I won't, sir, I promise.'

'You know "Dover Beach"?'

'Yes, sir.'

He cleared his throat. 'Ah, love, let us be true, To one another! for the world, which seems, To lie before us like a land of dreams, So various, so beautiful, so new, Hath really neither joy, nor love, nor light . . .'

He gave me a look that seemed to urge me to continue, so I did. 'Nor certitude, nor peace, nor help for pain; And we are here as on a darkling plain, Swept with confused alarms of struggle and flight . . .'

He smiled. 'Where ignorant armies clash by night.'

We stood for a few seconds, lost in our own thoughts.

'Sir,' I said. 'There's talk of a big push, perhaps even within a week. Is that what we're moving up towards?'

He took a cigarette out of that silver case and lit it.

'I can't say much,' he said, exhaling smoke into the room. 'But I'd rest now, while you have the chance. Write your letters. Do some reading. We won't be here for much longer.'

When I got back to our digs that night, I opened the book

209

and inside the front cover was an inscription in a gentleman's handwriting. It read simply, 'To our beautiful son. I look forward to your safe return. Your loving father.' For some reason, I found myself weeping.

### Daphne to Robert

You met me at Bridport station that final weekend before your journey to France. As my train arrived, I spotted you sitting on a bench beyond the bustling crowds, holding a cigarette, biting your fingernails. You were wearing your new uniform and seemed to be looking out towards something beyond the train tracks, beyond the whole of England even, your face empty of expression. But when you saw me alight, you smiled and, for an instant, I saw in your eyes what I had seen when we first met – that glimmer of charm and boyish delight. It took you a couple of seconds to stand and, by the time you were up, I was already with you. This close, it seemed that you'd aged in the few weeks since we'd last seen each other; your eyes deeper set and darker than before, your face made taut by some terrible internal effort. Around us, porters gathered cases and whooshed by on the way to waiting carriages and taxi cabs. There was laughter from a group of older uniformed men, newspapers under their arms.

You had booked us into a small hotel overlooking the harbour, using the names Mr and Mrs Woodbridge. It was an illicit thrill to watch you sign the register and for us to be accepted as husband and wife by the elderly lady at the desk. She looked me up and down with an odd expression but handed you the key anyway.

You asked, 'Daphne, would you like to see our room?' in a strange formal voice, and I nodded. You took my hand, and we walked through the hallway to the narrow staircase, and up to the first floor, where we almost collided with a maid pushing a wooden cart loaded with fresh linen. She looked us over and gave me a surreptitious smile. We reached the room and you slowly took out a key and unlocked the door, pushing it open and guiding me inside. Your hand was shaking. The interior was simple and homely; a floral carpet, a plump bed neatly made up with crisp sheets and a rather worn blanket. There was a sink in one corner. Through the window we could just see the harbour, the fishing boats bobbing at their moorings, and beyond them, the open sea. Neither of us spoke while we looked out. It was you who eventually broke the silence.

'I shouldn't have volunteered. You were right.'

'It doesn't matter now.'

'It does. I should have listened to you.'

'You did what you thought was right.'

'I didn't. I did what my father expected. I could have stayed out of it.'

'You couldn't,' I said, putting my hand on your arm. The cloth of your jacket felt stiff and scratchy. 'No man could.'

'Jim, another apprentice – he became a conscientious objector. Rattled off a bloody good speech to the military panel. Got himself a job in an arms factory in Gloucester. He'll never have to . . . ' You broke off for a second and grimaced at some thought of pain and terror. 'Well, he saved himself some trouble, that's for sure.' You tried to laugh, but it wouldn't come. Instead you started coughing. 'I'm sorry,' you said. 'It's just that I'm scared. I'm so damn scared.'

'It's all right,' I said.

'Do you want to go back downstairs? I've heard they do an excellent afternoon tea, despite all the shortages.'

'Robbie,' I said, putting my hand on your cheek as I had done that day in the church. 'I didn't come here for tea.'

There was no thought to what followed. It just happened. Nothing else of the world and its standards and expectations bothered us for the time we were together in that room. It was wonderful, Robbie, I can recall every moment. The idea that we were committing a sin seems ludicrous now. How could this small act of love be wrong, when across the Channel men are being slaughtered in their thousands for a few acres of land?

Mrs Lewis has come down with a chest infection and the doctor consigned to her bed for a week. Ethel has taken on most of her duties including dusting Father's study and I have seen that she is storing the key in a pot in the kitchen rather than carrying it about with her. My stepmother is visiting friends tomorrow and taking the boys, so the house will be almost empty.

Robbie, I am going to take the key. I am going to get into the study and I am going to find whatever is hidden there concerning my mother.


### Robert to Daphne

Back in the trenches again, the furthest east I have ever been. We are at the head of an arrow looking to pierce German territory. This time it is real. The attack is imminent. We will make a direct assault on the enemy position in less than a week. I have within me a growing feeling of fury. The thought that we have to wait patiently, like pigs led to the slaughterhouse.

The last few days have been quiet, with no shelling at all. An almost jovial air has descended. Last night, we could hear singing from the German trenches, and some of our lads started shouting requests. One of our reserve trenches has just been connected to a line the French abandoned a few months earlier, and a case of decent brandy was discovered.

George got tipsy. He talked endlessly of his daughter. 'She is too clever by half,' he said. 'She's got my missus around her little finger. She can read and count. She loves fairy tales, she makes up her own! My daughter – the writer!' He sat back on the little bench in our dugout, smiling broadly. 'The new world, after this war is done, it will be hers, all hers. God, I hope I get to see it. If I make it back, all I want is to watch her grow up.'

'You will,' I told him. 'I'll make damn sure of it.'

He gave me one of his daughter's drawings. A vivid squiggle of colours.

Later, Captain Seabright and I drank half a bottle of brandy in the candlelight of his bunker. He could tell I was becoming despondent and angry. He asked about you. He asked me to share a memory, the first thing that came into my head.

I told him about cycling with you along the lanes near St Cyprian. Dappled sunlight on the track, the scent of cow parsley. But forgive me, Daphne, what I truly pictured was that morning in the guesthouse, us lying in bed half-asleep, naked, the sun pouring in through the window, illuminating your body, like something holy. I watched you for many minutes, perhaps hours, and I knew I had never seen anything so beautiful in all my life. You brought your hand to my face. You said it was lovely and soft. It is rough and dirty now, the sort of filth that can't be got out with soap and scrubbing.

I told Guy that you carry books with you, wherever you go. You and he are alike in that. I wonder if you will ever meet? I hope so. I had this thought of us three having a day together somewhere after all the fighting is done, after enough men have been killed to appease the generals. We are strolling along a pebbly beach, or through a spring wood, the bluebells out, larks singing high above. We go for lunch, you two unpack your little libraries and read and talk. It is torture to imagine, yet my heart aches for it.

## Daphne to Robert

This morning I woke early, filled with trepidation about what I was planning to do. I went down for breakfast early and when Ethel brought in my porridge, I asked about the condition of Mrs Lewis.

'Oh she's still in bed, miss,' she said. 'She does seem somewhat improved from yesterday, but still very weak.'

'Give her my best wishes,' I said. This was good news – there would at least be no intervention from her today. The nanny came down with the boys and they sat at the table being raucous and annoying, so I excused myself, and went up to dress. I stayed upstairs while my stepmother emerged, took her breakfast and with the nanny, gathered the boys and left the house.

Then it was just me and Ethel.

I came down and sat in the parlour with a book, trying to affect a nonchalant demeanour as she cleared the breakfast table, then scampered about upstairs collecting laundry. I was sure she'd have to leave the house at some point, but after two hours, she seemed no closer to finishing her chores. The window of opportunity was closing. Finally, at a quarter to midday she announced that she was heading out to the butcher's shop. I waited for her to close the kitchen door behind her, and then ran to the parlour window to see her making her way along the long path to the road.

Darling, I have never moved so fast. I ran through to the kitchen, reached up to the shelf and took down the pot. The key rattled inside. I took it, putting the pot back where it was, then rushed upstairs, along the corridor. Just outside the study, I stopped for a moment and listened. I heard a noise from above, the squeak of bed springs and then several bumps. Was Mrs Lewis coming down? I stood petrified like a frightened animal for a good five minutes. It had been made clear to me on many occasions that if I

214

was ever discovered in this room, all my privileges would be taken: no more bicycle, no more days out with Eliza or anyone else, a prisoner until marriage. But when no further sounds followed, I put the key in the lock and slowly turned it. For a second, it got stuck and I had a swooping concern that this was the wrong key after all, but after rattling about, it suddenly turned and the latch opened.

As I opened the door, the room was slowly revealed to me: the polished bookcases running along the entire left wall, the large oak desk in the centre of the room with its rich red leather top and the matching leather-bound chair, the fireplace with the painting above it depicting Bath Abbey, the large Persian rug that my grandfather brought back from the Middle East. The air smelled of books, cigars and my father's cologne. It seemed unnaturally still, as though the room itself was furious at this trespass.

I checked all the drawers beneath the bookshelves first, sliding out each in turn, my hands shaking all the while. It was nothing but maps, charts and more books. A filing cabinet on the other side of the door held letters, bills and other documents that I didn't recognise or understand. I shuffled through them, looking out for my mother's name, but there were so many, all I could do was glance quickly at each page as the grandfather clock in the corner loudly ticked. When it started to chime for noon, I almost dropped everything in shock. But I found nothing.

There was nowhere left but the desk. I crept over, the floorboards creaking noisily beneath my feet. The desk surface was clear apart from several pens and a pot of ink. I pulled out the top drawer. A cigar box and a lighter. Second drawer. Monogrammed writing paper, neatly stacked. Third drawer, a battered leather folder, closed. I put my hand in to pull it out, when I heard voices from outside, boys' voices, and then a key in the front door. They were home. Panic struck me, Robert. I seemed to lose all feeling.

215

My first instinct was to bolt from the room immediately, but I had come this far, and I didn't know when I would have another chance. I took the folder, held my breath and opened it.

The first thing I saw was a photograph. It showed a beautiful woman in a long dress sitting on a chair holding a baby wrapped up in a christening gown – and standing beside her, his hand on her shoulder, was my father.

Tears pricked at my eyes. Here she was at last. My mother. And with me in her arms. I almost couldn't bear it. I wanted to examine every inch of the image, I wanted to run my fingers across her face. But there were voices downstairs and I realised then that Ethel was home too. I put the photo back and took out a document, a letter to my father from a Dr Arthur Wendle from the Bristol Sanitorium. I skimmed my finger down the page, until I reached this paragraph, which I memorised.

'In my professional opinion, it is likely Miss Redferne will be prone to periods of hysteria for the rest of her life. Her experiences that evening at St Cyprian's Court, and the tragic death that occurred, have placed untold stress on her mind. She is also convinced that a revelation which emerged that night concerning a curse on her family is true and accurate. I think this will continue to haunt her. However, I believe it is possible that under your care and close attention, she can make considerable progress towards restitution.'

I heard a door opening downstairs. The door into the hall. Then the unmistakable sound of footsteps on the staircase. Sheer panic, Robbie! I quickly leafed through several other documents, including my mother's birth certificate, and finally, there was a printed journal, a publication entitled *The Supernatural Sciences*. There was a note with it: 'my darling Daphne, I have thought long and hard about whether to share this with you, but perhaps you need to know. I will leave it with your father to decide. Forgive me.' Desperately, I flicked through the pages, hoping the footsteps would continue to the floor above, hoping it was Ethel going to check on Mrs Lewis. But I did not know what I was looking for and I was too mad with fear to focus. Until I came to one page, one headline.

This was it. Oh, Robbie, this was it.

'A most dreadful séance at St Cyprian's Court, by Camille Redferne.'

I started to read, but at that moment, I heard the footsteps again, louder now – not on the stairs any more, but coming along the corridor towards me. For a second, I felt an odd sort of resignation, almost a relief that the game was up, then the fear set in. I kept the journal but put the rest of the papers back into the wallet and put it back into the drawer. The steps were closer, passing the two bedroom doors en route without stopping. With the journal concealed behind my back, I ran out from behind the desk and stood in the middle of the room, waiting. In my head, explanations and excuses tumbled through my mind, but I knew none would suffice. I would be found and the journal would be taken from me, along with everything else. Footsteps outside the door now. A pause. I swallowed, and waited. I saw the door knob turning. Then a voice.

'Ethel!' It was my stepmother, but she was calling from downstairs. 'Where are you?'

'I'm upstairs, ma'am,' she said. 'I'm sorry, I must have left the study key inside the room yesterday as it's not where I keep it.'

'Sort that out later. Come down at once, one of the boys has spilled milk in the sitting room!'

The knob turned back and then I heard the sound of footsteps scampering away.

I stood there for a few seconds, trying to catch my breath, then

I carefully opened the door, checked the hallway and crept to my room. I hid the magazine in a small suitcase on top of my wardrobe, then I'm afraid I had to run to the bathroom where I was sick again. I will read it later, but I am scared, Robbie, I'm so scared of what it might contain. I need to be as brave as you are. How trifling this must all seem to you. How utterly absurd the world has become.

### Robert to Daphne

A bad night, Daphne. A bad, bad night. I was on an inspection tour of the frontline trench, ensuring the walls were firm. I made my way along the sunken depths, dodging the dozing bodies of other soldiers, nodding at the clusters of men standing awake and on watch. After a while, I bumped into George and Bert who were putting up more ladders along a stretch running close to the German line – the idea I suppose was to ensure that the men could climb to their slaughter as efficiently as possible. Burt crept off to the latrine, so I chatted to George and he was telling me about how his daughter was starting at school, what she was learning, and how bright she was. While I was bending down testing a fire step for rot, he lifted his head up, just for the briefest of seconds, to fix a roll of barbed wire. I heard a sort of whistling noise then a sharp intake of breath, and I thought perhaps the daft boy had pricked his finger. Then he slumped against me, his eyes wide in horror. A sniper's bullet had passed through his neck and blood was spurting from the wound in great red geysers. I dragged him into my arms and slowly lowered us both to the ground as his body convulsed and his hands grabbed uselessly at the air. I shouted for help, but I knew it was useless.

'I shoved me head up too high,' he spluttered. 'What a bloody idiot.'

'Shh,' I replied. 'You don't want them to take another crack at you.'

'I'm going to miss the big push,' he said.

'It doesn't matter.'

His body went rigid, then he grabbed my arm.

'You'll take a few out for me, won't you, Rob?'

'I will,' I said.

'Swear it.'

'I swear.'

He slackened in my arms.

'My girls,' he whispered. 'My girls.'

I dug around in his breast pocket and found the photo of his family, then I held it up for him to see.

'You're going home to them,' I told him. 'It's over now. You're going home, my friend. My good friend.'

And that's how his little life ended, squatting amid the blood and dirt, three miles from a French town he couldn't pronounce or ever have found on a map. In that moment, everything I had seen and experienced in this godforsaken country rushed into my brain, and I was so filled with homicidal rage, I wanted to drag a machine gun to the German trench and kill every single one of them myself.


### Daphne to Robert

Robbie, I am so dreadfully sorry to hear about your friend. I can't begin to imagine what you are going through out there. But please, you must stay strong, I have news. I had hoped to tell you in person, or at least to know for certain that you are somewhere safe away from the front, but alas, I must write now. Please, Robbie, if you can, please write to me after you have read what I have to tell you.

Two weeks ago, I began to feel ill. I was very tired and unable to eat anything without being sick, and then my stepmother commented that I was looking somewhat heavier. I discreetly made an appointment with our family physician, Dr Harrington, and he confirmed what I suspected. I am pregnant.

I feel so scared and alone. Dr Harrington has agreed not to tell my father, but it is only a matter of time before he discovers the truth. And then what? I am certain he will disown me. I will be thrown to the mercy of the church or some hostel for fallen women. The baby will be taken from me.

Don't tell me all will be all right, Robbie, because I have read my mother's article now. She did attend a séance at St Cyprian's Church in 1888 and I know what happened to her that night. I know what she was told, and what it means for me, for you, for our baby. Our baby. To write those words, it doesn't seem real at all, but it is.

I am cursed as my mother was cursed. I am a danger to you in a way I cannot explain. All I will say is that the dread I've harboured through my life has a genuine source. It is now clear to me that, for your own good, we cannot marry. My darling, I love you with all my heart, but you are in grave danger. You must not fight in that battle – find a way out. Ask Captain Seabright for compassionate leave, injure yourself, whatever it takes. I am desperate for you to live, Robbie, but it cannot be with me. She's coming, Robbie. She's coming for us.

Oh God, what have I done?


### Robert to Daphne

My brothers are dead. I got the news yesterday morning. A gas attack. They were found holding on to each other in the mud. At around 11 p.m. last night, Seabright called me to his quarters. I found him sitting at his desk, downing the contents of a battered tin mug. He grimaced and even though he heard me come in, he looked back down at his maps. 'The attack will be tomorrow morning at dawn,' he said. 'It will be proceeded by an hour of shelling.'

All I could say in return was, 'I see.'

He shifted in his chair, then took out his cigarette case, which he offered to me. I declined.

'There is, however, good reason to believe that the Germans are well-resourced and fully prepared for the onslaught,' he said. 'Their trenches have been reinforced and they have phosgene cylinders ready if the wind direction is in their favour. The plan from the generals is to go ahead with the attack anyway.'

He lit his cigarette and looked away, as though summoning the courage for something.

'I'm being shipped out tonight,' he said. 'I've been ordered back to battalion headquarters for reassignment.' He took a long drag and blew out a plume of smoke. I thought this was going to be it: the big goodbye. It's been nice knowing you, old chap, but off you go, into the maw. But that's not what happened.

'I need a batman,' he said. I noticed that his eyes were teary. 'I haven't had one since Ypres. Would you be interested in the role? I have permission to relieve you of your combat duty here and to bring you with me.'

I was momentarily dumbfounded into complete silence.

'I won't get you ironing my uniform or any of that butler nonsense,' he said. There was something unfamiliar in his voice, which took me a few moments to place. He was trying to be brave. 'You'd be running messages along the lines to and from other officers and battalion HQ. I'd need you to keep my rifle in good, clean shape, and you would fetch and collect mail. But your key responsibility would be to make sure my little library made it safely to each new posting. Naturally, you would be able to billet with me and the other COs.'

I stumbled for so long over how to reply, a look of disappointment fell across his face.

'You can have an hour to think about it if you like?' he offered.

For the briefest moment, I saw an image of you in that bed again, honey-toned in the searching sunlight. But then I saw my brothers' bodies, I saw George slumped against me, fading away in my arms in a stinking hole in the ground.

'I'm so sorry, sir, but I can't leave tonight.'

'What on Earth do you mean?'

'I have to fight with my unit.'

He stood at last, sending the tin cup hurtling across the table, staining the maps with the dregs of his drink. 'Do you not understand? This will not be a fair fight. The Germans know we are coming, they are ready. It's going to be slaughter.'

'I understand, sir.'

'I can get you out of it!'

'I know, sir, and I appreciate it. But I can't.'

He stared at me, his expression exasperated.

'What if I were to give you a direct order?'

'In that case, I would regrettably disobey and face the consequences.'

With a desperate, spurned look on his face, he scrabbled about on his desk and produced an unopened envelope, which he tossed at me.

'There is a new letter from your lady friend. I have not read it yet, but it is marked "urgent" on the envelope. You ought to see what it is before you make this decision.'

I don't know why but I couldn't face reading it, I couldn't face

222

you in that moment. I felt angry and inhuman. Nothing else mattered to me but the fight.

'I couldn't save George, but I can at least avenge him. If that will be all, sir, I will excuse myself.' I saluted, turned and skulked towards the exit. I was, at last, my father's son.

'You saved me!' he called, his voice cracking with emotion.

I stopped.

'That night I stumbled in on you and your pals, I'd just about had it. Almost the entire battalion was killed at Ypres. I sat for three days and wrote to the families of the men under my command, so that their mothers knew someone remembered them. But you see, I didn't. I didn't know them at all. I had a sergeant sit with me and feed me their stories. I was just another cog in the war machine, peddling lies to grieving mothers. I began to feel like an empty shell. But meeting you, that damn chat about poetry, it was like a little stove being lit inside me. I remembered what it was to be a human being.'

'Sir, I have to go. I couldn't live with myself if I snuck to safety in the night.'

'You're a damn fool!' he shouted. 'There is no honour in this war! All we have is luck and horror.'

'I have to fight with my pals tomorrow,' I said quietly, like a patient parent to a small child. 'But when my part in the battle is over, I will be honoured to serve as your batman. If you will still have me.'

'I will,' he said. With that, he handed me your letter.

Neither of us said goodbye.

Tonight I will sleep in the dugout with Burt and Teddy. In the morning, porridge and a cup of rum, then we'll cower with the other lads all lined up at the base of the ladders, knee deep in mud, none of us able to look in each other's eyes. We'll wait for the bombardment to be over and the silence will fall on us as deadly as any poison gas. Then the shrill note of the sergeant's whistle. Until the next men come along, the rats will have the place to themselves. Still, I'll have my vengeance. I have your letter, as yet still unopened. I fantasise about what it contains.

Don't be afraid. We will always be there at St Cyprian's in that hot summer. When you are next at the church, examine the lower section of the wall I repaired, on the east side of the porch. There is something of us there.

After I finish writing, I shall wrap all your letters together with my replies, and hand them to a messenger to give to Captain Seabright before he leaves. I have asked him one last favour. If anything happens to me tomorrow, he is to ensure their safe delivery to you. I am certain he will survive the war – somehow it never got into his blood as it did with the rest of us. Perhaps he is sitting with you now as you read these lines. If that is the case, I send my love to you from wherever I am.

### Daphne to Robert

I have received word: you are missing presumed dead. It had to come second-hand from someone in the village. No one knew to inform me. There is no hope apparently.

I am undone. My heart is broken. How I regret that last letter, informing you of the curse upon me and killing your hopes of marriage. I am certain I drove you to your doom. I may as well have fired the fatal shot.

Father wants to send me to Yorkshire to have this baby and to live in exile with his sister. If I cared any more, there would be ways to escape this fate. The contacts I made with suffragettes at Eagle House would surely lead to possibilities of freedom. But there is a greater force acting on my life than paternal shame. The thing that haunted and destroyed my mother will, I am certain, follow me, just as the monster followed Dr Frankenstein to the ends of the Earth. Already, I feel its claws in me. This is the fate I deserve for dragging you to your end.

### Daphne to Robert: unsent

I saw you yesterday, I am certain of it. I was riding along the track next to the church and I glimpsed you through the trees. You were in your working clothes, sleeves rolled up in the sun. I dismounted from my bike, letting it fall into the ground, and I walked towards the gate leading through the woods to the churchyard. You looked up from your toil and saw me. You smiled. I was running then, running through the trees. I kept losing sight of you amid the branches, but then you would be back, smiling still, but not moving, as I got closer and closer. My heart hammered in my chest as I ran. I could barely breathe. I knew that it made no sense – why would you be back here, at the spot where we met, as though not a day had passed? And then, finally, with just one tree between us, I lost sight of you again. I wrenched a branch out of the way and stumbled into the churchyard.

But you were gone.

And soon, I will be too.

Chapter Sixteen

# The Institution

I'd never heard a silence quite like it in this place. Once I'd finished reading the final letter, the church itself seemed to be holding its breath. Outside there was nothing, no leaves rustling, no wind rattling along the ancient iron gutters. It was like the whole world was waiting for some sort of resolution. But this was all we had – an increasingly desperate correspondence; a frightened young woman seemingly left alone to cope with a horrible situation. It was so unnerving to encounter my past in this way, as a series of catastrophes, like giant waves smashing into an ocean liner.

Here were all the familiar markers: a young woman falling in love, an eerie sense of disquiet, strange dreams and signals, a mother wondering whether to keep it all a secret but then inadvertently passing the curse down anyway. And then everything collapsing.

Daphne passed it on to Robert too in that final letter. He must have read it before the planned advance, hoping for salvation, but finding only fear and horror for their future.

At least now I had a direct link to the source: a séance. I whispered that word to myself and had an odd feeling, like I already knew this, I had already seen it somehow. Little images at the back of my mind. Lightning. Screaming.

I spent the next day trying to track down a copy of the journal Camille had written for. I went through all Lorna's books and papers again, just in case she'd managed to locate one, but if she did, it wasn't here.

On Friday evening, Justin was away again, so Nikki invited me up for a takeaway and something 'insultingly shit' on Netflix. I felt like I needed to wind down after the latest investigative frenzy. We sat on her sofa, a Marlborough white wine on the go, the coffee table groaning under the weight of Chinese food. But Nikki wanted to be kept up to date with what I was doing, so I told her about Daphne's letters and Camille's article.

'And you think this séance is the origin of it all?' said Nikki, piling mushroom chow mein into her bowl. 'You think, what? An evil demon escaped from the spectral realm and vowed to fuck up our relationships for evermore?'

I tried to match her light-hearted mood. 'This is why I don't come around for dinner more often,' I said. But I think she saw in my eyes how serious I was.

'Okay, what is your working theory?'

'I think something happened that night, but maybe the séance wasn't the origin of it, maybe it was just the conduit through which Camille was exposed to the curse.'

Nikki smirked. 'I'm sorry, but you sound like one of those paranormal investigation programmes.'

227

'Can you please just listen to me?' I said. 'According to Daphne's letters, Robbie was repairing damage caused by a lightning strike in 1888. That's the year séance took place. I think the two are connected somehow.'

'In what way?' said Nikki.

'I don't know, it's just . . . strange, right?'

'I think it only seems strange because you're actively looking for connections. Human beings have a tendency to see patterns and meanings where there are none. It's a survival mechanism.'

I was quiet for a few moments, picking at my food.

'Okay, there is one intriguing element of this,' said Nikki in a conciliatory tone. 'Your astraphobia. I mean, it's bad enough now, but when you were a kid, you would be literally paralysed with fear when a thunderstorm came. There were times Mum worried you were having some sort of seizure. You'd lie in the understairs cupboard, dead rigid, zoned out completely.'

'So?'

'So it's interesting that this story of yours may well begin with a storm – the very thing you're most afraid of.'

In bed that night, I couldn't stop thinking about Daphne. It struck me that I'd been picturing these stories as distant historical dramas, but they weren't. They were close by. These were my relatives, and these things happened in nearby places: the church, the village, the woods. Daphne and Robbie could be me and Ben. I had to start thinking on a local scale. And considering Camille's life and interests, I knew a good place to start.

The next morning, dressed as conservatively as I could, I stood outside the Bath Royal Literary and Scientific Institution on Queen Square. I knew this wasn't the building Camille would

228

been to; the Institution used to be in a grand Victorian edifice on Terrace Walk, but that was demolished in the 1930s to make way for a traffic island. Yet I still got a slightly eerie feeling as I walked into the reception area and spotted the first few exhibits, wondering if she had once seen them too. A man was sitting at a modern reception desk, watching me looking about. I felt a little intimidated by the place.

'Can I help you?' he asked.

'I'm not sure. I'm looking for a Victorian magazine that I think might have had something to do with this place. I just wondered if anyone here could help?'

He looked at me vacantly for a moment and I wondered if he was just going to ask me to leave, but instead he said, 'You're in luck. Our head archivist Rhea Bennett is just here.' Then he turned round towards a room behind him and called out, 'Rhea?'

A small thin woman in her fifties came out. She was wearing a bright violet suit, Nike trainers and red-framed spectacles. She looked me up and down suspiciously. 'A goth?' she said in a bright American accent. 'You're a little early for the talk on Mary Shelley – that's tomorrow.' I liked her immediately.

We sat down at a small table in the corner of the reception area, while she explained how she'd come to Bath on a temporary secondment from the Met Museum in New York, but that was ten years ago and she'd never quite got round to going back. 'This town,' she said, laughing. 'Once it's got its claws into you, it doesn't let go.' I showed her Daphne's letters and my research into Camille's role at the Institution, and she studied it all closely.

'I can tell you there were a number of talks during this period on the subject of the paranormal,' she said. 'There was a lot of interest in the scientific basis of ghosts and hauntings – it was seen as a respectable pursuit. You know that Arthur Conan Doyle was

229

obsessed with spiritualism and the supernatural? As was William Gladstone. Your ancestor was in good company.'

'Was it rare for women to have been involved in the Institution back then?' I asked.

'Not really. It's always been pretty forward thinking. We had a lot of women who were members and speakers throughout that era. Sounds like Camille would have fitted in just fine.'

'Is there any chance you might still have the journal?'

'We have quite an extensive archive of journals and pamphlets that have connections to the Institution and its members, but I'll need to search our records to track this particular publication down. Leave it with me. I'll call as soon as I find anything.'

We walked together towards the exit and when we reached the reception area again, she stopped me. 'Are you sure you've never been here before?' she asked.

'No, never,' I said.

Rhea regarded me with an odd questioning expression. 'You look kinda familiar.'

Then she disappeared back into the building.

# Chapter Seventeen

# **Flowers**

She didn't call the next day, or the day after that. I started to feel edgy again. I wasn't due to visit Ben until the following day but I had this overwhelming need to see him. I wanted to tell him about everything that had happened, though I didn't know exactly why. Was I trying to prepare him for horrible news? Or did I just need him?

When I got to the rehab centre, I bumped into Greg in the reception.

'How is he?' I asked.

Greg did the so-so gesture with his hand. 'He's frustrated with his progress. He's getting some movement back but it's very weak and patchy, and his brain is still foggy. He's been a bit down, to be honest.'

I had a terrible selfish thought that I could do without this. I could do without feeling responsible for someone else's mental health right now. Greg seemed to spot it in my expression immediately.

'Look, don't ever feel that you have to entertain him,' he said. 'You don't have to put on a show. He just needs different inputs and distractions. If that means a silent half-hour mope around the garden, that's fine. It's a silent half-hour mope with someone he likes, who isn't manipulating his limbs into weird positions or testing his reflexes. That's enough. It might be all he needs right now.'

As predicted, Ben was in his room, already in the wheelchair, looking downcast and despondent. He was wearing those institutional tracksuit bottoms and a baggy T-shirt, and his hair was greasy.

'So,' I said, as brightly as I could. 'Shall we go for a wander?'

He tried to shrug, but even that didn't work properly.

'I'm not really feeling it today,' he said.

'I know,' I said. 'Neither am I. But let's just give it a go. I'll grab the flower book. It'll do us both good.'

Outside in the gardens, the sky was a little overcast and there was a cool breeze that carried specks of rain. Only a few other patients were out, mostly dotted about on the front lawn watching a couple of gardeners trimming a hedge. Ben let me push him for once, which I took as a bad sign. This really was going to be a quick mope around the perimeter and then back inside.

'How are you doing?' he asked as we edged down the ramp on to the concrete path.

'Okay,' I said. 'Still tracking my family history, but I'm worried I've hit a bit of a dead-end.'

'I know how *that* feels,' he replied.

'You are going to get there,' I said to him. 'It just might take more time than you thought.'

'Have you been speaking to Greg?'

232

'Yeah.'

'He thinks he's good at managing expectations.'

'Come on, Ben, he's just trying to help.'

We got to the first flowerbed and I pulled up, put on the brake, and took the book out.

'Right,' I said, pointing to a cluster of small yellow flowers. 'Do you recognise those?'

He glanced at them. 'I don't.'

'We looked at them a few days ago,' I said, trying to sound encouraging.

'Cammy, I don't know.'

'Well, what about those? The red ones?'

'I can't remember.'

'Ben, I'm not sure that you're trying.'

'And you're not listening! It's gone, Cammy! It's fucking gone!'

I know I should have been more sympathetic, I probably should have turned round and taken him back, but I was pissed off and felt frustrated and angry, so I slammed the brake off and thrust the chair forward, stomping along the path.

'Just don't visit me,' he said. 'Don't come if it's so annoying.'

We passed an elderly man being pushed along by a nurse. He was wearing headphones, eyes closed, mouthing the words to whichever song he was listening to, completely oblivious to us. I had to swerve round him.

'It's not annoying,' I said. 'But you've got to keep trying.'

'I am trying! All I do is try! I try for twelve hours a day every fucking day!'

'I know,' I said. 'I'm sorry, okay? I just . . . '

We got to a little meadow area, which had been left overgrown for wildflowers to take hold. I stopped and grabbed the book again, ripping it open.

'Just what?!' he said loudly.

I flicked backwards and forwards in a blind rage. 'I just . . .'

There was a group of beautiful flowers in the midst of the tall grass. They had delicate blue petals and a yellowy white centre.

'What?' he yelled. 'What?'

'I just want to know what the fuck those are. We saw them one night, along the lanes when we walked from Sydney Gardens up on to the meadows, when it was so warm and we held hands, and your skin was tanned and you were wearing those stupidly expensive sunglasses and you looked so fucking cool and you were so funny and charming and I felt like you saw me and knew me! I want to know what those flowers are. I want to be back there!'

I felt guilty as soon as I'd said it. Because we couldn't go back, because Ben was different now. Unable to look him in the eye, I was still flicking through the pages, desperate to identify the flowers, but not really looking at the photos, not registering the section names.

'I do too!' he said. 'But it might not happen. Because I can't walk and I can't . . . I can't think straight. And I hate that I'm here and I resent you for being my carer, and for . . .'

Suddenly, I found the right section, the right page, but there were so many that looked the same.

'I think I've got it,' I said.

'Listen to me, Cammy, that version of Ben, he might be gone . . .'

'Is it a . . . wild hyacinth?'

' . . . he might just be a dream now and . . .'

'Oh no, wait, they have longer petals . . .'

'It's time to wake up . . . it's time . . .'

'Are they thyme snowdrifts? Little white petals . . . no, the centres are different . . .'

'OH FOR FUCK'S SAKE, CAMMY, IT'S YARROW!!'

We looked at each other, for a moment too stunned to speak.

'Latin name *Achillea millefolium*.'

The breeze died down and the air was still. There was warmth in it now.

'They flower well into the autumn and they were used in folk medicine. To heal wounds.'

Slowly, I looked down at the book and read the description.

'It is supposed to be a symbol of love ... of lasting love.'

'That's right,' I said. 'That's all right.'

He turned the wheelchair back towards the meadow. 'Those are autumn hawkbit,' he said, his voice still low and uncertain. '*Leontodon autumnalis*, they grow in ancient meadows, right up to November. The last colour of the year. Those are ... those are scarlet pimpernels ... *Anagallis* ... *Anagallis arvensis?*'

Almost in slow motion, I leafed through the pages. 'Correct,' I said. 'Correct.'

With sudden purpose and determination, he took the brake off and sped away, accelerating down the sloped path towards the more ordered beds. 'Come on!' he yelled. I ran after him.

'Blue vervain,' he shouted back at me, pointing as he passed. 'Toadflax! *Linaria vulgaris*. They were used long ago to ... to break curses.'

I was trying to look them up, fluttering desperately through the pages as I ran. 'Slow down!' I shouted.

'I can't,' he said. He was laughing. He was laughing now. We reached the herb garden and he was in through the gateway in the hedge, while I had to stop and get my breath. I could hear him shouting, 'Lemon balm, rosemary, sage! Cammy, come on!' And then he was out again and I was chasing. I closed the book because it was useless now, we didn't need it. Through a gap in the clouds

235

the sun rays caught the tops of the trees lining the gardens; they shimmered on the wet grass. Everything shimmered. We reached the woods, and he saw something that made him brake and swerve off the path. In one lurching movement he thrust himself forward in the chair so that he almost stood for a second before spilling out on to the ground. 'Ben!' I yelled, trying to pick up speed to get to him, but my legs were shot and I could barely breathe. 'Ben, wait, I'm coming.'

But he wasn't listening. He was crawling towards a cluster of luscious pinky-red flowers at the edge of a small clearing, and when he reached them he pulled himself on to his knees and put a hand in among them. When I finally got to him, gasping and wheezing, he gently picked one and held it up to me. 'These are red campion,' he said. 'This is the first wildflower my grandma ever taught me.' He looked up at me and his eyes were teary. 'They are also called Red Riding Hoods. Grandma told me that fairies used them to protect their homes from evil.'

I knelt down next to him and took the flower. 'You're back,' I said to him.

'I'm back,' he replied.

I took him into my arms and hugged him as tightly as I could. Then, not sure what else to do with it, I put the delicate, beautiful gift between two pages of the book and carefully closed it shut.

When we got back to the centre, Ben's psychologist, Sasha, was waiting for him. We told her what had happened and she hugged him too. And then, because it was becoming that sort of afternoon, she hugged me as well.

As I walked back to my car, I began to think that it didn't matter if I never got to the truth about the curse. Perhaps it would be for the best. The joy of the afternoon felt cleansing. I wondered if the past could be erased so that the future could become a blank slate, vast with possibilities. It felt, for a gorgeous moment, that I could be free.

When I got back to the studio I checked my emails and there was one from Rhea. The subject header read simply, 'I've found it'.

The flower is still there, by the way; still pressed between pages 118 and 119, even after all this time. The petals are dry and cracked now, and at least one has been lost along the way. But whenever I open the book to those two pages, I see a boy on his knees in the short grass, the memories flooding back to him like sweet scents on the breeze.

## Chapter Eighteen

# **The Journal**

It had taken Rhea a little longer to find the journal than she'd expected. After rooting through poorly labelled storage containers for the whole afternoon, she found it in a box containing a bundle of other Victorian magazines with connections to the Institution.

'The folder was last taken out twenty years ago, but then put back in the wrong place,' she explained as she guided me to the study room. 'The good news is, while I was looking I found another bunch of folders containing a lot of other interesting journals which had all been mislabelled – a real treasure trove. I don't think anyone has seen these since they were brought over from the old building eighty years ago. I actually started a spreadsheet cataloguing the collection. I'll email that to you when I'm done.' She was clearly delighted by the find, but I wasn't really taking it in. I was steeling myself for the article I had come for.

The article I now know all too well.

When we got to the study room, Rhea set me down at a small wooden desk and put the folder in front of me.

'Just be careful handling the journal,' she said. 'It's very delicate.'

She took it out and turned to the start of the article. 'I'll leave you to it. Just bring the folder back to my office when you're done.'

She had begun to walk away when she clearly remembered something else.

'This might interest you,' she said. 'The previous archivist kept a record of who borrowed items and when. The publication was last requested in 2001 by someone called . . . wait . . . Lorna Piper. Is she a relative of yours?'

Once again, I came face to face with a lesson I really needed to learn: the past demands to be found.

## 'A most dreadful séance at St Cyprian's Court' by Camille Redferne, *The Supernatural Sciences,* 1889

It is with some trepidation that I relate to you the events of March 29 of last year, a day that will haunt me for the rest of my life, and perhaps beyond. Naturally, I was already familiar with the phenomenon of the séance. I have had an avid intellectual interest in spiritualism since I first learned of the Fox sisters, who became famous around the world for their ability to commune with the spirits. In the pages of this very journal, I have read accounts written by distinguished gentlemen in which groups of curious peers have gathered about a table in hushed reverence and, guided by some sensitive medium, did consort with the dead. As a very active member of the Bath Royal Literary and Scientific Institution I have helped organise lectures concerning the science of the paranormal and have been fortunate enough to host lectures on the subject given by Henry and Eleanor Sidgwick and other great theorists in this area. Many of my peers have remained sceptical about the idea of communicating with spirits, believing most of the supposedly supernatural events taking place on such evenings to be the stuff of parlour tricks. But I was open to the idea that spiritualism could prove to be a new branch of science, which, like electricity, may be safely harnessed and used to the benefit of mankind. Such was the hubris that would lead to my downfall.

I should at this point provide some background. A year ago, my dear mother was taken from me, along with her second husband, not a month after their marriage. The two had planned a lavish and exotic honeymoon cruising the islands of the Caribbean, but two weeks into their adventure, the ship they sailed on, the RMS *Rhone*, was caught in a hurricane and sunk, taking 123 passengers with her.

On receiving the dreadful news via telegram, I confess that I broke down. I took to my bed for many days and wept. I would not be pacified, not by my maid nor by any friend or physician. Instead, I called out for the person from whom I had always sought comfort – the one person who could never give it again. My mother and I had been extremely close since the untimely death of my father twenty years earlier. We lived in a beautiful townhouse on Great Pulteney Street, filled with books and paintings. As a girl, I developed an interest in science and literature and a desperation to learn more. She was supportive of my ambitions. I attended the Bath School for Girls, then Cheltenham Ladies' College, and later Girton College, Cambridge. Although twenty-six years of age, I was in no hurry to find a husband, despite my sociable character, and although concerned, my mother felt no compulsion to force the issue. When I wasn't writing or studying, we went for long walks across the hills, took day trips to the coast, holidayed in Europe. We also attended many lectures and exhibitions at the

Institution, and it was she who encouraged me to get more involved as a member. We always talked freely, more as friends than mother and daughter. We relied on one another.

The weeks following Mother's death remain a disorientating blur to me – it was as though I was living within some terrible, poisonous fog. I would suffer appalling nightmares, then wake in the darkness absolutely certain there was someone in the room watching me. My aunt Beatrice, my mother's beloved older sister, took matters into her own hands; she sent her servants to collect me and bring me to her home at St Cyprian's Court, the ancestral seat of her husband, Lord Reginald Seymour. It was a vast, imposing building and its gothic grandeur had somewhat scared me as a child. Furthermore, something happened to me there, during a visit when I was nine years old, that had left an indelible mark on me. Pray patience, dear reader, for it was here that my history with that accursed building began, and I must relate what followed as it bears pertinence to the terrors that come later.

On that horrible afternoon, I had decided I wanted to be an explorer, so without telling a soul, I set off from the house and wandered into the woods alone. After a while spent following muddy paths through the undergrowth, I stumbled upon the small church that had served as the Seymour family chapel for hundreds of years and was for a long time also used as a parish church by the villagers. Hidden amongst gnarled trees, it was squat and solid, its stone walls slightly crumbling, its tower crooked and ugly. In the coming darkness, the windows looked almost black, their shape resembling eyes looking out at me. I recall noticing that the vast oak door was open, which seemed odd to me, and as I approached I felt a sudden sense of foreboding, as though something awful was waiting inside. A strong wind had blown up and it circled the trees above me, sending shivers through the dry autumn leaves. Rooks gathered in the branches, squawking loudly. Yet still I approached, compelled as though in a dream, and when at last I reached the door, I eased past it into the darkness beyond. There were five rows of old wooden pews, leading to a heavy stone altar, and beyond it the stained glass window at the rear. I walked slowly along the aisle, past a low bookcase filled with musty prayer books. A moth-eaten tapestry of the family crest was hanging from one of the arched beams above me. The atmosphere was eerie, but I did not feel afraid – not until I reached the centre of the nave, when suddenly there was a voice behind me.

'You don't want to be in here, young lady.'

The shock of it sent my heart pumping madly.

I turned slowly, dreading what I might see, only to find my aunt's head groundskeeper, Mr MacGregor, standing in the doorway, half silhouetted in the darkness. He was a tall man with a gaunt, haggard face and narrow eyes. I'd seen him roaming the gardens and woodland, with his dogs, but never this close. He took a few steps towards me and I wanted to back away, but in that moment the fear had utterly paralysed me.

'You know the stories of this place, do you?' he said. 'You know what they say about it around here?'

I could only shake my head.

His thin mouth upturned into a sneering smile that revealed his jagged teeth yellowed by tobacco. Then he came closer and knelt so that his leering face was close to my own and the stench of his breath and his dirty clothes filled my nostrils. 'This place is haunted. There is something here, watching. It hates young ladies like you,' he said. 'You feel it, don't you, girl? You feel it in the air. So stay in the house and the pretty gardens. Don't come round here again.' He lifted his bony hand and pointed at me. 'Now she has her eye on you.'

242

With that, he let out a horrible dry cackle, the sound echoing around the church interior, mocking me from every direction.

I ran all the way back to the house, and never told a soul about what happened, but the memory of it lingered with me. It left a mark. It's why I hesitated at the idea of staying at St Cyprian's again in my grievous state.

Yet Auntie was adamant that I stay with her during my convalescence. 'You must get out of the town if you are going to recuperate,' she said. 'You shall live with us until you are strong enough to face the future.' With little will of my own, I acquiesced. She put me in a lovely bedroom with a large window overlooking the ornamental gardens – not that I ventured from my bed to admire them. The view outside felt pointless and grey. I did not have the strength or will to lift the sheets. And besides, I knew that if I looked out of the window towards the south, I would see the church tower there, black as pitch beyond the trees.

My aunt came to sit with me every day. She was a strong-willed, imposing woman in her sixties, extremely bright and endlessly curious about the world. The manor had a large library and when she married Lord Seymour it soon became clear that due to pressing business interests in Africa, he would be absent for much of the time, so she began to work her way through it. Left alone for countless hours, she devoured everything from Bede's history to Sheridan Le Fanu's *Carmilla*.

Every day of my recovery, she would read to me. It might be something from the Brontës, Ann Radcliffe or the poetry of Elizabeth Barrett Browning. She would also share news from the village, weaving the lives of our neighbours into gentle tales.

'Mrs Jeffers the greengrocer is retiring,' she told me one bright morning, as I lifted myself up in the bed. 'She ran the store for thirty-five years. It is said she could sense when fruit was ripening.'

243

She took the armchair by the window and looked out over the lawn, towards the trees. 'Doctor Aitken has taken on a new trainee nurse, who is aiding with physical examinations, but apparently she has cold hands and there have been protests . . .'

I didn't know these people, but her voice was melodious and I found it calming to hear about a world going on beyond the confines of my grief.

'One of the stable lads was kicked by a horse and knocked clean out, but has thankfully made a full recovery. Our old grounds-keeper Mr MacGregor has retired . . .'

I looked up at her. 'Mr MacGregor?' I asked.

'Yes, you remember him?'

With a chill, I recalled our encounter. The sound of his voice in that place, his haggard face. What he said to me and how he cackled.

'I met him once when I was a child,' I confessed. 'I wandered down to the church alone and he came in and caught me. He told me the building was haunted.'

My aunt laughed. 'Oh yes, he is full of local legends.'

Her light manner emboldened me and I felt a wave of relief that I would be most unlikely to spy him out of the window, or happen upon him in the grounds.

'It's just a story then?' I asked.

Her smile faltered for a fraction of a second. 'You know how superstitious the country folk are. Something happens and over the years adornments are added to the tale. The landscape around here is filled with myths. There is something ancient and uncanny about this place. Perhaps that is why my spiritual evenings have been such a success.'

Spiritualism was an interest my aunt and I had in common. But while my fascination was theoretical, guided by the writings of

Henry Sidgwick, Frederic Myers and Edmund Gurney, Aunt's was practical. She too had taken an early interest in the mediums of the United States and once attended a séance given by none other than Maria Hayden, who helped bring the phenomenon to Britain. She also claims to have seen Daniel Dunglas Home levitate six feet into the air, and at one séance in the London home of a close friend, was astonished when the medium Georgina Houghton seemingly conversed with the recently deceased brother of one of the other participants, and then painted a perfect watercolour likeness of the gentleman. Soon after my aunt began to hold her own meetings where, she told us, the spirits spoke to her through table knocks, rapping out responses to questions offered by the group. The table itself would tilt or move, often enough so that the seated guests would have to get up and move with it. She'd recently heard of highly skilled mediums who were able to manifest spirits into the room so that they appeared to the guests in physical form – she was desperate to employ one. Her mind was open and generous to fresh perspectives and possibilities.

In my aunt's care, I began to feel better. I ventured from my room and took walks in the long gallery, where portraits of my uncle's ancestors lined the walls, watching me pass. I wandered the gravel paths of the formal gardens close to the house, and then took tea in the orangery among luscious tropical plants. But whenever I looked out of my bedroom window, no matter how beautiful the gardens looked, from the corner of my eye there was that goading tower.

I was, however, determined to recover, if only because my dear mother would have desperately wanted me to. I began to take longer walks in the woods bordering the estate. At first, I kept to the neat paths and always had the house in view. But each morning, I ventured further into the older woodland, tracing streams and fox runs, gaining strength. On one of these walks, I stopped in a glade enjoying the feeling of the sun on my skin, and caught sight of a figure on a horse, perhaps a hundred yards away among the shadowy oaks. The rider seemed to be watching me. I could not tell if it was a man or woman, just that their riding cloak was a dark shade of red. I walked a little closer, but the rider gave a gentle kick to the horse's flank and it rode off into the shadows. Although I was intrigued, I would not follow, as I knew where that track led.

Eventually, one morning, being careless with my orientation and getting somewhat turned around in the heat, I chanced upon the church. It stood in the clearing, exactly as I recalled, although now it seemed a little more decrepit. Vines clung to the grey stone causing it to crumble in places, and the arched windows were dirty and cracked. My aunt had only allowed a small amount of restoration work, enjoying the worn, haggard appearance of the building, which she felt was romantic. But it stirred in me old memories, quite apart from the already sorrowful mood of my visit.

Inside, it was very dark. A faint smell of wet stone and rot hung in the air, and as I walked further in, the door, which had been so reluctant to open, closed shut behind me seemingly of its own accord. The sudden, close silence made my ears buzz. I had the odd feeling there were others in here with me. A phantasmagorical congregation.

Though filled with trepidation, I carried on, feeling pleased with myself for my bravery. Eventually, I stopped and knelt down to read the inscriptions on the ledger stones. They brought to mind my mother's grave, the headstone glossy and black yet flecked with shiny particles, like a starry night sky. I recalled the words we had carved into its surface: *In memory of Esther. Beloved wife, sister and mother, who died at sea October, 1867, aged 54 years. 'Your word is a lamp to my feet and a light to my path.'*

Feeling the sting of hot tears in my eyes, I looked up. 'I miss you, Mama,' I said to the altar. 'I just want you to know that I miss you.'

When I stood, I gasped in shock. There was someone sitting in the pew at the very front, their back to me, their head hung low as though in silent contemplation. I felt a sudden, terrible sense of dread in my breast, like the vapours of some monstrous crypt escaping upwards to infect the air.

'Hello?' I said. 'I didn't see you there.'

As the figure turned and their identity was revealed, I felt so dizzy I had to clasp the corner of a pew for support. It was MacGregor, the groundskeeper. He was much older and more wizened, but as he got up, I saw that he was still that same tall and imposing man.

'I warned you, didn't I, not to come here?' he said. 'I warned you she was watching.'

In that moment the temperature in the church seemed to drop, as though someone had swung open the door and let in the cruellest winter gale. I saw shadows like spectres, swimming around me in the bleak light, edging in at the corners of my vision. Terror encompassed me like a thick, suffocating blanket. It was as though I was a frightened child again, frozen to the spot, utterly unable to move or even breathe. All around me was this awful, vaporous atmosphere of fear and grief, thick and ancient like the fetid air in a tomb.

'She will come for you,' he said.

With a jerk, my body seemed to come back to life and with all the strength I could muster, I turned away and staggered towards the door. Outside, the fresh air made my head swim, and with the softest of whimpers, I fell into a half-swoon. Then there were hands on my arms, gripping me tightly. I tried to fight, but they were too strong. If I could have screamed, I would have. Instead, I turned in silent anguish to face my captor.

And that, alas, is all I remember. I woke up hours later in bed, with my aunt sitting beside me.

'You fainted in the churchyard,' she explained. 'Quite by chance, you were found by a young gentleman who happened to be riding past. He saw you running from the building in some distress and went to investigate, but by the time he got to you, you were lying unconscious amid the graves. His name is Martin Blacklock. His family owns the large estate just beyond Bradford-on-Avon.'

Martin Blacklock. I dimly recalled having met him before at the Institution. We occasionally talked after attending the same lectures, although I could not remember the details apart from that we'd had a minor, rather trying disagreement about Mary Shelley's *Frankenstein*.

'What was it?' she asked softly. 'What happened in the church?'

'I don't know,' I said. 'Perhaps I merely over-exerted myself.'

I didn't want to tell her the groundskeeper had told me a scary story, or that I'd had a feeling of foreboding in that place.

Two days later, the same Martin Blacklock arrived to check on my health, and Aunt insisted that he join her for tea. The best I could manage was to wave at him from my window as he left. Later, she came up to tell me about the encounter.

'He was very polite and very concerned for your welfare,' she said. 'He told me that when he rushed to your aid that evening at the church, you opened your eyes momentarily and had etched into your face the most purest look of abject terror. He told the tale with such fiery emotion, I found it quite frightening!'

Through those tormented weeks, Mr Blacklock made several visits. Although I refused to accept guests, much to my aunt's sadness and vexation, he left packages of fine foods and bouquets of fresh flowers. He wrote letters filled with sympathy and support.

And then one bright morning in early spring, a maid came to my door and handed me a note, barely able to contain her excitement.

'It is from the gentleman,' she said.

'What gentleman?' I replied blearily, lifting myself up in bed and taking the note.

'The gentleman in the garden,' she said.

I opened the note and read it.

My dearest Camille. I understand your terrible sadness – my heart rends at the immeasurable loss you have suffered. But yet, it is such a beautiful morning, I could not resist taking the chance to call on you. Having sought permission from your aunt, I would like to invite you out into these beautiful gardens. If you could just look out from your window.

Yours,

Martin

For the first time in many weeks, something touched my heart that wasn't grief, it was curiosity. I climbed down from the bed, wrapped my shawl about me and padded gingerly across to the heavy, closed curtains, which had thus far kept the daylight at bay. I opened them just a little and, immediately, the brightness of the sun flooded the room, refracting through glass vases and across the mirror, painting rainbows of light across the walls. It took my eyes a moment to adjust, and when they did, I looked down to an astonishing sight. Martin was in the garden, standing by a dining table, loaded with food of every description. Though he was some distance away, I could see that he was smiling. He took a low, extravagant bow.

'Your luncheon awaits,' he called.

Gentle reader, I did go down to him.

We ate and talked, although in truth, he did most of the talking. He revealed that he had a passionate interest in the arts, particularly stage magic. He owned and managed a variety theatre on Orchard Street in Bath, where he told me he hosted some of the finest magicians and illusionists of the day, much to the frustration of his parents who had expected him to pursue a career in the military.

For a fortnight he came back every other day and Auntie would invite him in for tea. For some reason I cannot describe, I never quite warmed to him. Although he was amusing, attentive company, there was something about him I found rather trying. There is little doubt, however, that his visits gave me the strength and fortitude finally to reacquaint myself with Bath life, especially the intellectual bustle of the Institution, and for that I was grateful. For it was while attending a lecture on evolution that I met Mr Anthony Seward. He had asked a question on the theme of pangenesis, which I found fascinating, and as the audience filed out, I caught up with him to tell him so. He was dressed rather casually in a light linen suit and his curly dark hair came down almost to his shoulders, giving him a Romantic look. His face was dark and chiselled, but there was a glint of kindness about it, and he smiled warmly when I approached.

'You have an excellent knowledge of Darwin's theories,' he said after our short discussion. 'I hope we get the chance to talk on this further on some other occasion. That is, if you feel well enough to attend another lecture. I know that you lost your mother this year. I have heard she was a wonderful woman.'

He then reached out and put his hand on my arm, a gesture that, had any other man made it, would have felt entirely inappropriate. But from him, it seemed natural. The warmth of it emanated outwards like a healing balm.

'Thank you,' I said. 'I would very much like to speak with you again.'

I was aware of a hotness at my cheeks.

Over the coming weeks, he attended several lectures at the Institution. The two of us often discussed the content afterwards, but unlike other men who sought to explain the themes and theories of the guest speakers as though speaking to a child, he sought to understand my own views and interpretations. I discovered that he was studying at the Bristol School of Medicine and had a keen interest in science, particularly physics. He was fascinated by spiritualism but sceptical about its scientific value. Our discussions on the matter were vigorous but respectful.

We became friends. Accompanied by his mother and sister, we would often go on to a concert or for supper at a restaurant. The three of them gave me confidence. I began to spend a few evenings at my own home on Great Pulteney Street, which our housekeeper had kept in an excellent state of preparedness. However, on one such evening, something very odd happened.

Anthony had walked me back home after attending an afternoon concert at the Pump Rooms with his sister. We conversed for a while outside, then said our goodbyes. I went through to the kitchen to say hello to the housekeeper when I heard a terrible crash in the front room. Someone had thrown a rock through my window!

'It will be children,' the housekeeper assured me. But I was terribly spooked and, later that night, fled back to St Cyprian's.

To my delight, Anthony became a regular visitor there. He accompanied me on walks, at first around the gardens, but later into the surrounding meadows and further afield as my strength and resolve returned once again. He often stayed as a guest for lunch and sometimes dinner. Though my aunt rarely enquired

251

about the nature of our relationship, insisting she was just happy I was recovering, I knew she was curious. I learned from her staff that she had made subtle enquiries regarding Anthony's family and reputation. But still, I found it hard to consider courtship, or any future beyond my grief; the present was enough. For his part, Anthony exerted no pressure and expressed no expectations. He was simply there when I needed him.

Then on one overcast afternoon, as I sat with Auntie in the drawing room making a terrible mess of an embroidery, a maid came in to tell us there was a gentleman caller. Aunt Beatrice went through to answer, and when she returned minutes later, she said to me, 'You have a visitor,' and motioned for him to come in. In that happy moment, I felt sure it must be Anthony and I confess my heart skipped a beat at the prospect. But it was Martin.

'I am sorry to disturb you unannounced,' he said. 'But I have an invitation that I wanted to extend to you in person. We are putting on a rather lavish production of Shakespeare's *Macbeth* at my theatre tomorrow evening and I would be honoured if you would accompany me. Your aunt has graciously given her permission for us to attend unchaperoned.'

'Yes,' I stuttered. 'That would be delightful.'

In truth, however, I had barely given Mr Blacklock a thought over the last few weeks as my friendship with Mr Seward had deepened. There remained something in his character that I found disagreeable, a sense of contemptuous entitlement that set me on edge. Yet, I did attend the theatre with him and it was a most gory production with extremely elaborate technical effects, especially when it came to the appearance of the witches and the famed banquet scene. I saw many women in the audience look close to fainting with fear. Martin was clearly delighted and watched me throughout for my own reactions.

252

I had decided to spend the night at my own home rather than St Cyprian's Court, so he kindly walked me back to Great Pulteney Street, excitedly telling me about the production and how there was talk of transferring it to New York. But when we arrived at the house he became more serious.

'Camille, my dear friend, I have something I want to say. You are, I am certain, the most beautiful and precious woman I have ever met. Our friendship has brought so much light into my life. You have become a sort of obsession to me. Therefore, I would like to ask your aunt for permission to make our courtship official, with a view to engagement at a later date.'

Caught there, beneath the sulphurous glow of the streetlamp, I was utterly bewildered. I knew I owed Martin so much. He had rescued me in the church, and it was his kind act with the picnic in the garden that had roused me from my desperate grief. His family was wealthy and much respected, so it would certainly be an acceptable match to my aunt. And yet ... and yet, there was Anthony, his prospects more modest, but his character and kindness so bright, his intelligence so invigorating. Though he had made no such overtures, I believed, perhaps in a somewhat presumptuous manner, that he harboured for me the same ardent emotions that I now most certainly held for him.

'I am honoured,' I said, my voice halting and uncertain. 'Your friendship has been most valuable to me. But, my dear Martin, I am still recovering from the death of my mother. I do not yet feel ready to make any sort of commitment. I pray that you understand?'

For a few moments he did not respond, and there was a sort of twitch about his eyes that suggested anger. But then he adjusted himself and he smiled. 'I understand,' he said. 'Please forgive me if my proposal was insensitive.'

'Not at all,' I said. 'It was very charming of you. I am flattered.'

253

Silence.

'Well, it is rather cold,' I told him. 'I should be getting back inside. I am sure my housekeeper is at the window, wondering what we are doing out here so long.'

'Of course,' he said. He bent forward, took my hand and lightly kissed my glove. 'Goodnight.'

'Goodnight,' I repeated.

And just as I thought our evening was at an end, he said to me, 'Could I just ask one question?'

'Please do.'

'Might it be, perhaps, that your favour has turned towards another gentleman?'

I didn't see how he could know about Anthony. The two had never met as far as I knew. This must surely have just been some desperate fear on his part.

'No,' I said. 'No, I assure you that is not the case.'

And with that gentle lie, I took my leave of him.

I spent two days fretting over my decision to reject Mr Blacklock, pacing my bedroom late into the night, hardly sleeping at all. How I wished mother was there to guide me! How I missed her wisdom. I knew my aunt was keen for me to marry. She was so worried about me being left alone. And, as my closest relative and confidante, it was her to whom I needed to speak.

I travelled to St Cyprian's Court the next morning, and as soon as I saw my aunt I began to weep.

'What is it, my dear child?' she begged. She took me through to the drawing room and asked a maid to fetch tea while I told her everything of Martin's proposal and the complication of my feelings for Anthony.

'He treats me as an equal,' I cried, 'with none of the cloying reverence or patronising dotage of other suitors. I feel in my heart that mother would have liked Mr Seward. But I don't know, I don't know!'

Aunt Beatrice took my hand and looked at me with much sympathy. 'Now, I've told you, haven't I, of my regular spirituals?' she said. A strong breeze caught the curtains at the windows, causing them to billow into the room. 'We are having a meeting next week. I have found a wonderful new medium, a very skilled young woman who comes highly recommended. According to my close friends, she is able to let the spirits speak through her, using her voice as their own! If you were to attend, perhaps we could, if you feel able, ask the medium to attempt contact with your mother?'

In that moment, it felt like several elements of my life had come together into close and urgent alignment. My scientific interest in the paranormal, my overwhelming desire to hear from my beloved mother once again, my confusion regarding the proposal. Was it so mad to think that some resolution could come about through such a meeting? Wasn't there in any case an intellectual value in participation? Could I perhaps even address some of the fears that had cursed me through my life?

'Yes,' I said. 'Yes, I will attend.'

'Oh Camille, you won't regret it! It is the most fascinating and emotional experience, and there is no danger I promise you!'

And so, the invitations went out and over the next two days excitement grew. Word got out that my aunt had secured the services of a well-known medium and she was beset with queries and requests to attend, which she mostly refused. I decided to stay at my own home while my aunt fussed over the final arrangements, so as not to impede her work.

I made the journey to St Cyprian's on the morning of the séance and on arrival my aunt, seeming quite fraught, invited me straight into the drawing room to speak with her. A morning tea was already laid for us.

'There has been a slight change of plan,' Aunt Beatrice said. 'I invited the medium to the house yesterday, so that she could get the feel of the place. A beautiful creature, although somewhat unrefined. She spent some time walking around the building then went out into the grounds. When she returned, she asked if the séance could take place in another location, one that she had a very strong feeling about.'

She put down her cup and looked at me.

'It was the church,' she said. 'She wants to hold the séance in the church.'

That afternoon, Anthony called and asked if I would enjoy a walk along the canal with him and his sister. The weather was inclement, but I decided a gentle stroll would take my mind off the evening to come. At first, we wiled away the time on pleasantries – I asked about his work and family, he asked after my aunt. At the George Inn, we stopped to watch a barge pass through the locks there, and I took it as an opportunity to broach my intended subject.

'Aunt is having her spiritualist meeting this evening. I am thinking of attending.'

He nodded, but said nothing, so I continued.

'Partly, I am fascinated by the concept of the séance and this presents a perfect opportunity for me to experience it at first hand. But I do also wonder if there is something in me, some injury of the mind that has left me open to . . . ' I paused, unable to express what I felt. 'After the death of my mother, I experienced a bout of melancholy that left me bedbound. During those dark hours I began to suffer nightmares, as I had once done as a child, I . . . It

256

is as though my grief has opened up something in me that needs to be closed. Do you understand?'

'I think so. You believe that if you can make contact with your mother, if you can say goodbye at last, perhaps you will be freed?'

'I feel rather foolish about it.'

'You mustn't,' said Anthony. 'You have suffered a terrible loss. What you are experiencing is only natural.'

'There is another issue to consider. The séance is to take place in the old church on the grounds of the estate. I have had two extremely unsettling experiences in that place. The locals are convinced it is haunted. It frightens me.'

Tearful now, I looked into Anthony's concerned eyes and with a self-reproachful laugh I said, 'I am sorry, you must think I am insane.' I walked on and he followed.

'Not at all,' he replied, handing me his handkerchief. 'I have heard tales, too. I think perhaps that buildings are like people – they contain within them the fragments of long-lost experiences and emotions. The past lingers everywhere.'

It was typical of him to exhibit such sensitivity. He seemed to understand me in the most intimate way.

'I'd be happy to take a ride past the church later this evening,' he said. 'Just to ensure all is well. But only with your consent.'

I turned to him, burying my face in his shoulder. I knew at that moment that I needed him, that if there was to be light and strength in my life again, it would be with him at my side. Even amid my uncertainty and confusion, I found in that thought the kernel of some future happiness.

We walked on in silence, lost in our thoughts. We walked and walked, until the spires of the city were visible over the hedgerows.

*

I entered the reception room that night filled with nervous tension, but also hope – hope that I might be offered the chance to hear from Mother one last time. My aunt did her best to make me feel at ease, introducing me to the other guests, her close friends Lady Oates and Lady Blanche, and then Lady Blanche's daughters, Ann and Jane, who were eighteen and twenty respectively and seemed rather immature and naive. I stood alone by the window, sipping a glass of wine. Outside, a storm was gathering, and the rumble of distant thunder could just be discerned beneath the pattering rain.

'Apparently, it is a new medium this evening,' said Ann, shyly approaching me. 'She does not rely on table knocks or automatic writing, and she does not lock herself in a spirit cabinet like those Davenport brothers. Instead, she converses with the spirits, who speak silently in her ear, and then she repeats what they tell her. She has even been known to conjure physical manifestations!'

'That is most interesting,' I replied.

'And is there a particular spirit you are keen to make contact with?'

'No,' I said, not feeling comfortable sharing my grief and hopes with a young girl I barely knew.

At that moment, the door to the reception room opened, and my aunt's maid entered. 'Miss Abigail Cooper,' she said, gesturing to the vacant doorway. And then in she stepped. My first reaction was that some mistake had been made – Miss Cooper looked to be very young indeed, barely more than a child, and so small and pale I'd have taken her for a waif if I had seen her on the street. But her eyes held a steely look of confidence and intelligence, and her dark claret dress was certainly refined. She was also strikingly beautiful.

'It is a pleasure to meet you all,' she said in a soft voice. 'I hope that no one minds taking our party to the small church in your grounds? It has an extremely strong energy that I think will be advantageous to our communications with the other world.'

'Oh, I think it will be fun,' squealed Ann. 'Our own little gothic adventure!' Her sister Jane nodded enthusiastically.

'I have heard that religious buildings are extremely conductive, in spiritualist terms,' added Lady Blanche. Miss Cooper nodded and gave a curious smile.

When we finished our drinks, it was time to go. As it was raining outside, my aunt arranged for carriages to take us on the short journey down to the church. Our small party still had to walk through the graveyard, the footmen holding umbrellas above our heads as we navigated the winding path.

We stepped into that grim old building, shivering slightly from our brief exposure to the rain. The house staff had already arranged the space, placing a circular table in the centre, along with seven chairs. Candles were lit in every alcove, with one in the centre of the table, to the medium's specifications. There were no place cards laid out, so I took the seat nearest the door, and Aunt Beatrice sat beside me to my right. Miss Cooper was the last to sit, taking the vacant seat opposite me.

'Please could everyone put their hands face down onto the table, ensuring your fingers are touching those of your neighbours,' she said. We followed her example. 'In this way, we create a circle of the living, which will light the way like a beacon, for any departed souls who wish to speak to us. Now I must make contact with my spirit guide. I need you all to be silent and to think of those who you have lost, and who you wish to commune with.'

We all sat in silence, shadows playing across the faces of the others, making their expressions look strange and deformed. I thought of Mother, of happy moments together, I thought of the last time I saw her, the day of her departure to Southampton, smiling down at me from the window of her carriage. 'Although I will be far away,' she had told me, 'I will always be close, always.' Outside, there was a low rumble of thunder.

*I will always be close. Always.*

'Can you hear that?' the medium asked, her eyes closed, her voice barely a whisper in the darkened chamber. We all listened, straining against the almost audible silence, occasionally glancing at each other, testing the mood. Just as one of the women cleared her throat, seemingly preparing to make a comment, the candle on the table suddenly flickered and a breeze passed against our faces. I did not know if it was my imagination but it seemed the air had become more dense; I felt a sense of pressure and proximity, as though someone had crept up behind me and was now very near.

The medium opened her eyes and looked upwards towards the ancient wooden beams.

'There is someone with us,' she said.

I felt my heart skip a beat.

'It is someone who very recently passed ...'

Mother?

Miss Cooper closed her eyes again. 'Does the name ...' She strained, tilting her head as though trying to hear someone call from a long distance. 'Does the name Percival mean anything to one of you?'

Lady Blanche let out a gasp. 'My uncle,' she said. 'My uncle. He departed not two months ago. A heart attack ...'

Miss Cooper nodded, her face betraying no emotion.

'He knows the manner of his death was a shock to you all, but he wants you to know that he was ready and that he is at peace.'

Lady Blanche made a sort of sighing noise and then slumped backwards as though almost close to fainting. Her daughters put a hand each on her shoulders.

'Ladies, please,' rebuked Miss Cooper. 'Place your hands on the table or we will lose him.' They did as they were told.

'He wants to say that . . . ' She halted suddenly and in that same moment the table jolted; a small but violent movement. 'There is another presence with us,' the medium said. 'Whoever it is, they are . . . they are angry.' Her face took on a pained expression. 'Please. Wait your turn. No, you mustn't shout. You must be patient.'

The rest of us looked at each other. The medium, with her eyes tightly closed, continued. 'I was talking to . . . No, I will not hear from you until I am finished here. You mustn't . . . '

Then, a low tremoring sound, seemingly coming from around us, as though the room was vibrating. All of a sudden, Ann let out an awful scream and pointed to something just beyond the table. There were wisps of reddish mist appearing all around us, crawling across the floor of the church. I looked to my aunt for some sort of reassurance but, although she attempted a smile, she too looked frightened out of her wits. Outside, the storm seemed to be moving closer, the rain louder, water splattering on to the stone outside.

'This spirit who has barged into our circle – they have a message for someone here.'

The unsettling vibrations within the room continued, gathering in urgency, like an engine throbbing. The fog now crawled beneath the table and over our feet, bringing a foul stench with it. As it did so, the glances between participants grew more concerned. I felt Aunt Beatrice grip my hand. The rain battered the door, the wind rattling its hinges like a madman at the bars of his cell.

'The message is a warning.'

I could feel beneath my fingers that the table too was vibrating, as though filled with some barely contained emotion.

'There is a spirit that haunts this place, filled with fury. A lady, jilted at the altar by her lover who was seduced by another woman, a feckless harlot.'

All sound stopped.

The medium's eyes flicked open and to my horror I realised that through the gloom, she was staring directly at me. This time, it was I who gasped.

'The restless spirit has placed a terrible curse on this place,' Miss Cooper said. 'Any woman who marries here brings that curse upon herself, her daughters and their daughters afterward.' She closed her eyes and began to shake and groan, a horrible noise, the like of which I had never heard. 'Someone at this table has the curse upon them.' When her eyes opened again, her face took on a grotesque appearance. She raised her hand and pointed, as I knew she would, towards me. 'You shall not have love, you shall not marry,' she said, and her voice, a taunting guttural rasp, did not seem her own. 'Love will bring no happiness. Only tragedy and death. I will take from you as I took from your mother, and will take from your daughters too. Only dread and solitude shall ye know.'

With that, the door burst open and the full roar of the storm came into the room, the rain, like cold sleet, splattering the walls and furniture; an explosion of lightning so close it electrified the very air around us. The door slammed shut again. Lady Blanche and her daughters screamed, leaping from the table in fright, knocking their chairs to the floor. My aunt stood too, looking confused and horrified at the wreckage of the evening. Amid the maelstrom, there was the medium, standing, looking over at the only remaining guest at the table – me. I was frozen, unable to move. Then from outside, we heard a shout, a man's voice calling. At first it was indecipherable, and then as it got closer, I could hear it. 'Camille! Camille, where are you?'

It was Anthony.

I rushed to the door but it wouldn't open, it was jammed shut. 'Anthony!' I called, banging at the ancient wood. 'Anthony! Help us!'

Another blast of lightning, and we felt the air energise around us. Then, from outside, there was a mighty cracking noise, like a cannon being fired, followed by a gargantuan crash and the sound of falling masonry, as though the whole church was collapsing in on itself above us.

Then silence. Horrible silence.

One of the girls, Ann, I think, tried the door again.

'Will any of the others open?' cried my aunt. All but I rushed from door to door, tugging at them uselessly. Finally, we heard a banging at the devil's door, which was then wrenched open. Two footmen stood there, drenched to the skin.

'My lady,' one said. 'The storm has brought a tree down, it has damaged the porch. We must take you out at once.' We all of us staggered out into the night. The rain had stopped and the storm was passing. The fallen tree lay across the graveyard, the stump of it still smouldering. And then as we stepped closer, we saw something so terrible I can barely relate it – beside the huge trunk was the lifeless body of a young man, a deep wound to his head.

I could feel myself hyperventilating, struggling to get air into my lungs, as I walked towards it.

'My God, Camille,' Aunt was shouting. 'Camille!' But I could hardly hear her. I stepped closer and closer through the mud. A footman got there first and he gently lifted the man's bloody face to me.

And then, as more staff rushed over, some of them trying hopelessly to revive the stricken fellow, my eyes locked on Miss Cooper. She stared back across the darkness and in her face, too, I saw a look of sheer terror. She was looking up at the church tower.

I followed her gaze. And there, in the shadows of the belfry, I saw the woman in the red dress.

I fell to my knees.

'Do you recognise this man?' someone shouted to me.

'I do,' I said quietly. 'It is Anthony Seward.'

I could feel my aunt gripping my shoulder, shaking me, shaking, shaking hard, but the movement seemed far away as though my own body, like Anthony's, had become a dead and distant vessel. All I could do now was stare at the body of the man I knew I loved and would always love. I knew the image would seep into my soul. It would never leave me. Only one thing would remain of my life.

A curse.

A curse on my mother, on me, for all eternity.

# Chapter Nineteen

# Shellshock

I sat dead still for several minutes in a state of all-encompassing shock. I don't know what I'd hoped to find in those pages – something rational and reassuring, I guess. Perhaps Camille had suffered from an undiagnosed mental illness; perhaps it was simple grief for her lost mother that got the better of her in the end. But no. Camille was strong and intelligent and determined. What took her was something much more awful and unknowable. God, the terror she must have felt that night. The discovery that she was being stalked by something ancient and hateful. What do you do with that? We think we live in a universe of logic and rationality, but we don't. Something did come for Camille, just as it came for Daphne and Elizabeth. And then it made its way down the line, to my aunt and my mum, who never had love, and down finally to me and Nikki. The red bride was there our whole lives, waiting in the dark. And I had this horrible certainty that, by reading about the séance, I had drawn her attention even closer towards me. I could almost feel her looking into my soul and seeing what was hidden there.

At last, I closed the journal, put it back in the folder and got up, my legs giving slightly beneath me.

I went back to Rhea's office in a daze.

'Are you all right?' she asked when I handed the journal over.

'Yes, it was just a shock to read . . . '

'Quite a story, eh?' she replied. 'And I love the photo of her – did you see it?' She opened the journal to a black and white photograph on the page before the article and turned it towards me. It showed a group of people, mostly men, in ornate Victorian dress posing for the camera in an ornate hall. 'The photo was taken in 1885 in the old building,' she explained. 'It's a group of the trustees and supporters . . . '

I looked along the row of severe unsmiling faces until I stopped and gasped.

'You look a lot like her,' Rhea said.

On the second row, third from the right, in a black dress and black gloves, staring directly ahead at the camera was Camille Redferne. She was tall, thin, her black hair pulled back into a bun. But it was her face that was most striking. Dark eyes, heavy set above high sharp cheekbones, her expression locked in a foreboding scowl.

'Maybe it's why you thought you'd seen me before?'

'I don't think so. I'd never seen this photo before yesterday. I swear I've seen a photo of her someplace else, a long time ago. I just can't put my finger on it. It's driving me nuts. Are you sure you're okay?'

Outside, it had started to rain. It seemed bizarre that everything was still happening like normal. Shoppers bustling about looking harried, office workers rushing by, yelling into mobile phones, car

266

horns sounding. I felt like I was suddenly living in a different world from everybody else. I walked through Queen Square and, looking up into the branches of the looming ash trees, I saw rooks, silent, pecking at their wings. I was certain someone was watching me and found myself spinning around, trying to see them. There was a mother walking past, pushing a pram; a group of teenage tourists in matching backpacks; two men in charcoal suits carrying brown paper carrier bags from a nearby deli; joggers; a glimpse of a figure at the far end of the square . . .

And then I felt my phone buzz in my pocket.

Slowly, I took it out and looked at the screen. It was a message from Nikki.

'I'm coming to see you at the church. Be there. It's urgent.'

I felt my stomach drop through my guts. What now? Oh God, what now? When I looked up, the figure was gone.

I almost hit another car trying to swing too fast out of my parking space, raindrops lashing across the windscreen. The adrenaline was pumping through me like floodwater, sparking off catastrophic scenarios in my brain. I tried to tell myself I was being irrational – she probably just wanted to complain about a hard day at work, some colleague who didn't know enough about microthrusters. When I got to the church, her car was parked badly as though it had been abandoned. I drew up next to it and flung myself out, forcing the gate open then standing at the mouth of the graveyard. She was stood hunched and bedraggled in the doorway of the church, her long hair covering her face, like some vengeful wraith. I had to walk much closer before I was absolutely sure it was her.

'I need to talk to you,' said Nikki. 'It's about Justin.'

And then I knew it was all over.

\*

We walked inside in silence. I fetched a towel so that she could dry her hair, and a spare sweatshirt for her to wear. She dragged off her drenched suit jacket and shirt, and put it on.

'Can I get you some tea?' I asked and didn't wait for her reply before filling the kettle. I turned back and she had sat herself down on the sofa.

'You look like you've seen a ghost,' I said with a stupid little laugh. 'I'm sorry about the mess in here, I wasn't expecting . . . '

'There's a rumour going around the office that Justin's been sleeping with other women,' she said quietly. 'I got CCed on an email thread by mistake.'

Heart thumping.

'Shit,' I said. I sat down on the sofa, leaving a gap between us.

'I've been trying to call him but he's in back-to-back meetings. It's going straight to voicemail.'

'Did you actually speak to anyone else about it?'

'No. I just got up and left as soon as I saw the email.'

'What did it say?'

She put her head in her hands. 'Oh, it was something about a conference he went to last month. Jenna made a joke about his extracurricular activities with a woman who works for one of our tech suppliers. Someone else said it was pretty standard behaviour for him.'

Tentatively, I nudged towards her on the sofa and snaked my arm around her shoulders. She sank into me.

'Do you believe them?'

She didn't reply for a few seconds. 'We're going to see a wedding venue on Saturday,' she said. 'He's started a spreadsheet for all the things we need. It's colour-coded for urgency. So no, I don't believe it, I don't believe he'd do it.'

I got up and walked over to the kettle and she watched me go.

'I know you've never liked him,' she said. 'I've made my peace with that. But you don't think he could do that to me, do you?'

I poured the water into the mugs.

'Because, the idea that he'd be able to hide that from me, that he'd just carry on as if nothing had happened . . .'

Milk. One sugar for me. None for her.

'That would be fucking unbearable. If I married him and then found out afterwards . . . I think it would destroy me.'

I turned back to her, holding the mugs. Hands shaking. Tea splashing on to my fingers.

'Hey, it's okay,' she said, her voice full of concern. 'Oh shit, Cammy, look at you, you're crying!'

She ran over, took the mugs, and put them down next to the sink. She wrapped her arms around me and hugged me tight, like when we were little.

'You don't have to worry. It's office bullshit. Just stupid gossip. That's what I'm so upset about – they've shared these stupid lies on our work system for everyone to see.'

I let her hold me for a few more moments, a few precious seconds. Then I closed my eyes. I had to save her.

'I believe them,' I whispered.

'What?'

'I believe that he has slept with other women.'

She pulled away from our hug. 'Why would you say that?' she hissed. 'What the fuck, Cammy?'

She stood staring at me while I tried to get my mouth to move and my voice to work. And then I saw how her face changed from concern to bewildered denial. I saw the pieces fall into place. And then I made my confession.

269

# Chapter Twenty

# **My Bad**

It was so disorientating, leaving university. After four years in a big city living with artists and musicians, to suddenly find myself back in the real world, poor and homeless with no idea what to do next. I was so frightened. Nikki took me in, of course she did. But then I was in a tiny flat on a quiet little street, with no plans, no prospects – my brilliant sister's charity case. I was vulnerable, I was lonely. I'd never dealt with my grief over Lorna and that came back in a big way.

'The week you were away in the States,' I said. 'I'd hit rock bottom. I couldn't leave the flat, I was crying all the time. Justin was there, feeling sad because of some argument you'd had. He came down to the flat to check on me, and we just started to drink and talk, and a couple of drinks turned into several and then too many. Somehow, we started to kiss. God, Nikki, I don't know why or how. The next thing, we were in the bedroom, everything was swirling ... but I swear, before anything else could happen, the reality of it hit me. I sobered up in an instant. I told him to go, and he did, but I was devastated. I hated myself, I hated him. The next day he begged me not to say anything to you. I got really good at telling myself nothing happened. But it did. It did. And I'm so sorry, I'm so, so sorry, Nikki.'

She stared at me, open mouthed, almost a parody of shock.

'I need to get out,' she said, her voice quiet and controlled.

'Nothing ever happened again. I was sick with guilt, I still am.'

'I need to get out of here. Right now.'

'I had to tell you! You wanted the truth.'

'Not this. I didn't want this.'

'Nikki, please. It wasn't really me! You said it yourself – the person in that flat, it wasn't me. There's no way I would have done that to you! Don't you see? It was the ...'

'Oh God, Cammy, don't you dare mentioned that fucking *curse*. Don't you dare. You've always been strange, but this?' Her eyes were glistening now and I could hear the rawness of her emotion spilling over at last. 'You let me believe I had a future with him when you knew I didn't.'

'Oh God, Nikki, please, I'm so sorry.'

'I don't care, I just want to go!'

She barged past me, I grabbed her arm to stop her. 'Please,' I begged. But she yanked herself away, and then she came at me and shoved me hard – hard enough to send me staggering backwards against the sofa and then on to the floor. I let her. I wanted her to hurt me. In that moment, I wanted her to take something heavy and smash it over my head. But she didn't. Instead she just yelled.

'I gave you a home! I looked after you! All my life I've looked after you. Not any more! You're on your own!'

Before I could beg her to stay, she rushed out into the gloom.

271

I managed to claw myself up, half-blind with tears and shame, and stumbled out after her into the dead night. But I was too late. I heard her car starting and then pulling away. I followed the sound as she turned on to the road behind the trees, and for a few moments, the faint aura from the car headlights lit up the church.

The rain was torrential. I stood in the churchyard beneath the blackened sky, drenched and freezing cold, staring at the building. It all came back to this place, I knew that now for sure. What happened to Camille that night had brought a plague on the family, poisoning every branch, every blossom. I should have listened to my aunt, I shouldn't have dragged Ben into this. The unease I had always felt in here made sense now – it was the residual effect of that night, the séance. I knew there was no escape for me, for Nikki, but we could at least protect others.

We could save them from us.

I had this weird sense of clarity all of a sudden. I knew that the reckoning I had been waiting for was here at last. I understood what needed to be done. I had been holding on by my fingertips. Now I had to let go.

# Chapter Twenty-One

# Goodbye Ben

The drive to the rehab centre took longer than it ever had before. The roads were oddly busy, so many cars lining up in the endless rain, red brake lights reflecting off the drenched tarmac. I was in no state to drive. I felt utterly blank and abstracted, as though this was all some sort of performance. I felt as though I was enacting a premonition I'd already experienced a dozen times before. It was only when I pulled into the car park and saw the entrance that reality finally cut through and jolted me out of the trance. I sat at the wheel for a while, breathing deeply. I looked in the rearview mirror and wiped mascara away from my puffy, swollen eyes. This was the right thing to do, the best thing for everyone. He needed someone capable, honest, not haunted. I had to set him free from danger. That's what I was telling myself. I really believed it. I believed I was doing this for him.

Leaving the car, I felt heavy and unstable on my feet. I ghosted past the desk, barely nodding at staff I recognised; I couldn't stand the thought of indulging in idle pleasantries about the weather. When I got to his door, I had to pause again. I could hear the TV inside. I knocked and waited.

'Hang on,' he shouted. I heard the effort it took him to get up and slowly walk towards the door – it was like a rebuke and it solidified my resolve. It didn't matter that I had pain, actual pain in my heart. Then the door opened and he was right there, looking at me with his wry, lopsided smile. He was in grey jogging bottoms and a T-shirt. 'Sorry for the outfit,' he said. 'I've got an appointment with a running machine this evening. It'll be more like stumbling, but you know, baby steps.' He kissed me and he smelled of nice soap. It struck me afresh, as it always did, how soft his lips were. I could barely look him in the eye.

'Are you okay?' he asked. 'You look weird.'

'I always look weird,' I said with an awkward laugh.

'Do you want to do something? Go for a walk? Get a coffee?'

'No,' I said. 'Can we just stay here and talk?'

His smile faltered. 'This doesn't sound good.'

He stepped out of the way so I could go into the room. There were his clothes everywhere, and lots of his books on plants and gardens that I guess Meg or Rose must have brought in for him. I went to sit on the bed, but then changed my mind and chose the chair at his desk instead. He watched me sit down but didn't move himself. There was an awful pressure behind my eyes. I looked down at my hands locked awkwardly together in my lap. I didn't know how I was going to do it, so I just started.

'I know this is the worst possible timing after everything you've been through but I think I need to stop seeing you.'

Ben didn't say anything for a long time. Behind me, raindrops were pelting the window in a scattershot rhythm of increasing ferocity. It seemed they may even smash the glass.

'Is it something . . . have I done something?'

'No, I promise. It's nothing like that.'

'Is it the long drive up here? Because it's fine if you don't come as much. You don't have to come at all. I'll be out soon.'

'Ben, it's not that.' My throat hurt so much I could barely speak. 'The truth is, I should never have started anything with you in the first place.'

'What do you mean?'

'I shouldn't be with anyone at all. Trust me, you're better off this way. You'll be safer without me.'

'Cammy, this doesn't make any sense.'

'I know.'

'What the hell has happened?' He started to walk further into the room towards me, and I could see the pain and effort it caused him, just to move. 'You need to explain it. You owe me that.'

'I can't, it's . . . it'll sound mad. It's something my aunt told me.'

'Your aunt? What does your aunt have to do with it?'

I thought I may as well tell him. What harm could it do now?

'She warned me, on the day she died. She told me there's a curse on the women in my family. When we fall in love . . . it comes for us. That's what I've been looking into all this time. I was tracing it back, and it's true. It's all true. Your accident was my fault.'

He took the very slightest step backwards and, in that moment, I could actually see something in his eyes harden and cool.

'Are you serious?' His voice had lost all its warmth. 'Are you fucking serious! You're finishing with me because of a curse?'

'I know how it sounds. I know it's insane, but you don't know what happened to my grandmother, and her mother before her, and probably every other woman in my family, all the way back. When they fell in love, awful things happened. And the moment I told you how I felt about you, you almost died.'

275

He looked up to the ceiling and shook his head, the gesture filled with disbelief, incredulity and anger.

'Jesus Christ, the accident happened to me. To *me*, Cammy. It had nothing to do with you. This isn't your fucking tragedy, it's mine! And I didn't die. I *survived* and I'm putting myself back together.'

'I know,' I said. 'You're doing amazingly. But it will be better for you if I'm not here.'

'Why? Why would that be better?'

'Because I'm no good for you! I see you with Meg. She helps you, she actually helps you.'

'Oh my God, is this about Meg? We've been through this, she's just my friend.'

'That's not what I'm saying! I'm not jealous of her. But she is totally focused on you. She's one hundred per cent there. She's good. She's a good person. I'm not and I can't be. I don't have what you need. And I'm scared, Ben! I'm scared all the time. I don't want to put you through it.'

He walked away from me with his halting, uncertain gait, and I felt a wave of remorse so huge it seemed impossible that I wasn't crying.

'Sasha said this might happen,' he said quietly, his back to me. His tone was different now, almost calm. 'After a trauma like this, partners hang around at first because they feel they have to. Only a monster would finish with someone while they're in a coma, right? But once recovery begins, the reality sets in. Me and you . . . we'd only been seeing each other for a few months before the accident. You didn't sign up for this.'

'That's not it,' I said. 'It's not about your injury.'

'Do you know what? I really wish it was. Because at least that would make some kind of sense.'

'I'm frightened. I'm frightened that one way or another, I'll hurt you.'

'That's my risk to take.'

I went to leave and he lurched up off the bed. 'Please, Cammy, just wait a second!' he cried, grabbing hold of my bag strap. I wrenched it back off him and it snapped, dumping the contents of the bag on to the floor. A nurse passed by and was just about to say hello when she saw the looks on our faces. Instead, she hurried past.

I sank to my knees and started gathering up all my things.

'I know you think I'm crazy,' I said.

'I always thought you were crazy. Right from the very beginning. But I never thought you could be cruel.'

'I know,' I said. 'I'm sorry.'

I stood up, clutching my bag to my chest.

'Just go,' he said. 'Just fucking leave.'

I walked out of his room and heard the door slamming behind me.

And then it was just me once more.

I went to get into my car but I couldn't push the button on the key fob because my hands were shaking so much. I had to wait a while, leaning against the bonnet and breathing slowly, trying to calm myself down.

Driving away, I understood what Camille had felt, and perhaps what they all had felt when the end came. I just wanted to keep driving until there was no road left, and to not stop even then. I wanted to completely disappear.

Back at the church, I stormed across the lawn then wrenched open the wooden door so hard the hinges screamed. Inside, I went to the table first, sweeping everything off, the letters, the diary, the books I'd been reading, my own notes. Books spun across the room, pieces of paper fluttered into the air and cascaded around me – weeks of careful, ordered thinking and research obliterated in the maelstrom. I lifted the table on its side then pushed it over until it crashed upside down on to the stone floor. Then I stumbled to the bookshelves, grabbing the side of the nearest and dragging it forward until it toppled over, sending the contents tumbling across the floor. I climbed over the heaps of old hardback books, slipping on the covers until I got to the next bookcase and toppled that too, this one hitting the edge of my polisher with an almighty clang. Finally, I pushed the last of them too, but this time I was too slow and weak to get properly out of the way and it hit my shoulder on the way down, knocking me to the floor, my head hitting the ancient stone with a sickening crack.

And for a long time, I just lay there, too tired and concussed to move or even cry any more. The silence buzzed in my ears. Dust motes glittered in the dead air. I had no idea what to do next, I just knew I didn't want to be in this place. There was nothing here for me now, it was a poisoned chalice. I thought about cutting my losses; selling the place, moving far away.

But just as I rolled over to try and stand up, I caught that smell in the air again, that Lorna smell, patchouli and paint, thick and heady. I also felt a cool breeze across my face, coming from the direction of the now-toppled bookcases. Was it her ghost coming to say goodbye, or 'I told you so'? Then I spotted them, a row of three iron floor grilles that had been hidden under the units. I crawled over to them, pain hammering in my head, and then I peered down the first one I reached. It was some sort of vent leading deep down beneath the floor, and though I couldn't see far into the pitch darkness, I knew one thing: the breeze was coming from down there, and the smell was coming with it.

I grabbed my phone from my back pocket, switched the torch

on and pointed it through the grille. I could make out a pipe running along about a foot down, part of the old Victorian plumbing system. Beyond it, I had a sliver of a view into the crypt, and even though I could barely see, I knew one thing for certain. Lorna had told Margot that it was completely empty, just an earthen floor and a vaulted roof. But she had lied. There was something down there.

## Chapter Twenty-Two

# **Breaking and Entering**

I was out of the church then, half walking, half running along the path to the outbuilding – I'd hardly been in there since the day I arrived, but I knew exactly what I was looking for. The sledge-hammer. It was propped up against the wall where I'd last seen it. At the time, I'd wondered what it would ever have been used for. When I picked it up, I was caught off guard by the sheer weight of it, and wondered if I'd even be able to use it, but I was sure as hell going to try.

I marched back to the church, then navigated down the old stone steps to the bricked-up crypt entrance. I had no idea on technique. At first, I tried to swing it like a backhand tennis shot and it bounced uselessly off the brick, chipping only a few particles from the surface, the impact travelling all the way up my arm. I did this three or four times until my arms were trembling and I could barely lift the thing.

'Fuck!' I screamed. I threw the hammer down, then bent over and put my hands on my knees trying to get my breath back. I picked it up and tried again from a slightly different angle. Nothing. No give at all.

'Come on!' I screamed it, I was begging. 'Come on, please!'

And in my head, the events of the last month flashed out in one horrible super cut. Nikki on my doorstep in the pouring rain, the way she left me there, the way I went straight out and finished with Ben. There was a wind picking up behind me now, and it seemed to be pushing me forward. I heard rooks cawing, closer to me than ever. Everything seemed to be pushing me forward. I grabbed the sledgehammer again and this time I swung it like a baseball bat, using my whole body, using everything I had, with an explosion of anger and hurt and frustration. My eyes were screwed shut, but when it struck, the impact felt totally different, there was give. I swung again. I swung at the year I wasted in Bath, I swung at not having enough guts to come clean to my sister, for having done what I did to her, I swung at what happened to Ben and what I'd lost – a lovely boy, a friend, who would have been there for me. And I swung at Lorna, for putting me here, for indoctrinating me into her coven. I could have spent all those holidays with my mum and my sister, I could have fitted in somehow. But Lorna took me and showed me a different world, then she died. She died and left me, and I didn't want her to go, I wasn't ready. Oh Lorna, I wasn't ready to say goodbye.

I swung at all that and I hit. I hit.

A whole section of the makeshift wall in the doorway caved in, with a block of six or seven bricks disappearing into the cavity behind it. When I struck again, more followed, until eventually the structural integrity was gone and the whole thing collapsed on itself in a billowing cloud of reddish dust.

The swirl cleared and I expected to see the old crypt door, the wood soggy and rotten, covered in slimy moss. This, however, was a new door, stainless steel and sturdy, with a huge handle like a fancy refrigerator – Lorna must have had it fitted before she died. I cleared all the bricks out of the way, grabbed the handle and pulled, expecting it to be locked, but it clicked open easily. Beyond it, I could make out shapes in the dark.

I stepped inside, getting my phone out again to use as a torch. But as soon as I crossed the threshold, a series of wall-mounted LED lights automatically switched on, bathing the room in a soft blueish light. I stood and stared in shock and incomprehension.

The interior was still unmistakably a crypt, with its low vaulted ceiling supported by two ancient stone columns. But the floor had been repaired and resurfaced in an obvious attempt to limit damp. There was a cabinet in one corner, the sort with large shallow drawers for artwork, and mounted on one wall was a workshop storage unit filled with tools – scissors, knives, paint brushes, pencils, technical drawing pens. There was also a metal shelving unit, the same kind as upstairs, crowded with her unsold sculptures and prototypes, the ones I feared she'd burned. But she didn't, she brought them here.

It was a studio.

The centre was dominated by one feature: Lorna's old work-bench, the one she'd replaced with a four-poster bed when she was too ill to move. There was something large on top of it, covered by a blanket, the one Lorna always had on her bed when I was younger. I took a step closer and I could smell her familiar scent, patchouli and ylang ylang. This is what I had smelled in the nave all those times. It wasn't coming from the afterlife, it was coming from the cellar.

I reached out and took a section of the blanket in my hand. I felt a slight shudder pass through me, and then I pulled.

It was a large-scale model of St Cyprian's Church, intricately detailed and painted, every element rendered in balsa wood, paint and textured plastics. The tower, the arched windows, the oak doors, the scarred stone surface pockmarked with lichen, and beneath it the dark, low crypt. It wasn't some twee Hornby trainset diorama; there was a serious, architectural exactness to it – somehow it captured the imposing, haunted feel of the building in miniature. More strikingly, the north wall was completely cut away to reveal the interior, inside of which there were four scenes, like theatrical stage sets, populated by small doll-like figures. It took me only a second to understand what was being depicted – it was the story of our family. In the crypt was the séance: a table in the centre around which sat seven women in Victorian dress. Standing directly behind one of them, was another woman, dressed all in white, holding out her hand towards the nearest sitter. It was Camille and her mother – the mother she had attended the séance to see, but never did. So close, but an infinity apart. In the chancel was Daphne, standing in front of the old wooden pulpit, holding a baby to her chest. Lying on the stairs leading to the pulpit was the body of a soldier, bloody and lifeless, the pages of a letter scattered about him. In the nave was a woman in 1950s clothing, holding a toddler by the hand, stretching her other arm out towards Daphne. It was Elizabeth, with Lorna herself. And finally, in the tower chamber among the mess of discarded clothes and records was Lorna as an adult, standing looking into the large antique mirror. Here were all the moments that defined us, pointing back to that one night in 1888.

For a while, I just stared at it, unable to fully comprehend that I was seeing something new by Lorna. She had worked on it in secret, a last statement about her life and history, the tragedy that linked and cursed every generation. My God, there was a chance no one was ever going to see it, if I hadn't gone down there. As I examined it, I realised two things: it was modular in design and could clearly be separated into separate sections, which would make it easier to move; and that it was incomplete. There were pencil notes on the interior walls, which looked like marking for extra features that were to come. There were electrical wires feeding in between the walls and under the floors, suggesting plans for something with movement or interactivity, something like her work with Reggie. And on the workbench beside it was a thick sketchbook. I opened it and inside were pages of elaborate plans, sketches and notes that seemed to be written in code. Lots of numbers and measurements, arrows and footnotes. It was an instruction manual. It was a guide on how to finish it. I put the book down and looked once again at the church, studying each small scene in turn. I realised every frieze showed a mother and daughter – that seemed to be the message, the passing down of something from one generation to the next. I walked around, looking at it from different angles, and when I finally got in close to the tower chamber scene again, I noticed something peculiar. In the mirror hanging on the chamber wall, Lorna was not standing alone, there was a smaller figure beside her, a young girl, dressed exactly like her. The girl was looking up at Lorna and Lorna was looking back. Her face showed regret, guilt.

Mothers and daughters. In every scene.

Mothers and daughters.

*You're so alike, you two.*

I took out my mobile phone and, with trembling fingers, chose 'Mum' from contacts then hit call. She replied on the first ring.

'Cammy? What on Earth have you done? Nikki is devastated!'

I paused to catch my breath.

'Cammy? Are you there?'

Exhaling slowly, I looked at the sculpture again, trying to get to grips with this cosmic shift I was experiencing. Trying just to summon a few simple words. And then they came.

'Was Lorna my mum?'

No answer.

Oh God, it was so obvious. It was all so obvious now.

'Was she?!' I cried.

'I'll come and see you tonight. I'll drive over.'

'I need to know now! Please!'

Crackles on the line then dead air, as though we were on the verge of being disconnected.

'Yes. Yes, she was.'

# Part Two

# A BLESSING

# Chapter Twenty-Three

# **Broken**

The sky was dark for a week, the sun hidden behind a thick sludge of cloud. It was freezing cold, so I didn't go out. I was exhausted but couldn't sleep. Instead, I skulked about the church wrapped in old blankets, my hair knotted, the bottoms of my feet black with ancient muck. I wished that a tidal wave would come and wipe the church off the face of the Earth, taking me with it. Who would care? The people who had shown me the most love had already been obliterated.

On the fourth morning of my exile, Mum turned up. What was I to call her now? She didn't knock, she just let herself in then stood in the doorway for a few seconds looking around the church and then at me. I was lying on the sofa wearing jogging bottoms, a Joy Division T-shirt and a huge mohair cardigan. I waited, uncertain of what exactly she was here to do: berate me for what I'd done to Nikki? Disown me?

Then I saw that she was carrying two huge shopping bags. She walked past me into the kitchen and began to unload them on to the altar. I saw fresh fruit, vegetables, pasta, milk, bread, tea and coffee.

'You've got to eat,' she said. Her voice was stern, but not completely unkind.

I got up and walked slowly towards her. She stopped unpacking and looked at me properly for the first time.

'Oh, Cammy,' she said. 'What on Earth have you done?'

I could already feel my legs giving away, my shoulders heaving. She dropped the bags as I slumped into her arms. We stood like that for a while, me sobbing helplessly into her shoulder, until she guided me towards the sofa, saying, 'Come on, Cammy, come on.' She sat me down and let me hold her for a long time. Neither of us said anything for a while. One of the bags toppled off the counter and a dozen red apples rolled out across the stone floor. This, it seemed, was Mum's cue to talk.

'When Lorna found out she was pregnant, she was in a very bad place, mentally. She and Reggie had split up, she was struggling to work and extremely depressed. Everything was caving in around her. Despite all of that, she was determined to keep the baby, to keep you. But when you were born, it was just too much for her. I offered to look after you for a little while, to help her get herself together. A little while became a long while. By the time Lorna was feeling better, you were a toddler. Cammy, I wouldn't let you go.'

She had tears in her eyes now, something I hadn't seen in years.

'Lorna understood. She knew it was better for you, and for us, if things stayed as they were. She begged me never to tell you – she wanted to do it herself. But she couldn't. She just couldn't. She was worried she would lose you, and she loved you so much. She really loved you.'

I sat for a while in her arms, trying to make sense of everything, as thoughts and emotions bombarded me. Then something new struck me and, in a burst of anger, I wrestled myself free and stood up.

'Is that why Dad left?' I said, trembling with the effort of it. 'Did he leave us because of me?'

'No!' she said, standing to face me. 'No! It was difficult at first, of course it was. But he did what he always did – he put in minimal effort and carried on regardless. He was always a selfish and unavailable man. And he didn't leave us, Cammy, I told him it was over.'

This was the Mum I knew: in control, holding all the cards, dealing them as she saw fit. She tried to put her arms out to me, but I wouldn't let her.

'You should have told me the truth! You should have told me everything!'

'I know. I know. I wish I could go back and do it all differently. At least then you would have had a choice.'

I started pacing madly around the room, not knowing how to process my feelings through my body. There was too much coming in: my sister, Ben, now this. Memories flashed up – Lorna and me shopping together, exploring museums and galleries, gigs and press events. I looked so much like her, how could I not have seen it? The way she taught me how to draw, to put on make-up, to cope with boys, to be comfortable expressing myself, to be me. To be me. How could I have not seen that she taught me in the way only mothers do – with complete, unending focus.

And one thought was rocketing through the rest, catastrophic and utterly unavoidable.

'My mum died,' I said, almost in a whisper. 'My mum died and I didn't know.'

Stupefied by the grief of it, I trudged to my room, crawled into bed and tunnelled under the duvet as deep as possible. There, I slept for sixteen hours.

When I woke, there was a note beside the bed. 'I didn't want to wake you. Had to go back to London, but call me if you need me. I'll come right away xx.'

We hadn't even talked about Nikki and what I had done to her. Suddenly there was just far too much to talk about. But it was there in the background for me, as it had been since that awful night. Although the guilt had always been in my head, I'd become skilled at deflecting it, at pretending it wasn't there. Now it was finally out, uncontrollably out, and there was no relief in that at all. I tried everything I could to contact Nikki. Having maxed out her voicemail inbox with tearful apologies, I sent long emails and dozens of WhatsApp messages. I sat in my car outside her house three evenings in a row, but the lights never came on. I thought of Ben, too, the sadness in his face when he found out it was over. At least now, I thought, he'll be saved from my reckless influence, my rotten legacy.

On the sixth day of moping, an unexpected thing happened: a call from Meg, asking to see me. I figured why not? What is there to lose? It would be the first time I'd stepped outside in five days.

We met the next day at the Society Café in Kingsmead Square, me with a black Americano, her with a decaf latte.

'I just wanted to let you know,' she said as we sat down at a little table by the window, 'he's going out to live with his parents in Abu Dhabi.'

Another gut punch of loss. Another self-inflicted blow. I didn't know what to say or how to respond. Instead, I sipped the coffee too quickly, burning my lips. My mind flashed back to the times we'd met up after work, his clothes grubby, dirt under his fingernails, big stupid grin on his face. I hadn't really taken in the extent of the damage to his life; I'd been too caught up in my own psychodrama.

'Poor Ben,' I said, knowing it was a ludicrous understatement. 'I fucked everything up.'

She stared at me. 'Why did you do it? Why did you break it off?'

'I thought I was bad for him.'

'Why?'

I shook my head. 'I thought there was something wrong with me, with my whole family. I've just been so stupid. At least *you're* happy now?'

'Happy? Happy that my best friend has left the country because someone broke his heart?'

'You never liked me.'

She tutted wearily. 'He told me you thought the accident was your fault, that you messaged him, or something? Here's the thing, you weren't the last person to talk to him before the crash. He called me. He wasn't sure if he should keep seeing you – he was worried about how much he was feeling. I told him he was an idiot, that if he liked you he should stick with it, give you a chance. After the accident, I had my doubts, I'll admit that. But the afternoon you brought him the book of flowers, I saw you both out in the garden – you were pointing things out and looking them up. I thought that was such a beautiful thing you did for him.'

'Why didn't you say?'

'I didn't want to get involved. I knew you were wary of me. To be fair, I don't always come across well. I'm way too protective of my friends.'

'Now Ben is going, and it's my fault.'

With this, she seemed to soften.

'You're not the only reason he's leaving. He had to resign from his job – he's never going to be up to it physically.'

293

She looked at her watch and pushed the half-drunk latte away.

'I'd better go,' she said, standing up. 'His dad is coming to collect him a week on Saturday, they're leaving mid-afternoon for Heathrow. I guess you have nine days to decide whether you want to try again. But I'm telling you, don't go and see him unless you're sure, you're absolutely completely sure, you want to be with him. Don't fuck him around again.'

I wanted to ask if she really thought there was still a chance, but she was already making her way out. For a second she stood outside on Kingsmead Square, looking up into the sky as though in disbelief at something silly she'd done.

I skulked home, head full of caffeine and grief. What kept me going was work. I had a lot of commissions to finish and, for some reason, I couldn't face letting down these completely anonymous customers who existed to me only as usernames and bank accounts. And so for two days, I drank industrial amounts of coffee, I worked and I ignored the calendar on my desktop, ticking the days down to Ben's departure.

And then an email came in from Christopher Erwitt, the curator from Bristol Museum. It was entitled 'Reggie Macclesfield article'. I opened it.

Hey Camilla

Hope all is well with you.

I'm not sure if you'll remember, but I mentioned during our chat last year that I was planning to write a new article on Reggie Macclesfield partially based on my mother's unpublished interview with him. I'm happy to say I got to speak to Reggie myself last month, and have now published the resulting piece in the *Bristol Museum*

*Magazine.* I've enclosed a PDF, as I thought you might be interested in some of what he had to say.


My finger paused above the download button, but I was in no state to read anything. I had no interest any more. What did it matter what he had to say?

I drank all day instead, and spent the night on my phone, trying to find evidence of Nikki's life on her friends' social media feeds. And then I started to feel angry. Just ferociously angry. At myself, at my futile search into the past, and at the church – the cauldron of the whole mythology. Somehow everything started and ended here, the way it whispered stories and conspiracies to me, the way I listened. Almost out of spite, I opened Christopher's article.

And then everything changed.

## Chapter Twenty-Four

# What Reggie Knows

For the first few paragraphs, I couldn't understand why Christopher had sent it to me. It was a lot of background about Reggie – how he had a very privileged, conservative upbringing, and how he was the odd, lonely misfit in a family crammed with thrusting Tory bankers. He got into programming in the mid-1970s, building his own computers, then learned about artificial intelligence and computer art. I wasn't really interested until the article reached his first meeting with Lorna, and then it finally hit me: this is my father.

'I met her at the Grafton Arms near Fitzroy Square,' he says. 'I was with some guys from the experimental art lab as well as a few computer science and medical physics students – we were all into computer graphics. Just a bunch of nerds really, ahead of our time. The school had the idea that programmers could be artists and we appreciated that, but most of the other students didn't. We had to form our own gang. Anyway, Lorna walks in with this other girl, and she just looked amazing, totally punk rock, loaded with attitude. I knew her work; I knew she was making these weird sculptures influenced by folklore and the occult, loads of cool dark shit. I didn't think she'd be at all interested in my work.

'We got talking about art, technology, horror . . . all the good stuff. She was so smart, so interesting . . . and, you don't realise how beautiful she is until you get close. Those eyes. I was in awe. But I was just completely intimidated. When she invited me back to her place, I kind of knew it was just to keep talking. I mean, she couldn't possibly have been interested in me, you know, sexually. She had her pick from anyone at the Slade. I made my peace with that from the outset. And then, I think it was while we were doing some press for *Zoltan*, all these journalists kept asking if we were a couple and I could tell it was really getting to Lorna, so I told them I was asexual and that our relationship was totally platonic, and that kind of became our thing. We were like these two emotionless cyborgs. I think the art press really dug that. But it's not how I felt. It's not how I felt at all. I was in love with Lorna all along. I just didn't know how to tell her, and soon it was far too late.'

I sat for a second, trying to process what I'd just read. Could it be true? Could it be that Lorna had completely misunderstood Reggie? In the space of four or five sentences, all her years of heartache had become a terrible misunderstanding. They were for nothing. He liked her too. It just seemed so cruel.

'This is why I needed to see your mother. Because the way Lorna told it, my perspective was totally different.' He lights a cigarette and blows smoke out into the space between us, shaking his head. 'I was in love with Lorna from that first night at the pub, through everything that followed; through all those nights in our studio in south London, sleeping together on that mattress, not daring to touch. It would be funny if it weren't an utter tragedy.

'When she left for Brighton that night, I thought it was because she'd grown tired of me,' he continues. 'I was devastated. But then, she came back, and we started kissing. So I went with it. That's where it all unravelled. I didn't understand, really, what the hell was going on. So I did what I thought she wanted. I pretended it hadn't happened.'

Then came another revelation. According to Reggie, two years before she died, she called him and asked to meet up again. This is something she never told us. She hid it from everyone.

She told him she had been diagnosed with cancer but immediately dismissed all his platitudes of sorrow and sympathy. She hadn't called for that, she wanted him to meet her the next day at the Grafton Arms. Where else? He immediately agreed. 'I walked in and she was standing at the bar with a pint,' he recalls. 'It was like a vision of the past. She looked exactly how she had done the first night we met. All that attitude and confidence. The years seemed to fall away. For a while I just stood there, unable to move, caught in the memories. Finally, she looked up and saw me. She smiled and said, "Oh Reggie, don't look so upset. Come and have a pint."'

Lorna told him the cancer was aggressive and that she was starting chemo, but it was a long shot. She might have a couple of years, she might not. He recalled that Siouxsie and the

Banshees were playing in the background. They sat in silence for a few seconds, listening to the music, supping their pints, and then they began to tell each other stories – about the things they did and saw back then; about the opening nights, the long hours of restless work, the first-class flights, the celebrity parties. They laughed together, they talked about art again. The time between them seemed to condense and fall backwards.

Once again, the things I knew or thought I knew about Lorna were wrong. That part hurt, like a spear through my gut. I'd always hated him for betraying her, but it was more ambiguous than I ever realised, and in this bleak new light, I was as bad as him: I was guilty of the same crime, the same mistake. I'd created my own story around the evidence I'd collected about my ancestors. And I was just as ruined by it. The story of Lorna and Reggie was more complex than the tragedy I had constructed – the one where he broke her heart, then turned up at the church six years later, then disappeared from her life for ever. I read on with a sense of something crumbling away to reveal yet more fresh truth, as though Lorna was turning from the page and talking to me.

For a few paragraphs, Christopher went back to Reggie's later career, the vast installation pieces he was making for global banks, mega corporations and Silicon Valley billionaires. But then the interview returned to Lorna one last time.

Reggie won't say much about what the two of them discussed that night – she swore him to secrecy. But it was a project. She wanted to talk to him about art again.

The possibility hit me like an express train: there was a chance, a *chance*, that she'd discussed the sculpture with him. Maybe he

299

could understand her notes, her vision. I didn't pause. I flipped open my laptop, went to Reggie's website, found his email address and sent him a message. History was being rewritten faster than I could keep up.

I wasn't really expecting to hear back from him personally; if I got a reply at all it would probably come from a PA in about three weeks' time. I was already thinking of different ways to meet him – turning up at one of his openings, maybe. I'd convinced myself that it would be a dead-end and that I'd need to find some other way to investigate. I was hunting through my contacts for Lorna's agent, when my laptop pinged.

It was a reply to my email.

It was direct from Reggie.

He wrote, 'Come and see me.' There was a Google Maps link.

'When?' I replied.

'How does tomorrow sound?'

And I immediately thought: does he know? Does he know about me? And if he doesn't, do I tell him?

# Chapter Twenty-Five

# Deep Down

Reggie Macclesfield's studio was based in an ex-MOD nuclear bunker complex in the North Devon countryside. I had to park next to a completely anonymous hut-like building, then get an elevator down. I was met by one of his assistants who showed me to a reception area and offered to make me a coffee. He later returned with a thimble-sized cup of steaming espresso. There was a promo video playing on a huge LED screen. Reggie's voice was explaining that in order to be ecologically sustainable and carbon neutral, his work would now be almost entirely digital, accessed through VR headsets and augmented reality displays. The voice-over said he was employing a team of programmers and 3D artists to create his innovative new cyber-sculptures, but none of them seemed to be around today so it would just be me, Reggie and the assistant, thirty feet underground.

We'd never spoken much – I was far too intimidated by him

when I was a girl, and he and Lorna broke up by the time I was old enough to understand their art, or what had happened between them. He was just this shadowy eccentric who haunted my aunt. I was only waiting for a few moments before he appeared in another doorway wearing silvery trousers made from some sort of fire-retardant material, a white T-shirt and work boots. His curly hair was long, grey and unkempt, and his thick-rimmed glasses hid bloodshot eyes. But he still had about him a certain damaged masculine beauty.

This was my father. My dad.

'You look a little like your aunt,' he said, puffing on an e-cigarette. It was immediately clear he didn't know.

'To be fair, I'm wearing her clothes,' I replied.

'No, you have that same look in your eyes: defiant but sort of . . . hunted.'

He guided me down a long narrow staircase, and along a low corridor into what he called his office, but which looked like some sort of sci-fi control chamber or spaceship. The walls were glossy white and lined with hidden light sources. His desk was domi-nated by an expensive-looking PC and three giant monitors. One showed a video of him setting light to the sculpture that won him the Turner Prize. We sat on large black leather swivel chairs and awkwardly watched it for a few seconds.

'The Turner Prize was a disaster for me creatively,' Reggie said. 'I never recovered from it. The trendy little galleries we used to love exhibiting at were no longer interested in me, I'd become too mainstream, but the larger places still didn't understand my work. So I basically started mass-producing robotic sculptures for corporate clients – Dubai mega hotels, Silicon Valley tech compa-nies, Russian oligarchs. I did one piece entitled *Trash Compactor*, which was placed in the reception area of a bank in New York – it confused the shit out of the customers. When is art not art? When people think it's a fucking cash machine.' He laughed joylessly. 'Oh, the irony.'

He continued, 'Nothing I've done since Lorna has been good. The spark died, you know? If only I'd had the courage to tell her how I felt. But I didn't.'

He sat watching me.

'I'm not good at small talk,' he said.

'Okay.'

'You've got some questions for me?'

'Yeah.'

'Fire away.'

I thought, if this is the way he wants it, then I've got to play the same game. No polite chat, no edging towards the point of our meeting. I just have to get straight to the meat.

'After your reunion night at the pub, you met up again?'

'Yeah, we started seeing each other regularly. We didn't tell anyone because we didn't want it to be about art, it was just about us.'

'You were together?'

'In a manner of speaking we were. All the way until the end. It was a privilege.'

'She didn't tell me.'

'No.'

'She made me believe we were cursed. That we couldn't be in love.'

'Oh, she believed that until the end. I suppose, after the diagnosis, she felt she didn't have much to lose. But if you're asking me if she was cursed ... Not any more than anyone else who was unfortunate enough to fall for an immature, emotionally unavailable prick. As far as I'm concerned, if there was a curse in her life, it was me.'

'And she never questioned it?'

'What do you mean?'

'It's just, I've started to discover things about the other women in our family – my grandmother, my great grandmother. Their lives didn't turn out the way we thought.'

He sat back in his chair with a quizzical look on his face.

'Interesting.'

'What?'

'In the last few months I started looking back through her family tree; spent hours on that Ancestry site, searching for birth and death certificates, all that shit. It was hard, not least because I was tracing the female line, not the male line. I got back as far as the sixteenth century.'

'And what did you find?'

'Nothing,' he said. 'At least nothing to corroborate that old story about an ancestor of yours pissing off the local ghost. There were no records of women dying in mysterious circumstances in or around the church. This didn't dissuade her at all – she believed it in her bones. But when she told me about the séance, a few of the details reminded me of something. I'd been working on a horror movie about Jack the Ripper, and I got friendly with one of the historical experts who was advising on the script. We had a lot of long, fascinating discussions which I've forgotten now, but . . . I don't know, something about the séance reminded me of him.'

'Who was it . . . this expert?'

'I can't remember the dude's name.'

'Okay, but what was he an expert in?'

'Special effects of the Victorian theatre.'

He took out his vape pen and started inhaling deeply. I had this inkling of a thought, a half-memory lurking in the back of my head that I couldn't quite place . . . something I'd been told recently that seemed relevant here.

'You don't recall anything else?'

He shrugged. 'It was a long time ago. A lot has happened since then.'

'You're so like her,' I said. 'Everything is a puzzle.'

He laughed. 'That's what it was always like between us. Everything *was* a puzzle. She held half the pieces, I held the rest, and without ever really explaining anything, we'd start building. It was magical.'

I wanted him to keep talking, to give me more details. But it was only partly about the curse. I also wanted to spend more time with him, figuring him out.

'It's such a tragedy that you never worked together again,' I said.

With this he turned to me, his mouth curling into something approaching a grin.

'Ah,' he said. 'That's not quite true.' He took another hit on the e-cigarette and sat back deeper into his chair.

'What do you mean?'

'That night at the pub, just after last orders, Lorna became serious for a moment. She told me she was planning one final piece, something big to leave behind. She asked if I'd help. I didn't ask any questions. I didn't even need to think about it. I said yes. "Hear me out," she says. "We're going to need to be discreet. It's a secret. It's not something we'll be able to exhibit straightaway. Perhaps it will never be shown." I know this sounds odd, I just want to be as honest as I can with you. We just discussed the technical logistics, I don't know how she intended to apply them. I don't know if she ever actually constructed it.'

I kept staring at Reggie, desperate to tell him everything I knew.

'She did make it,' I said.

He lurched forward. It was the first time he'd shown any emotion. 'You've seen it?'

'It's in the crypt at the church.'

'Holy shit.'

'It's not finished though.' I took Lorna's notebook out of my bag and handed it to him. 'She left this. Do you understand it?'

He took it from me gently, as though it was an ancient holy relic, and started leafing through, his expression a contradiction of excitement and confusion.

'It's our language,' he said. 'It's how we worked together.'

'What does it say?'

'It'll take me a while. Can you leave it with me?'

He was up, pacing about, flipping through pages. I'd become invisible. Our meeting was coming to an end.

'There was just one more thing I wanted to talk about,' I said.

At that moment his assistant came through.

'Can you show Cammy out?' said Reggie. 'I've got to go through to the studio.'

'But—' I started.

'Got to go,' he said. 'Art waits for no man.' He put out his hand for me to shake. 'Stay in touch, yeah? Let's talk again when I've deciphered this.'

The assistant took me back to the elevator and then I was out in the real world once again.


While driving home, I ran through everything Reggie had said. He had found no evidence of what Camille was told during the séance, but the story had dislodged an odd half-memory in his addled brain. Lorna had allowed Reggie back into her life, but she clearly hadn't told him about me. It was getting harder and harder to separate facts from stories, reality from mythology. The air was heavy with signs and portents.

A weather report came on the radio. I was barely listening until the presenter mentioned that a huge storm was crossing western Europe; experts stated it was one of the biggest to hit the continent for several years. 'Is it coming in our direction?' laughed the DJ.

'Yes,' was the answer. 'The Met office is predicting winds of up to sixty miles per hour and dramatic lightning storms over the southwest. It should hit us in a week.'

A horrible feeling of foreboding came over me. I switched the radio off.

# Chapter Twenty-Six

# Confessions

The following day, everything seemed heavy again. The air in the church felt dense with something uncanny. It was as though my own mood, my sadness and confusion, were haunting the building. I was the ghost.

I spent a lot of time stalking Ben's Instagram, studying the photos of him in the gym. I didn't know whether to hit Like on any of them or not; it felt sort of intrusive and immoral considering what I had done. But I did like them, I liked that he seemed to be getting better. I liked seeing his face. It physically hurt me to think he would soon be thousands of miles away. Meanwhile I heard from Mum – what else was I to call her? – that Justin had moved out of the house, and that new tenants were in the garden flat. Nikki still wasn't responding to my messages.

At 11 a.m., there was a knock at the door, quiet and unurgent.

I wondered if it was Mum back again, or perhaps even Nikki. My heart leapt at the thought.

'Come in,' I shouted.

The door creaked open just a little, and a face looked in.

It wasn't Mum. It wasn't Nikki. It was Joan Pendle. I'd almost forgotten about her. She smiled at me, as though everything in the world was completely fine. And, as she stepped into the room, a few weak rays of sunlight crept in behind her, reflecting between the windows and off the wet stone floors.

'Is it ready?' she asked. I had to think for a second, then I recalled that I'd set the stones and buffed the ring with a pendant mop to start giving it a proper shine.

'Yes.'

'Good girl,' she replied, delighted. 'I knew you wouldn't let me down.'

It was so odd, and I don't know why, but I almost burst into tears when she said that. Sometimes people say exactly the right thing – the one thing you really need to hear – even if they don't know they're doing it.

For as long as I live, I'll never forget those words.

She walked into the nave, once again seeming somehow both old and young. She was wearing the same beautiful scarlet coat, this time over a mustard wool dress that looked ruinously expensive. I took the ring out of a little box in my workbench drawer.

'I was passing,' she said. 'I thought I may as well check up on your progress.'

'I'll just give it a quick polish,' I said. 'Then it's ready for you.'

I went to the polishing motor and she followed me, looking around the nave, as though searching for something specific. There was an odd energy about her. Something static. I pressed the button and began running the ring gently along the mop.

309

I wanted it to be just right for her. I figured it must have some emotional significance, some meaning beyond merely being a nice object. I was weirdly nervous about her seeing it. While I worked, she wandered over to the table where all the papers were spread. I'd picked them up after my tantrum, but they were in a mess.

'What's this?' she asked.

'Oh, it was just a sort of project of mine. I was tracking my family history, trying to get to the bottom of an old legend.'

'And how are you faring?' she asked.

'I've stopped now. I feel like I'm still missing lots of pieces, but to be honest, there were too many sad tales.'

'May I take a look?'

'Sure.'

She began idly sifting through the papers as I finished up. I guessed she was just enjoying the chance to interact with someone else's life, or maybe the old photos had a familiar look to them – the fashions, the hairstyles, the make-up. She circled the table, her fingers gliding fleetingly over the newspapers and magazines, nothing holding her attention for long. But then she came to an abrupt stop. She was looking at Elizabeth's journal.

'That is my grandmother's diary,' I said. 'From the fifties. It's quite a story.'

'I know,' she replied.

I glanced up, wondering if I'd heard her correctly. Perhaps she just meant that she remembered the era? I went to the desk and got out a presentation box, placing the ring carefully inside. I found that I was walking over to her with the box held out, but I was going so slowly, like in a dream where you're trying to run, but it's like you're wading through treacle. I watched her. I didn't say anything, I just watched as she opened the cover of the diary, then slowly started turning the pages. She ran her fingers over the handwriting. Almost imperceptibly, she nodded.

'Sorry, did you know her?'

She gave me a strange look, as though this was something I should have known. 'Yes,' she said. 'Very well.'

My mind was spinning through possibilities, recalling the diary, the cast of characters, trying to work out where this demure old lady could possibly fit in. As I was thinking, she took a seat, crossed her legs and sat with perfect poise as though waiting to be interviewed, and I recalled what I'd thought when I first saw her – those high cheekbones, the thin, tall frame. She must have been beautiful once, I had said to myself. She could have been an actress. She could have been a model . . .

I felt a spasm of shock, like every synapse in my brain was firing at once. I felt as if I was in a theatre, in front of a hushed audience, all waiting for me to say the next line. Waiting and expecting and knowing.

'Lea,' I said.

# Chapter Twenty-Seven

# **The Ring**

For a moment she didn't respond and I thought I'd made an idiotic mistake. But, at last, she nodded. 'Lea is my middle name,' she said. 'I always preferred it. Pendle is my maiden name, my professional name.'

I couldn't believe a piece of my family history was here in front of me. Not a diary, or a magazine article, but a person.

'You look like her,' she said, still holding up the diary. 'The same dark eyes, the same serious, rather sorrowful expression.'

I was beginning to feel swamped, the grief threatening to explode through the barriers I had hastily constructed. But it was necessary to remain professional. To not show the bewilderment and panic I was going through.

'How did you find me?'

'I needed to replace the ring, and a young friend found your advertisement on the internet. We looked you up and there was your photo – I saw Elizabeth straightaway. I was rather hesitant about coming, I wasn't sure how I would feel. But then I saw your beautiful jewellery and I had the feeling you would do a good job for me. It was a sign. Life is full of signs, isn't it? You just have to learn how to read them.'

'Why didn't you tell me when you came the first time?'

'I wanted to get the measure of you.' She looked towards the diary again. 'Have you read it?'

'Yes. Have you?'

'No.'

'Do you want to?'

She reached into her bag and took out a packet of cigarettes. 'Do you mind if I smoke?'

I said I didn't. She lit one and held it in the elegant, mannered style of a Noël Coward character.

'Ashtray?' she asked.

I handed her a mug from my desk. She took it and flicked ash into the coffee dregs. Then she sat in silence, looking at me expectantly.

'Can I ask you about her?'

'Do you think I might be able to see the ring first?'

I'd almost forgotten about it, and now I was half petrified to hand it over. Her manner wasn't exactly unfriendly, but it was brusque – she was clearly used to getting what she wanted. What if the ring didn't match her expectations?

I brought it over to her and Lea took it gently between her thumb and forefinger, turned it around, examined it from every angle, watching light glint from the stones. She did this for what felt like an age, her face locked into a scowl. Then, finally, she looked at me.

'It's perfect,' she said. Her eyes were teary now. 'It's *perfect*.'

313

Slowly, she slid it on to her finger, her hands shaking with emotion. 'Just looking at it again, I see it so clearly. I see the day she gave it to me.'

'Elizabeth?'

'Who else?' She put out her cigarette in the mug, then took off her coat. 'Can you hang this up for me?'

I took it from her and hung it in my wardrobe. When I went back, she was sitting down on a chair beside my workbench.

'Well,' she said. 'How can I help you?'

For a few moments I was utterly tongue-tied. Here she was, offering me Elizabeth, offering me the chance to tie up another loose thread in this miserable tapestry. I thought, perhaps, it would help me process everything – to have it confirmed to me, from an eyewitness, how the curse had indeed ruined everything.

'I'd like you to read the journal.'

'I shall need a cup of coffee.'

And as I went off to fill the espresso maker, she started to read. She read for an hour, often running her fingers along the handwritten lines, sometimes smiling, sometimes on the verge of tears. Then she put the journal down on the desk and I waited. I waited for her to confirm the story of their doomed relationship.

'So,' I said. 'Is it the truth?'

'Most of it. But the way she writes about me ... I wasn't the person she thought I was back then. There were things she didn't know. Important things.' She lit a cigarette and took a long drag. 'Let me tell you a story.

'I was born in Hampstead, my parents both worked in publishing. They were rather a bohemian couple, lots of parties, lots of booze. There were always people around at our house – actors, musicians, politicians. I'd lie awake in bed listening to them downstairs, music blaring, laughter, things getting smashed. Sometimes a couple would sneak into the spare bedroom beside mine. Believe me, I heard everything. It was an odd childhood. I understood that my parents loved me, but I also understood I was an inconvenience to them and their lifestyle.

'Then our house was bombed and my father was killed. We found him in his study, still sitting at his desk in front of the typewriter, the room obliterated around him; half his head was missing. Mother and I had to get away, so we moved to Edinburgh. I went to university there. At that time, I knew there was something different about me. I dated boys, but I liked girls too. I couldn't tell anyone, it had to be a secret. I felt there was no place for me – it was stifling. When my mother died, there was nothing really keeping me here, so I cut my hair very short like Audrey Hepburn and left for Paris. God, the delusionary confidence of youth! I fell in with quite a wild crowd, and found myself modelling. I had my first relationship with another girl. I met her at a fashion event. She was a little older than me, very experienced. It didn't last, but it helped me to understand that I wasn't alone. That was what I needed to know – just that I wasn't all alone in the world.'

She took a sip of her coffee, then put the cup down, slowly and deliberately.

'But I was a disaster really. Lots of late nights, alcohol, amphetamines. I'd wake up in strange apartments with strange men. A psychiatrist would probably say I was making a deranged attempt to recreate my childhood. It felt like fun for a while. But then I started an affair with a very well-known photographer. He was married. When his wife found out, they had me excommunicated. No more modelling, no more parties. I was alone again, and with no money to pay for rent I was almost homeless too. I spent days wandering the city, hungry and frightened.

'And then Arthur came along. When I like people and want

315

them to think the best of me, I tell them Arthur and I met in a bar, but that's a lie. We met in a park, the Bois de Vincennes. I saw him sitting on a bench reading a newspaper. He looked sort of paternal and harmless. For some reason, I sat beside him and lit a cigarette and then started crying. He was rather shocked, but he consoled me, then he took me for coffee. We sat for hours and he just let me talk and talk. I told him everything and he wasn't shocked at all. He told me he was in Paris for business – it was only later that I found out he was with the secret service. He was odd and funny and rather mysterious, but not at all threatening. He was the first man I ever felt I could be friends with.

'Anyway, over the next week he cleaned me up, he made me feel almost human again, and when he had to return to London, he offered to take me back with him. And that's when I told him I was pregnant.'

'You were pregnant before . . . ?'

'Yes. But you see, he didn't care. He was not interested in women – or men for that matter. Yet there was pressure from his family, from his work even, for him to marry. So we helped each other. He said, "I know our relationship won't be the same as other people's." And that's *all* he had to say. We both understood. So I went. And, at first, I loved the safety and normality of it. It felt like I was a child playing at being an adult – I took pleasure in the most mundane things. I had this idea of living the suburban dream as a family. That's what I thought I wanted for Noah, for me. But I was still playing, I think.

'We had only been in St Albans for a few days when part of me knew it was a mistake. The house was too big, the town too small, Noah hardly slept, Arthur was spending most of his time in London. There I was with a baby and no friends and no life of my own. Everything started to cave in on me. And so when Elizabeth writes about how sophisticated and relaxed I was, that's not true. And when she says that I saved her, that's not the whole story either. She saved me right back. That day she came to see me, holding a cake, Lorna in tow, I saw it in her straightaway – something like me. Something hidden. She looked complicated. Those days we spent decorating the house, talking, dancing to the radio, were bliss. I don't think you ever realise the depth of your happiness at any point in your life until much later. It's a cruel trick – we can only see it in retrospect; the sun is too bright the first time around.'

'I met her husband Donald,' I said. 'He's in a care home in St Albans. He told me he'd found the journal. Do you remember what happened?'

She smiled. 'Ah, yes. We heard raised voices from next door that night, then there was a bang on the door, just after ten p.m. Arthur and I were in the living room listening to the wireless. We looked at each other, but before we could say anything there were three more bangs, hard enough to make the wall reverberate. Arthur got up and walked into the hall. I heard him unclasp the latch and open the door, and then there was a barrage of shouting – a man, absolutely apoplectic with rage. "Where's that bitch of yours?" the voice yelled. "Where is she?" It took a good few seconds for me to realise it was Donald. I rushed to the hall and was immediately confronted by a bizarre scene: Arthur was having to physically hold our neighbour back as he fought his way beyond the door and into the house. He was clutching what looked like some sort of notebook and sobbing like a baby. It was awful.

'Elizabeth came over and led him away. There were neighbours watching and naturally it blew up into a big local scandal.

I knew we'd have to leave – Arthur couldn't be at the centre of gossip, his job was so secret. So we moved back to London, and then he got a placing in Washington, so off we went across the world, leaving Elizabeth and Donald to patch things up. She was worried that if there was a divorce, Donald would get custody of Lorna – that would have destroyed her. And she really didn't want to hurt him. So they stayed together, but the marriage was a shadow of what it had been before. They had another child, your mother, but they separated soon after. And that was that.'

'And the ring? I guess it was a valuable heirloom?'

She scoffed a little. 'The day we arrived in Bath on the train from St Albans, we spent the afternoon exploring the town. Elizabeth went into a dusty old antique shop on Old Bond Street, and saw a ring with a split band that ended in two entwined blue stones. It was just a piece of costume jewellery, but she liked it, she desired it. I encouraged her to buy it for herself.

'On the day we moved, I went to see Elizabeth. I gave her the necklace I'd lent her that night at the hotel. In return, she took that ring from her finger and gave it to me. I wore it for fifty years, but I have started to lose weight and one day it must have slipped from my finger unnoticed. I need it. I need it with me, even if it is just a copy. It's all I have of her.'

'So, it wasn't platinum? The stones were fake?'

'Yes, but isn't it odd how we ascribe worth? That trinket was by far the most valuable thing I ever owned. But this beautiful ring, the one you have made, it finally has some of that value within itself.'

She stood up, slowly and with effort, and walked to the windows. 'Come and see,' she said. 'It's a lovely bright afternoon outside.'

But I didn't move, I was wallowing in the story, in this confirmation. The past had come for them too, and it had taken its toll.

'There's nothing you could have done,' I said. 'It was always going to end that way.'

She gave me an odd, almost disappointed look. 'The ancient

Greeks had a phrase, "know thyself". The greatest crime Oedipus committed as far as they were concerned was not knowing his own past. If we accept our fates, without discovering the truth ourselves, we will make all the same mistakes over and over again until the end of time.'

'I don't understand. What do you mean?'

She turned and walked back to me and perhaps it was my imagination, but the room suddenly seemed lighter somehow. 'You're assuming it ended between us that day,' she said. 'But, Camilla, it didn't.'

Casually, she flicked ash into my mug.

'We met up at least once a year, sometimes more – a day here, a weekend there. We kept seeing each other until she died.'

'How . . . how do I not know about this?'

'Elizabeth never told. She kept it a secret all her life. She always felt that she was in hiding, I think.'

'From what?'

'Society, perhaps. She never got over how her parents reacted to finding her with Heather. She grew up in St Albans in the forties and fifties, homosexuality was illegal. She believed she had harmed Lorna by leaving Donald. She didn't want to cause any more upset. But I also think she was afraid of the same thing you are. She hoped she could protect her girls from it if they didn't know about me.'

'You don't believe in the curse?'

'No, because when we were together we were happy! She made me happy! She gave me my confidence back. I flourished because of knowing her.'

'But you never got to be truly together.'

'Oh darling girl, that's nothing to do with a curse, that's life! Some people get to have the fairy-tale version of love – marriage, a life together, a family. But sometimes love is fractured, the

319

moments have to be stolen. So that's what we did. We were in love, we didn't have a choice. It's true, we had to be careful, there was always subterfuge. Even when Lorna was older, it was still a secret. I used to come and stay with Elizabeth when she moved to Brighton.' She laughed. 'I remember one occasion, Lorna had turned up unexpectedly, and I was on my way for a visit. Elizabeth managed to get a telegram to me, asking me to book into a hotel until her daughter left. I walked by each evening and Elizabeth watched for me in the window. It was farcical, really, but she was determined to keep her secrets.'

Lea lit another cigarette. 'I think she almost needed it, though – the curse. It was a connection for her, to her mother, her family, her past. Even if it was destructive. This is what you have to understand. We all tell stories about our lives. But stories cast shadows. They often hide as much as they reveal.'

It was so odd to be confronted with this new tale. The curse didn't destroy them. They fought back. It felt like a glimmer in the darkness, a lighthouse in a perfect storm.

Lea stayed with me for another hour, and I showed her the other evidence I had accrued. Camille's article, the piece on Lorna, the letters. It was while reading the latter that she stopped and looked around the room as though trying to remember something fleeting and elusive.

'What is it?' I asked.

'Oh it's ... it's probably nothing, just a strange coincidence, perhaps.'

'Yes?'

'When your grandmother died, she had a very small funeral. Your mother was there, and I introduced myself to her as an old friend of Elizabeth's. But among the very small crowd of friends and well-wishers was Dame Ursula Conrad.'

320

'Who?'

'Dame Ursula Conrad. Her husband was military top brass, she supported a lot of charities, but she had no connection with Elizabeth as far as I could see at the time. But now . . . ' She held up one of the letters.

I took it from her and looked at it. 'I don't understand,' I said.

'Oh, it might be nothing, nothing at all, but this Captain Guy Seabright who befriended Robert Woodbridge during the war . . . Ursula Conrad is his daughter.'

## Chapter Twenty-Eight

# What Ursula Knows

The blackness of the curse seemed to be lightening into a shrouded grey. Lea and Elizabeth reforged their relationship. They had to make sacrifices, but they managed to have something approaching love. If only Lorna had known, perhaps she too would have started to doubt the curse. *Stories cast shadows. They often hide as much as they reveal.*

It wasn't hard to corroborate what Lea had told me. I did a Google search for Seabright and the first result was a short obituary on the website of a military charity in Cheltenham.

It is with great sadness that we announce the death of Captain Guy Seabright, at the age of eighty-seven. Seabright, who attended Rugby and Oxford, served with distinction during the First World War, as a Captain in the Somerset Light Infantry First Battalion, earning the Distinguished Service Order and Military Cross medals for valour. After the war, he travelled widely, writing a series of books about his journeys through the Mediterranean and Persia. He returned to Cheltenham in 1926 and became involved with several charitable institutions. Captain Seabright is survived by his daughter Ursula Conrad.

It only took another hour of browsing to find an address and phone number for her. I called several times, leaving increasingly desperate messages. Somehow, I was finding the energy to be motivated again. I told myself that it was just a distraction, a way to keep my mind off what I had done to my sister and to Ben. But then I had an inkling of an unfamiliar feeling, and after a while I recognised what it was. Hope. Perhaps there was more good news to be found – perhaps the curse was cracking apart. And if it could be beaten, there may be a chance for Ben and me. But the clock was ticking. There were four days until his flight.

The next day, storm warnings were all over the local news. The Met Office was now giving a likely window for it to hit the West Country: Sunday morning. The presenters warned of travel disruption and likely building damage. I thought of the séance. The tree falling, the porch caving in. And then with a jolt, I thought of Lorna's art in the crypt. It was ridiculous to worry – a million-to-one chance, surely. But I was running on dread now and there was an uncanny feeling in the usually still and fetid air of the church – a feeling like static. The buzz of something coming. Little orbs of light danced along the windows. The trees outside were empty of birds. I had the sudden understanding that I needed to get it out of there, but it was delicate, I couldn't just hire a Transit van and lob it all in. I'd need a special removal team and a warehouse to take it too. How was I supposed to do that in two days?

Roland. Lorna's old manager. That was how. I took out my phone and called him. He answered in one ring.

'Hello, Cammy,' he said. 'How can I help?'

He was a man who liked to get straight down to business so I gave him the basics as quickly as I could: I'd found a new Lorna Piper work. It was very large, though thankfully modular in design, and currently lying in a crypt beneath the highest building in the area with a huge storm on the way.

'I see,' he said. 'Okay, I'll sort it. Do you have any storage crates there?'

I remembered there were a dozen in the shed from when she'd had her work stuff brought to the church.

'Yeah,' I said.

'Can you pack the sections up ready?'

I'd helped Lorna do it in the past. It brought a lump to my throat, remembering her patiently showing me how to wrap delicate objects in acid-free paper, then bubble wrap, double-boxing if it was going anywhere near boats or planes. Those moments would have to be reframed and recontextualised. Aunt and niece to mother and daughter. Did it make them more special or less? What did our time together mean?

'Are you still there?' he asked.

'Yes, sorry. I can pack them up.'

'Great. Be careful with it, and don't try to move it out yourself. I'll get a van and a warehouse sorted, and bring some professionals with me. Sit tight, darling.'

The call went dead.

I went out and bought bubble wrap from a DIY store, then spent the afternoon packing up the individual rooms of Lorna's sculpture, writing the names of my respective ancestors on each crate. It kept my mind focused. It kept everything else at bay. I boxed her art materials and the rest of her sculptures. I also found a large number of sketches and computer print-out artworks in the cabinet in the corner of the crypt, and packed those too. I moved that stuff to the outbuilding – I figured it had all been heaved about before, so what harm could I do? When I finished, only the workbench and the crates containing Lorna's final piece remained.

Ursula Conrad called me back the following morning. I told her I was doing some research into the war and that it had led to her father. I thought this was easier than trying to explain the whole situation with the letters and the curse. I asked if I could chat to her about him. The line went silent for a few moments and I wondered if I'd have to repeat everything again or whether she was just trying to think of a polite way to decline. But then she said, 'Yes, I suppose I can speak with you,' in perfect received pronunciation. 'But not over the phone, my hearing is not what it was. You will have to come here. I'll fetch my appointments diary.' She was gone for almost a minute and all I could hear was a dog barking a long way off. I was starting to think she'd simply abandoned the call.

'I'm busy for most of the week,' she said, and I tensed up. 'But I can see you Friday afternoon.'

Her home was a large Georgian townhouse with a grand portico entrance on a quiet treelined road in the Montpellier part of Cheltenham. Its box-like shape, ornately decorated window ledges and perfect, cream-coloured stucco made it look like a huge wedding cake. I buzzed the old-fashioned doorbell and then there she was.

'Camilla Piper,' she said.

'Yes,' I replied.

She was clearly ancient, but there was nothing about her that looked in any way decrepit. Dressed in a smart grey wool skirt and a jacket, she looked sharp and businesslike, and I felt immediately intimidated.

'Do come in.'

And she disappeared inside.

I found myself in an airy hallway, with exquisite mosaic floor tiles, the walls painted in some expensive Farrow and Ball version of green. In the corner next to the door stood an antique wooden umbrella stand and, beside the wide staircase, a vast aspidistra plant, which had been conspicuously well cared for.

'Through here,' she called loudly, and I followed her into a giant living room. It looked like something out of one of those coffee-table books on classic English interiors: polished oak floors, a vast open fireplace and two gigantic settees covered in a luxurious striped fabric, arranged in an L-shape around an antique leather ottoman. What I was most struck by, however, were the walls. Every available area of space was covered with framed photographs, hundreds of them, a mix of colour and sepia-toned images, some very large, some the size of miniatures. Grouped family portraits of unsmiling Victorians; Edwardian families on breezy beaches; children in flowing garments. I just stood near the doorway and gazed around for a few moments, taking it in. Ursula sat down on an armchair at the far end of the room beneath a window overlooking a large rear garden. At her feet was a sleepy Labrador, which lifted its head for a moment when I walked in, but then sunk back into its snooze.

'Are these all family photos?' I said.

'Family and friends. Most of them long gone. I prefer to have them around me, rather than in an album somewhere. A sort of benevolent haunting.'

She slowly leaned down and scratched the Labrador's head.

'Tell me more about this research,' she said. 'You're looking for information about my father?'

'Yes, I wondered if he told you much about his time over in France? Did he have any stories?'

She looked at me almost disdainfully. 'My father rarely talked about the fighting, so if you are here for tales of derring-do, I fear you've had a wasted journey.'

'No, I'm not here for that, I promise. Sorry, I know it's unusual, a complete stranger coming to your home and bothering you.'

'It's not a bother. It's been a while since I have had the chance to talk about my father. It was all such a long time ago . . .'

Her voice tailed off.

'I'm actually interested in a friend of his, Robert Woodbridge – I have some of his letters here.' I reached into my bag and took them out. 'I just want to find out what happened to him, and I wondered if your father knew.'

'Robert Woodbridge?' she repeated, a quizzical look on her face.

'Yes,' I said. 'I totally appreciate this all happened a hundred years ago and I'm sure your father had many friends and comrades, but I just . . .'

'He talked about Robert Woodbridge all the time,' she said.

I sat forward. 'He did?'

'Oh yes.'

I gulped, unsure where to go with this unexpected success. 'Do you know if Robert survived the war?'

'No,' she said. 'No, I'm afraid he never came home. At first, he was declared missing, and then later, dead. His body was never found. There is a cross for him at the military cemetery in Étaples. My father visited every year until he became too frail.'

'Okay,' I said, totally unsure now of how to proceed. It seemed that this tragedy was certainly complete. Daphne fell in love, and her partner was lost, and then her baby was taken away. God knows what happened to her after that. I'd come here to try to challenge the curse, but all I had done was confirm it. I couldn't get away from the fact that he had died on that final assault, and that Daphne's future died there too.

'There is a photo of them together,' she said. 'Would you like to see it?'

I said that I would. She walked me over to the other side of the room and stopped at a single, faded black and white photo beside the fireplace. It was of two men relaxing in what looked like a small bunker. Both were reading books, clearly comfortable in each other's company. 'That is my father,' she said, pointing to the one sitting on a wooden chair beside a small stove. 'And that is Robert.' He was lying on a narrow camp bed, his arm resting behind his head, a cigarette between his fingers. Beside him, I could just make out what looked like the pages of a letter, scattered out across the mattress.

'What is your interest in Robert?' she asked.

I thought I may as well be honest now.

'He's my great grandfather.'

She swung around to face me, then gripped my arm as though to steady herself. 'Really?'

'Yes. He had a daughter with my great grandmother, Daphne – that's who he wrote to during the war. But the baby was given up for adoption. God, are you all right?' I asked.

I held her elbow and helped her over to one of the sofas. The dog came and nuzzled her.

'I'm fine,' she said. 'You just caught me by surprise. Why didn't you tell me on the phone?'

'I wasn't sure you'd see me if you knew the real reason I was here.'

'Which is?'

'I read Daphne and Robert's letters. I think my family is cursed. I think Robert died because of it.'

'Robert died because he was fighting in a war – like millions of other young men.'

'But he had a way out,' I said. 'And he didn't take it.'

'No,' replied Ursula. 'No, he didn't.'

'I don't get it.'

'You have to understand the pressures he faced, his upbringing. There is nothing harder for a man to escape than the expectations of his father.'

'But if he loved Daphne, if he really loved her . . . ?'

She shook her head, silently. 'It's all in the distant past now. History took a different course.'

'He died. Daphne lost everything.'

Ursula turned to me with an expression of confusion. 'What do you mean?'

'From what I've been able to piece together, she gave up the baby for adoption, and was then ghosted away to live with an aunt in Yorkshire. For all I know, she lived her whole life there, alone and forgotten.'

'My dear girl,' she said. 'You really have no idea, do you? You have it all terribly wrong.'

Then she walked over to a wooden bureau by her armchair, opened a drawer and took out a folded letter. It was old and delicate, and unmistakably written in Daphne's hand. 'This is one you haven't seen.'

Gently, I opened it.


## Letter from Daphne to Robbie, 1921

My dear Robbie,

It has been three years since I lost you. Not a day since then has passed without me thinking of our time together. Sometimes, it feels that you are still with me, so close, yet just out of reach.

I glimpse you from the corner of my eye. I see you in the faces of passing strangers. But although I feel you close by, I need to tell you in my own words what has happened to me since we last exchanged letters.

The months following your death were the darkest of my life. The moment my father discovered the pregnancy, he concocted a plan to have me spirited away to my aunt's house in Haworth. He did not mean to be cruel, his hope was to spare my reputation, but my aunt's home was a cold grey place, and she resented the presence of a sinner such as me. Six months later, I gave birth at a mother and baby hospital, and while I recovered, the tiny girl was put forward for adoption. One morning, she was gone.

I cannot bring myself to describe the wretchedness that followed. The twofold grief of losing you and my baby girl, the loneliness and isolation of my life. It seemed unending.

Then, on a cold afternoon in January 1919, there was a knock at my aunt's door, and her maid came to tell us a gentleman was here to see me. I expected my father but, instead, a stranger was shown in; a tall young man in a good suit, with darkening blond hair and an affable face. He informed us his name was Guy Seabright, your commanding officer, and that he had made the journey from his family home in the Cotswolds in order to fulfil a promise he had made to you.

'I first arrived at the address Robbie had given me in Batheaston,' he explained. 'Your father kindly redirected me.' But it seemed that he had not told Guy the reason for my absence.

Guy had with him a satchel containing my letters to you, as well as your battered copy of *Jane Eyre*, the pages all loose and torn and mottled with mould. Apparently, during the long journey, whenever he wondered to himself why on Earth he was travelling the length of the country to see a woman he had never met, he put the letters to his nose and breathed in. Immediately, he was taken back to the trenches winding along the Western Front, to the toil and boredom, the horror, but also the friendships. It was, he said, his duty to deliver these artefacts, his final duty as a soldier and a pal.

'Won't you stay for tea?' my aunt asked in a grudging tone. She was a small mean woman with a shrewd face and pinched nose that gave her a permanent expression of distaste. I am certain he took an instant dislike to her, though he never showed it. She complained bitterly about how difficult it was to find domestic help these days since all the young girls had gone off to work in factories. She disappeared into the kitchen to bully the maid and he stood in our cold little parlour, unsure, I think, of what to do.

'Please sit down,' I said.

He took the armchair by the window, the pale sunlight behind him. His smile was full and genuine and unguarded. We sat and looked at each other for a few moments, unsure of how to behave.

'Robbie described you perfectly,' he said.

'He talked about me?'

'All the time.'

'And what did he say? If I may ask?'

He fiddled with the satchel on his lap. 'That you were the finest woman he'd ever met.'

Robbie, I was wearing a dark, plain dress, much repaired. My skin was pale, my manner timid, due to a complete lack of social contact.

'You must understand,' I said. 'He had a very vibrant imagination.'

Guy burst into unguarded laughter. 'On the contrary,' he replied. 'As soon as I walked in, I saw you exactly as he described. I could have picked you from a crowd.'

It was at that very moment I saw in him exactly what you had written, something untarnished and beautiful.

My aunt came back with the maid and tea was set at a small

table between us. She sat on the sofa beside me. Guy told us about your evenings in various billets and tiny French villages, and rare quiet afternoons in the trenches when you had time and peace enough to talk and read.

'There were long literary discussions,' he said. 'A few recitals of half-remembered poems. We could have been in a university dorm room. These were the moments that got me through the war.'

He looked circumspect for a moment, and I was sure I saw in his eyes a slight glistening that brought my own feelings to the surface. So I told him about the day you and I met, and the walks we took. 'Robbie always brought bread and great hunks of cheese, enough for an army,' I said. 'Food and books, that's what he loved most. Food and books.'

'And you,' he added.

It was almost too intimate, but you know him, don't you – how easily he says what others would struggle with? It was there from the beginning.

As we talked, I could feel inside myself the stirring of something like life, a small seed somehow germinating in the darkness. Hopeful shoots, reaching out. We did not see evening draw in until my aunt impatiently informed Guy that it was late and that he ought to get on. He stood with good grace, and handed the letters and book to me.

For a moment I felt bereft that this momentary glimpse of life would soon be gone, but as we showed him to the door, he turned.

'I'm staying the night in a small inn down the road,' he said. 'Could I perhaps return tomorrow and take you both for a stroll and some lunch?'

My aunt agreed, if only for the chance of a free meal.

The next day, we took a walk up to the moor, my aunt following behind with a friend of hers, both watching us with hawkish intent. Our discussion was much as it had been the afternoon before – literature, nature, music, but it always led to you. Our memories of you.

'What will you do next?' I asked, as we looked out over the town. 'Do you have plans?'

'I'd like to travel,' he said. 'Go out and see a few bits of the world we didn't destroy. Perhaps write about them. And you?'

I looked away from him. 'I have no plans,' I whispered.

What was I to say? That I was a fallen woman who was now earning her keep as a seamstress working late into the night, sewing in the weak glow of a gas lamp? For some reason, I desperately wanted to tell him about our baby. There was something in him that made me trust him, but I had known him barely forty-eight hours. It would have been utterly inappropriate. A scandal.

And yet, somehow, he read me.

'I know,' he said gently. 'I know what you've been through. I saw the letter.'

My first thought was to look around and see if my aunt was listening in, but she and her friend were sitting on a rock a hundred yards away.

'I cannot talk about it.'

'I understand.'

'Not without the grief breaking me apart in front of your eyes.'

'I would hold you together.'

The sun was high and warm. A pleasant breeze blew across our faces. I felt for the first time in many months that I was part of life.

'They put her in my arms,' I said. 'She was mine for an hour. Without making a sound, she looked around the room with a great look of curiosity and wonder, her tiny fingers clenching and unclenching. Robbie was there in her eyes.'

I couldn't go on. My shoulders heaved and I made a sound of

anguish I did not think it possible for a human to make. Without hesitation or abashment, he pulled me to him and he held me, just as he said he would. My aunt raced towards us through the long grass.

The next morning, I knew that Guy was boarding his train back to the Cotswolds. He had invited us to see him off, but I couldn't bear it. In just two days, he had unlocked a part of me that had been closed away for so long. Now was I to shut it again? I paced the floor in the parlour, looking at the clock. It was 8 a.m. and I knew his train was departing at ten. My aunt was at church. The house was quiet. I paced and I paced. The clock ticked.

At 9.35 a.m. there was a knock at the door. I rushed to open it, hoping, hoping, almost knocking the maid for six. But it was the butcher's boy with my aunt's order. My heart sank.

Yet, with the door open, I saw the world outside. The sun brightening the dark stone walls of the buildings, children in their Sunday best, a man walking by, a pile of books under one arm.

And I ran.

I had to lift my skirt and wind through people, often losing my step on the cobbles. The station was a good twenty minutes from the house. I suppose those years of cycling had ensured I still had the capacity for physical exertion, despite my meagre months in that house. I ran. Past the shops and carriages, the inn Guy stayed at, over the bridge, the river running beneath.

The train was pulling into the station as I arrived. The platform was quiet, a couple of porters lounging in the shade. I saw him at the far end. Coat over his arm, the satchel across his shoulder. He was opening a door and stepping aboard.

'Guy,' I called.

For a second, he disappeared on to the train, the door closing behind him. Then it stopped and opened again. And he was there, looking back at me.

He leapt down. I walked quickly towards him, and he to me.

When we met, I was crying. 'It was my fault,' I said. 'It was my fault he went into that battle. In my last letter, I told him it was finished!'

'No,' he said, holding my arms. 'He never read that letter. It was brought to me unopened. He never saw it. To my shame, it was me who opened it. He died knowing you loved him, certain of it.'

The porter blew his whistle. 'All aboard,' he shouted. The steam bellowed around us, the great noise of the engine was deafening.

'Come with me,' he said. 'Come with me now.'

'Guy, that is madness.'

'Come back with me to the Cotswolds. We have a large jolly house, there are plenty of rooms. There are always guests. You would be under no obligation. Just . . . come aboard now.'

Obviously, this was lunacy. The mere idea broke every rule of etiquette and social cohesion. I got on.

I got on the train.

His father greeted us at the platform and drove us to the Seabright home. No one saw me as an escapee, a shamed woman, I was just another guest, a friend of their son's. I was told I would be most welcome for however long I wished to stay.

Three months later, Guy proposed. When I mentioned the curse, he simply laughed.

'I've been through hell and come out the other side,' he said. 'I've seen horrors beyond imagination. Do you think I am scared by some churchyard ghost? If it comes for us, I'll bloody its nose. I'll send it scuttling back to the grave.'

We married in the spring.

*

335

That was two months ago. Yesterday evening I arrived safely in Bath after a long and rather troublesome train journey. The suite Guy booked for me at the Grand Pump Room Hotel is rather large and ostentatious for my needs, and it appears to have a door adjoining to the room next door, though thankfully I can lock it my side.

This morning I took the tram out to Batheaston. It was odd to be back, a lot has changed since I left. Naturally, I went to see my old family home – it looks much the same, though the garden has fallen into disrepair; my father would be furious. I can't say how I felt to stand there and look up at the place. The girl who lived there, the girl who was so desperate to live and learn, is gone now. Long gone. Then, I summoned my courage and started the walk up to the church. It was a pleasant stroll, the weather sunny but not too warm, which was fortunate as the lane is steep.

It was a shock to see it. Even more ancient now, and uncared for. The repairs you made have started to discolour, so the stone now matches the rest of the building, but the bramble bushes are coming right up to the walls and the graves are being swallowed. Whatever will happen to the place?

Inside it was cool. The unlocked door groaned on its hinges as I opened it. The pews were gone and there was a smell in the air of decay. But there was a beauty to it. I traced our steps from the afternoon we kissed, I remembered the excitement we felt. The trepidation. Darling, I hope you are comfortable reading this, but I need you to know.

I came to the pulpit, the last piece of wooden furniture still left in the place. I had to test the first step with my foot, to make sure it wasn't rotten. It was soft but it held. I climbed the staircase and I remembered how you had followed me that day, how you had reached me and how I took your face in my hands. The world opened to me, I think, in that moment, or at least something in me opened to the world. There was no going back.

I took the letters from my bag and I put them in the small cupboard beneath the lectern. I left them there for you, Robbie.

'If you wander this way again,' I said outloud, 'perhaps you will find them and read them, and you will remember you were loved. How I loved you, Robbie Woodbridge.'

I sat for a while on that little platform, and I cried for you. It was only then and there, with little circles of coloured light streaming in through the stained glass, that I realised something. Perhaps there was no curse in this place, no lingering dread – had I instead brought it in with me? Nothing supernatural was required for you to be taken, just the men who started the war and then fed it with young lives. I thought about what you could have been, I thought about you as a father, a grandfather. Stories that would never be told.

So I decided to take out my pad and pen and write you this last letter. I'll leave it with the others. Afterwards, I will walk around the church, back to the section you repaired. I will fight my way through sharp thorns and twisted vines to get to the place I need to see, at the base of the wall – the message you had carved for me. 'R. W. & D. R. In love. 1915. For ever'.

We didn't quite have for ever, but then, who does?

# Chapter Twenty-Nine

# The Truth about Daphne

'I visited St Cyprian's Church much later,' Ursula said. 'Mother once told me she had hidden the letters there. I'm afraid I took that one to remember her by.'

She walked to the large photograph over the fireplace. A family portrait. It showed Guy beside a beautiful woman with a warm unguarded smile. 'That's Daphne,' she said. 'My mother. Your great grandmother.' She smiled an odd sort of smile, like a shared joke, 'which makes you my great niece.' I couldn't even begin to take it in, this whole new branch of my family tree sprouting in an instant. Perhaps sensing my bewilderment, she turned her attention back to the photograph and pointed to a baby in Daphne's arms, swaddled in a long white christening gown. 'That's my older brother, Robert. I arrived two years later. Now you are up to date at last.'

Questions circled my brain. My tea sat on the tray, untouched, cold now.

'They were happy?' I asked.

'Yes,' she said. 'They were happy. We moved to Somerset when Robert and I were young. Father was very interested in radio technology. He invested in a company called Anderson Wireless, and Daphne campaigned for women's rights and set up a shelter for unmarried mothers. They were inspirational. I cherished them.'

'Did she . . . did she ever mention the curse to you?'

'When I was fifteen, she told me she once thought there was some ancient evil hidden away in her family. Some cataclysm they all had to fight with. She mentioned the article her mother had written. But she came to doubt it. It was her father who took her baby away, it was the war that took Robbie. Those were more powerful forces than any curse.'

'But that final letter she wrote to Robbie – she told him she loved him but that they couldn't be married. She passed the curse on to him when he read it! That's why he fought in the battle when he could have been safe.'

'No,' she said simply. 'Darling girl, he never read that letter. It was returned to Guy unopened. He opened it later. Robbie chose vengeance; he chose to follow his father and brothers. My mother's only regret was that she could never contact her daughter to tell her that she need not be the victim of a tainted history, that she was free. A few years after Mother died, I tracked Elizabeth down, but by then she was gravely ill. She passed before I could see her. But I did make it to her funeral.

'I shall tell you what my mother desperately wanted to tell Elizabeth. You are safe. You can be happy. My mother and my father were in love their whole lives. They were wonderful parents. I miss them every day.'

Then she took my hand. 'Do you understand? Whatever poison

was in her family, she beat it. And you can beat it too. The past is not a window, it is a prism – it reflects and refracts the truth, it bends and splits it into myriad new colours. You need to look hard at what you have right now, right in front of you. Because the future is *there*.'

Gradually, it seemed the certainties of the dark history I had constructed were falling away. Elizabeth did not lose Lea, Daphne did not die alone. I'd only found the saddest sections of their stories: the happiness had been hidden from me.

But for some reason, when I got back to the church, I still . . .didn't feel safe. There was something in Camille's story I was missing, something that would provide the closure I needed. Her voice was in my head, and it was telling me: keep looking. Keep looking. With just a day until Ben's departure, I had so little time to work it out. The silence was getting to me, so I switched on the radio. I read Camille's article over and over again. I lay on my bed and thought about the things Reggie had told me about Lorna: that she was beginning to ask questions about the curse, and something else. She had asked Reggie about Victorian theatre. Were the two connected? And why did the subject of stage magic seem so familiar?

The news came on and the approaching storm was the main story. It had gathered strength in its short journey across the Channel, and the police were telling people in Devon, Dorset and Somerset to cancel travel plans. My fears bubbled to the surface. Everything was coming for me at once. I checked my phone to see if Roland had been in touch about the van, but nothing. Would I have to be here when the thunder and lightning started?

Thunder and lightning.

*When shall we three meet again?*

*In thunder, lightning, or in rain?*

Martin Blacklock's production of *Macbeth*. It suddenly came to me. Martin had taken Camille to a production of *Macbeth* at his theatre in Bath, and he had enthused over the elaborate effects, explaining how they were achieved. She wrote that he had been fascinated by magicians and escape artists. Reggie said that when Lorna told him about the seance, something in it reminded him of an expert he'd once met while working on a Jack the Ripper film. An expert on Victorian stagecraft.

But how could that be relevant? Martin was a peripheral figure, a one-time suitor who respectfully faded away after Camille rejected him. Or did he?

This was the point at which the slow slip and slide towards the truth became a sheer, plummeting drop.

## Chapter Thirty

# What Martin Knew

For the rest of the night, I investigated this man. I spent hours on Google, I searched the newspaper archive and the census records. Nothing of any use. The whole thing was hampered by the fact that his father, Peregrine Blacklock, a notable politician and a confidant of Disraeli, utterly dominated any search results for the Blacklock name. I gave up and switched my search to him, hoping that somewhere in the mass of material, the thousands of newspaper reports, the entries in *Who's Who*, the lengthy biographies, there would be something about his son. I wasn't finding much about Martin, but I was certainly learning more about the British aristocracy.

It was about 3 a.m. when I settled down to read a book entitled *Ruthless Gentlemen: The Dark Side of Victorian High Society* that I'd found on an obscure academic database. It was mostly scurrilous tales about sordid affairs and colonial war crimes, but then I came across this passage:

Although Lord Blacklock's eldest son, Viscount Charles Blacklock, went on to become a much-respected statesman, younger sibling Martin Blacklock (1853–1911) was a very different character. A theatre practitioner, journalist and co-owner of a literary magazine, he entertained questionable friendships with actors and performers of low repute. Furthermore, he is said to have written several candid autobiographical articles which brought great scandal on the family.

It was everything I'd been looking for in one paragraph. I remembered that Rhea at the Literary and Scientific Institution was compiling a spreadsheet of all the historic journals in their collection – she said the index would contain dozens of Victorian periodicals, with the spreadsheet listing the major articles and writers.

I phoned her at 9 a.m., and when she answered I breathlessly tried to explain what I'd been looking for and what I'd found.

'Whoa,' she said. 'Slow down, and run that all by me again – and then remind me who you are.' I did.

'Do you think you might have any articles by him in your index?' I asked.

'Let me look,' she said. And I could hear tapping on a computer keyboard. 'Martin Blacklock, you said?'

'Yes!'

More tapping. Time seemed to extend outwards. 'It looks like he co-owned and contributed to a magazine entitled *Black Ink*. It was published between 1886 and 1912, but we only have fourteen issues in the archive. I'm not seeing anything relevant in the index. A piece about Houdini, something about a French guy named Ruggieri? I don't think ... oh wait. He had a big piece in the final issue. "A confession concerning the events at a séance at St Cyprian's Church near Batheaston".'

'Oh God,' I said. 'That's it.'

'When would you like to come and see it?'

'Now,' I said. 'I'm coming right now.'

When I arrived at the Institution, Rhea was waiting at reception for me. I was breathless and dishevelled, having run from the car park. I had four hours until Ben was leaving the rehab centre. There's no way I could go to him until I discovered something solid, something that obliterated our doom-soaked family narrative.

'Come this way,' she said, showing me through to a reading room. On the table was a copy of the magazine, open and ready for me.

Okay, Martin Blacklock – what *really* happened that night?

## 'A confession concerning the events at a séance at St Cyprian's Church near Batheaston' by Martin Blacklock, *Black Ink*, November 1912

Every crime committed against a person has two witnesses: the victim and the perpetrator. If the act is observed, or if evidence has been left, justice may be served – a trial, a sentence, then prison or the gallows. But sometimes there is no such resolution. The criminal remains at large, the victim silenced eternally, and so the truth of the act festers under the surface undetected, like some awful contagion. My story falls into the latter category. What follows is a confession to a crime. I will likely never face fitting punishment in a court of law for what I have done; my solicitors have been instructed to release this article for publication only after my demise. Perhaps I do not deserve understanding or forgiveness, but I hope that by recording the true facts of that fateful evening at St Cyprian's Court, I may afford modest relief to at least some of those affected, even though it is too late, far too late indeed, to make recompense to my victims. That is something I will have to live with, though live I shall.

I will not forget the night of the séance as long as I live. It comes to me in my nightmares. I can picture the darkness of the church nave, the figures huddled around the table, candles fluttering as the medium conducted her gruesome opera. Then the surge of the storm outside and the dreadful close of the evening. What I saw of it is frozen in my mind: the guests departing in terror from the building, Camille's aunt dragging away her niece, hysterical with shock, and then the felled tree beneath which lay the bludgeoned corpse of Anthony Seward. Beyond them all, I saw Miss Cooper half in shadow, lit only by the burning embers that lay about the scene. She was glaring out, her black eyes unblinking and resolute.

And I knew full well. I knew her stare was for me.

I first encountered Camille Redferne at the Royal Literary and Scientific Institution, during an interesting lecture on the future of telegraphy given by the inventor David Edward Hughes. I was there to research a possible article on the subject and, as always, I sat myself near the front of the room so that the speaker was aware of my presence; I felt that it benefitted visiting professors to know that their subject matter was of interest to an esteemed writer and editor such as myself. At the end of his lecture, the professor asked if there were any questions, and before I could raise my arm, he had already pointed to an audience member behind me.

'Do you think . . .' began a high voice, and immediately I and several gentlemen around me turned to discover the source of the query. Although it was becoming more common to see ladies at the lectures, it was exceedingly rare for them to ask questions. And this was not the usual dowdy bluestocking. As soon as I laid eyes on Camille, I was struck by her beauty, and the almost childlike enthusiasm of her face. 'Do you think that one day we may see telegram printers in private homes?'

I do not recall the speaker's reply, nor anything else of the following questions – all my thoughts were focused on the ravishing Camille. At the close of the meeting, I distractedly joined in the applause, and then as the audience stood and began to file out towards the tearoom, I jostled through the throngs, desperate to get to her and introduce myself.

'I say,' I called as I edged closer. 'That was an interesting question you put to our speaker.'

She turned slowly to face me, unrushed and unperturbed by my approach.

'Thank you,' she said. 'When in the company of a luminary such as Mr Hughes, it would be a shame not to take full advantage.'

'You know his work?'

'Yes, of course. I am very interested in the subject of telegraphy and the development of codes of communication. His work regarding the microphone effect is fascinating.'

I was astonished at her knowledge and the clarity with which it was expressed, although naturally, she lacked my expertise. 'You may find,' I said, 'that there will never be a market for teleprinters in homes, due to their limited use compared to the telephone. Besides, the cost of such machines would be prohibitive.'

She smiled briefly and then moved away into the crowd, no doubt cogitating on my helpful intervention. I was certain I had made an indelible impression.

Sadly, I was unable to make a formal introduction that day as we seemed always to be at opposite sides of the crowded room, but I did make subtle enquiries with several mutual acquaintances. I discovered that Camille was unmarried and lived with her mother in a house on Great Pulteney Street. Her father, now deceased, had been a much-respected solicitor who enjoyed powerful connections throughout the city. Her aunt had married into the Seymour family and was now Lady Seymour at the grand St Cyprian's Court. Camille was widely admired, but also viewed as somewhat subversive, often expressing challenging views and ideas during meetings at the Institution where she was a member and subscriber. This information only made her more fascinating to me and I resolved that evening to meet her again.

From this point on, I attended every lecture at the Institution, even those I had no interest in – and each time, I took the opportunity to greet her, and talk a little about the subject at hand. Throughout this period, my ardour and admiration grew with every encounter and I was certain these feelings were mutual, though nothing had been expressed. After several weeks of this, I decided to attempt a more formal expression of my feelings. It was in the exhibition room at the Institution, after a rather arduous lecture concerning that disgusting *Frankenstein* novel, that I made my move. Camille was examining a new display of ancient human skeletons, her face close to the glass case in concentration when I approached.

I leaned in towards her and whispered, 'Miss Redferne?'

I had not meant to startle her, but on hearing my voice, she lurched instinctively away from me with a loud gasp.

'Mr Blacklock!' she exclaimed. 'My goodness, I did not know you were there.'

'My apologies. I did not realise you were so absorbed.'

'Your approach was extremely quiet. If you were an assassin, I would be dead on the ground with my throat slit.'

I chose to ignore this gruesome image. 'What did you make of the lecture?' I asked.

'Very interesting. The novel is a favourite of mine.'

'Really?' I tried to hide my displeasure. 'You don't think it monstrous?'

She began to walk on, and I followed.

'It is certainly monstrous,' she said. 'But that's rather the point, isn't it?'

'I suppose I prefer more subtlety in my reading matter.'

'It is a book about the fear of death, and of the dead being brought back to destroy us. I'm not sure there is much room for subtlety there?'

'You think literature should explore such outlandish topics?' I was shocked by her analysis, especially coming from a woman.

'Literature should explore all topics. Besides, there is nothing outlandish about the fears and desires the book expresses. I have some personal understanding of them.'

She started to walk a little faster, although I'm certain she meant me to keep up.

'I was wondering,' I said. 'I would very much like to call on you before the next lecture and walk with you to the Institution.'

'Call on me? At my home?'

'Yes. If it is not too forward.'

She looked around distractedly, and I was concerned that she was afraid for her reputation, of being seen in this intimate conversation with a suitor.

'No, no,' she said. 'That is fine, I suppose.'

'Excellent. I shall call on you at twenty past seven on Thursday evening.'

She nodded and hurried away, leaving me alone amid the fossilised remains of long-dead creatures.

In the days leading up to our appointment, I was riven with excitement and trepidation. Barely able to sleep or think of anything but her, I was neglecting my many writing and theatrical pursuits and had become an object of ridicule in my household. I was so restless. I took a trip to London to pick up a suit I had recently been fitted for and which I felt would make a good choice for Thursday evening. I bought a new shirt and new shoes, caring nothing for the cost.

As I approached Great Pulteney Street that evening, the weather was clement, the sun coming in low over the tops of the beautiful Bath stone buildings, lending them a sort of honeyed glow. At the door I was met by an impertinent maid who refused to announce me.

'I'm sorry, sir,' she said. 'But Miss Redferne has received some terrible news – her mother has died. She is in mourning and does not wish to see anyone.'

Turned away in such a fashion, I felt most disappointed. I called again a week later but this time I discovered that she had gone to stay with her aunt at St Cyprian's Court, which complicated matters greatly. Unperturbed, I took to riding out to the estate almost every day, obviously keeping a respectful distance from the manor. It was on one such reconnaissance that I finally spied her walking through the woods alone. She looked so pale and beautiful I was certain in that moment that I must have her by any means. For several days I followed and observed her, and each time she got little closer to the clearing where the church stands, looked at it for a while, then rushed away. Intrigued at last, I dismounted, tied my horse up and went to investigate the building, but it was little more than a wreck. I was just about to leave when I bumped into a tall, rather frightening countryman taking his dog for a walk. We chatted, and I discovered he was the old groundskeeper of the mansion. Seeing a chance for some useful information, I offered to take him to the pub for lunch and ale. He readily accepted. It was during this clandestine meeting that I learned of his dislike of the Seymour family and of Camille who he saw as entitled and 'too clever by half'.

'I once gave her a scare in the church,' he said, laughing to himself. 'When she were little. Told her the place was haunted. Put the fear of God into her I did.'

'It's haunted?' I said.

It turned out the locals had some vague idea that something supernatural lurked in the building and the land around it. People felt they were being watched. It was deemed unlucky to go near, which was one of the reasons the church had fallen into disuse. Camille was clearly still terrified by the place. A devilish plot came into my head.

'Do you pass the church often?' I asked.

'Every day,' he replied. 'I live in a cottage nearby.'

'I have a feeling she will be back there tomorrow. Be ready inside the church. I'll pay handsomely if you do exactly as I tell you.'

Just as I thought, the next day, she led me to the old church, and this time she went inside. I hid in the trees, attempting to invent an excuse for my presence. To my great fortune, it was not needed: I heard a terrible scream, and on venturing towards the building I found her collapsed on the stone floor. I went to lift her and she struggled in my arms, giving me a frisson of excitement. Then she fainted. The groundskeeper emerged, looking pleased with himself.

'I told her the tale just as you said.'

'Good man.'

I paid him and he assured me of his discretion. Afterwards, I set out to find help, ecstatic that I now had a legitimate claim on Camille's attention.

The next day, I visited the house and had to suffer an

interminably dull tea with her ancient aunt, and I feared that it may be weeks before Miss Redferne would be willing to meet with me. But, in the carriage on the way home, I came up with the audacious idea of a surprise picnic to lull her out of her bedroom. I put this to her aunt in a letter and to my surprise she agreed. I went straight into action, employing my father's senior kitchen staff to plan the most lavish feast that could possibly be enjoyed out of doors. On the designated day, I arrived in my carriage with a large willow picnic hamper stuffed full of various meats, soft fruits, cheese and a fresh lobster.

What can I say of that glorious afternoon? It was the best of my life. It was I who managed to lull her out of her self-imposed exile, and though she looked tired and somewhat ill-prepared, I played the magnanimous host to the best of my abilities. As I left St Cyprian's, with the sun falling low behind the trees, I was certain courtship would follow. Indeed, I visited several times after, always receiving a warm welcome from the whole household, and finally, Miss Redferne told me that she was ready to face society again and would be attending a lecture the following week. Little did I know, it was all about to fall asunder.

To this day, I have no recollection of who spoke at the lecture that night or what it was about – I spent the whole hour in a nervous state. My plan at the close was to walk with Camille into the conversation room and invite her on a Sunday trip with my family to Bradford-on-Avon. After the talk was done and the applause faded, I stood to follow her out, but was stopped by my damned friend Mr Melton who wanted to discuss something about the illusionist John Maskelyne. I tried to put him off politely but the incorrigible fellow would not take the hint, until at last I blasted at him, 'Good God, man, can this not wait? I have important business to attend to!' Thankfully, this stunned him into silence, allowing me to slip away. I rushed out into the foyer expecting to find Camille waiting patiently for me. Imagine my frustration, then, when I saw that she was in mid-conversation with another gentleman, whom I did not recognise – a tall, broad, superficially handsome man in the sort of pale suit one might wear to a sporting occasion. Not only were they extremely animated, but this man had the temerity to take Camille by the arm.

I was struck with rage. I had never known such anger; it erupted inside me like molten lava. I rushed home, ignoring Mother, and went straight to my room. For the next month, I couldn't bear to be among other people and rarely strayed from the house. I handed control of *Black Ink* to my fellow founders and cancelled all my appointments. Locked away from society, I festered in my sorrow, cursing Camille for her cruel and capricious nature, damning the day I ever set eyes on her. Mother was most perturbed by my withdrawal, and friends sent letters asking if I had fallen ill. And the truth was, I had – I was suffering a terrible sickness of the mind, a seething, jealous malady that seemed to know no cure.

A curse.

There were whole days like this. I wandered about the house, not bothering to eat or dress, hating her but also desperately hoping that she would contact me, that she would apologise and beg forgiveness. But she never did. I pictured her with Mr Anthony Seward, debasing herself and laughing at me.

Finally, I heard that she was back at her own home on Great Pulteney Street, so I resolved to pay a visit so that I could reinvigorate our friendship. It was a pleasant afternoon and the streets of Bath were quiet, as though the whole town understood my sweetly sombre mood. On my way, I stopped at a florist's for a posy of carnations, and dallied at Pulteney Bridge for a few moments to admire the view. I felt a somewhat giddy sense of purpose and anticipation: soon I would be able to take up the subject of our courtship once again.

Imagine my disappointment when I knocked at the door only to be told by the housekeeper that Miss Redferne was out attending a concert.

So I waited. I did not go home, I did not want to miss her. I wanted to be there when she returned. I loitered about on the bridge, I walked down to the gallery and back again. It was dark when I eventually saw her approaching the house, and a horrifying image assaulted me. She was with Anthony! At the door, they talked for a several minutes and then she took his hands in her own with obvious affection. I stood transfixed, barely able to assemble my emotions. The flowers fell from my hand, scattering across the road. I must have remained there for several minutes as my hopes and plans fell about me like theatrical scenery. I felt myself plunging back into the depths of fury and despair. Why would she do this? Why him, when I had been so respectful, so accommodating? I'll admit I let my fury get the better of me. I picked up a loose rock from the street and aimed it at her window, only meaning to make a din, but the glass pane shattered. I scuttled away.

It was obvious to me that Mr Seward was exploiting Camille's fragile state in order to ingratiate himself further into her life. Yes! That was it. The scoundrel was taking advantage of her. All I had to do was intercede.

The very next day, I arrived at St Cyprian's with an invitation for Camille for a performance of *Macbeth* at my theatre, which I knew to be an arresting and fiery production. I felt the fear and emotion of that experience would push her gently back into my arms. I would then propose a formal courtship and we could put Anthony Seward in the past. But you have perhaps read her account? After the thrilling performance, I propositioned her, and she refused me.

I was undone.

My disappointment turned once again to fury, and now it was directed at her. She had lied to me. Her affections for him were now obvious. She was a harlot. A whore. I determined to take revenge.

For days I cogitated on this state of affairs. Unable to rest at home but keen not to bump into friends, I ventured out in the evening to wander the unlit backstreets of the city – the crisscross of narrow lanes between the abbey and the White Horse pub, the marketplace at Walcot Street, the stinking quayside. I became a solitary creature of the night, festering with resentment, surrounding myself with the scum of the city. It was on one such skulking excursion, along the alleyway leading from Edgar Buildings, that I turned a corner and almost walked straight into a man in a black cloak and black hat who turned out to be Major Philips, who I knew from my club.

'Goodness,' he said. 'You startled me. You are out late. Have you been playing cards?'

'No, I find myself unable to sleep. Walking helps me to cogitate. And you, sir?'

He gave me a most unsettling look – a kind of smile, but with no humour nor kindness in it. 'I am just returning from dinner with Lord and Lady Blanche and their two daughters. Fascinating family.'

'I see. Very good.'

'Are you acquainted with them?'

'Vaguely. I have seen Lady Blanche at society lectures. She has a keen interest in the occult, I believe.'

'She does indeed,' he replied, his dark eyes showing a glint of excitement. 'In fact, she is soon to attend a séance at St Cyprian's Court, to be held by Lady Seymour.'

By now, I was keen to get away. 'Well, it has been pleasant to see you, sir,' I said. 'I must bid you good evening.'

I started to walk away, but he only continued his discourse, raising his voice a little so that I could still hear. 'Quite an interesting little group, by all accounts,' he said. 'Lady Seymour, Lady Blanche and her daughters, Miss Camille Redferne . . .'

I stopped. 'Miss Redferne?'

'Why, yes. You know her, don't you? An intriguing young woman.'

We stood in silence in the narrow alleyway for a moment, his eyes never leaving mine.

'Well, it is indeed late,' he said at last. 'I'll be on my way.' With that, he turned back and walked away towards the Assembly Rooms, leaving me to consider this titbit of news.

I resolved to find out more about this meeting. I discovered from a mutual friend that it was taking place a week hence, and that, yes, Camille would be attending. What's more, the medium for this séance was to be a very young lady, barely more than a girl, and a newcomer to the area. A fresh plan for vengeance formed in my fevered brain. I discovered her name was Abigail Cooper and that she was currently renting a room on Corn Street in Bath's sodden slum area, a hive of immigrants, thieves and drunkards, all packed like lice into those shameful tenements. I sent a message to her, asking for a meeting and hinting that discretion was of paramount importance. She replied, agreeing to see me and suggesting the Shamrock Inn, just round the corner from her building, at 8 p.m. the following evening. Although I was loath to visit such a notorious drinking establishment, I knew I had to do whatever was necessary to make Camille realise her mistake.

I decided to walk to the pub that night rather than take a coach, so as to draw as little attention as possible. As soon as I veered off Southgate Street, the stench of damp filled my nostrils. Each time the River Avon rose, the whole of this wretched area would flood, and whatever the stagnant waters left behind would remain there to rot in the streets. It was almost unbearable. To my left, the quayside factories and warehouses loomed, casting everything in darkest shadow. As I walked, I passed figures hunched in blackened doorways, rough men in working clothes, leering out at me in a most unsettling way. I tried to keep a steady pace as I approached the Shamrock, not wishing to betray my discomfort to any lowlifes looking for easy prey. It was a relief to grasp the door and get inside, although what greeted me was a similar scene of degradation. In the low light of the meagre gas lamps, groups of men huddled, muttering together over bare wooden tables, the smoke from their pipes filling the air like fog. The damp stone floors were filthy, the plaster walls rotten and cracked. I bought a pint of weak ale at the bar and looked about, finally spotting a lone woman sitting in a dark corner snug at the opposite end of the room. She was wearing a simple cotton dress, her jet black hair uncovered and pinned up loosely so that curls fell out about her face, which had, I admit, a pale and foreboding beauty. Venturing over, I took great care not to make eye contact with any of the other inhabitants.

'Miss Cooper, I presume?' She nodded. 'This is quite the venue,' I said while lowering myself gingerly on to a rickety wooden stool.

'It's close to my place,' she said quietly. 'I know it. It's safe.'

'Well, you have nothing to fear from me,' I said lightly. 'I am a gentleman.'

She smiled. 'Oh sir, it is the gentlemen I have learned to fear the most.'

I chose to ignore this bizarre interjection and moved on. 'You are holding a séance at the home of one Lady Seymour next week, is that correct?'

'It is.'

'There is a sensitive matter I'd like to discuss with you. Can I be assured of your discretion?'

'Most assuredly.'

'One of the guests at the evening is Miss Camille Redferne. She is a very good friend of mine, an exceptional lady, but I'm afraid also somewhat vulnerable. She has in the past been prone to hysteria ... and she recently lost her mother in a terrible accident.'

'I'm sorry.'

'The tragedy has left her in a somewhat confused state, and unfortunately there are men willing to exploit such circumstances for their own gains. In short, a certain very unsuitable fellow has wheedled his way into her affections, much to the shock and concern of her relatives and closest friends, who only want the best for her. We have tried to talk to her, we have begged her to break off contact with this man, but in her brittle state of mind, she is refusing all counsel.' I took a sip of my drink. 'I'm afraid desperate times call for desperate measures.'

Behind me I could hear the raised voices of two men with strong Irish accents, arguing over some sort of wager.

'The church is said to be haunted. During the séance, I want you to tell Miss Redferne that you are being contacted by the ghost dwelling there, and that it has an ominous message for her.'

'Mr Blacklock, I can never guarantee which spirits will be drawn to me during a séance, nor the nature of the messages they may wish to impart.'

Her dark eyes hovered on me, waiting.

'I appreciate that, Miss Cooper,' I said, glancing around the room, as though anyone I knew could possibly be there. 'Which is why I am prepared to offer you a significant sum of money to do what I tell you to do.'

Behind me, the argument was becoming more furious until

there came the sound of clattering chairs and a physical scuffle, accompanied by shouts of encouragement from the other drinkers. I turned round, just as the publican ran out from behind the bar and dragged the men apart. When I turned back, Miss Cooper was still studying me, unperturbed by the violence erupting around us.

'You want me to lie?' she said.

'It is a sort of white lie,' I replied. 'For I am absolutely certain this would be her mother's wishes, if she were still alive.'

'It will be a costly lie if I am suspected,' she retorted. 'Surely you understand that trust is a vital element in the relationship I have with my clients.'

It was both amusing and alarming to hear this little girl using the terminology of business, as though she were a respectable bank clerk. I had to stifle my distaste.

'I do understand,' I said. 'That is why I am willing to pay you a reward of two pounds for your charity.'

For the first time her wry smile dropped and I thought for a moment that she had taken offence at the offer of payment.

'My charity is more costly than that.'

'Five pounds. That's my final offer. A most generous amount for an evening's work.'

With a sort of shrewd half-smile, she thrust out a hand and I found myself shaking on the deal with the errant child.

It was then I told her my plan and her role in it.

'But you must take care,' I cautioned, while taking out my wallet and handing over the payment. 'She is extremely intelligent and sceptical. You will have to be convincing.'

She glared at me as she took the notes. 'Don't worry,' she said. 'Your friend will get the message.'

But I *was* worried. I was not convinced that Miss Cooper's revelations would be enough on their own. I wanted this séance to be a spectacle, I wanted it to chill and terrify. I had access to exactly the sort of theatrical equipment that could deliver certain special effects, and the experts able to use it. All I had to do was ensure the séance was moved from the house to the church – the site of the ridiculous haunting. From there, I could manipulate the whole evening.

The following night, I undertook a reconnaissance mission to the building, and discovered there were grilles along the edges of the stone floor that covered holes leading down into the crypt below. My theatrical mind whirred with the possibilities. I went back to Miss Cooper with the enhanced plan of action – it would be up to her to confect a reason why the venue should be altered. The minx demanded more money, and I conceded. Two days later she confirmed the change. The trap was set.

Dear reader, if you have read Camille Redferne's own account of the séance you will know about the supernatural visitations she experienced that night and the agonies of terror she went through. The intrusion of the phantom bride; the ghostly vapours rising around the table. But none of it was what it appeared to be. I had taken a simple peasant superstition about the church and added pertinent detail: a ghostly lady, a tale of thwarted love and cursed retribution. I had gained access to the crypt the day before with an acquaintance of mine, the French pyrotechnician Monsieur Jean Ruggieri, who set beneath the floor grilles a series of fireworks enti-tled Bengal Fires, which would emit a thin reddish smoke when I lit them. As the *coup de théâtre*, I had two of my stage hands climb the tower with a mannequin in a red dress, which they posed in the belfry in such a way as to resemble a figure. The medium was to draw Camille's attention to the spectral vision as the party left the building. When I discovered that a thunderstorm was forecast for that very night, it seemed my desire for spectacular vengeance would be more than sated. What could cement the horror of the night better than a display of lightning?

As the noise of the storm erupted and Miss Cooper's performance reached its crescendo, I stole out of the crypt to peer in through the main door. I saw the terror Camille was experiencing, I saw the other ladies scream. Having locked the doors from the outside, I meant to steal away undetected, satisfied by my work. All I could envisage was the triumph of my anger. But then I heard a voice from the darkness of the graveyard.

'Who goes there? Come out!'

It was Anthony Seward. My most hated nemesis. I stepped into the moonlight and we faced each other across the mud, surrounded by fog and headstones.

'You've come to check on your harlot?' I spat.

'Who the devil are you?' he cried.

'Her true love. One who was spurned in favour of a charlatan!'

Deafened by the howling wind, half-blinded by the rain, we circled each other like fighting dogs.

'I have no argument with you,' he said, wiping the rain from his face. 'I don't know what has happened here, but there seems to have been a misunderstanding. If we could go inside and talk.'

'No,' I shouted. 'It is far too late for talk!'

With that, I charged at him, my boots slipping on the wet earth. Pulling back my fist to strike, he weaved to the side in a flash and thrust his hand into my chest, knocking me over in the mud. Incensed, I scrambled to get up but could gain no footing. The bastard even put out his hand to help me up. Just then, out of nowhere, there was a deafening explosion and a blast of white light that lit up the whole estate. A lightning strike, barely fifty yards from us. Moments later, the sound of something huge splitting and cracking, followed by an image I'll never forget: the tallest tree on the edge of the woods, its upper branches aflame, falling towards the church. Anthony turned just in time to see the mammoth thing smash into the porch, obliterating the ancient stonework. Now mad with fright and fury, I grabbed a rock half buried at my side and while his back was turned I struck him over the head with it, meaning only to knock him from his feet. But when he turned to me, his face was a mask of blood. He stood stupefied for a few wretched moments, then his lifeless body dropped into the mud by the felled trunk. Staggering to my feet, I threw away the incriminating weapon and fled.

With no witnesses, save myself, the death was recorded as accidental. Camille was consigned to a sanitorium for several months. The news of her condition spread throughout Bath society, drawing much gossip and speculation around her peculiar state of mind – many blamed her high level of education and her almost manly intellect for the hysteria she suffered. If I had pondered fully on my plans that night, perhaps I would have considered the dangers, the many permutations that could lead to tragedy. But, I regret, I did not. How could I know that Anthony would come into my theatrical production unbidden? How could I know that in the midst of the savage storm, my anger would be so electrified?

We do not always appreciate the damage we have wrought upon the lives of others until much later. Sometimes far too late. What madness led me to make my pact with that damned harlot Miss Cooper? What cowardice ensured that I never told a soul until now? Camille believed an ancient curse was on her family, but there was no such curse apart from the one I placed there myself. In a rotten pub on a dark street many years ago, I made a thoughtless bargain that had consequences far beyond my understanding, like a boy throwing a pebble into the sea, not realising that the ripples may somewhere become waves big enough to swallow ships whole.

Please be charitable in your judgement of me. I know now how terrible my actions were. At home, after the séance, I was riddled with guilt.

But as I ruminated on the events, I realised that, though certainly a crime was committed that night, Camille had surely been exploited by Mr Seward. Wasn't my original motivation to do the best for her? I was no common murderer. Furthermore, I began to realise that my route to redemption would surely lie in devoting myself once again to her protection. She doubtless still held feelings for me, the man who once brought her out of her sickbed to taste life once again. And true, though it pained me that, on leaving the sanitorium, she married a dull man and had a daughter with him, I was certain the marriage was not a happy one. It was now my solemn duty to rescue her.

And so here I sit at my writing desk, finishing this confession with a promise to win back her affections. My anger at Camille has had time to dissipate, and the feelings of ardour I always had for her have returned. When the Seymour family moved from St Cyprian's Court, I bought the place as it allowed me to be close to her new home in Batheaston. This way I can insinuate myself into Camille's life again, confident that she will be glad of my interest and thrilled to revisit the home of her beloved aunt. And if she remains wrongly devoted to her husband and her child, perhaps an accident could befall one or both of them. Whatever is necessary to ensure her flight from that loveless home.

My servant is waiting to take this confession to my solicitor for safekeeping, so I must finish. I am optimistic for the future, and hope when this article finally surfaces, I will have redeemed myself. It is unsettling, though, that since moving here I have begun to feel ill at ease. An eerie sense of abjection lingers about me. On several occasions over the past weeks, I have looked through this window and seen a figure watching me from the edge of the woods, a woman in a red dress, exactly the same as the one I hung in the bell tower. Every time I go out to investigate, no one is there. It is beginning to prey on my nerves. A horrible feeling of dread is rising in me. I have tried to placate myself: saying out loud, 'What tricks our minds play on us while we're vulnerable!' But just now she was there again. This time holding a lamp. I cannot shake from my mind the feeling that I will soon face the consequences of my actions.

But why? Why do I deserve to feel such torment? Certainly my act against Anthony Seward was wretched, mad and violent, but surely my only crime was to love too much?

## Chapter Thirty-One

# Oh Ben

It was all a lie. The séance was a hoax, the fucked-up stage performance of a spurned, jealous man. I could barely process it – how someone could be so cruel and conniving, how so much machinery could be brought into play just to terrify and humiliate one woman.

But it wasn't just one woman. It was all of us. We'd carried Camille's trauma – Daphne, Elizabeth, Lorna, me. It was embedded from birth. A hidden inheritance. We should have challenged it, but instead it was passed down, we shared it with each other like a story, sometimes explicitly, sometimes through our actions. And by believing the story, we conjured it into existence. We cursed ourselves.

It was almost funny, the ultimate sick joke: we thought there was a vengeful spirit after us, but rip the mask off and it's just some guy who felt hard done by. And I'd sacrificed everything out of fear that

I'd be next and that I'd take Nikki and Ben down with me. Ben had relied on me; he was maybe the first person who ever did. I knew then, in that moment, that I loved him. The certainty of it was overwhelming.

I checked the time. 11.30 a.m. Meg said they'd be leaving in the afternoon – there was a chance I could make it. I had no idea what I was going to say, I just had to see Ben, I had to try to explain, in the hope that I could keep him.

But when I got outside, I froze in shock. The sky was already dark: vast blackened clouds blocking the sun. Curls of wind whipped in the air, carrying droplets of rain. And as I stood at the edge of Queen Square, there was the low rumble of distant thunder, like bombs detonating somewhere in the city. The storm was coming. It was coming far too soon. I checked my phone's weather app. The Met Office had issued a red weather warning for Bath and northeast Somerset, starting now. High likelihood of building and infrastructure damage. There was a message from Roland. He was on his way with the van but stuck in dense traffic on the A303. His text said, 'Change of plan. Church is right in path of storm. Crypt could flood. Or worse. Move Lorna's artwork if you can!' People were running back and forth around me, clearing the street, funnelling into shops and pubs, accentuating the feeling of impending disaster. What was I to do?

Ten minutes later, I was in my car, roaring through the Bath traffic, running on adrenaline or instinct. I wasn't thinking, I just had the route in my mind – towards the A46 and, from there, the rehab centre.

Off the M5, it took fifteen minutes to get out of the snaking country lanes. First, a tractor idling its way from farm to field, then temporary traffic lights guarding some large excavation in the road that no one seemed to be working on. I kept checking the clock on my phone, knowing I couldn't miss him. I couldn't. Because then where would I be?

The rain came in suddenly, splashing off the windscreen, blurring the world beyond. Every time the traffic ground to a halt, I tried to call Ben's mobile. Voicemail again and again. I looked out beyond the road, wondering if it would be absolutely crazy to just veer off, through a hedge and over the fallow fields. But then, thankfully, we started to gather speed and, at last, I could swerve on to the first in a series of unpopulated B roads that would get me to Ben.

The car park was full when I pulled into the grounds. I had to drive around circling the bays until I spotted a vehicle leaving. I accelerated fast, but then had to screech to a halt when someone with a walking frame stepped out in front of me. The space was too narrow, so I parked ridiculously close to a spotless BMW and then climbed across the passenger-side door to crawl out.

Then running, already drenched to the skin. Running through the gardens where Ben had come alive again, across the paths we'd walked so many times over the last few months. I was imagining what I'd say, how I'd explain what had happened, how I'd met Lea, her story, the ring, Ursula, Martin. And we'd go into the canteen and he'd give me his own story at last. And maybe, maybe, maybe, he'd change his mind about going, if we were still friends, if I hadn't abandoned him.

The automatic doors at the entrance were moving horribly slowly, so I squeezed between them while they were barely a foot apart, and half fell into the reception area. I pictured catching him saying goodbye to his physios and therapists, I saw myself standing there breathless and dishevelled. I'd say, 'Don't go,' and he'd listen.

He wasn't there.

Maybe he was still in his room? Still packing. That would give me much more time. But as I passed the desk, I looked over to the waiting area with the nice settees and the water cooler, and into the canteen – and there was Meg, sitting alone, studying her phone. She looked up and her expression was a curious half-smile, half-frown. In that frozen moment I had time to think, how typically oxymoronic of her.

Then I realised, somehow.

It was a physical feeling, a punch in my stomach that left me breathless and aching.

He'd already left.

He was long gone.

My heart was still beating fast as I walked over to her.

'I'm too late, aren't I?'

She nodded. 'They left half an hour ago because of the storm. He saw he'd missed some messages from you but it was a bit of a scramble to get away. I stayed behind to pack up his stuff – I'm taking it back to the flat for now.' She caught me glancing out of the doors towards the car park. 'Don't try to go after him. Cammy, this isn't *Love Actually*. Let him go.'

I stared at her, my adrenaline and crushing disappointment making my legs feel weak and shaky.

To my surprise, Meg pulled out a chair for me and sat me down on it.

'It's not all bad,' she said. 'His parents have built him a gym. They've hired a personal trainer. Maybe it'll be good for him to be away from it all.'

She took my hand in hers.

'Do you think he'll stay?' I sounded like a frightened child desperately looking for reassurance from an elderly relative.

'Maybe, I don't know. I think he'll be there for a while. He needs it.'

We paused for a moment, watching the receptionists chatting idly about last night's TV.

'Oh, I have something for you,' she said. She rummaged in her bag and drew out a book. It was Ben's sketchbook. 'He wanted you to have this.'

I looked inside the cover and there was a note in Ben's handwriting.

When I was at my lowest, you gave me a book and it brought me back. Here is one in return. You never think you're good enough. You're wrong.
    With love,
    Ben

I opened the book and flicked through a couple of the pages. The sketches were wild and slipshod, the flowers billowed over the pages, they seemed to spill out beyond the paper. I flicked through to find the sketch he had made in the churchyard, and when I saw it, I found that he had put me in the background, leaning against the wall of the church, looking at my phone. He had captured something in me, that underlying thing of mine. I was the only person in the book, sharing space with the things he loved. On the last page was a watercolour. It showed him and me sitting at a pub table. I'm wearing quite a glamorous dress and we're drinking something honey-coloured from tumblers. It was the Grafton Arms. He'd imagined us there, fulfilling the promise we made that day, a promise we'd now never fulfil. He was beautiful and I had lost him.

*

I left Meg talking to some of the staff and managed to get outside before crying. I made it to my car and clambered inside, sliding on to the seat, sobbing hopelessly, clutching the book to my chest. Ben didn't know it, but I had been right, I wasn't good enough. I betrayed Nikki because I was sad and drunk and lonely, and I let Ben down because I was scared and stupid, and now I was paying the price. This was the real curse – the one I inflicted on myself and my sister. I didn't deserve Ben or anyone, but even still I would have given anything to have got there an hour earlier, to have seen him again, to have at least said goodbye. Now I was alone. Even though I was in the middle of a mess I'd created, I just wanted someone to take care of me.

But the art. I still had a chance, at least, to save that. Nothing else mattered now.

The roads were quieter than before. No one else dumb enough to be out in this. Driving way too fast, strong gusts of wind buffeting the car around on the sodden road. Local news on the radio – lightning strikes in the Bath area. With a lurking sense of doom, I made a hands-free call to Nikki.

'I know you've heard it before, but I am truly sorry. I'm on my way back to the church. I think something bad is going to happen. Thank you for always being there. You're my hero.'

When I weaved off the roundabout towards Batheaston, there was an explosion of thunder and lightning above me so close the car shook. I screamed in fear, almost aquaplaning off the road. Panic detonated inside me. Heart speeding up. A dead tingling feeling in my hands. Then another detonation of lightning, just to my left, striking further up the hill. The hill to St Cyprian's.

A direct hit.

I turned into the lane and started climbing, wheels spinning in the mud. It was when I came around the last steep corner that I could finally see it. Above the treeline, a billowing plume of thick black smoke just visible in the darkness. I approached another car, travelling slowly down the narrow road towards me, and jammed my fist on the horn, hoping to somehow make them aware of the unfolding tragedy. They sounded their horn in return, clearly thinking I was just some road-rage idiot. Closer now, the wipers intermittently obscuring my view, I at last saw what I had expected. Lower down between the black branches – the unmistakable flickering orange and red of flames. Surely someone else had seen it and called the fire brigade? But then, there were no other houses nearby and who would think to check on the building? The locals would be happy to let it burn.

I accelerated around the final corner to my parking spot, hitting the brakes too late on the wet surface, smashing into the wooden fence around the layby. Out of the car in one violent lurch, I could see flakes of ash and burning embers drifting about in the air. I staggered on through the gate and into the graveyard and, once there, finally, I looked up and gasped.

# Chapter Thirty-Two

# **Armageddon**

It was a vision of hell. The church was engulfed in acrid smoke, the stone of the tower almost entirely blackened, fire pouring out of a gash in the side and from several of the smashed arched windows along the nave. Around the building, trees were flaming, too, the branches turned to gigantic torches. Great black birds were abandoning their roosts, squawking with panic in the red air, before disappearing beyond the smoke. The noise was like some terrible battle, a machine-gun onslaught of crackling flames and splintering wood. I tried to get closer, but the heat was like a physical force field, pushing me backwards. I ran around the edge of the churchyard, until I could see the entrance to the crypt, tufts of smoke already beginning to emerge from the interior.

Standing there, I had the presence of mind to call 999. It was a struggle to hear the operator on the other end, and their questions seemed nonsensical. My own voice sounded shaky and distant in the buffeting wind.

'We're dealing with a lot of callouts presently,' the person explained. 'Is there anyone in the building?'

'No.'

A pause. Fast typing.

'St Cyprian's Church?'

'Yes, please hurry.'

'I've logged the call, we'll get an engine there as soon as possible.'

'When will that be? There's stuff inside I need to save.'

'Listen to me,' she said. 'Do not attempt to enter the building.'

I staggered on through the gate and into the graveyard. This was madness. To even think of going in there. And for what? To save some art?

Yes. To save some art. Lorna's art. The last thing she worked on. Her final statement.

In a ludicrous act of self-defence, I put my hood up, took three deep breaths, then rushed to the crypt.

Inside, there was more smoke, not as dense as above, but enough to make it difficult to see. I collected the Elizabeth section and got her outside, just as glass rained down from the last of the windows and a belch of flame spewed out above me. Making it to the shed, I put the crate down on the floor and went back through the rain, shivering with cold, coughing. Inside the crypt again, I lifted the Daphne box, my arms already starting to ache at the weight and effort, muscles burning. The same short, scary run to and from the outbuilding. When I got the Camille crate, I started to think it was going to be okay. But on stepping outside, there was a terrible groaning, cracking noise from somewhere in the building. I looked up and, in one bizarrely silent and graceful motion, the rest of the tower fell in on itself. I felt in that instant a sort of cool breeze on

372

my face, as though the building was letting out one last breath. Then all hell broke loose. A deafening cacophony of crashing stone, the substructure imploding under the weight of hundreds of tons of falling stone. I fell back on to the ground and screamed.

I should have given up then. I should have retreated beyond the treeline and back out onto the road. A sane person would have.

But I didn't. I wasn't. Instead, I clambered to my feet again, dropped off the crate, and tore back into the swirling vortex of destruction. The art was all that mattered. I'd broken everything else.

As soon as I re-entered the vault, I saw that the far end had collapsed beneath the weight of the dead tower, allowing the fire an entrance point. I put my arm over my mouth and charged forward, grabbing the crate of Lorna's sketches. A section of wall fell inwards and, suddenly, I could see up into the building, I could see my things all on fire, the workbench, the record player, all of the books, and I was sure, for one split second, that I could see Lorna's four-poster bed at the centre of the nave. The floor was now covered in smouldering embers like a field of stars. I didn't care any more, I felt that what would be would be; this was the only place I'd ever felt comfortable, even though it seemed to exude something hateful. There was no curse, no ancient hex upon the family. What I'd done, I'd done alone. I was the witch and the church was my coven. So wasn't this apt? Wasn't this an apt fate for me? Outside again, I saw headlights passing on the distant road and hoped it was a fire engine or maybe Roland with the van at last, but they passed by.

I had one final piece to retrieve: Lorna. But now, as I stepped inside, the flames were rolling in through the collapsed floor, seething across the roof of the crypt like a glowing sea. I could hear above me the terrible groans of foundational walls giving in to the heat. I had minutes, maybe seconds. The smoke was so thick now I couldn't see anything; I got down on my hands and knees, trying to stay below the worst of it, feeling my way across the floor, gagging and coughing, my eyes burning. I got to the crate and tried to haul myself up it, but I slid down uselessly. I tried again, but found I could barely move my legs and arms. My chest felt like it was filled with molten lead.

I made one last try to reach up, putting every ounce of what I had left into the motion. But part of me knew it was too late, far too late now. As I slumped back down to the ground, my breath coming in tiny pathetic wheezes, it occurred to me with barely a jolt of surprise that I didn't care. A weird calm had descended. I was here where I belonged, where I had always been, and now what light I could see was fading at the edges like a photograph tossed in a fiery hearth. The world was pulling away and I didn't have anything left to grasp it back. Instead, I turned. I curled my arms around the crate, holding it in a close embrace.

And I gave in.

But while lying there in the flickering light, I opened my watering eyes and saw a figure bathed in light, distant at first, but getting closer and closer to me through the blackness. I knew it was Lorna.

'You're here,' I whispered.

'I am,' she said.

I tried to hold out my arm. 'I missed you so much.'

'I missed you too.'

'Have you come to take me?'

'Yes,' she said. And she took my hand.

In that moment I was transported back to the first time Ben and I held hands, walking around Sydney Gardens in the late afternoon sunshine. The naturalness of it, completely unforced and comfortable, but also tingling with excitement. Some people say the world opens up when you fall in love, like petals unfurling. I remembered thinking, yes, yes, now I understand what they mean. Now, lying alone in the crypt, I thought, what a shame. I loved that boy. I really did love him.

Then I felt myself move.

I had thought my mother would lead me gently away. But no.

There was a huge yank at me, and then another. Not soft at all but angry and determined.

'Come on!' a voice screamed. 'Come on!'

The shock of it roused me out of my stupor. A rude awakening, a 5 a.m. alarm call. I felt my body being dragged over the surface, dragged by something superhuman. I was aware of the crackling flames and the heat on my face, but all I could feel was the dirt and stone and grit beneath my body, scratching at me as I moved. For a little way, I was still dragging the crate with me, but weakened now, and given over to this determined new force, I let go. 'No,' I whispered. 'I have to . . .'

But the grip, if anything, tightened, and the dragging sensation continued. Then I felt myself bumping up over some big immoveable obstacle. And finally, on my face, something cool and light.

The air. The night air.

I tried to open my eyes, but they seemed to be swollen half shut. Through the blur of tears and grime, I could just make out someone kneeling above me; they had their fingers in my mouth. They were saying something.

'Wake up! Wake up!'

But I was too tired and sore to wake, I yearned to slip back into the warmth and mist. It's what I wanted and what I was destined for.

Hands grabbed my shoulders and shook me. Again. Again. And that voice was back, yelling, 'Come on, Cammy, come on!'

In the background, the terrible destruction continued; the sound of walls bulging and then collapsing inwards, and oak beams, hundreds of years old, snapping like twigs and giving up their loads. The force of so much falling, so many tons of it, sent rumbles through the ground like an earthquake, like an angry god. The death roar was so loud I thought my eardrums would burst. I realised I wasn't really breathing. I was certain that if I gave in to it, I could still float away. But an arm was thrust under my head; it pulled me in close, as though trying to keep me from drifting up into the clouds. And amid the chaos and tumult, I heard her say over and over again. 'Please, oh please. Oh, please don't do this to me.'

And that was what did it. That's what kept me down. I blinked hard and tried again to open my eyes, and this time it worked.

'Oh God,' the voice said. 'Oh, thank God.'

And there she was. Nikki, my big sis, whose life I helped to destroy. She was in a sweatshirt and pyjama bottoms, all black and filthy, her face covered in soot and snot. I managed to somehow arrange my face into a smile.

'You look awful,' I whispered.

'You're a terrible human being,' she said to me. 'You always were.' She bent down and kissed my forehead.

'I know,' I said. I went to say something else, but she stopped me.

'The ambulance is on its way,' she said. 'You *will not* die. You owe me that much.'

I nodded feebly.

'I can't believe you came to get me.'

'What else was I going to do? You're my sister,' she said.

I shook my head. 'I'm your cousin.'

'No, you're my little sister.' She wiped my hair away from my face. 'You're our baby girl.'

I tried to cry but it hurt too much.

Then everything went black.

376

# Chapter Thirty-Three

# Lorna is Back

It was a warm autumn night in Fitzrovia. All the restaurants along Charlotte Street had tables out next to the pavement, with crisp white covers and candles that flickered as people walked past. The sound of gentle conversation and piped jazz music floated in the evening air like a familiar scent. I was standing outside the Slate Gallery on my third glass of champagne. Inside, art collectors and journalists as well as a few C-list celebrities were swanning around the crowded space, cooing at the rediscovered works on display. The exhibition was entitled *Ashes to Art*, a Bowie reference Lorna would have been pleased with. Dozens of her sketches, paintings and prototypes were for sale, all the stuff we'd rescued from the crypt, but the centrepiece was the now completed version of her final piece, mounted on a revolving platform surrounded by spotlights. Amid the throng I could see Reggie Macclesfield, quaffing wine in his trademark silver trousers and mirror sunglasses, no doubt telling any who'd listen what a genius Lorna was.

I checked the time on my phone, then reached into my bag, pulled out my inhaler and took a long hard puff. My lungs had taken quite a bashing in the fire, but there was no really serious damage. I was out of it for a couple of days afterwards. I remembered the inside of an ambulance, a mask being put on me, kind voices I didn't recognise, dreams about being strangled. Then I woke up in a hospital bed and I was fully conscious at last. The curtains around me were closed, and it was dark. My throat felt like I'd swallowed a fistful of razor blades. I tried to call out but the only noise I could make was a pathetic painful squeak. Yet, somehow, a nurse heard me. He parted the curtains and smiled, then took my wrist and checked my pulse.

'You're okay,' he said in a low voice. He had a soft Scottish accent, and it made everything he said sound doubly reassuring. 'You're at the RUH. You were suffering from smoke inhalation, so you were given a bronchoscopy to check your airways, that's why your voice is a little hoarse. You've burned your throat and there's a little scarring on your lungs but nothing major.'

'. . . Nikki?'

'Is that your sister, aye? She's fine. She saved your life, so I think you owe her a decent Christmas present this year. She and your mum have been in twice to sit with you today. They're coming back in the morning. You should try and get some more sleep.'

But I didn't really sleep. I was going over and over in my head what I needed to say to Nikki, the best way I could say sorry so that it meant something. When I saw Mum walking through the doors in her smart suit, her hair tied back, it all disappeared and I found that I was crying. She leaned in to hug me and I took her arm with both my hands and pulled it into my chest. She let me. I don't think I'd ever needed anyone so much in my life as I needed her then. For the next few minutes, I just sobbed painfully while she stroked my hair and said, 'Silly girl, silly girl,' in a voice I hadn't heard since I was seven years old. Her maternal voice. Then, in a jolt I realised something and looked up and around.

'Where's Nikki?' I said. For a horrible second I thought that even though she'd saved my life she still wanted nothing more to do with it.

'Don't worry,' said Mum. 'She's here, she's just on the phone to work.'

Just then she walked in, and in stark contrast to Mum she was dressed down in scruffy jeans and an old Snoopy sweatshirt. She looked drawn and pale.

'I'll get us some coffee,' said Mum, and she left us alone.

The door to the gallery swung open and Roland walked out. He gave me a peck on the cheek and lit a cigarette, blowing smoke out into the London night.

'This is nuts,' he said.

'I know.'

'There's a lot of interest from collectors. Are you ready to be a millionaire?'

'Lorna used to say, it's not about money, it's about immortality.'

'But money is nice though – and, unlike immortality, you're definitely going to get it.'

'Yeah.' I shrugged. 'Thanks to you.'

'Just doing my job,' he said and smiled.

He had turned up at the church a few hours after I was taken away in the ambulance. While fire crews doused the flames, he and his accomplices painstakingly collected and packed all the crates, including the Lorna section which my sister had gone back

379

to retrieve before the whole crypt collapsed. They took them to a storage facility and made sure restorers got a good look at it all to prevent any secondary damage. He had also dealt with the insurance details so I didn't have to worry about the reams of paperwork while I recovered. When I met up with him to discuss it, he told me the payout would be sizeable. 'It's rather odd,' he said to me. 'When we were setting up the policy many years ago, Lorna made me check that it specifically covered lightning damage. Isn't that fortunate? It's as though she saw it coming.'

There was a big cheer from inside and we both turned around to look in through the slightly steamy windows. Reggie had got up on to the little stage and was obviously making some sort of speech. I didn't begrudge him taking the limelight. It shifted the focus away from me and he deserved it anyway. It made Lorna furious that she couldn't work without him, but it was obvious he couldn't work without her either – it's just that art buyers remain curiously receptive to white male artists, even when their work is second-rate production-line bullshit. Lorna had forgiven him his success, and a lot of other things, so I could forgive him too. I'd learned a lot about forgiveness after all.

When Mum left Nikki and I sitting on the ward together, I smiled weakly at her and opened my mouth to apologise yet again, this time for everything. But she stopped me.

'I've got to say something. The day of the fire, I met up with Tricia from work – she had the whole story on Justin. He'd slept with at least two other women. It happened at office parties or weekend conferences. They were always younger. It was his MO apparently.'

She paused for a second to take a couple of deep breaths. 'This was the man who brought me breakfast in bed and supported my career and remembered every birthday and anniversary. I felt betrayed and stupid. Just so fucking stupid. But what hurt the most was that I couldn't come to you about it.'

'I know,' I said to her. 'I know.'

'I'm still furious with you. It hurts my heart to think of it. But I know you were in a terrible place and so did he. You were a victim too. That's how I see it now. So I'm going to try. I'm going to try very hard to forgive you.'

Just then Mum walked back on to the ward carrying two cups of coffee.

'How are you both?' she said. 'You've had a chat?'

Nikki nodded and took the cup. 'I've told her that I will try to forgive her.'

'Excellent,' said Mum. 'I think saving her life was a good start.'

We decided that afternoon that I had two mums. Lorna and the mum who'd always been there, in her own complicated way. And I definitely still had a sister.

Roland stubbed his cigarette out on the wall of the gallery and opened the door. 'Are you ready to get back into the fray?' he said.

'Not really,' I replied, but I followed him in anyway.

The interior was hot and stuffy and loud, a great swarm of people in expensive clothes, shouting at each other while a DJ played the Sisters of Mercy. The first person I spotted was the gallery owner, Sian Hoffman, who had first exhibited Lorna and Reggie's work thirty years ago.

'You're the one who saved Lorna's art from the inferno?' she asked in a thick Brooklyn accent.

'At great risk to her own life,' said Roland.

She nodded. 'It's a lovely work.' We all followed her gaze. In the centre of the room was Lorna's piece, St Cyprian's Church looking imposing and grand under a thick bulletproof glass case, with a neon sign displaying the title she gave it: *Love is a Curse.*

Reggie turned up at the hospital two days after the fire. He brought a bunch of sunflowers and a four-pack of some Japanese health drink.

'I hear I have a daughter,' he said, sitting down in the chair. 'This is going to take some mental readjustment.' Then he put his feet up on the bed. 'Let's get to know each other.'

We did that in the best way possible: we finished Lorna's final piece of art together. He arranged for it to be transported to his underground art bunker and we worked on it for several weeks. At first it was awkward, but we started to talk and compare stories, and something like a working relationship emerged. He translated the instructions, and understood what she wanted, but I also added my own elements. A family project.

It was when looking over the rooms of the *Love is a Curse* sculpture with Reggie that I discovered the USB stick, stuck to the inside of the Lorna section.

Carefully, I lifted the tape and removed the drive. Plugging it into my laptop, I found there were a few video files, one named, *For Cammy.*

And there was Lorna on screen, sitting in her vast four-poster bed, wearing Ray-Bans and a 'Bela Lugosi's Dead' T-shirt.

'If you're watching this, I am dead,' she said, lighting a cigarette. 'I've always wanted to say that.' She puffed out. 'But seriously, this is for Cammy only. If you're not her, stop watching and go and get her. Everything in this crypt is hers, legally – the paperwork is in one of the drawers. Go fetch it, have your lawyers check it or whatever, I don't care.

'Cammy, I hope it's you. I hope *you* found it. I feel like I left enough clues, or at least I knew that when you read about Camille, you'd be curious enough to break down that wall and go inside. I'm sorry I lied to you about who you are.' She stopped for a second. It was impossible to read her emotions through the darkness of the shades. 'I let you down. I let myself down. Nothing I say can ever make up for what I did. Handing you to my sister like that. But the person who gave you away, it wasn't the person you came to know. You helped make me again. You brought me back. But by then, it was too late for me to be your mother. Perhaps one day, you will forgive me.' Another long pause.

'You may ask yourself why I did this final piece,' she said. 'Art is like life, darling, it's all about narrative. Everything has to be an event. When you show people this stuff, maybe it will mean something again, for having been buried. It's yours now, to do with as you wish. One thing. The piece is not finished. That's your job. Reggie will help, but you must add yourself to it. My final collaboration.

'I hope you are happy, my girl, my favourite girl. I almost beat the curse. I got so close, but I ran out of time. You can do it. Get out there, Cammy. Get out there and show them.'

The video ended. I watched it again. I put my fingers on the screen to touch her face. I said, 'Goodbye, Mum,' through my tears. As heroes go, she was weird, challenging and sometimes cruel, but she was mine.

We kept Lorna's scenes more or less as she made them. Reggie added little working gaslights and a smoke machine for the séance, as well as robotic effects. On the walls, instead of windows, are LED screens showing videos that Lorna made, of the woods and the grave-yard, and the rooks in the trees. We placed a button on the stand in front of the model, like an exhibit at the Science Museum. When you press it, the marionette characters in each scene move their heads and watch each other. Some turn to look out at the viewer. At times, a shadowy figure dressed in red is projected on to the rear of a scene like a wraith. It is hypnotic and weird and unsettling.

But the sculpture also turns on a revolving table and on the other side is a mirror image of the piece, with a different version of each scene – these I made myself. In the crypt, now, is Lorna, working on the sculpture, cigarette between her lips, Joy Division playing on the stereo. Behind her, a little girl watches, enraptured. Proud, so proud. In the nave, Daphne and Guy, visiting the church, laying the letters down on the pulpit. In the tower chamber, Lea and Elizabeth, wearing their evening dresses from the hotel. And in the chancel are Ben and me, the stained glass windows created from his sketches, the colours of the flowers shimmering across us. Through another of the LED windows, the spectator can see the manor in the far distance. It is on fire. A funeral pyre for the man who tried to destroy us and failed.

'So what are your plans now?'

Sian had come up behind me and was now standing looking at the sculpture too. I had a sense of claustrophobia and, for a second, it was almost as though I was back in the church, where I had sometimes felt that presence, right in the centre of the nave, of dread and grief.

'I don't know. I've got a few ideas, but nothing seems real. I feel sort of blank. I always believed there was some dark destiny in store for me, and it became like a crutch. Now I don't have it and I feel . . . adrift.'

'You've got time,' she said, putting her arm through mine. 'You're still recovering.'

She spotted someone and disentangled herself from me so that she could rush over. On her way she shouted back, 'Will you give a little speech later? The masses want to hear from you.'

'I'll think about it,' I said. Then I found I was checking the time on my phone again. Stop it, I told myself. But the thing on my mind wouldn't go away.

It felt suddenly as though the crowd was pushing in against me.

I took another hit on the inhaler, then reached into my bag, delving around until I found it. The sketchbook. My comfort.

That's when Rhea Bennett came over. For a moment, I forgot that I'd sent her an invite, but I was glad to see her – she was the catalyst, after all. Besides, she blended in well with this crowd in her eccentric vintage suit and bright orange trainers.

'I've got something to show you,' she said, reaching into her handbag for a manilla folder. 'Sorry, do you have time? I'm not good at parties.'

'Yes,' I said. Anything to keep me occupied.

'You remember the photo of Camille that accompanied her article? Hang on, I have a copy here.' She handed it to me. 'I said to you at the time that Camille looked familiar, right?'

'Yeah. And we decided it's because she looked like me but in a nice dress?'

'Well, hold on, because I don't think that's it. When I first started at the Met I was given the job of sourcing materials for an exhibition we were planning on the history of women at the museum – notable curators, conservators, benefactors, yada, yada, yada. I came across an interesting story about a woman named Cordelia Radford. She was guest curator on an exhibition of occult art in the 1920s, and went on to become an important member.'

'Okay?' I said, looking around at the bustling crowds and wondering where this was going.

'So I found a photograph of her.' She flipped through the folder and drew out an old photo, slightly faded, worn at the edges. 'Look.'

She handed me the image, but it was hard to focus amid all the noise. It was another old photo of a smartly dressed woman.

'I tried to look into her history, but . . . well, there is not a lot of it. She basically just seemed to turn up in Manhattan society in the early 1900s.'

It was a few seconds before it really hit me. The eyes, the jet black hair. *No body was ever found.*

'Shit,' I said. 'It couldn't be, could it be?'

'I mean, the dates fit. It's possible. The thing is, she also wrote a bit, mostly short stories. In one of her collections there's a tale about a woman who seeks revenge on a man who has ruined her. She burns his house down with him inside it, then escapes to start a new life.'

We both stared at the photos looking from one to the other and back again. This is what the past does, I thought: just when you think you know it, there is a shift, like sand blowing along a dune, creating new shapes, new ripples. Nothing ever remains set in time and space, everything is fluid.

'Anyway, I'd better go,' said Rhea, breaking the spell. 'Last train to Bath is in half an hour. I'll keep looking into it. Drop by anytime.'

Then she was gone and I was alone in the noise.

But only for a second. When I turned round, there was Nikki. She was wearing a beautiful Galvan dress that we chose together in Liberty.

'You look amazing,' I said. 'Sorry, this isn't your scene at all. '

'Are you kidding? I'm having a great time! You see that guy over there in the sky-blue suit? He gave me his business card. He's a techbro with some sort of AI start-up based in San Francisco. I'm not sure whether he wants to ask me out or offer me a job.'

'Do you have a preference?'

She shrugged. 'I'm not really into narrowing down possibilities these days.'

There was a buzz on her phone and, while she studied it, I decided I may as well look at mine.

'What's going on?' Nikki asked.

'What do you mean?'

'You keep checking your phone. I've seen you.'

'It's nothing. Just nervous about the speech I'm supposed to make.'

She looked at me shrewdly. 'I thought we'd agreed: no more lying.'

I sighed.

'Oh it's just . . . when I took Ben to the Grafton Arms, he said that whatever happened to us, we should meet there again, in one year's time, at nine-thirty in the evening, and we'd drink Old Fashioneds. He made me promise. That was exactly a year ago.'

'Shit,' she said. 'You've got to go.'

'He's not going to be there,' I said.

'How do you know?'

'He's in Abu Dhabi, Nikki.'

'You promised. You made a commitment. You've got to go. Besides, you're desperate to go, look at you! It'll give you an excuse to escape for a bit. Reggie can hold the fort here.'

When she said that we both looked around for him and saw him in a corner by the bar, talking to Mum. They were very close and clearly deep in conversation.

'Oh no,' said Nikki in mock horror. 'You don't think?'

'Let's just not go there,' I said.

'So are you going to the Grafton or not?'

'I don't know! After all that I've done, I don't deserve him anyway.'

'When will you ever learn? It's not about what you deserve. It's about what people are willing to give to you.'

At that moment, the opening bars of 'Love Will Tear Us Apart' started playing. Something gave way inside me.

'I suppose it would be good to get away for a bit,' I said.

'Then go,' she said.

Outside, I hailed down a cab and watched through the grimy windows as the city passed. The beautiful Edwardian buildings with their muted colours and pristine paintwork, their sides plastered with faded ghost signs for long-gone hotels and lost drapery stores. Such a haunted city.

A little way from the pub, the road got snarled up with traffic. I looked at my watch. It was now almost twenty past nine. This was pointless, surely. But something in me said, 'Oh, what the hell?' and I climbed out, into the night. I was running then, weaving in and out of drinkers and tourists, my lungs protesting at the unexpected exercise. But there was a fair wind behind me and people seemed to be parting out of my path. Two hundred yards away, I could see the lights of the pub sign; there were people gathered outside with pints and cigarettes, laughing, chatting. I stopped at the door to catch my breath and before I could talk myself out of it I swung the door open and went in.

It was odd to see it, this old place. It seemed somehow both smaller than I remembered and much larger. What was I doing? It felt so ridiculous to be here all by myself. It seemed clandestine and ill-augured. When I walked into the main bar, I half expected the people inside to turn on me and say, 'What are you doing here? You've no right. You don't belong. He's not here.' But they didn't. The room was crammed. I looked around, but I couldn't see him. I struggled my way through to the other room. No sign. My heart sank; the giddiness I had been feeling turned to nausea. I'd lost him again.

I decided to sit at the bar like some sad loner in a movie, drowning their feelings in cheap Scotch as the gentleman bartender dried glasses and shared wise platitudes about life. But the young woman who came over to me had a big smile, dyed red hair and multiple face piercings. 'What can I get for ya?' she asked in an Australian accent.

Behind me I heard the door swing open, and I swirled round in a giddy moment of dumb optimism, but it was just a young couple in preppy clothes. They yelled 'Hi' to someone else in the bar and went over. I turned back.

'An Old Fashioned, please,' I said.

'Sure.'

She started off to get it, then stopped and turned back to me, looking confused.

'Wait . . . are you Cammy?'

'Um . . . yeah.'

The door opened again, and again I turned. This time it was an elderly man in a corduroy suit jacket, a newspaper rolled up under his arm. He waved to the bartender and she waved back.

Her attention returned to me. 'He's over there, mate.'

Slow motion. Whenever I look back and try to remember that night, it always happens in slow motion. I get down from the stool and walk towards the corner of the room that was hidden behind a group of office workers drinking fizzy wine. As I push through, memories of the last year flood in, the things I'd discovered, the people I'd met, the stories of love and loss, winding their way through time. The sounds in the room, the music, the chatter become suddenly crisper and brighter, like light hitting a stained glass window and dispersing in rainbow shards of colour. I look up slowly, almost not daring, as though terrified I will be confronted with empty space.

But he was there. Ben was there.

He was tanned, his hair was a little shorter. He was wearing jeans and a baggy cardigan. He looked lovely. There was a wooden walking stick propped on the seat next to him. I stood staring at him, stunned into silence.

'You're here,' I said.

'I am.'

'How?'

'A really expensive flight . . .'

Finally, with some effort, he stood up. I pulled him towards me and buried my face into his chest. I folded my arms behind his neck. I felt him embrace me in return. And I cried. Great long, silent sobs, right into his heart. The room faded into nothing around us and the ghosts faded with it. When he lifted my head to kiss me, I closed my eyes and I saw us walking along that quiet lane in Batheaston, hand in hand, the scent of cow parsley in the evening air, I saw us sitting together at the edge of the cliff, just beyond the campsite, sharing cheap wine as the sun fell below the waves. It was as though these things had just happened. It was as though they were yet to happen.

'You're here,' I said again.

'I was always here,' he replied.

That, I felt, must be what love is: permanence. No matter what. Love continues despite time, despite loss, despite war, despite tragedy, despite ourselves.

It was an ironic moment for my phone to buzz loudly in my pocket. I broke off to look.

'It's Reggie,' I said. 'They want me back at the gallery to do a speech. Will you come?'

Ben downed the drink and we caught a cab. Wrapped up in each other's limbs in the backseat, the city passed unseen this time. I was no longer a lone spectator, we were participants. We were included.

We spilled out of the car at the kerb outside Slate and tried to tidy each other's clothes. My legs were weak. I felt high.

'Please stay,' I said to him. 'Please stay with me.'

He held my hand and smiled. 'I have to. I love you. And I only bought a one-way ticket.'

As soon as I got inside, Sian came over, coiling her arm around mine and dragging me away. 'Come on,' she said. 'The natives are getting restless. Everyone wants to hear from the hero. They want to know what happens next.'

Did I know? I'd not really had chance to think about the future. I'd spent so long dwelling in the past, it seemed weird and alien to look forward.

But deep down, as I stepped on to the stage, the inkling of an idea was beginning to form.

# Epilogue

# Love is a Blessing

It is spring, and the bluebells are beginning to flower, lending the woodland a lush purple carpet. The air smells of wild garlic. Somewhere amid the yew trees a thrush is singing.

I'm sitting on a new wooden bench on the lawn beside the gravestones, looking up at the church. It is almost unrecognisable now, and in a few weeks it will reopen as something entirely new. A thrilling metamorphosis.

Here is what I said that night at the art gallery: 'I'm setting up the Lorna Piper Foundation – it will help young creators working in experimental art and emerging media. The church will be rebuilt. Not exactly the same. It's going to be a combination of the old building, and something fresh. Artists will be able to work there for free. I'm still coming up with the details, but that's the broad picture. I want people to be inspired by Lorna, in the same way I was.'

That was five years ago. In truth, the process took longer than I expected. It wasn't the funding, that part was easy. The sketches, print-outs and prototypes I saved from the crypt sold for a modest fortune. Great Aunt Ursula also insisted on making a donation. But there was the small matter of a global pandemic, and a few other unexpected snags here and there. It was slow going, yet we made it in the end. It helped that I hired a brilliant if sometimes exasperating architect who oversaw the entire project with an air of cool detachment. Yeah, it was Deborah Piper. My mum.

I call her Mum because that's what she is, in all practical definitions of the word. Lorna was . . . Lorna. A teacher, a friend, a hero. She was eccentric and difficult, and mystical and brilliant. The universe she inhabited was something she sculpted herself and she taught me how to see it, for good and bad, as something magical. So I just call her Lorna, and that's fine.

Once all the ruins had been stabilised, Mum's team constructed the foundations of the new build. They built a dazzling modernist edifice of glass and steel, right on top of the ancient remains. It should be ready for the autumn when the first residents arrive. I couldn't sell the church sculpture in the end. Instead, *Love is a Curse* will form the centrepiece of the new space. It will be placed where Lorna's workbench had once been, and where she decided to spend her last days in that monstrous four-poster bed. Something of her will always be present.

It had been weird to come back here, to stand where the nave had been, in the place that contained so much history. I still felt it in the air, a kind of presence just out of reach. Early on, when builders were clearing the rubble of the tower, one of them freaked out – he thought he'd found a body. But it was just an antique mannequin wearing a very tattered old red dress.

We decided to create a sculpture garden in the church grounds, a combination of nature and art. I'd found a few of Lorna's unfinished plans in the crypt. With Reggie's help, I completed them. I hired a team of five gardeners to do the landscaping. There was only one man I wanted to manage the project.

Then I spot him, emerging from the woods.

Ben. My Ben.

He is a little less bouncy and strident now, but he doesn't need a walking stick any more. Mostly, he orders the gardening team about, but sometimes he gets stuck in with the physical graft, though he still gets dizzy spells so can't operate any of the heavy machinery, to his frustration. As he walks out into the sun, I see he's not alone – he is hand in hand with a little girl, and they are chatting amiably. She is another reason the work on the church was somewhat delayed. We named her Mabel after Ben's grandma, and she is almost three. She has dark eyes and hair like mine but a wide friendly face like his.

After the exhibition, Ben and I bought a cottage on the outskirts of Batheaston. It's small and very old. A neighbour warned us it was haunted, but that didn't put us off. Ghosts don't scare me any more. I have a workshop at the back of the house and sometimes I'll go out there to work on some new sculpture or piece of jewellery while Ben potters about in the garden. We laugh about being premature pensioners. But when I need to, I escape into London. I'll meet Nikki or Reggie, we'll got to nice bars and art exhibitions. The doom that once scuttled after me usually stays in the shadows now. Although I do still dabble in family research; I can't help it.

Idly one quiet evening, I searched the newspaper archive for the medium Abigail Cooper. One story stood out. She had been accused of fraud by the Society for Psychical Research. Although adamant that her psychic abilities were real, she admitted that she had been paid to fake a single spirit encounter.

The young lady told our investigator that after the disastrous séance at a small village outside of Bath, she went to see one of the attendees, who had since suffered a breakdown due to fright. Cooper allegedly informed the lady that the evening had been a hoax perpetrated by a spurned lover. Further investigations revealed that this lady was none other than Camille Redferne, once a respected member of the Bath Royal Institution, who is believed to have perished in a house fire several weeks after her visit from Miss Cooper.

That's how Camille found out the truth about Martin. And when he bought St Cyprian's Court she must have realised she'd never be rid of him unless she did something drastic. Something magnificent.

I was fifteen when I found out my family is cursed. And although the evidence tells us that wasn't entirely accurate, there is something in it, some nagging half-truth. Every family has its own folklore, its own creation myths. Every family is a haunted house. It contains within it the ghosts of everyone who went before, their traumas, their crimes, their hopes and ambitions. They whisper to us through the years, quiet but inescapable. They are there in our fears, our phobias, our nightmares and our dreams. On top of those spectres, we add our own.

I sometimes worry Mabel carries the seed of the curse within her. Trauma, it seems, echoes downward through the years, like aftershocks from an earthquake. But if it's there, I will help her beat it.

When work is over, the three of us walk to the Black Dog Inn. Ben goes off to get drinks, while Mabel and I take a table in the little courtyard outside. She climbs into my lap.

'The book,' she says. 'The book.'

I know which one she means. I reach into my bag and pull out the battered guide to trees and flowers that I bought for Ben all those years ago.

'Flower,' she says. 'See the flower.'

So I turn to the page where I put it all those years ago. And I tell her, once again, how Daddy was poorly, but then he found this flower and started to get well again. And I think about the damaged boy from that afternoon, vulnerable yet also defiant and determined, and how for a few dark days I felt I needed to leave him. But I never really did.

This is the story I will tell her about our lives. There will be no dread. I will make sure she knows she is safe to love whoever she wants.

Because the tales we tell about ourselves, our parents, our grandparents, about long-dead ancestors, they are important. They are more than stories, they are maps. They are toolkits. What I will tell Mabel is that Camille, Daphne, Elizabeth and Lorna were heroes. They all hungered for something, and they got it, one way or another. Whatever they faced, they had determination enough to care for people and not let go.

That is the curse; that is what I have inherited.

We finish our drinks and walk back towards the old church, Ben and I either side of Mabel, holding her hands, swinging her in the summer light, her laughter filling the warm air. Above us skylarks sing, the fields are filled with daisies. Everything glows.

If you must be cursed, let it be with love.

# Author's Note

While some elements of this novel are based on real places and genuine historical figures and events, much has been fictionalised, including the workings of the Bath Royal Literary and Scientific Institution and the exact effects of traumatic brain injury.

# Acknowledgements

Thank you to:

Andrew Ziminski, author of *The Stonemason,* for taking me on wonderful church hunting trips and making me climb up rickety ladders and down ancient spiral staircases.

Daniel Musselwhite for jewellery advice even when hungover.

Paul Brown for memories of Slade School of Art in the 1970s.

Catherine Freeman for her expertise on girls' education in the Edwardian era.

Richard Irwin and Jyoti Evans for their knowledge of physiotherapy and brain-injury rehabilitation.

Gavin Fuller for exploring the *Telegraph*'s archives and uncovering stories about Victorian séances.

The Bath Royal Literary and Scientific Institution (especially Rob Randall), for sharing their history with me.

Rob Dwiar for gardening tips.

Frome Library, where I wrote much of this novel.

Everyone at Sphere and Little, Brown, especially: Howard Watson and Zoe Carroll; Jessica Purdue, Louise Henderson, Zoe King and Lana Beckwith in Rights; Ben Prior in Design; Tom Webster in Production; Sarah Shrubb in Audio.

And Thalia Proctor, always.

My editor, Ed Wood, who immeasurably improved this book, as he did with all my others.

My agent, Eugenie Furniss, who got me through it all with wise words and nice meals.

My friends and family.

Catie, my chief medical advisor.

Morag, Zac and Albie, who are everything.

I have created a Spotify playlist of songs that inspired this novel. You can listen here:

http://bit.ly/love-is-a-curse